The Prophet
and the
Pharoah

Carol Corwin

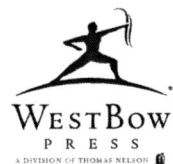

WestBow
PRESS
A DIVISION OF THOMAS NELSON

the Prophet and the Pharaoh

Copyright © 2011 Carol Corwin

All rights reserved. No part of this book may be used or reproduced by any means, graphic, electronic, or mechanical, including photocopying, recording, taping or by any information storage retrieval system without the written permission of the publisher except in the case of brief quotations embodied in critical articles and reviews.

WestBow Press books may be ordered through booksellers or by contacting:

WestBow Press
A Division of Thomas Nelson
1663 Liberty Drive
Bloomington, IN 47403
www.westbowpress.com
1-(866) 928-1240

Because of the dynamic nature of the Internet, any web addresses or links contained in this book may have changed since publication and may no longer be valid. The views expressed in this work are solely those of the author and do not necessarily reflect the views of the publisher, and the publisher hereby disclaims any responsibility for them.

ISBN: 978-1-4497-1320-1 (sc)
ISBN: 978-1-4497-1321-8 (dj)
ISBN: 978-1-4497-1319-5 (e)

Library of Congress Control Number: 2011924987

Printed in the United States of America

WestBow Press rev. date: 3/30/2011

People of Ancient Egypt

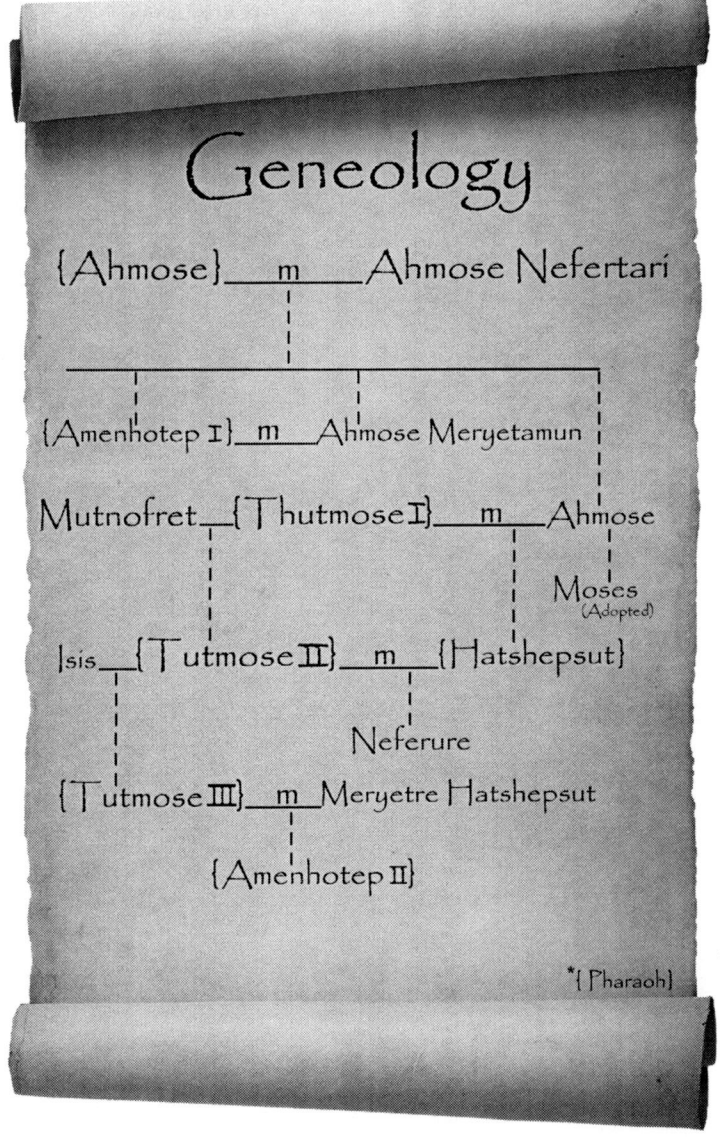

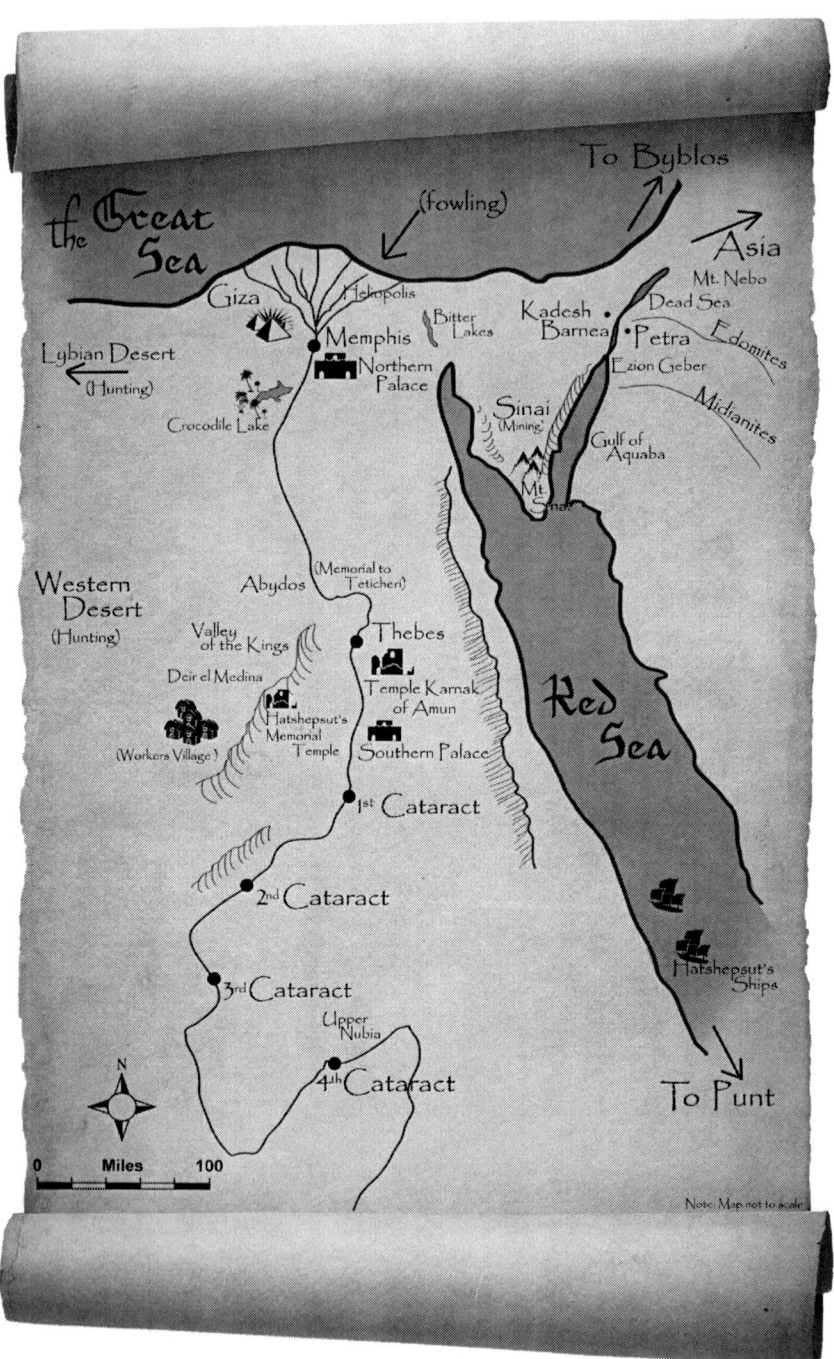

Introduction

A millennium after the great pyramids were built and 1500 years before Queen Cleopatra sailed the Nile, there was a period in Egyptian history called the *New Kingdom*. Pharaoh Ahmose I had driven out the *Hyksos*, invaders from the north who had advanced from the delta and nearly taken over Egypt.

As our story opens, a golden age of relative peace and prosperity has dawned in Egypt. There is one cloud on the horizon, however. Another delta group of people, the *Habiru*, have so greatly increased that pharaoh considered them a threat to Egypt. After failing in previous attempts to control their growth, Pharaoh Ahmose has devised a new plan that will have consequences for his family and for Egypt that he could not have imagined.

Thebes
1526 BC

Ahmose I and Queen Ahmose Nefertari were enjoying a glass of wine on the terrace of their palace overlooking the Nile. The queen suspected that her husband had brought her on this trip up the river from Memphis to protect her from what was to come.

"Do you have to kill the babies?" she pleaded. Pharaoh looked at his beautiful sister-wife, whom he had known all his life.[1] She was tenderhearted, unlike their powerful mother, the Royal Queen Mother Ahotep, who had been fiercely supportive in the fight against the Hyksos, even though it had cost her the Pharaoh she loved. "Do you realize how close we came to being defeated by the Hyksos?" Ahmose asked, reminding his wife of the threat the delta people had been. "If we hadn't intercepted the message from the Hyksos king in the north requesting an alliance with the Nubian ruler in the south, Egypt could have been squeezed in the middle. The other delta people, the Habiru, have become so numerous. What is to prevent them from uniting with one of our enemies to attack us?"

She knew he was right. All of Egypt trusted and revered him as a hero. They were calling his reign the New Kingdom. The Hyksos, who had formed their own government in the delta, were gone at last. Ahmose had fought them all the way to the land of the Hittites in Canaan. Now Egypt was united and powerful.

"Listen," Ahmose told her firmly, "do you think I enjoy ripping babies from their mothers' arms? I thought it would be better if they never held their babies, so I tried another plan. I called the Habiru midwives and instructed them, 'When a Habiru woman sits on a birthing stool, if a male

---
1   In Egypt the royal custom of marriage between siblings was practiced to emulate the gods and to strengthen the royal line.

child is born, take him away and kill him immediately.' Sometime later, when I heard that the male babies lived, I called for the midwives and asked them why they had not followed my instructions. They explained to me, 'Your Excellency, the Habiru women are not like the Egyptian women. They give birth before we can get there.' So I sent the midwives away and devised a new plan of sending my soldiers to throw the male babies into the Nile. What else can I do? Even increasing the workload of the Habiru has not reduced their numbers."

Later that evening, as Queen Ahmose lay in her bed with her head cradled on a headrest, a soft breeze stirred the bed curtains. Though the air was warm, the queen shivered. She could imagine the Habiru mothers clutching their infants as the soldiers came to take them away. It was happening right now in the delta. Her own son, Amenhotep, was asleep and safe, but a sense of dread entered the queen's heart; she hoped no finger of death would ever enter the palace to touch her own son. She thought of her fifteen-year-old daughter, Princess Ahmose. How would she explain this dreadful event to that sweet young maiden who would surely hear about the babies? She was her mother's daughter, gentle and sensitive. The suffering of an animal could sadden her for days.

For now, the queen would hold her family close. Next week, they would return to their palace in Memphis.

Three months later and back in Memphis, Princess Ahmose, accompanied by her servant girls, went down to the Nile to bathe. The morning was bright and fresh. Sending the girls ahead to inspect the reeds for any lurking crocodiles, Ahmose opened her arms and lifted her face to the sun, welcoming the day. She enjoyed this morning ritual before the sun grew hot.

Suddenly, her reverie was interrupted by a cry from her servants.

"What is it?" called the Princess, hurrying to the edge of the river. "Did you find a croc?"

"No," they replied, and they lifted a covered basket from the reeds. "There is something in here; we heard a cry."

The Princess carefully removed the lid, and all exclaimed at the same time, "A baby!" The chubby infant looked to be about three months old.

"It must be one of the Habiru babies," said Ahmose. Just then, the beautiful baby scrunched up his face and began to cry. Princess Ahmose's heart was touched. She lifted the baby into her arms, and soothing him, she said, "I will call him Moses, and I will raise him as my son."

The baby's elder sister, Miriam, had been standing nearby and keeping watch over the basket to see what would happen to her brother. Her parents could no longer hide the baby at home, and putting him into a carefully sealed papyrus basket, a tiny ark, was their desperate attempt to save his life.

"Would you like me to get one of the Hebrew women to nurse the baby for you?" Miriam asked.

"Yes, go." the Princess answered. Miriam ran to bring the baby's mother, Jochebed.

Pharaoh's daughter said to her, "Take this baby, and I will pay you to nurse him for me."

With Miriam in tow, Jochebed hurried home, clutching her own baby and thanking God for saving him in such a marvelous way.

"Only you, Almighty Lord, could have worked out such an excellent plan. Your ways are far above what we can imagine. You have given me back my precious son as though from the dead."

Back at their little mud-brick house, Jochebed and Miriam settled down on the comfortable floor cushions. "You have done well, Miriam," her mother said. "You patiently watched over your brother. You were courageous to approach the Princess and very clever to suggest a wet nurse. God has blessed us this day, and I am thankful to him and to you."

Miriam was glad. Sometimes she felt her mother didn't give her enough credit, but now she knew her father would hear a good story about her when he came home from work, which was important to the ten-year-old girl.

Jochebed opened her robe, because she could see that her baby was hungry. As she began to nurse him, three-year-old Aaron stood at her knee. Newly weaned, he longed to be on his mother's lap, but patiently stood by, watching his brother nurse. Jochebed reached out to him with her free arm and drew him close.

"Someday," she told him as she kissed his little head, "you will be glad we got your little brother back."

To baby Moses she said, "My precious baby, you will be mine for at least three years."

In her heart, she knew God had something special in mind for this child who was nestled safely in her arms.

MEMPHIS
1525 BC

"You did what?" Queen Ahmose Nefertari asked her daughter in disbelief.

"Please, Mother, don't be upset," replied Princess Ahmose. "You should have seen him—so precious and helpless."

"My daughter, this is not some little stray animal you are talking about. This is a baby. Have you thought of how this might hurt your father? This is in direct defiance of his orders."

"Do you have to tell him, Mother?" replied the princess anxiously. "He hasn't been well. Moses won't be old enough to come to the palace for several more years, so why disturb Father now?"

Queen Ahmose pondered her daughter's suggestion. On the one hand, she wasn't in the habit of keeping anything from her powerful husband. On the other hand, she was loath to disturb him as he lay ill in his bedchamber. The doctors had applied a poultice of many herbs as well as animal fats and lizard's blood. To help cure his setyt, or stomach illness, they gave him warm milk and had him breathe the steam from powdered plants, *Te'an* and *Amamu*, heated over the fire. Still, he grew weaker day by day.

The decision not to disturb Ahmose with the news of Moses was a wise choice. Within the month, Ahmose joined his fathers in the afterlife. The mummification process took seventy days.[2] When the body of Ahmose

---

2   In mummification the body of the pharaoh was dried out in natron, then wrapped in many layers of linen bindings. The internal organs had been removed and were stored in a canopic jar labeled with a cartouche (or name) of the king. During preparation of the body, the chief embalming priest assumed the identity of the god Anubis and wore the mask of the jackal.

was ready, his face was covered with a mummy mask and he was placed in a coffin.

A canopied shrine sheltered the coffin, which rested on a boat-shaped bier drawn by a team of oxen. Noblemen and courtiers, dressed in white robes and sandals and wearing white bands around their heads, led the procession. Immediately after the shrine of Ahmose I, came the royal family, carried on litters within curtained canopies.

Professional mourners followed, wailing lamentations, "Our great shepherd is gone." They beat their chests and tore their clothes, tossing dust over their heads.

Bringing up the rear were the people who mourned their hero from their hearts.

Pharaoh's sarcophagus was waiting to receive his coffin at the tomb. After the sarcophagus was lowered deep into the vault, workers sealed the tomb and covered it with soil to hide the location.. Nearby, a large tent had been erected, and beneath it a feast awaited the mourners.

During the procession, Queen Ahmose Nefertari, Amenhotep, and his sister-wife, Meryetamun, kept their composure. However, Princess Ahmose could not prevent the tears from smearing her kohl-lined eyes and streaming down her cheeks in long black streaks. Her heart was heavy for all she had lost and for what her father would never know-- the joy of meeting her adopted son, Moses.

Memphis
1524 BC

Miriam liked to take Moses to visit the princess, who was kind to her and seemed interested in her life. Miriam was always careful not to give away the secret that Moses's wet nurse was actually his mother. Their visits usually took place in the courtyard. Each time, the princess would bring a new toy for Moses to play with.

On one visit, when Moses was two years of age, the princess brought a carved wooden lion. When Moses pulled the string, the toy lion's mouth opened wide, revealing its teeth. Moses chortled with glee as the princess made a soft roaring sound. Soon Moses was roaring too. Princess Ahmose watched him as he toddled around the courtyard with his new toy.

Princess Ahmose longed to keep Moses, but she knew the time was not right for him or for her family. Her brother, Amenhotep, was now the pharaoh, and she would need his permission to adopt Moses. She had hesitated to ask her mother to intercede for her, because her mother was still grieving over her father's death. However, she wanted Amenhotep to get to know Moses before she brought him to the palace. She loved her brother and hoped he would be like a father to Moses. His wife, Queen Meryetamun, was her older sister, whom she adored. What a handsome couple they had made at their coronation. She hoped they would both be equally accepting of her adopted son.

It was six months before Princess Ahmose finally asked her mother to speak to Amenhotep. Her mother was now the great Royal Queen Mother, highly honored. She had her own property, which was administered separately. The people of Egypt now considered her divine.

Queen Mother Ahmose Nefertari requested to be ushered into the presence of the pharaoh, her son.

After the initial greetings, she broached the subject of her daughter. "Princess Ahmose is alone," she said. "She has neither mate nor child. You have the throne and the wife you desired."

"That is true, my dear and honored mother, but what is your wish?" replied Pharaoh.

"Your sister, Princess Ahmose, has a request to make of you. It means very much to her. She has rescued a Hebrew baby, now two years old, and she wants to raise him as her son."

Pharaoh asked in surprise, "Where is he?"

The Queen Mother explained, "He is with his wet nurse in her home and will be there until he is three years old. In the meantime, I would like you to see him. In another year, your sister wishes to bring him to live in the palace with us. For her sake, please grant your permission and welcome him as your nephew."

Pharaoh replied, "Have you thought of what this means? If I should have a son, he must come first."

His mother assured him, "Of course, but they would be raised together. I want you to discuss this with Meryetamun and reassure her. The country is united now because of what your father accomplished. I want to be sure that nothing divides the royal family."

"Rest assured, Mother. You know I love the princess, and if this will make her happy, it's the least I can do. There already are other children, sons of the nobles, being educated in the palace," said Pharaoh.

"I know," replied his mother. "I want to be sure that Moses will be accepted by them too—as an Egyptian."

Several months later, the pharaoh met Moses in the courtyard with Princess Ahmose. The curly headed cherub lifted his little arms to be scooped up by his uncle. It was love at first sight, and Moses's adoption was sealed.

Memphis
1523 BC

Jochebed was always happy to see the pharaoh's entourage moving toward the Nile to board the royal bark, because she knew that meant they were leaving for their palace in Thebes. It could be for a festival at the temple or for a royal funeral, but whatever the reason for their trip, she knew that she wouldn't have to let Moses see the princess for a while.

The time was drawing near when she and Moses's father, Amran, would have to give Moses over to the princess for good. Life had become easier for Amran since they were paid to care for Moses. He had risen to the position of foreman and was not as weary now when he came home. He had to work for the Egyptians, but he also acted as priest for the Hebrews. He tried to spend as much time as possible with Moses and taught him to praise Adonai.

"Adonai is one God," he would tell Moses, and the little boy would point one finger to the heavens. "Adonai is great," he would say, and the child would spread both arms upward.

Jochebed could hear Amran pacing the floor at night. The first time she found him weeping in the dark, she had tried to comfort him.

He asked her, "How can we give him up?"

Jochebed steeled herself. "We must," she said. "The princess considers him her son. She seems like a good person. Already she loves him. Besides, God chose to save Moses. He could have been food for the crocodiles or drowned in the Nile. At least he is alive. God must have a purpose for his life. He will be given all the best that Egypt has to offer."

Although her words had been hopeful for her husband's sake, Jochebed's heart was breaking. Any day now, the princess would call upon her to give up her son.

Jochebed made the most of her time with Moses. She taught him about the one true God. As the breeze came off the Nile, she would say, "Do you feel the wind? We can't see it, but we know it's here. We can't see God, but we know He is here. He loves you." Then she would put his little hand on his heart. "Adonai," she said.

And Moses replied, "Adon." He could not say the whole word. Jochebed knew he was bright, but he was slow to speak. She remembered Miriam and Aaron speaking clearly at his age. She wondered if he had been stunted by the shock of being set adrift on the Nile. Then she caught herself, remembering that fearful day. What else could she have done? And anyway, God had intervened.

Moses was observant. Sometimes Jochebed, watching his eyes, would wonder what he was thinking. It was as though his speech could not catch up with his brain. She loved to tell him stories about the Hebrew patriarchs. He especially liked the story of Joseph. His favorite part was Joseph riding in the pharaoh's chariot. He had watched the chariots at the palace, so he could picture the scene in his mind. He would sit on his mother's lap and grasp her arms as though they were his chariot reins. As Jochebed increased the speed of her bouncing knees, he would shout "Osef, Osef," mimicking the accolades given so long ago by the people to Joseph as he rode through the countryside in the pharaoh's chariot.

Miriam and Aaron would join in calling, "Osef, Osef."

Memphis
1523 BC

What a joy it was to finally have Moses at the palace full time!

It was a comfort to both Princess Ahmose and her mother, Ahmose Nefertari. The death of the princess's father had been difficult.

"Not enough years, not enough years," Ahmose Nefertari kept saying. "He was younger. I should have gone first, but Amun called him." The Queen Mother's faith in Amun was unshaken.

As she held Moses, her new grandson, she said to her daughter, "What a fine child, so sturdy and beautiful of face. No wonder you could not resist him, even as a baby."

"But you are a big boy now," she continued to the three-year-old child as she nuzzled his neck and made him giggle. Then she grew serious, for his education into Egyptian ways should begin without delay.

"Who is God?" she asked the child, "what is his name?"

"Adon," Moses replied.

Ahmose Nefertari put her finger gently on the boy's lips to stop him. "Look at my lips," she said as she held them together to emphasize the second syllable. "A-mm-un."

"Adon," Moses pronounced plainly.

"Ah, well, my child, there will be time to get it right," she said as she handed the boy back to her daughter, Princess Ahmose.

Suddenly the queen was tired. Grief was like that, she thought. It was like walking in the black Nile mud at flood time—difficult to put one foot in front of the other, fearing you could be sucked under at any moment. That was the problem with marrying a younger brother. She had known him all her life. They had the same father and mother. They were bound together in so many ways. Now she doubly felt the wrenching of the separation.

Ahmose Nefertari wanted only to lie prone on her bed, but she thought, *I must be strong for my son, Amenhotep, the new pharaoh. He is so young. My husband was much younger when he ascended the throne at only sixteen. Our mother, Queen Ahotep, was a strong support for both of us. For sixty years she reigned, first as Queen consort and then as Queen Mother. Now I am the Queen Mother. I must be strong like a limestone pillar for my son. Yes, a limestone pillar.*

I can do that, she thought as she felt a cold numbness at the core of her being. *I can do that.*

The next morning, Queen Mother Ahmose Nefertari arose as her servant girl brought her a breakfast of warm bread with honey and hot brewed herb tea. When she stepped into the bathing room, her handmaidens poured warm water over her, wrapping her in soft towels afterward. Other servant girls stood by, holding her fine linen robes.

Seated at her dressing table, she studied her countenance in the polished silver mirror. Ahmose was surprised that she looked rested for the first time in years. A little kohl around her eyes, some rouge on her lips and cheeks, and she would be presentable. Her elaborate wig, jewelry, and crown completed her ensemble. The queen mother had arranged for a meeting with her son in the main salon, after which she would seek out her daughter and play with Moses for a while.

The meeting was good. Amenhotep was happy to find his mother taking an interest in kingdom affairs. She was very knowledgeable and had been a supportive consort to his father. For the first time since his father's death, his heart was encouraged and the burden of his position felt lighter.

As Ahmose Nefertari left the salon, she was suddenly aware that she was more alive and responsive to her surroundings. The feeling of coldness she had felt the night before was gone. It seemed that her decision to move forward had given her strength and somehow released her senses.

Now, as the light streamed from the clerestory windows above her and, slanting down, illuminated the colorful tapestries on the opposite wall, she could appreciate the intricate weavings. Entering the corridor, she heard the lilting voice of her daughter lifted in a song of joy. Following the sound to the sunny courtyard, she found her daughter with Moses.

"Such a happy child," the princess said, as she turned to look at her mother. "Oh, Mother, you look wonderful this morning," she said, rising with a slight bow, followed by an embrace. "Come sit with me," invited the princess, now eighteen years of age and more beautiful than ever.

As the princess pulled Moses onto her lap, he grasped her arms and started bouncing vigorously. "Osef, Osef," he called.

"Mother," asked the bewildered princess, "who is Osef?"

"I have no idea," she declared as she watched the insistent bouncing boy.

"Osef … Osef!"

The Delta
1885 BC

Approximately three and a half centuries earlier, Joseph, the man whom young Moses called "Osef" lay in the prison of Pharaoh's palace. Joseph could not sleep. He thought back over his thirty years of life and how he had come to this place at this time. His family came to mind: his ten half brothers and his beloved father, Jacob. He thought fondly of his only full brother, the young Benjamin. Their mother, Rachel, had died giving birth to Benjamin. The family was aware that Rachel had been Jacob's favorite wife. The favoritism had extended to Joseph, prompting insane jealousy in the half brothers. When Joseph was only seventeen years old, they had thrown him in a pit and had subsequently sold him to a passing caravan headed for Egypt. From the depths of the pit, Joseph had heard them plot to kill a goat and smear his multicolored coat with the goat's blood. This would provide "evidence" to their father that Joseph must have been killed by a wild animal. Joseph shuddered as he remembered the terror he had experienced as he listened.

In Egypt, Joseph had been sold to Potiphar, a nobleman of the pharaoh's court. Joseph had been entrusted as manager over all Potiphar's possessions and had fared well until he was falsely accused of misdeeds by Potiphar's wife. Joseph had managed to evade her seductive advances for years, but one day she sent all the servants away so there would be no witnesses to her attempts to entrap him. When spurned by Joseph, she lied and accused him of attacking her. Potiphar believed his wife and had Joseph thrown in jail.

In prison, Joseph felt that God was protecting him. The head of the prison guards liked Joseph and put him in charge of the other prisoners.

One of those prisoners had been troubled by a dream. God revealed the meaning of the dream to Joseph. The prisoner was grateful, because a positive outcome was predicted for him. Joseph asked the man to remember him to the pharaoh when the man was restored to his position as cupbearer to the King. That had been two years ago. Joseph wondered if the cupbearer would ever remember him.

One day, the ruling pharaoh, Senusret II awakened from troubling dreams. In the first dream, he had been standing by the Nile when out of the river came seven fat cows, followed by seven gaunt cows. Then the gaunt cows ate up the fat cows. Another dream followed in which seven scorched, thin heads of grain swallowed seven healthy heads of grain. The pharaoh was so disturbed by his dreams that he called for all the magicians and wise men of Egypt to interpret them, but they were unable to tell him the meaning.

The chief cupbearer said to the pharaoh, "Today I am reminded of my shortcomings. I was once imprisoned by Pharaoh. A young Hebrew was there as a servant of the captain of the guard. He interpreted a dream I had. He said it meant my position as cupbearer to the King would be restored, and just as he said, my dream came true."

The pharaoh sent for Joseph, who was quickly brought up from the dungeon. When he had bathed and shaved off his beard, he dressed in new clothes that had been provided and was brought before the pharaoh.

Senusret II said to Joseph, "I had a dream and no one can interpret it. But I have heard it said that when you hear a dream, you can interpret it."

"I cannot do it," Joseph replied to the pharaoh, "but God will give Pharaoh the answer he desires."

After the pharaoh related his dreams, Joseph explained that the dreams were one and the same.

"The seven fat cows and the seven healthy heads of grain represent seven years of abundant harvests," Joseph interpreted. "The gaunt cows and the parched grain are seven lean years in which there will be widespread famine. By giving you two dreams with the same meaning, God is emphasizing that the events are sure to occur and that they will come to pass very soon."

Joseph advised the pharaoh to appoint a wise person to supervise the storing of grain in the good years in order to provide food for the people in the years of famine that would follow.

Pharaoh declared, "Where in all the land would I find a man as discerning and wise as you who can tell me the meaning of my dreams with the help of God? You shall be in charge of my palace, and my people will submit to your orders. Only with respect to the throne will I be greater than you."

Then the pharaoh put Joseph in charge of the whole land of Egypt. He took his signet ring off his finger and put it on Joseph's finger. He dressed him in fine linen robes and put a gold chain around his neck. The pharaoh put Joseph in his chariot as second-in-command, and men shouted before him, "Make way!"

Pharaoh told Joseph, "Without your word, no one will lift a hand or foot in all of Egypt."

As time went on, Senusret II noted that Joseph was handsome as well as wise. "You must have a suitable wife," the pharaoh said. "There is an exquisite young woman of excellent character nearby in On. She is the daughter of Potiphera, the priest of On. Her name is Asenath. I will send for her." When the pharaoh saw that Joseph was stunned by the beauty of Asenath, he gave her to Joseph to be his wife.

Joseph went throughout Egypt collecting grain and storing it in the towns. After several years had passed, the pharaoh was succeeded by his son, Senusret III. Joseph remained second-in-command, and his administrative ability was greatly admired. By the end of the first seven years, there was so much grain that the scribes stopped recording because the amount was immeasurable.

During that time, Joseph had two sons by Asenath. He named his firstborn Manasseh,[3] because, he said, "God caused me to forget the trouble from my father's household." He named his second son Ephraim,[4] saying, "God has made me fruitful in the land of my suffering."

After these seven years of abundance, in 1877 BC, there was a "poor flood." The waters of the Nile had slipped to six and a half feet below the normal level; one third of the valley was dry. In the famine that resulted, Joseph sold grain to the people of Egypt. All the surrounding countries came to buy grain from Joseph as well, because the famine was widespread. When the people ran out of money, they brought their livestock, pleading, "Give us grain for all these animals." This greatly expanded the herds of the pharaoh. Finally, the people offered their lands and themselves in servitude to the pharaoh in return for grain.

In this way, Joseph broke the power of the *nomes* or provinces and centralized the government, making Egypt a stronger nation. The people

---

3   Literally *making forgetful*
4   Meaning *fruitfulness*

were allowed to work the land but were required to give 20 percent to the pharaoh.[5] Only the priests could keep their land, because they received their allotment directly from the pharaoh.

In the second year of famine so many people were suffering that Joseph became concerned whether his father's family had enough food in Canaan.

---

5   This system continued to modern times.

Canaan
1876 BC

In the second year of the famine, Jacob said to his sons, "Why do you just sit around looking at each other? I've heard there is grain in Egypt; go there and buy some for us. If conditions continue like this, we will die, for the famine is severe."

So ten brothers of Joseph went down to Egypt, leaving young Benjamin at home with their father.

When the brothers arrived in Egypt, they were directed to Joseph, the governor of the land. They bowed low before him with their faces to the ground, but did not recognize him. He recognized them but pretended they were strangers and spoke to them harshly, accusing them of being spies. They said they were honest men of Canaan who had come to buy grain. As Joseph insisted that they had come to spy out the land and see where it was unprotected, they became anxious and gave Joseph more information about themselves.

"We are twelve brothers, the sons of one man who lives in Canaan. The youngest is with our father and one is no more."

Joseph told them he was going to test them. He held them in custody for three days, after which he told them, "Do this and you will live, for I fear God. Take food to your starving families, but leave one brother here in prison until you come back with your youngest brother so that I may know you are telling the truth."

The brothers talked among themselves. They did not know that Joseph could understand them, as he was using an interpreter. "Surely we are being punished for what we did to our brother. We did not listen when he pleaded with us for his life. That is why this distress is come upon us."

One of the brothers, Reuben, spoke up, "Didn't I tell you not to sin against the boy? But you wouldn't listen, so now we will be held responsible for his blood."

Hearing this, Joseph was moved. He turned away from them and started to weep but steeled himself and turned back to them, ordering that one of them, Simeon, be bound and taken away. In secret, Joseph gave orders that each man's sack be filled with grain and the money they had paid for the grain be put back in the sacks. Provisions for their journey were also given. The brothers loaded the grain on their donkeys and left for Canaan.

When they stopped for the night, one man opened his sack for some grain to feed his donkey. When he saw the silver, he was alarmed and told his brothers. They exclaimed, "What has God done to us?"

The brothers returned home and told their father all that had transpired.

When they opened the other sacks and saw that all their money had been returned, they were frightened. Jacob said, "What have you done? Joseph is gone. Simeon is held prisoner, and now you want to take Benjamin from me? I will not let him go! If harm comes to him it will send me to my grave."

As time went on and the famine continued, Jacob and his sons ran out of grain. With great difficulty, the brothers persuaded their father to let them go back to Egypt with Benjamin. "For," they said, "the governor will not see us or sell us grain unless we bring Benjamin with us."

"Why did you tell him you had a younger brother at home?" Jacob asked.

The brothers answered, "He questioned us at length asking about our family. How were we to know he would demand to see Benjamin?"

They explained to Jacob, "If we take Benjamin, the governor will let Simeon go, and he will sell us grain."

The brother, Judah, offered to be responsible to see that Benjamin was returned safely.

Jacob said, "If it must be done, then take the best products of the land as a gift—balm, honey, spices, myrrh, almonds, pistachio nuts—and more silver, in addition to the money that was returned to us."

When Joseph saw Benjamin coming with his brothers, he called his steward and told him to take the men to his house, slaughter an animal, and prepare a feast, for he wanted them to eat with him at noon. The steward brought the men to Joseph's house. They were frightened because of the money that had been returned to them, so they explained that the money had appeared in their sacks, and they were returning it. The steward told them not to worry, because their God must have given them the money. Then he brought Simeon to them, fed their donkeys, and gave them water to wash their feet. As the brothers waited, they prepared their gifts for Joseph. Then they were ushered to a table, apart from the Egyptians. Marveling that they were seated in order of their birth, they asked each other, "How did they know our ages?"

When Joseph entered, they bowed to the floor before him.

He asked them, "How is your aged father you told me about?"

They answered, "He is well."

Searching out Benjamin in the group, Joseph asked, "Is this the younger brother you left at home last time?"

Joseph wanted to embrace Benjamin, but he restrained himself and hastily left the room, looking for a place to release his emotions. He went to his private chamber and wept. When he felt he could control himself, he washed his face and returned to the dinner.

"Serve the food," he ordered the servants.

After the meal, the brothers thanked Joseph and left for their home. Now Joseph had ordered his steward to return their silver again and also to take his own silver cup and place it in Benjamin's sack.

When the men had gone a short distance, they were apprehended by the steward, who ordered them to open their sacks. To their horror, the governor's silver cup was found in Benjamin's sack.

Back in Egypt, Joseph was waiting at his house. "How could you do this?" demanded Joseph, "Didn't you realize I have ways of finding out these things?"

Falling on their faces before him, the brothers pleaded for their lives.

Joseph told them, "I will spare your lives, but the one in whose sack the cup was found I will keep as my slave."

Judah spoke up, "My Lord, you asked if we had another brother at home, and we told you truthfully. Our father was devastated to let Benjamin go, but you would not sell us grain unless we brought him back with us. We did not take the cup, but how can we prove it? Please let Benjamin go. Take me instead. I swore to my father I would be responsible for him. Let me stay here to be your slave. I could not bear to see my father's misery if we do not bring Benjamin back safely. Benjamin is all my father has left of the two sons his wife Rachel bore him. One is dead, and if Benjamin is not returned, our father will die of grief."

At this pitiful plea, Joseph could no longer control himself, so he ordered his attendants, "Everyone leave my presence."

Joseph told his brothers, "Come close to me. I am your brother, the one you sold into Egypt. Do not be distressed or angry with yourselves, because God meant it for good. He has sent me ahead to provide for you. For two years there has been famine in the land, and for five more years there will be no plowing or reaping. It was God who sent me here, not you. God made me father to Pharaoh, and ruler of all Egypt, in order to preserve you as a remnant on earth."

Joseph's brothers stood in awe, trying to absorb what he was saying.

Joseph continued, "Now hurry back to my father, and tell him Joseph is alive. God has made me Lord of Egypt. Come down to me. Don't delay."

Then Joseph threw his arms around Benjamin and wept. Benjamin embraced him, weeping also. Joseph kissed all his brothers and wept over them.

Pent-up emotion burst from Joseph in such loud weeping that the Egyptians heard it, and the news of his reunion with his family reached the pharaoh's household.

When the pharaoh heard that Joseph's brothers had come, he and all his officials were pleased. Pharaoh called for Joseph and told him, "Tell your brothers to load their animals and return to Canaan. Bring your father and your brothers back to me, and I will give you the best of the land of Egypt and you will enjoy the fat of the land. Take carts along from Egypt for your wives and children and your father."

Joseph sent his brothers back with these instructions, giving them provisions, new clothes, and money for their journey.

So it was, that with the blessings of the pharaoh, the children of Jacob [Israel] were settled in the land of Goshen, the rich eastern delta area.

With great rejoicing, Joseph met his father there upon his arrival and enjoyed seventeen years with his father in Egypt. Before his death, Jacob blessed his children, including Joseph and his two sons born in Egypt. Then he asked to be buried with his father, Isaac, and grandfather, Abraham, in the cave of Machpelah in Canaan.

God had appeared to Jacob in a dream on his journey to meet Joseph in Egypt. Jacob told Joseph, "God assured me that he would be with us in Egypt and that he would make us a great nation here. Then he told me he would surely bring us back again to Canaan, and that you, Joseph, would close my eyes with your own hand." And Joseph did. He had his father embalmed in Egypt and then, accompanied by the adults in the family and by a large contingent from the pharaoh's court, he buried his father in Canaan. The lamenting of the large company was so great that the inhabitants of Canaan thought it was remarkable.

"The Egyptians are holding a solemn ceremony of mourning," they said.

After their father died, Joseph's brothers were afraid that, finally, Joseph would exact revenge on them for their earlier mistreatment. Joseph wept when he heard that and he reassured them that though they had meant harm for him, God had a higher plan. God had accomplished good for all of them, so they need not fear Joseph. Speaking kindly, he promised to provide for them and their children. Before his own death, Joseph made his people swear that when God came to their aid, as he surely would, they would carry his bones to Canaan with them. Joseph's years were 110, a number deemed to be the ideal lifespan in ancient Egypt. The Egyptians considered it a divine blessing on Joseph.

And that is the story of how a family from Canaan came to live in the delta region of Egypt. There the people flourished for over four centuries and greatly increased in number. A new pharaoh, Ahmose I, who did not remember the story of Joseph came to the throne of Egypt. By this time the children of Israel had been forced into slavery and they cried out for release from their oppression. After the death of Pharaoh Ahmose I, a descendant of Jacob (Israel), came to live in the palace of Egypt as the adopted son of Pharaoh's daughter, Princess Ahmose, and nephew of the new Pharaoh, Amenhotep I.

Memphis
1522 BC

"Where is Uncle Tep?" four-year-old Moses repeatedly asked his Egyptian mother.

Princess Ahmose told him his uncle was fighting a battle with his bow and arrow. She knew Moses greatly missed his uncle, Pharaoh Amenhotep. When he was at home in the palace, he would give Moses rides on his broad shoulders, loping around the courtyard to the excited laughter of his little nephew. Amenhotep and Meryetamun, his sister-wife, did not have any children yet, so they were delighted to give Moses their undivided attention. It was Amenhotep to whom Moses was most drawn. Princess Ahmose was pleased, as she had hoped her brother would be a surrogate father to Moses. He was a brave man, yet sensitive and kind.

Princess Ahmose took a toy chariot drawn by two horses down from a shelf in the play area. Next, she opened a large storage basket and pulled out a carved soldier with a bow and arrow, placing him in the chariot.

"See," she told Moses, "here's Uncle Tep fighting the battle."

"No," said Moses, "where is his crown?"

Princess Ahmose summoned her servant girl to bring her a small piece of papyrus, a little paste made from flour and water, and a flint knife. When the girl returned with the items she had requested, Ahmose took the knife and cut a small strip of papyrus, forming a point in the center. Then she rolled the strip with her fingers to form a small, conical crown, securing the edge with paste. Ahmose placed the tiny crown on the head of the toy soldier. "Uncle Tep, Uncle Tep," cried the delighted child.

* * * * * *

Meanwhile, in the Libyan hill country on the edge of the desert, Amenhotep sat before the leaping flames of a campfire. He missed his wife. The fighting that day had yielded spoils, including a number of beautiful girls. His soldiers offered Amenhotep his choice of these young women, but waving them away, he refused such favor to the reigning victor. He only wanted his Meryet[6]. Earlier, his chief officer had brought him a sealed papyrus that the queen had slipped in with her husband's provisions. The note wished Amun's blessings on Amenhotep and, besides her prayer for his safety, included an Egyptian love poem:

I am thy first sister,
And thou art to me as a garden,
which I have planted with flowers
and all sweet smelling herbs.
I directed a canal into it,
That thou mightest dip thy hand in it,
When the north wind blows cool.
The beautiful place where we take a walk,
When thine hand rests within mine
With thoughtful mind and joyful heart
Because we walk together.
It is intoxicating to me to hear thy voice,
And my life depends upon hearing thee.
Whenever I see thee.
It is better to me than food and drink.[7]

Meryet added, "Come home to me soon, my love, my life."

Amenhotep remembered their courtship. They had been raised in different parts of the palace. He had been in the princes' quarters, called the shep. Their mother, Queen Ahmose Nefertari, had kept them apart as they entered their maturing years. That was not difficult to do, as Amenhotep had sought to be outdoors whenever he could. There was so much to do for a growing boy in Egypt. He was gone fishing, hunting, or exploring when he wasn't in classes. The queen understood Amenhotep's love of adventure, so she had provided a little mystery for Meryet and Amenhotep. By the time he was grown, he still thought of his sister as a little girl.

---

6   Amenhotep's nickname for his wife, Merytamun
7   Erman, *Life in Ancient Egypt*, 389; The Harris Papyrus, 500, 10, 9ff.

Then, one memorable evening at a palace celebration, he caught sight of a gorgeous young woman across the room. Captivated by her appearance, he asked an attendant, "Who is that young woman talking to the harpist over there?"

"My Lord," replied the surprised servant, "she is your sister, Meryet."

In subsequent months, he had courted her with precious gifts and Egyptian love poems.

He wrote to her:

Seven days and I've not seen my lady love.
A sickness has shot through me,
I have become sluggish,
and I have forgotten my own body.
My heart will not be comforted with their remedies,
My lady love is more remedial than any potion.
She's better than the whole book of medical lore.
If I see her, then I'll be well.
Distracting is the foliage of my pasture,
The mouth of my girl is a lotus bud,
Her breasts are mandrake apples,
Her arms are vines,
Her eyes are fixed like berries
Her brow a snare of willow, and I, the wild goose.[8]

Amenhotep smiled to himself as he remembered how his lovesickness had been remedied by their marriage and the passionate nights of lovemaking that followed. Now they were King and Queen of Egypt and still in love. Thinking of his queen, he could not wait to get home to the palace, to the arms of his lovely wife, and to the warmth of his family.

I'll bet little Moses misses me too, he thought. *He is nearing the end of his fourth year, the end of childhood in ancient Egypt. Soon I must see to his schooling, as he is entering boyhood.*

---

8   William Kelly Simpson, "The Gift of Writing," *In Ancient Egypt, Discovering Its Splendors,*152

Memphis
1520 BC

Moses was now a schoolboy. Clad in a simple linen kilt, he wore the traditional side lock of hair hanging down along his face with the rest of his head shaved—the custom for Egyptian boys. He sat cross-legged on the floor of the palace classroom, surrounded by his palette and inks, his water pot, his case of rush brushes, and his erasing stone. On his lap was a writing board, which had been coated with gesso so that it could be erased and used many times. Moses had a sharp mind and a diligent spirit, which spared him from the cane that the palace instructor kept by his chair and didn't hesitate to use on his pupils. It seemed the teacher took seriously the Egyptian saying, "A boy's ears are on his back, and he listens when he is beaten."

The writing and exercises were slow and tedious, but Moses was mastering them as he patiently copied the texts from the book of Kemyt over and over. Soon he graduated to copying stories, which he found to be much more interesting. In this way, Moses was learning to read and write at the same time. As he wrote in the cursive hieratic script, his hand moved from right to left across his board.

On this day, Moses had been working since early morning and was ready for a rest. During the lunch break, he enjoyed playing a game of ball with his classmates, most of whom were sons of Egyptian noblemen. The others were foreigners, sons of tributary rulers. They were treated very well in Egypt, but they were actually hostages, kept as insurance against rebellion by the foreign rulers. Once the young princes had been trained in Egyptian ways, they would be returned to rule in their own countries.

Over lunch, Moses enjoyed hearing about these foreign lands. Now his team was winning in the game of hitting a leather-wrapped ball along the ground with long sticks. After lunch, it was time for a lesson in ethics. Egyptians began teaching their children moral values at a very young age. The "wisdom texts" from the Old Kingdom, such as the teachings of Ptahhotep, described expectations for behavior of an Egyptian. Respect for parents and superiors was fundamental, but inferiors were also to be treated well. They were not to be humiliated by persons of a higher rank. Instead, their respect was to be won by understanding and polite words. One must resist jealousy and envy. A person should always be generous and treat friends well. If he has nothing interesting to say, a person should be silent. Such admonitions, and others, formed a system of values that was the basis for the good behavior toward which each student was expected to strive.

Memphis
1517 BC

At nine years of age, Moses was a sturdy boy, taller than most of his classmates. His studies now included mathematics. He enjoyed the calculations that were applied to practical problems, such as how long it would take so many men to build a brick ramp, how much grain a silo of a certain size would hold, or how many provisions it would take to supply a military unit for an expedition to Syria. There were no multiplication tables to learn. All mathematical procedures were based on the underlying process of addition or subtraction. The hieroglyphic decimal system had symbols for 1, 10, 100, 1000, and 10,000. Intermediate numbers were written in multiples of the single number. Procedures for fractions were based on the addition and subtraction of unit fractions.

Moses had now progressed to the learning of *hieroglyphics* or sacred writings. He was allowed to use papyrus, a paper made from the plant that grew long the Nile. The plant fiber was stripped and pounded into sheets. Because Moses had such a steady hand, his teacher told him he should consider becoming a chief scribe. Moses had seen the scribes at work, endlessly recording details and inventories. He would rather write stories and poems.

Now that he was older, his classes ended earlier, and a tutor took over for religious studies. This was an area in which Moses had shown an early interest. His uncle had cautioned him to respect the tutor, even if he didn't always understand or believe everything about the god system that was being explained to him.

Moses asked his uncle why Egypt needed so many gods.

Pharaoh replied, "Think of them as aspects of the god of gods, Amun-Re. Amun is the one and only true god. This is what the educated people believe and especially the people of Thebes. But remember, the nation of Egypt is spread out for a great distance along the Nile; all the little towns along the way, and also the cities of the delta, have their own gods, because the people of Egypt want it that way. I personally would like there to be one god, but I doubt that the people of Egypt are ready for that."

"The animals are what people know," he continued, "so we have Bastet, the cat god; Hathor, the cow goddess; and Sobek, represented by the crocodile. Each god is given a special function. You will learn more about the Egyptian god system when you are older. I think the stories of Osiris, Isis, Seth, and Horus are especially interesting. In the meantime, I'd like you to think of Amun as the god beyond the natural world who was there before the world came into existence. He had the idea of the world[9] and created the world by his word[10]. He is the "hidden one" as the midnight sun. His glory is seen in the daytime as Amun-Re, but he is the same god. All other gods emanated from him as did all the creation. Remember, Moses, this is the highest form of religion that Egypt has to offer."

Moses pondered his uncle's words. He had a faint memory of someone telling him there was one God. Could it have been his Hebrew father or mother? he wondered. He still thought of his mother as Princess Ahmose, but she had recently told him that he had Hebrew parents who had saved his life by putting him into a papyrus boat on the Nile. Then she told him how she had rescued him and taken him in as her precious son. He loved to hear about how he came to live in the palace. He couldn't imagine his life without his dear Egyptian mother and his beloved Uncle Tep, but sometimes he wondered about those other parents who had loved him too and had sent him to sail on the mighty river.

Moses was spending more and more time sailing little papyrus boats on the Nile. Princess Ahmose told Pharaoh Amenhotep, "Sometimes I can't help but wonder if it was because I told Moses how I rescued him from a little papyrus boat on the Nile."

"All boys like to sail," her brother told her. "I did too, but I can see your concern if he is slipping away to the river by himself."

"Yes," replied the princess. "What if he should lean out to retrieve a boat and topple into the water? He doesn't know how to swim."

---

9   perception
10   annunciation

"That is easily remedied, and I should have done it before this," her brother said. "I will see that he receives swimming lessons immediately, which is a good idea anyway, because I am planning a fishing trip."

"Just for the two of you?" she asked.

"With a few attendants," he replied, "but don't tell him yet. I'll use it as a reward for learning to swim quickly."

"There is one more concern I have," she said. "If he learns to swim, there is still a danger of crocodiles. And it's not only the river. Sometimes he just wanders off on an *adventure* as he calls it, and he forgets to take along an adult."

Amenhotep replied, "He needs his freedom. The boy has to have room to breathe without always having someone looking over his shoulder. I remember what it was like growing up in the palace. I'll tell you what, suppose I get him a greyhound, a *slugi*? That could be protection for him. Besides, it would do him good to train him as a hunting dog, with my help, of course. We can take him along when we go hunting."

"Excellent" exclaimed his sister. "I knew I could count on you. You are so good to me and to Moses."

"Now, I have three surprises for Moses," he responded. "Swimming lessons, a fishing trip, and the dog!"

Moses was off on one of his adventures again. He had several getaways or hideouts; the most secret one was in the reeds and brush beside the Nile, under an old willow tree that had low-lying branches. Another one was a fort, made with limestone blocks from a pile of stones being used to repair a palace terrace. His classmates had helped him move them on his small sled. Moses's favorite getaway was in the guard tower. The guards agreed to keep his secret if he behaved himself. They acted a bit stern because that was part of their job, but they actually enjoyed his presence. The guards accommodated the young lad by pushing two small tables under a window as a lookout platform for him. Moses dragged cushions up the stairs of the tower and put them on the tables, forming a comfortable place where he could kneel and look out the window to survey his kingdom. He could watch the boats go by on the Nile, a major highway for travel and commerce. There were boats of every size and shape. Soon his uncle would take him on one of those boats, because they were going fishing. Uncle Tep had a surprise for him, too. He wondered what it was.

* * * * *

The sun had just risen as Moses and his Uncle Tep boarded a boat on the Nile. Moses was amazed as he watched the boatman hoist the sails. The man was so nimble! He thought this might be a good job for him when he was grown and said so to his uncle.

"No, Moses, you aren't going to be a boatman. Someone who is not as privileged as you needs that job," said Uncle Tep, leaning toward the boy. In a low voice he said, "Who knows, Moses, you could be Pharaoh someday!"

Amenhotep thought to himself, *There, I've planted a seed!*

The boy's eyes widened, and he whispered as though it were their personal conspiracy, "Just like you Uncle Tep?"

"Yes, just like me," his uncle replied. "That would please your mother, and it would make me happy too."

"What about Aunt Meryet?" asked Moses.

"Your aunt and I wish we had a child of our own, but so far Amun hasn't blessed us with one," Amenhotep said. "He has brought you to us instead; so maybe that's what he wants—you to be the next pharaoh."

As the boat moved forward under the billowing sails, Moses asked, "What about Adonai? Is that what he wants too, Pharaoh?"

Amenhotep marveled at the boy's sensitivity, to call him by his formal title in the hearing of the attendants. Moses was looking at him expectantly for an answer.

"How should I know, Moses" he asked. "Adonai is your God, but he doesn't speak to me. Does he speak to you?"

"Not out loud," replied Moses. "He speaks to my heart," he said simply.

Amenhotep had no reply to that. How could one doubt the simple faith of a young boy?

"Come now," said Amenhotep, changing the subject "It is time to get our spears ready. The fish are waiting for us."

With that, he took hold of a thin spear, almost three yards long, which had two sharp points attached firmly to one end. Then he picked up a smaller version for Moses.

"Watch me Moses," he said, demonstrating the proper stance. "It is important that you stand just like this so that you do not lose your balance and fall into the water. Even though by now you are a good swimmer, that's not what we are here for, is it?"

"No, sire," said Moses. "We are fishermen!"

"All right then, come over here, and let me show you how to spear a fish," invited his Uncle Tep.

Amenhotep showed Moses how to hold his spear. Then, standing behind him with one arm around the boy's waist and holding his spear arm with the other, he practiced the thrust of the spear again and again with Moses. Next, he indicated that Moses should watch him before trying it himself. The voices around them rose in a cacophony of sound. The boatmen were singing, traders were calling out to passing barks and hawking their wares, and travelers were hailing people along the shoreline. Moses could hear the distant singing of the farmers, busily harvesting their grain in the fertile fields. Soon the annual inundation would take place, flooding the fields, so they wanted to get their crops in. Other farmers were taking advantage of the dry riverbanks to cultivate small patches of chickpeas, lentils, and onions.

"Look, Moses, just past that clump of palm trees over there," said Amenhotep, motioning for the helmsman to steer toward the bank so Moses could get a good look. "That farmer is using a *shadoof*," he added, pointing to a farmer who was dipping water from the Nile with a bucket levered by a weighted pole. "That shadoof," he continued, " is a fairly new invention that has made it easier for the farmer to irrigate his fields. Still, he must work from dawn to dusk to get it done."

"The farmer must not mind so much," commented Moses. "I can hear him singing with joy."

The man was singing an ancient paeon to the Nile: "The fields laugh—the visage of man is bright."

The sunny spring morning was filled with bird song too. Moses was quiet, but his heart was singing along with the birds and the people. He was on the mighty Nile with his Uncle Tep, and he was going to spear his first fish. The sailors searched for a quiet spot that was shallow enough to make the fishing easier. It wasn't difficult to find, as the Nile was at its lowest level. Moses watched for a little while as his uncle thrust his spear into the water and came up empty. Finally, Amenhotep speared two big fish at once, much to the boy's delight. Then it was Moses's turn. Though it took a long time, his patience paid off, and sure enough, Moses speared his first fish.

It was midday when Uncle Tep and Moses made their way to the palace, an attendant carrying their creel full of catfish and perch.

"Have the cook prepare those for our midday meal," ordered Pharaoh.

To Moses, he said, "Wash up for lunch. After we've eaten and had a rest, I'll give you the surprise I told you about."

"I'm not tired," said Moses eagerly.

"Well, your old uncle needs a nap, but I'll make it a short one," Amenhotep promised.

Moses was ready and waiting when his uncle walked into the garden where he had been passing the time by trailing his fingers in the cool water of a small pool.

"I thought I'd find you out here," said his uncle. "Do you have any idea what the surprise is?"

"No, I don't," replied Moses.

The pharoah clapped his hands, and a male attendant came walking out with a beautiful greyhound on a leash.

"Oh!" gasped Moses. "Is th-th-this dog mine?" he stuttered.

"If you want it to be," said Amenhotep.

"Oh, Uncle, thank you," his nephew said, wrapping his arms around the pharaoh's waist in an embrace of gratitude.

Amenhotep was deeply touched by this spontaneous burst of affection from Moses. Brushing away a tear, he said, "Now, it is time this animal has a name. Think carefully, Moses, and choose an appropriate name for your new dog."

Moses gazed at the graceful creature. "She reminds me of a gazelle," he said, "so I will name her Bekah'e."[11]

"An excellent choice," exclaimed Amenhotep. "Bekah'e it will be; maybe Bekah, for short," he suggested.

"Perfect," said Moses. "Here, Bekah," he called to her. Kneeling beside her, Moses hugged her neck and stroked her narrow back. In response, Bekah licked his face eagerly with her long tongue.

Moses laughed, "That tickles, Bekah!"

Amenhotep could see his nephew was wrapped up with Bekah. To get his attention, he said, "Moses, I have the time now, so I thought we might start Bekah's training this afternoon. Bekah is old enough to learn obedience," he continued. "Here, Moses, you take her leash and, Khasha, you come along too," he told the dog's handler.

As they walked to the archery field near the palace, Amenhotep spoke to Khasha, "I want you to schedule regular training sessions. Check with my scribe as to when I am available, and check when Moses is free from classes. I'm not sure Moses realizes how much work the dog requires. I want Bekah to bond with him, so it is important for Moses to be responsible for the dog as much as possible, but I'd like you to stand by. Make sure that

---

11   *Bekah'e* is the Egyptian word for a gazelle.

Bekah has the best of care as this is a new experience for Moses. Do you have any questions?"

"No my Lord, I understand," replied Khasha.

Nodding, Amenhotep continued, "Princess Ahmose will check on Bekah also, simply because she loves animals so much. You've probably heard how she has this uncanny sense when something isn't right with one of our animals, even before it comes down with an illness. I've learned to trust her instincts."

They had reached the archery field, so he called Moses over. "Moses," he said with a serious tone, "before we start the training I want you to remember this. In a dog pack there is always a leader, a chief dog. It is instinctive for the dog to have a leader. You must show Bekah that you are that leader. Do not yell at her, but make your voice loud and firm enough in your commands so that she knows you are in charge. When she performs well, that is, when she obeys you, praise her and give her a morsel of food from your hand. Do you understand?"

"Yes, Pharaoh," replied Moses with gravity, suddenly realizing his uncle was entrusting him with authority over a creature, who might not always do what he wanted her to do. Yet he was eager to start on this new adventure. After all, how hard could it be?

Moses had been working with Bekah for three months now, and she was always at his side. As Moses walked into the palace kitchen in the first light of dawn, he was warmly greeted by Cook, who, as usual, was as jolly as he was robust. The place was redolent with appetizing aromas.

"Well, well, look who is up already. Our favorite boy. Are you off on an adventure, Prince?" Cook queried.

"Yes, sir," he replied. "May I have a snack to take along?"

"Of course you may," replied Cook, looking at Bekah, who gazed back with soulful eyes and gave a short bark as if to say "Me too!"

"How about pocket bread with a tasty meat filling, some fruit, and a piece of honey date cake?" Cook continued. "Have you had breakfast?"

"No," answered Moses, "that will be plenty for breakfast and a snack too. Do you have something for Bekah?"

"Indeed I do," said Cook turning to give orders to his helpers. "It's a good thing you are here early today. When all the produce and game arrives for tomorrow's New Year's celebration, we will be so busy we won't know up from down."

Moses watched the cook's helpers deftly chop the roast fowl and mix it with chopped onions, tomatoes, cucumbers, garlic, and spices to stuff in the freshly baked bread. His mouth began to water. He would eat that first, he decided. Once the food was ready, he filled his skins with water. He would need extra for Bekah and to wash sticky hands after eating honey cake. He thanked the kitchen staff and set off to his favorite hideaway with Bekah in tow.

The summer day was bright with promise as Moses looked out the window of his guard tower hideaway. Just as Cook had said, boats were arriving and being unloaded. The carts and litters were loaded with delicious foods for the celebration tomorrow. Pharaoh had said Moses could attend the party. It would be his first big adult affair. His uncle, the pharaoh, would be presented with the most marvelous gifts from the nobles, which was the custom at the New Year. It was the onset of the inundation of the Nile. Moses had learned in school that Sopdet[12] appeared as a morning star after several months of invisibility. Moses smiled. It wasn't only *he* that liked to hide away. Even the stars did it sometimes. When Sopdet reappeared at the onset of the inundation of the Nile, the joint events marked the beginning of the Egyptian New Year. Everyone said the party would be great fun, with acrobats and lots of music. Maybe Moses could write a song for the festivities. There would be a wrestling match too. Moses wanted to watch the wrestlers' moves, as his uncle said the activity would be good physical training for him to have. Moses finished his food and fed Bekah. He started to write a song, but his full stomach and the heat of the day began to make him drowsy. As he sank to the cushions, his brush rolled onto the floor, startling the dog who was already snoozing under the bench. As midday came and went, Moses dreamed he was directing Bekah in all kinds of tricks at the party, while musicians played the song he had written.

---

12 Sirius

Memphis
1514 BC

Twelve-year-old Moses was having his side lock shaved off, a sign that he was entering a new stage of life in Egypt. Ordinarily, he would also be circumcised at this time as a rite of passage. However, Moses's Hebrew parents had circumcised him when he was only eight days old, according to the Hebrew religious tradition.

Moses would also have a change of dress. Instead of a simple linen kilt, he would now wear a short loincloth under a long robe of transparent, pleated linen cinched at the waist by a colorful sash. Around his neck, he would wear a pectoral, a collar of gold, studded with semiprecious stones. This was his formal dress, and he would soon be wearing it to the Beautiful Festival of Amun at Thebes.

The attendant fitted an elaborate, curly black wig on Moses's freshly shaved head. Over the wig, he would wear a wide woven band decorated with more gems. "Now you look like a true prince of Egypt," said Pharaoh Amenhotep, supervising his nephew's transformation.

"What I wore before was more comfortable. The collar is heavy, and the wig is hot."

"Yes, Moses, we sacrifice comfort to appear as adults, but don't worry, you won't be wearing that all the time. Let us go. We will be leaving soon for Thebes, and we will be gone for a long time, as the festival lasts eleven days. Your mother will see to the preparations for the journey, and she will tell you what to take along. We must get a good rest tonight, as we will be leaving early in the morning. It is a long trip, but I think you will enjoy it, Moses."

At dawn the next morning, Moses called for Bekah, "Come on, girl," he said. "We are going on an adventure. Want to go? Want to go?" The greyhound recognized those last words. She sat before Moses, wagging her curly tail and thumping it on the stone paving. Her eyes alight with excitement, she started bounding round and round.

"All right now, settle down," said Moses as he accepted the dog's leash from Khasha. The attendant would be going on the trip to stay with Bekah while they were at the Temple of Amun-Re at Karnak.

ON THE NILE

The main royal bark, *Star of the Two Countries*, bore the same name as the bark of King Khufu, builder of the Great Pyramid, some fifteen hundred years earlier. The huge boat was made of Lebanese cedar. Her tall masts held rectangular shaped sails, now furled, as the vessel sat at the dock awaiting the passengers. The three royal women, Queen Ahmose Nefertari, Queen Maryetamun, and Princess Ahmose were carried on elaborate litters down the broad flight of stone steps leading to the impressive limestone portico on the Nile. From there, the women were helped to board the bark, which had already been staffed and loaded with provisions and all of the baskets of clothes and toiletries they would need. Moses and Amenhotep walked down the stairs with Bekah on her leash.

The royal bark was a beautiful sight to see in the morning sunlight. The large central cabin was painted on the outside with colorful designs. The keel swept up at the stern in a graceful curve between the two steering oars and then recurved steeply at the end to form the shape of an open papyrus head.

Once aboard, the royal family was ushered to the comfortable cabin where the servants served them refreshments. Moses, however, wanted to be outside with Bekah. There was so much to see! He watched the helmsman at the stern use his long pole to push away from shore.

Moses reached down to pet his dog. "We are on our way, Bekah," he said as he watched the boatmen scrambling to unfurl the sails. The cool morning breeze filled the sails and caused them to snap open. Moses felt his own body snap to alertness. He did not want to miss anything on this trip.

The sail from Memphis was with the prevailing north wind, which moved the boat along at a smooth clip. Sometimes oars were used but only as a complement to the sails. As the royal bark sailed along, Moses watched the farmers riding their donkeys along the Nile bank to check on their fields. The flooding had receded, leaving a thick deep layer of fertile mud, which the workers would soon scatter with seed. Then the farmers would drive their goats over the fields to tamp down the seed. To direct and control the river water, the farmers used small canals and sluices. In that way, the floodwaters could be more evenly distributed in the water basins that would provide irrigation for a long time after the Nile water receded.

Moses could hear laughter emanating from the boat's cabin and ducked in to see what it was all about. His grandmother had reminded his mother and aunt of Moses's antics as a small child in the palace. Moses smiled and kept saying, "I don't remember that," or "No, I didn't really do that, did I?" which would make them laugh all the more. Then his uncle chimed in with tales of Moses's achievements as a boy. Moses became embarrassed and excused himself.

Amenhotep remarked to the women, "Moses is so humble. Actually, I like that about him."

"Yes," agreed the women. "It is a virtue of his."

Amenhotep joined Moses on the deck and pointed out the large rudder oars at the stern, which were painted with wedjet eyes. "Do you see that, Moses; do you know what the wedjet means?"

"It stands for fractions of the self, does it not?"

"You are right, Moses, the eye is the symbol of the whole person," said Amenhotep. "The story behind it involves the falcon god, Horus, the son of Osiris. The eye of Horus was ripped out in a battle with Seth, his enemy. Seth took the eye and tore it to pieces, but the wise Thoth, who was Horus's friend, put it together again. Each part of the eye, the pupil, the white parts, the eyebrow, the cheetah tear trail, and the falcon's cheek mark under the eye, are all fractions. When the shine from the eye is added, it becomes a whole eye corresponding to a complete, functioning person."

"But why are the oars decorated with the wedjet eyes?"

"It is the symbol of guidance and protection in the afterlife, but it also means the protection of the pharaoh in this life." Moses thought about that.

"In other words, I have my eye on you," said Pharaoh smiling. "So don't do anything foolish."

"Like what?"

"Like jumping in the Nile for a swim."

"Hah! I would sink like a stone with this collar round my neck."

"Seriously, the wedjet just means: "have a safe journey!""

"Our main purpose for this trip is the festival, of course," said Pharaoh, "but, there is something else I want to do while we are in Thebes."

"What is that, Uncle?" asked Moses, wiping his brow. He wished he could take off his wig or go for a swim without his heavy collar.

"I'd like to take another look at the western cliffs on the other side of the Nile. They are shaped like a pyramid. The valley below may serve as a necropolis, where we could bury our royal family members. That would be simpler than constructing pyramids, don't you think, Moses?"

"Anything would be easier to build than the Great Pyramid," said Moses, who had learned about the pyramids of Giza in school.

"The Queen Mother first thought of the idea, and I've been mulling it over. General Thutmose[13] thinks we should build a village nearby for the craftsmen and artisans who would work on the tombs and mortuary temples. Well, I know you don't care about all that, but I just thought you and Bekah could accompany me as I check it out."

"Sure, could I go without my wig and this?" he asked, tugging at his pectoral.

"Oh, all right, Moses, take them both off now. But remember, as soon as we get close to our destination, you must put them back on."

"Oh, thank you, Pharaoh," said Moses with relief as he went into the cabin to shed the oppressive symbols of adulthood.

All morning the royal bark sailed past towns and villages. By the time the midday meal was served, Moses was famished. He was often hungry lately. He guessed it was because he was growing so tall. After the meal, everyone rested, leaning back on the cushions in the cabin.

Everyone, that is, except Moses. Having refueled, he was back on deck, munching on figs and dates as he watched the world of the Nile pass by. He fed Bekah and gave her fresh water. Then, taking a long draft from his water skin, he watched the helmsman handle the pole at the stern. The boatman was using the pole to sound the depth and push away from sandbars that threatened to ground the boat. There wasn't much danger of that on this trip though with the water level so high in the inundation. They were passing a stretch where the settlements were sparse, and tangled brush lined the banks of the river. The countryside was wild here. There was little cropland, but back beyond the brush Moses could glimpse herds of cattle in the rough pastures and bush country. The terrain stretched for miles toward desert hills in the distance.

---

13   Chief army officer of Amenhotep I.

Dusk fell, and the servants began to prepare the evening meal.

"Where will everyone sleep?" asked Moses.

"Your grandmother and mother and aunt will be in the cabin. You and I will sleep on the deck, Moses," said his uncle.

"Oh, that will be great!" said Moses. He thought that he and his uncle would talk under the starry sky, but that didn't happen. Moses was very comfortable, curled up with his dog under a light covering, and he fell quickly and soundly to sleep.

Thebes
1514 BC

Finally, after many days, they were nearing Thebes. Moses, wearing his collar and wig again, stood on deck with his uncle, who pointed out the tallest parts of the temple of Amun-Re which was coming into view. "Those are the entrance pylons" said Pharaoh. Since the time of Senusret I,[14] there had been a temple at Karnak.[15] However, this temple of Amun had become more important in the New Kingdom (Eighteenth Dynasty), and every pharaoh added to it during that time.

"The temple is huge!" exclaimed Moses as he stared at the long, narrow building.

It had been a long trip, and everyone was looking forward to the comfort of the lovely Theban palace, which was close to the temple. They were welcomed by the servants who lived there and maintained the palace. Moses was tired and the bed felt good, but it took him a while to get to sleep, because he was excited about what the next day might hold. Bekah was snoring at the foot of his bed.

She can sleep anytime, anywhere, Moses thought.

The next morning, the family gathered in the dining hall for a light breakfast. There would be much feasting later in the day. Moses was dressed in his formal attire, with a fine linen skirt and a wide linen sash angled over his bare chest. The sun would be warm today, so the dress was slightly cooler than the full linen robe. However, he was wearing his formal collar and wig.

Amenhotep had joined the temple priests earlier in the cleansing rituals, which were required before entering the temple.

---

14 Joseph's time
15 The hypostyle hall had not yet been built, nor had the temple at nearby Luxor.

Pharaoh looks splendid, Moses thought as his uncle joined them at the table. He was wearing the triangular kilt of royalty. It had a colorful sash, which complemented his pectoral collar. From his waist, in the back, hung a real lion's tail, which swayed as he walked. He wore wrist and arm bracelets, jeweled sandals, and the tall cobra crown of Egypt. Both queens wore crowns and the princess wore a tiara. Their fine linen robes and matching long sashes were bordered with bands of intricate needlework. The royal women wore their finest jewels.

After breakfast, Amenhotep I led the dazzling family group as they left the palace to walk to the temple next door. People lined the short route, throwing flower blossoms at the feet of Amenhotep. As the family passed by, the celebrants placed clusters of lilies in the arms of the royal women and put a necklace of lotus blossoms around Moses's neck. The group entered the temple courtyard, proclaiming, "Hail to you, Field of Offerings." This was one of the few areas open to the public. It was a place where offerings were deposited, some for the gods and some for the dead. Only the pharaoh was permitted to enter the temple. The priests were waiting for him at the entrance between the towering pylons. Over the door, an engraving displayed the words, "Serve the god, that he do the same to you."

As Pharaoh disappeared into the heart of the sanctuary, Moses glanced toward his mother for direction.

Princess Ahmose reached out to him, "Come this way, Moses," she said. As they stood in the outer courtyard, Queen Ahmose Nefertari offered her lilies to Amun and to her husband, the great Ahmose, who had gone before her. Then Princess Ahmose and Queen Meryetamun offered their flowers to Amun, all three women laying their bouquets on the stone pavement. Moses looked around him. It was as if he was standing in a forest of tall flowers that had turned to stone. All around him stood pillars, symbolic offerings carved as flowers. Following the women's example, Moses placed his lotus necklace at the base of one of the pillars, but he offered his sweet smelling flowers to Adonai. The women strolled around the gardens adjoining the temple. Royal guards escorted them, and Moses trailed behind until his mother beckoned him to walk with her. She took his arm and told him, "I am so happy you are here with us this year, Moses."

It seemed a long time passed before Pharaoh emerged from the temple carrying a bowl of incense. Behind him marched a line of priests bearing the sacred bark of Amun, which was adorned on both prow and stern with a ramshead.

"Where is Amun?" whispered Moses to his mother.

"He is in that small linen-wrapped cabin in the middle of the boat. Remember he is the Hidden One. We never see him."

"Who are they?" asked Moses, referring to two additional groups of priests behind the first. They were carrying two smaller sacred boats.

"Those are the barks of Mut, consort of Amun, and Khonsu, their son," explained Princess Ahmose.

Temple musicians joined the processional, playing their harps and flutes. Young women in flowing dresses and long black hair danced along as they played the jingling sistrums. The people cheered and joined the processional as it moved on toward the small building apart from the temple. A sanctuary, the white chapel had been built by Senusret I for his Sed festival in the thirtieth year of his reign. This jubilee had served as a rejuvenation of Senusret's role as the link between the human and the divine.

Amenhotep halted at the base of a ramp leading up to the sanctuary. At this point, the priests put the sacred bark of Amun on a sled and dragged it up the ramp behind Amenhotep to the altar inside the chapel. The other barks were brought back to the temple. More rituals were conducted inside Senusret's chapel. Then Pharaoh led the procession to the sacred lake near the temple, where the bark of the Hidden God was put to float on the water, which was used at other times for the priests' cleansing rituals. All the celebrants gathered at the edge of the lake. The musicians sang a hymn of praise, celebrating the god of creation. The lake symbolized the primordial flood before earth was created. Moses thought the music was beautiful and inspiring. Then the singing changed to pleas for provision. What bothered Moses was that the singers sounded demanding, as though they were instructing Amun what to do. Moses decided he would ask his uncle about that later.

There was a small chapel at the back of the temple that was open to the public.[16] Moses escorted his mother to the chapel; she wanted to pray to Amun. He wished he could worship wholeheartedly as she did. In the deepest part of his being, Moses felt that he had the potential to give himself to adoration of Adonai, but he just couldn't do it in this place. His spiritual longings remained unsatisfied as he left the chapel with Princess Ahmose.

After the lake ceremony, the royal family retreated to the palace for a rest before the feast.

---

16   It was later called "the Place of the Listening Ear" and enlarged by Ramses II.

"Ah," murmured Moses as an attendant poured warm water over him in his bathing room. "That feels so good," he exclaimed, lathering himself with the Egyptian equivalent of soap—animal fat mixed with chalk and limestone dust. He had been glad to shed his clothes in his palace chamber. In his private toilet, he had relieved himself into a hole in a bench elevated above the chamber pot. As soon as he left the toilet, an attendant popped in and whisked the pot away to empty it into a pit outside the palace. Now, as another servant rinsed him and then handed him a towel, Moses felt refreshed.

The morning's spectacle played back in his mind as he rubbed his body with lightly scented ointment. He donned a fresh loincloth and lay down on his bed. Moses thought about Uncle Tep and what he had been doing so long in the temple. Was it all right to ask him, he wondered, or was it a secret?

At home in Memphis, there was a small chapel in front of the palace. It was Pharaoh's daily routine to bathe in the Nile and then to bring his offerings to Amun in the chapel. Once when Moses thought no one was in the chapel, his six-year-old's curiosity got the best of him. He entered the dim space and was startled to see Ahmose Nefertari, his "Grandma Nefer," there in the chapel, praying before the altar. He stood frozen as she looked up and saw him.

"Moses," she said, "It's all right. Come here." She invited him to join her.

"Amun," she whispered, and nodded to the small linen wrapped figure on the altar. On the table before it, flickered two incense oil lamps. Between the lamps, lay offerings of round bread and choice fruit. Moses bowed his head and silently prayed to Adonai. When he told his uncle about it later, mentioning how quiet it was in the chapel, his uncle quoted from an ancient saying,

"In the sanctuary of God
Clamor is an abomination to him.
Pray for thyself with a loving heart
in which the words remain hidden,
that he may supply thy need, hear thy words
and, accept thine offering." [17]

Now, as Moses lay on his bed in Thebes, he thought that maybe Uncle Tep had been bringing food offerings to Amun in the temple that morning.

The evening feast was the largest Moses had ever seen. He remembered the table manners he had learned from his mother and at school. One was

---

[17] Erman, *Life in Ancient Egypt*, 273; Papyrus de boul.,i.17, I ff.

not to eat greedily as though eager to get the lion's share of the food. So, even though there was an abundance of food at the festivities, Moses ate slowly, savoring the great variety of tastes. Wine and beer flowed freely. Moses was allowed a little wine, and he was not tempted to take more, because he had seen what happened to people when they drank too much. He also had noted that his uncle was not one of those people.

It was the end of August, and the sun did not go down until late. However, the servants lit the lamps on the tables before darkness fell, so that the celebrants could enjoy the aroma of the scented oil. Later, as torches on stands were lit around the large courtyard, musicians and dancers filed in. More praises to Amun were lifted to the stars, the people joining in with the temple singers.

For the eleven days that the festival lasted, there were daily offerings in the courtyard and temple. The feasting and music continued into the evenings for the duration.

Amenhotep took Moses aside one day and told him they were going across the river to see the western cliffs. Moses was to wear his formal dress until they got to the boat, where he could change into something comfortable and cool. He was to have Bekah ready to go also. They slipped away between the morning ceremonies and the evening feasting. When they reached the west bank of the Nile, they traveled by donkey and sedan chair. An attendant walked beside the pharaoh's chair, waving a tall plumed fan to cool the king. Moses, sitting beside the pharaoh, felt the stirring of air around him too. Bekah ran alongside the donkeys, her tongue hanging out as she panted in the heat of the day.

The royal party was escorted by armed guards, ready to spring into action should the group be threatened by the wild animals that were known to prowl these parts. The thousand-foot high, lion-colored cliffs rising above them were pyramidal in shape, just as Amenhotep had said. It was an adventure for Moses as he jumped down from the donkey perch and scrambled with Bekah over the dusty, rocky ground.

"Be careful," called his uncle, "that limestone scree is loose and slippery." Bekah stopped to inspect every cranny. Moses tried to keep up, for he didn't want her encountering a lion or dropping into a dark hole in the rocks. He called her back, because his uncle wanted to move on. They climbed up into the sedan chair again and continued on their way around the back of the cliffs.[18]

---

18 This area would one day be called *Valley of the Kings*

On the other side lay a smaller valley where Amenhotep envisioned the workers' village. "That is where the houses and shops would be built, close together," said Amenhotep, pointing out the site. "We should surround the whole place with a wall that would provide security. That rise to the right could be used for the workers' tombs, which they could build and decorate when they had the time."

"It's quite desolate, don't you think?" Moses said, thinking of the artisans who would live and die here.

"Desolate, you say," said Amenhotep. "Well, so is the road of the afterlife. People here could wear the wedjet eye for protection."

"Maybe they could also make a level road," said Moses, thinking practically.

"Good thinking, Moses," declared his uncle. "Maybe you would like to help build the road. That would be a good project for you."

Moses searched his uncle's face for the telltale smile that was a clue of his uncle's teasing, but found no sign. Then his uncle let out a roar of laughter that startled the attendant standing by. Amenhotep had been staid and formal for over a week, and he was letting loose.

"Moses," he said, still laughing. "You should have seen the look on your face when you thought you would have to build that road. You are getting used to the comforts of the palace, aren't you? Well, in six years you will have military training. That will toughen you. Come now, let us hurry back to the palace. Maybe there will still be time for me to grab a nap."

Back at the palace, Moses asked Khasha to give Bekah a cleansing shower. She had been thrilled to explore the dusty areas of the future necropolis, but she would need a bath before she could share his bed.

The last day of ceremonies was especially festive. The sacred barks were carried by the priests down to a larger bark on the Nile. The royal family boarded their own boat, which towed the sacred bark. All this was done amidst the common people and nobles, who sang and praised the gods as they followed in smaller boats. They also praised the pharaoh, whom they believed to be the instrument of Amun on earth. The Nile cruise was leisurely and joyful. A midday meal was served onboard the royal bark. The waterborne procession was headed for a specific southern destination, Luxor.[19]

---

19   Several generations after the reign of Amenhotep I, there would be erected at Luxor a big, beautiful, temple complex connected by a sphinx-lined walkway that stretched nearly two miles to Karnak. There would also be built at Luxor, the *Opet* (southern harem) where the god, Amun, would symbolically consort with the Queen Mother to give birth again to the pharaoh. In this way, the pharaoh's life and reign would be rejuvenated for another year, it was thought. In future the celebration would be called the *Opet Festival*.

In Amenhotep's time there was only a small shrine in this area south of Karnak. When the boats docked below, the sacred bark of Amun was again placed on a sled and dragged up the ramp to the altar where Pharaoh and the priests performed another ritual. Pharaoh and the Amun statue (still wrapped in linen) were then welcomed back onboard their barks by their respective families for the return sail to Karnak.

That evening something very different took place: the precursor to the Opet event. In front of the palace an elaborate enclosure was erected. This was for the Hidden One, who would symbolically pay a conjugal visit to Queen Mother Ahmose Nefertari in her palace chamber that night to provide the rebirth for Pharaoh Amenhotep I. Of course, Moses had to ask about the enclosure in front of the palace.

"What's that for?" he said. When he heard the explanation, he was sorry he had asked. *That is really strange*, he thought.

The next morning, Moses looked at his uncle. Did he look refreshed—like he had a new lease on life? A rebirth? Nah, Moses thought, shrugging off the idea. *This stuff is getting to me. It's time we went home to Memphis.*

The Nile
1514 BC

When it came time for the family to leave, people lined the bank above the royal bark, shouting, "Hail to Pharaoh. Safe journey to all."

Moses was standing on deck with Bekah. As they pulled away from the dock, the dog lifted her head and sniffed the morning air. *She is smelling the breakfasts being prepared by the fishermen and trades people in the boats surrounding us,* Moses thought. Scratching behind her pointed ears, he said, "Let's get you something to eat."

The sails of the royal bark remained furled as they headed north to Memphis against the wind. However, the current was with the boatmen who labored hard at the oars. They would stand to dip their poles in the water and then plop back on the benches as they stroked. They had cleverly sewn pads on the seat of their pants to cushion the impact of their plopping. Amenhotep pointed out the fields as they passed.

"Look, Moses," he said, "the farmers are seeding the fields now. Over there they are already driving their goats to tamp down the seed. In the time that we have been gone, the water has receded sufficiently for the farmers to work their fields. They don't waste any time getting their crops in." Then he began reciting an ancient hymn to the Nile. Moses joined in as he remembered learning it in school:

"Hail to you, O Nile!
Sprung from Earth
Come to nourish Egypt
Food provider, bounty maker
Who creates all that is good."[20]

---

20   Butzer, Karl W., *People of The Nile*, 32

About midway through the next day, after rounding the big bend above Thebes, they arrived at Abydos. The royal family disembarked there in order to pay tribute at a little chapel. Amenhotep's father, Ahmose, had erected a chapel and dedicated it to his grandmother, Tetisheri. She was married to Taa II, who began the war against the Hyksos. The stele inside the chapel honored Tetisheri as mother of a king and wife of a king. Amenhotep explained to Moses: "My grandmother, Tetisheri, played an important political role in the reign of her husband, Taa II. She must have been quite a woman," he added proudly. The golden stele they were studying, pictured Queen Tetisheri wearing the tall double feather crown of Egypt. Her son, Ahmose I was depicted standing before the seated queen. He was wearing the double crown of upper and lower Egypt. Their names were in cartouches above them.

Moses left the chapel before the others to check on Bekah. When Amenhotep came outside, he found Moses laughing at the dog, who was running round and round the chapel.

"You silly dog," said Moses, as he opened his arms to her. "Why are you running in circles? We aren't on the boat now."

Bekah sat looking at Moses with her head cocked to the side as if to say, "Well, you didn't invite me inside, what else was I supposed to do?"

"Let's go," said Amenhotep. "I want to travel a good distance before we stop for the night."

Moses enjoyed another night with his uncle under the stars, but this time they did talk. As they lay on their cushions, Bekah asleep beside them.

"Uncle Tep," Moses began, "I have some questions about the festival."

Amenhotep was pleased that Moses wanted to discuss the experience they had just shared. He hadn't had a chance until now to ask Moses what he thought of it all.

Moses began with the part that he had observed. "I liked the music, especially the singing by the lake. After the praises though, the singers seemed to be telling God what to do."

His uncle replied, "God can do what he wants, but he chooses to act through the pharaoh, Moses. He helps the pharaoh give the people what they need."

"That sounds like a big responsibility for the pharaoh."

"Yes, Moses, it is. It certainly is." After a pause, Amenhotep continued, "You see, Moses, in the tomb, man reaches toward God. In the temple,

God reaches to man. But he wants people to tell him what they need. Did you notice the engraving over the door of the temple? *Serve the God that he do the same to you.* The service is reciprocal. The people have brought their offerings, so they have expectations that God, through the pharaoh, will meet their needs."

Moses was quiet for a while looking, at the stars above.

"Are you asleep, Moses," asked Pharaoh, softly.

"Oh, no, Uncle. I was just thinking. Do you remember how you told me that Amun created all things by his word, by just announcing what he wanted?"

Amenhotep was surprised that Moses remembered that. "Yes, Moses," he said.

"The people were worshiping the Creator God by the lake, were they not?"

"Yes," said Amenhotep, wondering what Moses was getting at.

"Well," said Moses, "if God created all things by his word, then why did he need a wife?"

Ah, there it is, thought Amenhotep. Moses, with his inquiring mind and good sense of logic, had found a contradiction in the system.

"To be honest, Moses, I don't think Amun did need a wife, but perhaps he wanted one, or more likely, the people didn't want him to miss out in the pleasures of a mate. You see, the people sometimes attribute human emotions and activities to the gods." In the dark, he could not see Moses's face clearly, but he could imagine his puzzled expression. "Does that make any sense to you, Moses?"

"I'm not sure," said Moses, "but you said God can do anything he wants to do."

"Yes," said Amenhotep. "That reminds me. I've been meaning to have a talk with you about love and marriage."

"Oh, I'm not ready for a wife, Uncle," Moses quickly replied.

Amenhotep laughed, "I guess not, seeing that you are twelve years old. Nevertheless, it's not too early to have this talk. Now I know you have watched me breeding Bekah to a male greyhound, so we could obtain puppies to add to our own hunting pack. I know you have an idea about how impregnation happens."

Moses remained silent.

His uncle continued, "And of course, there are always one's classmates, who love to share that kind of information. I know how it goes, Moses. I was a boy once."

Moses was glad it was dark. *This is getting embarrassing.* He thought he had better say something though. "Yes, Uncle, I know how it goes too."

"All right, but there is a lot more to it than putting a stake in a hole, like that game Jackals and Hounds [21] that you like to play." His uncle waited but there was no response from Moses, so he went on. "I'll give you an example, Moses. You remember the musicians at the festival, how they used their fingers on the harp, and their mouth and fingers on the flute to create the music?"

"Yes, Uncle," replied Moses, more comfortable talking about music. Moses felt himself relax as though he were floating on the Nile.

"All right, then," continued Amenhotep. "Someday, when you have a beloved wife, just like the musicians, you must use your fingers and your mouth to explore her lovely body to create pleasure for her."

Oh, no! Moses had not seen that coming, but he listened, wondering what was coming next.

"You must bring her to the point of great desire before you enter her. During the time of caressing and kissing, you may have to struggle to control yourself, because you will find your own desire mounting. It takes practice, Moses, just like anything else. But you will learn the ways of your beloved. Remember, when you give your mate pleasure, you will have pleasure too," Amenhotep said, thinking of his lovely Meryet.

"Listen, Moses, for I am working backward as I am telling you about lovemaking. I've told you about what should happen before you enter her body. Now I will tell you what should happen before you enter her bedchamber.

"You must treat her with understanding, kindness and affection during the day. Let me give you another example. If you had a friend who was rude and uncaring toward you all day, and then he came knocking at your door that evening, would you want to let him in? You might do it, but you wouldn't feel like it, would you?"

"No," said Moses.

"Well, that is the way it is with a wife. If you treat her without compassion during the day, she will not open her door to you with passion in the evening. Have you heard the wise sayings about how to treat a wife?"

"No, Uncle," replied Moses.

---

21 Amenhotep was referring to a table-height game that was supported by four cow-shaped legs. The surface of the table was punctured by round holes in which were inserted long wooden poles, their ends carved to resemble either the head of a jackal or a hound.

"You should be a leader, always treating her well."

"But what if she doesn't do what I want her to do?" asked Moses.

Amenhotep laughed, "Oh, that will happen, Moses. I promise you—that will happen. You may not agree with her, but you must be wise and patient. Let your wife be in charge of the household, but don't let her take charge of you, or she won't respect you. When she is managing the household, do not criticize how she does it. The writings of Ptahhotep instruct us: "If you are a man of means, able to establish a household, love your wife at home. Fill her belly and clothe her back. Make her happy as long as you live. When you take a wife, remember how your mother gave birth to you and how she raised you. Don't give your wife cause to blame you. Don't supervise your wife in her house, if you know she is doing a good job. Don't say to her, *'Where is it? Get it for me!'* when she has put it in the proper place."

"These are wise sayings, Moses, so remember them. They will serve you well. You see that I have a happy marriage with your Aunt Meryet. I have chosen not to have a harem, although it is common for a king or even a nobleman to have many women. However, the wisdom literature advises to 'marry and enjoy the wife of your youth.' I think they are right, for I have been satisfied with one wife. You see, Moses, the joyful experience in love is not found in many women. When you go down that road, it is never enough. Rather, true joy is found in creating many ways to love one woman. But it is important, Moses, to find the right one!"

Moses was in no hurry. If all that his uncle said was expected of him as a husband, he was willing to wait until Adonai guided him to the right one.

"Moses," said Amenhotep, "we have strayed from the subject of the festival in talking of love and marriage. Perhaps you have other questions about the festival."

"I do, Uncle," replied Moses, "but is it all right to ask about what happens inside the temple, or is that a secret?"

"No, not at all, Moses, you may ask what you want."

"You were inside the temple for a long time, Uncle. Were you bringing offerings to Amun?"

"Yes, Moses. I first directed the changing of Amun's robes by the priests. They dressed the image in fresh clothing and concealed his small chamber with new linens. Then I presented the offering of bread and choice produce. After that, came the meat offerings of fowl and haunches of beef. I burned incense and presented Amun with bottles of the finest wine. This was all done in the holy place. The image of Amun is in the Holy of Holies, at the farthest end of the temple. In the sanctuary of Senusret I, I poured out the drink offering," Amenhotep added.

"What does the big temple look like inside?" asked Moses.

"Ah, it is magnificent!" said Amenhotep. "The ceiling is painted blue with gold flecks for stars, the walls are white, and the pillars are mostly green. The paintings are colorful and detailed. They depict the accomplishments of Pharaoh and show Pharaoh bringing offerings to Amun."

"Are you in those paintings too, Uncle?"

"A few," replied Pharaoh. "Perhaps someday, you can have more added when you are the pharaoh."

Moses could not picture himself as a pharaoh, but he said, "The festival was certainly elaborate."

Amenhotep thought that Moses did not want to think about a time when his Uncle Tep was not around. That was true, indeed, but for once Amenhotep had missed the deeper meaning behind Moses's deflection of his uncle's remark—namely, that Moses *did not want to be pharaoh!*

After many days on the Nile, Moses knew they were nearing Memphis when on the opposite bank, to the west of the river, he could make out Crocodile Lake in the distance. A tributary of the Nile fed the lake and a large oasis of palms, willows, and fig trees. Not long ago, Moses had gone with his uncle in a boat on the Nile and then across to the oasis. They had enjoyed picnics under the trees during their campout. At that time, they had also visited the nearby alabaster mine where Amenhotep had showed Moses the source of the material that was used in so many objects of daily use, such as bowls, goblets, perfume flasks, and table tops.

The palace at Memphis was midway between the oasis and the delta. In three more years, Moses would be travelling away from the other side of Memphis, going to the delta university, the House of Wisdom at Heliopolis, the Ancient On.[22]

---

22 Where Joseph had found a wife

Memphis
1514 BC

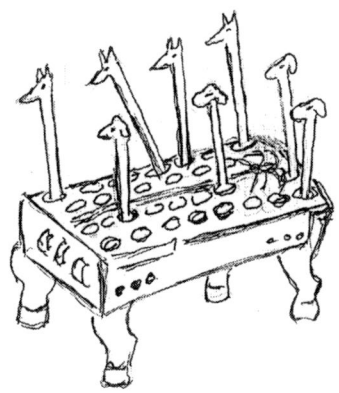

The holiday was over, and classes in the palace had resumed for Moses. He was learning more of the wisdom sayings with Ineni, his private tutor: "If you desire your conduct to be good, refrain from all kinds of evil. Beware of an act of avarice; it is a bad and incurable disease … it alienates fathers and mothers … it drives wife and husband apart."[23]

In his group classes, Moses was solving geometry problems. Surface measurement was necessary to the Egyptians because of the destruction of so many field boundaries in the inundation each year. Egyptian methods for calculating angles, circles, and volume produced results that were less than exact, but who can fault a people who managed to build the Great Pyramid?

Moses enjoyed his classes in classic literature. His favorite story was the *Tale of Sinuhe,* which was about a distinguished courtier of King Amemenhat I. Moses could identify with that, as he was a distinguished member of the court of Pharaoh Amenhotep I. Unlike Sinuhe, however, Moses did not fight alongside royalty in Libya. Moses would have fought the Libyans alongside Amenhotep, but he was too young for military service at the time.

---

[23] A millennium later, the Instruction of Amunemope also emphasized proper conduct and ethical behavior: "Give your ears and hear what is said; give your mind over to their interpretation. It is profitable to put them in your heart." Scholars have noted that the thirty sayings from the wise in Proverbs, 22: 17 to 24:22 of the Bible, contain similarities to the thirty sections of the "Wisdom of Amunemope." The personification of wisdom may be compared with the personification of abstract ideas in Egyptian writings of the second millennium BC. The biblical verses were written a millennium later, in the time of David and Solomon. The format of these philosophical passages was that of a father instructing his son in wisdom.

The story of Sinuhe continued with the account of the pharaoh's death. When the news reached the military camp in Libya, Sinuhe believed, for some reason, that his life was in danger, so he fled from Egypt. His route of escape took him to the eastern frontier of Egypt. He crouched in bushes awaiting darkness, because he was fearful of being seen by guards on the roof of the watchtower. The fort had been erected as a defense against the Bedouins. By night, Sinuhe fled into the desert. The next day, when he reached the Bitter Lakes northwest of the Red Sea, he was seized by thirst and his throat burned. He knew he should not drink the water, but he was desperate. Just in time, he heard the lowing of a herd and saw an Asiatic herdsman, who gave him water. Sinuhe also boiled some milk, offered by the herder.

He went with the Asiatic to his people, spending almost two years going from tribe to tribe. Then Amue'nshe, prince of the upper land of Retenu,[24] took him in and asked him to remain in his land because he had heard of Sinuhe's valor.

The prince asked Sinuhe, "Why have you come here?" surmising that something must have happened at the court of King Amemenhat, who had gone to heaven without its being known how or why.

Moses thought that Sinuhe was clever in his answer: Sinuhe described Egypt as being a great power and told the prince that the reigning king was very strong. Then he offered his own services as a mediator in case Egypt threatened to attack the prince's land.

That sounded like a good idea to the prince, who lavished Sinuhe with gifts. He gave his daughter to him in marriage and bestowed on him the choicest part of his lands. Sinuhe was provided with an abundance of daily food, and he was made prince of a tribe. He spent many years in the land "flowing with milk and honey," a land that had more wine than water and numerous olive trees.

Moses was very interested in this part of the story, because he knew that the Hebrews came from that land, and he was aware of his own Hebrew origin. In the story of Sinuhe, his children flourished and became heroes and heads of tribes themselves. Sinuhe gave hospitality to everyone and defended the country in battle. There was a story of jealousy, too: A local hero, who envied this outsider's success, challenged him in a battle, intending to take his honor and possessions, but Sinuhe prevailed.

After many years, Sinuhe was not content in his new land, longing to return to Egypt. He wanted a proper burial and preparation for the afterlife,

---

24 Palestine

so he wrote to the new pharaoh, Senusret I, pleading to be forgiven for his unauthorized absence. Pharaoh's reply was favorable, inviting him home, so Sinuhe left his possessions with his children and returned to Egypt, where he was welcomed back as a hero.

He was given a private audience with the King, in his inner court, the "house of adoration," where the king's sons lived with him. Then Sinuhe was provided a room in the house with a prince. Servants attended to his every need. His rough Bedouin garments were exchanged for fine linen robes, and he was anointed with the finest oil, so that he looked young again. When he died, he was mummified and given a stone pyramid as a tomb amongst the pyramids.

Moses was amazed that Sinuhe would leave his own children and all his possessions in the most fertile land of Palestine (Canaan), just to be buried in Egypt. He discussed this with Amenhotep, who still supervised his studies.

"Uncle, why do Egyptians care so much about burial and the afterlife?"

"It has always been so," replied Amenhotep. "The tale of Sinuhe is a universal story. Everyone wants to go back to the place from whence they came; that is home! The Egyptians love this tale so much because Sinuhe longed to come home to Egypt."

Moses paused thoughtfully before speaking, "It wasn't only Egypt that Sinuhe was thinking about. It was the afterlife, but no one ever comes back to tell us about the afterlife."

"True," said his Uncle, "that is why the people sing:

Spend the day merrily!
Put ointment and fine oil
to your nostrils and lotus
flowers on the body of your beloved.
Spend the day merrily
and weary not therein.
Lo, none can take his goods with him.
Lo, none that has departed, can return again."[25]

Moses smiled; he enjoyed poetry and so did his Uncle Tep.

Pharaoh said, "We have some of the day remaining. Let's spend it merrily!" The song had reminded Amenhotep of how much Meryet loved flowers.

---

25 Barbara Mertz: The Pleasures of Life In Egypt, 102

"Go get Bekah. We will go down to the Nile and gather lilies for your Aunt Meryet. Then I'll play you a game of Jackals and Hounds."

Moses enjoyed the game even if he lost. The best part was being with his uncle. Now, as he watched Bekah bounding through the sedge while they searched for lilies, he thought with satisfaction, *We are spending the day merrily!*

Memphis
1513 BC

"Moses, you are getting the feel for the bow. Your arrows are on target most of the time," said Amenhotep, encouraging his nephew in his archery lesson. "With regular practice like this, you will soon be ready for that hunting trip I promised you."

Pharaoh noted the developing muscles in Moses's arm as he stretched the bow and took aim. "Bull's-eye," he shouted as the arrow hit center target. Moses reached in his quiver to draw out another arrow. "When we are finished here, I've arranged for a chariot driving lesson," his uncle told him.

Before the hunt, Amenhotep wanted Moses to be proficient with the chariot, should his uncle need him. There would be guardsmen and other servants along on the hunt, but he didn't want to depend on them. Instead, this would be a teaching opportunity for him with Moses. A short time later, he called an end to the archery lesson, as he had heard the sound of horses' hooves approaching. The chariot pulled up in front of Pharaoh. Moses was eager to mount the chariot as the attendant stood holding the horses' reins.

"Just a minute," said his uncle. "First I want you to greet the horses. Stand in front of them and speak to them gently. They need to get used to you. Stroke their necks. That's it." Then Amenhotep mounted the chariot, took the reins, and motioned for Moses to join him.

"Today we are just going to circle the archery field. Watch me carefully as I handle the horses and instruct you as I go. Then I will let you take the reins, standing close to me. We will be practicing for many lessons on the field before taking to the road."

Amenhotep showed Moses how to manage the team with various tugs on the reins, how to get the horses to speed up and slow down, and how to handle the turns. Finally, he allowed Moses to hold the reins as he stood next to him, ready to grab the reins if the need arose. He cautioned Moses to keep the horses in a steady gait for this lesson.

"Don't lose your focus, Moses, the horses need to feel you in control at all times. These are spirited horses, which I wanted to use for the lesson, so you can learn to handle them."

Moses surprised his uncle with his command of the horses.

Why, he is a natural, thought Amenhotep. Little did he know that Moses had been envisioning himself driving a chariot from the time he had grabbed the arms of his Hebrew mother and cried, "Osef! Osef!"

Memphis
1512 BC

Moses could hardly believe that he and his uncle were actually on their way to the antelope hunt. He had looked forward to this, and he felt he was ready after all his practice in archery and chariot driving. As they traveled westward from Memphis toward the open desert reaches, they passed by barley fields waving in the morning breeze. Moses thought he saw a lake in the distance.

"No, Moses," said his uncle. "There's no lake out there. That blue expanse is a flax field in blossom."

"It's beautiful here, Uncle," said Moses, raising his voice over the clattering of horses hooves.

"Yes, let's spend the day merrily," said Amenhotep, urging the horses on. They had reached the margins of the floodplain. The fields and settlements were behind them now. Amenhotep pulled up on the reins.

"Are we here?" asked Moses.

"Not quite," answered his uncle, "but we need to slow down and check out the area." Amenhotep called the other hunters over. They formed a good-sized group, including the servants carrying provisions and others handling the pack of hunting dogs.

Moses looked for Bekah among the greyhounds. He left the chariot and walked over to pet her, but he left her with the other dogs, knowing that she would soon need to work in unison with them in order to worry the prey.

"Let's go on foot into that wadi over there. Gazelles like to wander in such places," Amenhotep told the hunters. "Take some of the dogs around to the other end and leave the rest here. That way, if there's anything in there, we will be able to flush it out."

"Keep the dogs quiet," he cautioned. After waiting for the hunters to reach the other end, Amenhotep said, "Come on, Moses, take your bow and quiver. Let's go."

They descended into the wadi and moved along the walls as quickly as they could, with Amenhotep leading the way. Suddenly, he turned, motioning for Moses behind him to be still and arm his bow. He stepped back and pointed to a gazelle, partially hidden behind a thorn bush.

Moses waited until he could get a clear shot, and then brought the animal down with a well-aimed arrow.

"There you are, Moses, your first kill." Moses went over to make sure the animal was dead, and then lifted it over his shoulders.

"Are you all right with that, Moses, or is it too heavy?" asked his uncle.

"No, it's good," replied Moses, as they slowly made their way back to the others.

The servants cheered and clapped their hands when Moses and Amenhotep emerged from the wadi with the game. Later, Amenhotep killed an antelope from his chariot, while Moses took the reins. The other hunters killed an ibex, another gazelle, and several hares. Then Amenhotep told the others he wanted to take an antelope alive to fatten with his cattle. He instructed several hunters to beat the bushes and drive the prey toward him. As a beautiful Oryx antelope leapt out of the brush, he took his lasso—a long rope weighted with a ball at one end—and skillfully threw it toward the antelope. Just as he intended, the rope encircled the animal's legs and ended up twisted in its long curved horns. With one perfectly timed jerk, Amenhotep brought the Oryx down.

"Uncle, that was amazing!" exclaimed Moses.

The dogs ran to the animal but halted on command. Amenhotep wanted this antelope alive. He would keep it in his menagerie. The attendants secured the animal for transport. Back at camp, it was time for a meal. While the servants were preparing the food, Moses went over to the dogs.

"Your dog performed well, Moses," said the hunter who had taken down an ibex with Bekah's help. "She bit the animal's heels and slowed it down."

Moses grinned proudly. "Good girl, Bekah," he told her.

The dog wagged her tail and licked Moses's hand.

Amenhotep invited Moses to get his food and join him under an acacia tree.

"Moses," he said, "some of the servants will transport the game and the live Oryx back to the palace. They will use their flint knives to butcher the game and scrape the hides. We will stay here. I told you we would camp out tonight. Tomorrow I would like to get that antelope I want to fatten."

Moses was chomping on the leg of a wild hare that had been roasted over the fire. He licked his lips and asked his uncle, "Will we have a campfire?"

"Yes, Moses. We will have guards, of course, but campfires are a good deterrent to wild animals. What do you think of that Oryx, isn't she a beauty?"

"Sure is," agreed Moses, "especially those long graceful horns."

That evening, Amenhotep and Moses sat before a campfire in front of the comfortable sleeping enclosure that the servants had put together with poles and skins, carpets, and cushions.

"This was such an exciting day," said Moses. "Was it difficult to learn how to use that lasso?"

"Practice, Moses, it's all about practice. It is effective, though, especially when you want to take the animal alive."

They sat watching the leaping flames. Then Amenhotep spoke, "What's really exciting, and dangerous too, is the hippopotamus hunt. That's done from boats, using spears."

"What's dangerous about it?" asked Moses.

"The hippo tries to take you under water with him. Those hippos have been known to attack boats, too. Did you know it was the hippopotamus hunt that started the Hyskos war?"

"No," said Moses. "How did that happen?"

"This was when the Hyksos controlled the delta completely and had even extended their power into middle Egypt. The Hyksos king, Alepi I, wrote to the Theban ruler, Taa II."

"Your grandfather," Moses said.

"That's right, Moses. You remembered," replied his uncle. "Alepi I asked Taa II to abolish the hippopotamus hunt practiced by the Thebans. You see, they believed the animal was the earthly incarnation of the Hyksos major deity, Seth, which they equated with the god of their homeland, Baal. Now you know, Moses, that in our religion, Seth represents all that is chaotic and evil. He killed his brother, Osiris, and tore out the left eye of Horus, son of Osiris. The Hyksos picked an appropriate god to relate to Baal. I've heard that in their homeland the Hyksos actually sacrificed their babies on the red-hot metal arms of Baal."

"How awful!" exclaimed Moses.

"Anyway," continued Amenhotep, "my grandfather, Taa II, refused to stop the hippopotamus hunts and war broke out."

Moses asked his uncle, "But was it so important—that hippo hunt I mean? There are so many other animals to hunt. Was it worth a war?"

"It wasn't just the hunt," explained Amenhotep. "The Hyksos were foreigners, and they were taking over more and more. When they tried to change our way of life, they had gone too far. If we yielded on the hippo hunt, what would be the next thing they wanted to change?"

Amenhotep continued, "That is why we have to watch the Habiru. They are foreign too."

In their defense, Moses asked, "But they haven't tried to change the Egyptian way of life have they?"

"Not yet, but that's because we keep them working so hard."

Moses was silent, but he thought, *So these people are being treated like slaves for something they haven't done yet.* What convenient logic to justify this oppression and get free service at the same time. It didn't seem fair to Moses, but what could he do about it? He decided to enjoy the time with his uncle.

The next morning Moses got a chance to see Bekah perform. With an explosion of energy, she raced toward an ibex and brought it down in minutes.

Amenhotep told Moses, "Greyhounds are bred to release quick bursts of energy to chase a target like that, and they can do it without guidance. They know what to do. It's in their blood to chase things, so you have to watch her around other animals. It's a good thing we don't have a cat," he added.

After a successful morning of hunting, the hunters returned to the palace. Amenhotep checked on the Oryx. *Yes, she is a beauty all right*, he thought.

The Oryx was buff-colored with a white belly. Her markings were distinctive, including black-and-white stripes on her face and a black stripe running along her flank and encircling her forelegs. The servants told him the animal had eaten the plants and tender shoots they had put out for her.

"Good," said Amenhotep. "She must be adjusting to her new surroundings."

"Pharaoh," he heard his sister calling him as she approached.

"Princess Ahmose," said Pharaoh, "you are looking happy today."

"Oh my brother, she is such a beautiful creature. I am so glad you brought her home alive," she gushed. The Princess reached through the wooden slats of the cage, as she cooed to the startled animal. "Oh, look at the poor thing. She is trembling."

Then Ahmose said, "You must have had a good hunt. Moses is ecstatic."

"He had his first kill. Did he tell you?"

Princess Ahmose winced. "No, he didn't. I suppose he knows how I would feel about it. Please don't give me the details," she said as she put up her hand. "By the way, Meryet is looking for you."

Amenhotep wanted to bathe before he joined his wife, so he hurried to his chambers. After the servants had helped him with a cleansing shower, shave, and fresh linen robes, he sent for Meryet. When the queen appeared, she was followed by a servant holding a covered basket.

"Welcome home. I have a gift for you, my Lord," she said, motioning to the servant to come forward with the basket.

"Well, well! What have we here?" said Pharaoh, thinking that Meryet herself was enough of a gift for him. He reached into the basket and lifted out a large amphora. The jar was decorated in the new style, with brightly colored leaves and flowers. Below the lip there was an antelope's head in relief, protruding from the neck of a beautiful double handled vessel.

Amenhotep laughed with delight. He dismissed the servant. Sitting down on a cushioned chair, he said, "Come here my dear," and drew the lovely queen onto his lap.

"I've missed you," he said as he breathed in her enticing scent of lotus blossoms and then kissed her deeply

Memphis
1512 BC

Moses wanted to visit the quarries below Memphis. The closest one was on the east bank of the Nile, just south of the capital. Until now, Princess Ahmose had discouraged such a visit, because the quarries were dusty, rough places, swarming with men driven by overseers who were pressured to supply material for one building project or another. It was no place for a boy.

But Moses was a young man of fourteen now. Amenhotep argued that Moses would be safe with Ineni.

"Besides," he said, "the weather is cool right now before the harvest season. Those quarries can be unbearable when it is hot."

With the reluctant consent of the princess, early the next morning Ineni and Moses set out in one of the royal chariots. When they reached the quarry site, Ineni called for the attendants to hold the chariot.

"From here we walk," he told Moses. While they were still some distance from the main site, Moses could hear the shouts of men calling directions and warnings: "Watch out! Ready, Heave! Step it up, you lazy bastards!"

Then they heard the crack of a whip.

"What's that?" asked Moses.

Ineni stopped and looked at Moses. "My son, what you are about to see will not be pleasant. But this is the harsh reality of life. The fine temples and monuments of Egypt do not rise magically from the sands. They are built on the backs of the common people and slaves. I do not come here unless I have to. Today I am here to select the blocks for one of those monuments," said the noted architect, whom Moses respected as his tutor. "Believe me, I won't be here any longer than necessary."

Moses followed Ineni around the top of a rock face, which the workers had sectioned off for cutting. Moses saw that grooves had been hammered around the sides of the rocks to be cut. Now the men were working with copper tools to chisel down the back. Moses could see wooden wedges protruding from the bottom of each rock. Ineni explained that the wedges had been soaked in water so that when they expanded they would split the rock free.

"This is a good cliff," said Ineni.

"This rock is just what I need for my project," he told the master cutter. "How soon will this lot be ready?"

"Let me check with my scribe." Moments later the master gave Ineni an estimate.

"Good," replied Ineni. "By that time, I will be ready for another load."

"Come, Moses, we can go now," said his teacher.

But Moses did not hear him, because his eyes were fixed on some workers who were struggling to load a large stone on a sled. They looked like Hebrews. Their overseer was bullying them and using his whip when the men were obviously doing the best they could.

Can't he see that? Moses thought. *A man wouldn't treat a donkey like that!*

"Moses, I've been calling you," said Ineni as he came alongside the young lad.

"Oh, I'm sorry, teacher," replied Moses, and, after one last look at the workers, departed the quarry with Ineni.

In the chariot, as they were returning to the palace, Moses was unusually quiet. Imeni asked him if anything was wrong.

"Yes," said Moses. "I am so sad for the workers." Then he turned to Ineni, speaking directly, "It makes me angry to see the workers treated so badly when they are doing their best!"

"Ah, Moses," replied Ineni. "I have felt the same at times, but remember, those task masters are working under difficult and dangerous conditions. They know how to wring that last bit of energy from the men and at the same time maintain control."

Moses wasn't convinced, but he fell silent. The remainder of the trip he spent trying to square what he had seen at the quarry with the teachings of Ineni about kindness to one's fellowman.

Memphis
1512 BC

"Will you please have a talk with Moses?" Princess Ahmose asked her brother. "Next year he will be going to the House of Wisdom. Don't you think he should have a focus for his studies? When I ask him about it, he just says he doesn't know." She looked worried. "He has been withdrawn since his visit to the quarry," she added.

Amenhotep responded to her concerns, "In regard to his studies, I think he has plenty of time to make that decision. You know Moses likes to ponder things."

He paused as his sister looked at him expectantly. Amenhotep knew she wanted him to say something about Moses's mood, but how was he supposed to know what was going on in the boy's mind?

"You say Moses has been withdrawn lately?" he began. "I wonder if something is bothering him. Perhaps it would be good to get away for a sail tomorrow. We can talk then; Moses seems to enjoy the river."

He was rewarded by the look of relief on his sister's face.

The next day, Amenhotep and Moses stood on the deck in the morning breeze, sipping the steaming mulled wine that the servants had prepared. They had started out early and enjoyed breakfast on board.

Bekah had been eager to come along. Now, standing at the prow of the boat with her body erect and her nose pointing due north, she looked like a prow decoration for the vessel. Suddenly she turned, ran to Moses, and let out a sharp bark.

"What is it Bekah, what do you see?"

"There," said Amenhotep, "on the left bank." Moses looked and saw several dogs running after a herdsman driving his cattle.

"She probably misses running with the pack like she did when she was hunting," Moses told his uncle. Then he bent down and ruffled Bekah's neck.

The boatmen were working the oars as they moved toward the delta. Pharaoh had decided to show Moses the Great Pyramid from a western tributary of the Nile. That should inspire him and lift his spirits.

They had come to the fork of the river when he said, "Moses, see we have come to the place of decision. If we go left, we will pass close by the pyramids, but if we go right, we will arrive at the House of Wisdom, where you will study next year. I have decided to take the left fork today," he said as the helmsman turned into the left tributary. "Now what about you, Moses, have you decided which way to go in your education?"

"What do you mean, Uncle?" asked Moses.

"There are some subjects every student learns, but there are others that are designed to prepare you specifically for the occupation you will pursue in life. Some of the positions that are appropriate for a prince of Egypt are: chief of the treasure house, chief scribe, or chief priest. The study of law may lead to being a judge, even a chief judge or governor. A few princes choose the arts, but those pursuits are more often chosen by the middle class. However, there are architects, chief sculptors, master painters, and such," his uncle enumerated for Moses's consideration.

At this point, Amenhotep stopped talking about Moses's future studies, because they were drawing nearer to the pyramids. Moses had seen them from a distance, but it was another thing to see them up close, looming above them as they pulled into a dock below the pyramid complex.

"We won't be staying long, Moses, so don't go far," his uncle called as Moses and Bekah scrambled up the river bank.

As Amenhotep watched them go, he reflected on all the work he had waiting for him. It seemed that there was never enough time.

Here I am, standing in the shadow of these pyramid tombs, he thought. *Death will come soon enough. What is really important?* And he knew he wasn't wasting time spending this day with Moses.

The area was a vast expanse of sand and pieces of shale. There were a few people on donkeys, riding around the complex, and others were on foot. Here and there, guards patrolled the area. The white limestone surface of the pyramids gleamed in the midday sunlight. Moses walked around the huge structures, so he could see them from every angle. Bekah was chasing her tail in joy as though she was celebrating the genius of the ancients. Moses wondered aloud, "How did they do it? How in the world did they build those pyramids?"

Then Moses heard his uncle calling, "It's time to go."

As Moses and Bekah joined him, his uncle asked, "Does your neck hurt, Moses?"

"Why should my neck hurt?" asked Moses.

"Because you were walking around with your neck craned like this," he said, demonstrating how Moses had spent the last hour gazing up at the pyramids.

Moses laughed, "Well, they surely are something to see, Uncle. Just imagine, they have stood there for over one thousand years!"

Back on board the boat, Pharaoh and Moses sat down to a lunch of hot lentil stew served with bread and beer. Bekah lay on the cushioned bench beside Moses, looking at him with hopeful eyes. Every now and then, Moses would slip her a piece of bread as he ate and talked to his uncle. A servant came around with more stew. Moses accepted another bowl, but Pharaoh said he was full and leaned back against the cushions of the cabin.

"You see, Moses," he said, "it was a good thing I told you to put more kohl around your eyes this morning. The glare of the sun on those pyramids was enough to blind you."

It was a common problem in Egypt to suffer diseases of the eyes because of the prevalent sun and dust. The *galena* in the kohl ointment served as a protection against these afflictions.

Moses was full of questions about the pyramids.

"We don't know much about them, nor about the people who built them," Pharaoh explained. "For everything we learn raises more questions. They are so imposing and yet such a mystery."

Amenhotep and Moses went out on deck as the boat approached the main channel of the Nile. They were sailing with the prevailing north wind and making good progress. Amenhotep returned to the subject of Moses's education.

"What did you study, Uncle?" Moses asked.

"I studied literature and law," he replied.

"That is what I will study," said Moses.

While Amenhotep was pleased to hear this, he didn't want Moses to take up those studies simply because he had done so.

"Is that what you really want for yourself, Moses?" he asked.

"Yes, Uncle, you've told me I have a good sense of what is fair. Isn't that what law provides—a system of justice? Maybe I will be a judge someday. Literature is where my heart is though, because I like to write stories and poems and songs."

"Well put, Moses, I see you have given it some thought. I've underestimated you. Your mother was wondering if you were considering architecture, because of Ineni being your tutor."

"Architecture interests me too, but I wouldn't care to design temples or tombs. I think mother is worried that I care about the Hebrew slaves. I've talked to her about the harshness of the taskmasters. As you said, I have a sense of fairness. Sometimes I think the slave drivers like to bully and humiliate the people. Do you think that is necessary, Uncle? I remember learning in my first years at school that one must not humiliate or mistreat one's servant."

"Ah, you are right, Moses! That is the ideal, but often in the real world there are those who abuse power."

"But, can't you do anything about it, Uncle? You are Pharaoh after all. You have great power."

"Yes, but I am not god, even if people think I am. I cannot be everywhere at once."

"If I were in charge of the quarries and the building projects, I would not allow that kind of mistreatment," stated Moses, adamantly.

"So you would be at all the quarries and all the building sites, at once, Moses?" asked his uncle.

Moses began to see the enormity of the problem of oversight. "I would appoint overseers who would answer to me," he said.

"And what if the overseers didn't report their harsh behavior?"

"Then I would hold hearings for the people, so they could tell me about any abuse."

"Don't you think they might be reluctant to bring their complaints to you for fear of reprisal—even harsher treatment—because they had brought charges against their taskmaster?"

Continuing his argument, Amenhotep asked Moses, "And what if the taskmaster lied? How would you prove it? It is said, Moses, that even when men stand before Maat, the goddess of justice, in the afterlife, they often lie in their confessions."

Moses knew his uncle was asking questions to teach him, to make him think, nevertheless, he was becoming aggravated because this was a subject he really cared about. "I know that it wouldn't be easy, but I would find a way," said Moses.

Amenhotep understood the implication that he, as pharaoh, hadn't tried hard enough to relieve the burdens of the common people, particularly of the Hebrews. Maybe he hadn't, but he didn't like hearing it from Moses, even in an indirect way. They had arrived at the dock in Memphis. "It's time to go," he said, trying to suppress the irritation he felt.

"Did you talk to him?" asked Princess Ahmose as she met Pharaoh in the corridor of the palace.

Her brother looked exhausted after his day with Moses. "Yes, I talked to him, for all the good it did," he replied.

"What do you mean? Didn't he listen to you?"

"Oh, Moses is always respectful, but I feel he's off in his own world and that my words don't have as much impact on his thinking anymore. Do you remember how he used to hang on every word I said, so happy he was to be with me?"

Ahmose placed her hand on Amenhotep's arm. "Brother, look at me. Moses loves you. He is almost fifteen years old. It's only natural that he wants to think his own thoughts. But you still matter to him. Now tell me, did you get any indication of what he wants to do?"

"Yes, he would like to study law and write songs."

"Well, that's good. I'm relieved he doesn't want to be the chief of the treasure house or an architect, because either of those professions would need more time spent at the quarries," said the Princess.

"Oh, but you haven't heard the rest of it," replied Amenhotep. "Moses has the ideal plan to end all mistreatment at the quarries. He laid it all out for me on the boat."

Ahmose heard the sarcastic tone in her brother's voice. This wasn't like him. He must really be hurt.

"Pharaoh," she said gently, "Moses is really giving you great regard, if you stop to think about it." She paused to let her words sink in.

"In what way, Sister? I'm afraid I don't see it that way," he said.

"No, I know you don't, because you are thinking he is being critical of you, when he is actually looking to you as the answer to his concern. He truly thinks you can turn the situation around."

"But he implied he could do better. How is that, giving me regard?"

"Were you asking him questions, as you do when you are teaching something?"

"Well, yes."

"And usually, that is good. But if his heart is in a matter, and you keep asking questions—" she broke off and paused again. "Do you see how that might frustrate him?"

"I don't know, I suppose so."

The princess could see that Amenhotep was tired and clearly out of patience now, so she said, "It's enough, come now, refresh yourself. Have a nap, and you will feel better. I do appreciate your taking Moses out today. I know it isn't easy in your busy schedule. Now here is something you can look forward to—Meryet has arranged for the cook to prepare your favorite dishes for dinner this evening: roast goose, bread made from Turet corn, and good wine from Charu."

Amenhotep felt better for having talked to Ahmose. She was as sensitive and nurturing as Meryet was a delight. It was ironic that he had started the day planning to lift Moses's spirits, and he was ending the day needing a lift himself. He had let Moses get under his skin, but his sister was right. Moses did love him. He was just impassioned for a cause, like any idealistic young man. Moses would soon be going away to school, and then he would have other things on his mind. Maybe he would forget about the Hebrews.

Memphis
1511 BC

Amenhotep and Princess Ahmose were having one of their rare arguments. It was about how many attendants to send along with Moses when he went away to college. Amenhotep maintained that Moses should have more freedom.

"Moses needs to develop some independence away from the cocoon of this palace," he told her. He felt that one guard was enough.

The Princess countered that it would take two people to accomplish everything that needed to be done: cleaning quarters, fetching supplies, cooking and serving meals, doing laundry, and keeping Bekah on her strict schedule of frequent exercise runs, all while Moses attended classes.

"Besides," she argued, "if one guard is ill or busy, the other would still be at hand for protection. Aren't you concerned for Moses's safety?"

The guards in question were twin brothers who had been enlisted in the palace service several years earlier. They were five years older than Moses and had proved to be the right choice. Well-trained, conscientious, and alert, they had also turned out to be pleasant company, according to Moses. The sight of the three of them walking together made heads turn. The guards were good-looking identical twins, and when they flanked the handsome Moses, it was like seeing a jewel with matching side gems. The twins were named "Khent," meaning *to go upstream,* and "Khed," meaning, *to go downstream.* The young men related a story their mother had told them about when they were little boys. When their mother had held up the bronze *see-face* or mirror for the first time, one of the two-year-old twins named his brother instead of himself, pointing to his own reflection. His brother had done the same. Since then, even though they were close and seemed to enjoy each other's company, they had each developed their own personality. Most important to the royal family, the brothers were devoted to Moses.

Princess Ahmose maintained that since the three young men got along so well together, it was a perfect arrangement to have them both continue as Moses's attendants while he was away at school. Amenhotep's wife, Meryet, agreed with her sister that both twins should go.

Finally, Pharaoh decided to consult Queen Mother Ahmose Nefertari. *She will support me*, he thought, but he was wrong.

"My precious grandson should have two attendants while he is away at school," she said firmly, as though by decree.

"What is the use of being pharaoh of the Two Lands of Egypt if three women of the palace make my decisions for me?" grumbled Amenhotep to himself as he strolled around the garden. To cheer himself up, he decided to visit the Oryx. There were two of them now. He had brought the female a mate and ordered a larger, more natural enclosure to be built for them. The female was carrying a calf, so it was a good thing he had built the enclosure. She would build a nest of brush for her calf, and when the calf was born, the mother would try to hide it for four to six weeks. Now she would have the room to follow her protective instincts. Pharaoh was carrying a treat for the Oryx pair. He had stopped at the palace kitchen and picked up a wild melon and some onions.

The princess had named the female Oryx "Isis" and her mate "Osiris." So, he supposed, if the calf were a bull, it would be "Horus." Princess Ahmose didn't seem to have any qualms as to possible irreverence in naming the animals after the gods. He remembered that she had explained that the gods were all manifestations of Amun anyway. After all, she hadn't named any animal after Amun, including the ram that was sometimes used to represent the Hidden One. "Besides," the princess had told her brother, "Amun created all the animals too, so why should he care if I name them after the gods?"

"What?" she said, looking at him.

"I didn't say anything. I haven't breathed a word. You are doing all the talking," said Amenhotep.

"It was the look on your face," she said.

If he lived a thousand years, he would not understand women, he thought as he approached the animal enclosure. *Ah, she's close*, he observed. *She will drop that calf any time now.*

He hoped it would be before Moses went away to school.

* * * * *

Princess Ahmose and Amenhotep accompanied Moses on the royal bark to the House of Wisdom. Bekah stood at her favorite post on the prow of the boat, while the twins kept their eyes on her. The royal family sat in the cabin going over last-minute instructions and arrangements. As their boat entered the eastern delta, the three came out on deck to enjoy the scenery. In some areas the banks of the Nile were soggy, but in other places verdant pastureland extended as far as the eye could see. Herds of cattle grazed contentedly.

Now they were passing a great pond lined with tall reeds and papyrus. Other sedges were filled with blue and white lotuses on the banks.

"Oh," exclaimed Moses's mother, "Meryet loves those."

"Why don't we just pull over and you can gather some for her," said Amenhotep as he pointed to a huge crocodile sunning itself on the bank. Two more crocodiles joined the first.

"I think I will decline that offer, thank you," declared his sister. A little farther along they saw a hippopotamus pond teeming with the large creatures. Stately flamingos were stalking in the shallows. They saw ducks, geese, ibises, and other waterfowl. Above their heads flew flocks of birds, as this area was on a major migratory route. The lapwing's or *rekyt* were so common in these marshy delta areas that the term was sometimes used to describe the common people: *rekyt*.

Moses's mother and uncle accompanied him to his new school. After Moses was settled in his new quarters, he bade goodbye to his family. He saw that his mother's eyes were full of tears.

"Mother," he assured her, "I am not far away. It only took a day to get here. I'll be fine."

Princess Ahmose dabbed at her eyes.

"I know, Son, it is just that you have grown up so fast. At least you have the twins to help you," she said, smiling at the brothers as though she was appealing to them to do a good job of taking care of her son.

The Delta
1511 BC

As it turned out, it was to Moses's advantage that both twins were sent along with him. One of the brothers was always left to guard him when he sent the other on an errand. The most important errand he had in mind was an idea that had come to him some time ago, and that was to find his Hebrew family.

Moses wanted to know if they were still alive and if they were faring well. He had many questions he wanted to ask them. One of the most important to Moses was how did they come to believe as they did? Another was what was their hope for the future? His own future was so uncertain for him. Growing up, he had felt just like any other Egyptian, however privileged he was in the palace. He knew his Uncle Tep and his mother, Princess Ahmose, saw him as an Egyptian and still held out hope that he would be pharaoh. However, Moses wasn't so sure who he was.

Am I Egyptian? Or am I Hebrew? he asked himself. *Certainly, I know more about Egyptian ways. In Egypt, I am a prince and could be pharaoh. Why would I want to be Hebrew and be a slave?*

But he didn't feel Egyptian as much as he did when he was a child. Another thing that puzzled him was why did being pharaoh seem so foreign? His Uncle Tep had been the best of fathers and he was pharaoh. Why couldn't he see himself as pharaoh?

His head began to ache, so he dismissed these confusing thoughts. He would take Bekah out for a run to clear his head. Amenhotep would be pharaoh for many more decades anyway, so he would have plenty of time to figure it out.

Little did he know that not even one decade would pass before Pharaoh's time on earth would be over.

Despite Moses's troubling thoughts, he was determined that once he was settled in school, he would try to find his Hebrew family. Maybe they could help him in his quest to understand himself better. He felt that there was no one who he could share these thoughts with, not even Uncle Tep.

He breathed a prayer, "Adonai, please help me. I feel so alone."

Moses settled into his comfortable quarters at school and was absorbed with beginning his classes. He liked the way the instructors addressed the pupils with respect, almost as peers. The classes were not just about assimilating endless facts. Instead, the students were invited to think about what they were learning and to give their own opinions and ideas. They sat around in seminar fashion and had stimulating discussions.

Moses found he was getting better at expressing himself, though he still was not as confident in that regard as the other students seemed to be.

As for Moses's search for his Hebrew family, he had heard that there was an enclave of Hebrew people living close to his school in Heliopolis.[26] Hebrews lived all over the delta, but Moses thought that On was a good place to start his search. He had plenty of money from the Prince's Fund.[27] Moses told the twins of his plan and swore them to secrecy. He assured them that Pharaoh would be informed of the mission but that he wanted to be the one to tell him.

Khent and Khed seemed to understand. They had experienced their own identity issues. The twins discussed how it must feel to be of two origins. At least they were Egyptians with only one set of parents. They took turns searching for almost a year. It was Khent who finally brought back news to Moses that he had found the home of Amran and Jochebed and that his parents were alive. Khent had not spoken to them, but their neighbors were willing to answer his questions when he reassured them that he bore a message of good news for the family and that the tidings had come directly from a prince of Pharaoh. He had revealed his badge of status as a member of the Royal Guard.

On Moses's first break from school, he had not been scheduled to return to the palace, so he seized the opportunity to visit his Hebrew family. Moses took the twins and Bekah with him and asked them to wait outside the house. He had sent a message that he was coming. Having

---

26 The ancient On.
27 A special fund which the royal family maintained for the personal use of the princes.

heard from the neighbors that a prince of Pharaoh's court wanted to bring good news, they barely dared to hope it was Moses. When they received Moses's personal letter, they rejoiced that their prayers to see Moses again were about to be answered. When Moses knocked on the door, his parents were overwhelmed at the sight of the tall, handsome young man who stood before them. Once inside, Moses was smothered with embraces, kisses, and tears.

Jochebed exclaimed, "Twice Adonai has given me back my son, first from the Nile and now from the palace. Praise be to Almighty God!"

Amran, tears streaming down his cheeks, simply embraced Moses, patting him on the back and repeating, "My son, my son, at last my son."

Miriam and Aaron, Moses's older siblings, stood back while their parents were welcoming their brother. Then they came forward with hugs and kisses also.

Finally, Jochebed declared, "You must be hungry, Moses. Come, Miriam, help me serve the meal."

They sat at the rough-hewn table, which was loaded with bowls of side dishes. Jochebed served Moses a generous helping of roast veal. There were roast tubers, fresh cucumbers and tomatoes, and a wonderful shraak, straight from the oven. The delicious Bedoiun-type, flat bread was doughy in the middle and crispy on the edges as Moses broke it apart.. Jochebed saw that Moses enjoyed the bread, so she gave him another big piece.

Moses thanked her, but was not sure how to address her. When he told her, "This food is better than the food in the palace," her eyes shone with delight.

Then she declared, "Nothing is too good for a prince of Egypt."

At that, Aaron and Miriam, sitting at the end of the table, bent their heads together and started snickering behind their hands. Moses noticed it and made a decision. He stood up and went around the table to his Hebrew parents.

"Father, Mother," he said, "in this house I am not a prince of Egypt. I am simply your son." Then with tear-filled eyes, he hugged them both.

After that, he walked over to his siblings. "Sister, Brother," he said, "I would like to get to know you better." They weren't laughing now; they were touched.

Moses turned to his parents, "I will visit you again. There is much I wish to discuss with you, but right now I would like to introduce you to some of my friends. They helped me find you."

Moses's father exclaimed, "Are they outside? Oh, they must come in and have something to eat. There is plenty."

Jochebed nodded, saying warmly, "Yes, yes, bring them in," as she quickly moved the platter of veal out of Aaron's reach.

Moses opened the door and beckoned to the twins to bring Bekah and come in. As his parents were welcoming Khent and Khed, urging them to sit down and eat, Miriam and Aaron were fussing over the dog.

"This is Bekah," said Moses. "You should see her hunt!" Miriam and Aaron had never had a dog. Their parents said there wasn't enough to feed a dog too.

Now Jochebed was bustling about, reheating food and baking fresh bread.

"You have to try that bread," Moses told the twins. "It will melt in your mouth."

Later, after a round of date cakes for dessert, Moses and the twins stood up to leave, but Bekah hesitated. She was wrapped up in all the attention and affection she was getting from Miriam and Aaron. Usually, when she wasn't racing around, she was sleeping, conserving her energy, but not today.

Moses laughed at her, for she was still soaking up the warm welcome. "Come on Bekah, you spoiled girl," he said

As the twins took the dog outside, Moses reached into his money purse and pulled out a handful of gold coins which he pressed into Amran's hand, saying, "This is for you."

"No, no my son," protested his father.

Moses said firmly "If you want me to visit you again you must take this. To me it is a small amount, but I'm sure it can be useful to you." He pleaded, "Please do not refuse my gift, Father."

So Amran accepted the gold and embraced his son, thinking, *I already have my treasure.*

The Delta
1510 BC

Moses was finishing his second year of school at the House of Wisdom. As often as he could get away, he would go to see his parents in the Hebrew community. During these visits, his father told him about the Hebrew religion.

At this point in time, the Egyptian system of worship was fully developed, whereas the Hebrews had no specific place of worship, no active priesthood, and no separate system of law. The Hebrews had an oral tradition, stories passed down by the patriarchs. Though they believed that a blood sacrifice was required to cover their sins, the Hebrews could not practice this kind of sin-offering on a large scale, as that would be offensive to the Egyptians.

Instead, they would slaughter a calf or a lamb without blemish and make an offering within the confines of their own homes. Extended families and friends would meet to share a meal of the roasted animal and offer prayers of petition and thanksgiving to Adonai. Moses had attended some of these quiet gatherings of worship, and in contrast to his experience at Thebes, he had been deeply moved. In fact, the holiday for the Beautiful Festival at Thebes had given him the opportunity to have several long visits with his Hebrew family. The royal family understood when he declined to go on the long trip to Thebes. He promised he would go the next year after his graduation.

By this time, Moses was well-known in the Hebrew neighborhood. The twins felt comfortable leaving him and Bekah at his parents' house, and so they could have the day off and pick up Moses and the dog later.

Taking Bekah out for her frequent runs provided breaks in Moses's long day of discussions with Amran. Part of the time, nineteen-year-old Aaron was off with his friends. Miriam, in her twenties now, stayed home, helping her mother to prepare the meals and, at times, joining in the discussion. Bekah lay sleeping between runs and was no trouble at all.

Moses and his father compared creation stories of the Egyptians and Hebrews and found some similarities between them. Both set forth the belief that God created the world by his word. However, the way the first human beings came to inhabit that world was very different in the two systems. There was a difference in the offerings too. Hebrews believed a blood sacrifice was required, which involved sprinkling the blood on the altar and presenting the burnt offering. Egyptians brought the meat to the gods, already roasted, as if providing a meal.

"Why is a blood offering required?" asked Moses.

Amran explained, "Actually it all started in the Garden of Eden. Let me tell you the Hebrew story of the first family. Adam and Eve were created to be perfect and pleasing to God. They must have been quite a pair! God placed them in a beautiful garden. He gave them free will, but he did not want them to become acquainted with sin. Therefore, he told them not to eat of the Tree of the Knowledge of Good and Evil or they would surely die."

"So he gave them the ability to choose," said Moses.

"Yes," his father replied, "but in this case, he warned them of what to avoid. He wanted them to trust and obey him. There were plenty of other fruit trees."

Amram continued, "However, Satan in the guise of a serpent, tempted Eve to eat. She did, and then she offered the forbidden fruit to Adam, who also ate it.

"Instantly they became aware that they were naked and were ashamed. They covered themselves with fig leaves. But you see, that was not adequate to cover their sins, so God provided them with animal skins that had required the shedding of blood. They were banished from the garden so they would not eat of the Tree of Everlasting Life."

"God wouldn't let them eat of the Tree of Life, because they had eaten the fruit of that other tree and they were going to die?" said Moses.

"That's right. I'm sure you will recognize a common trait of mankind when I tell you this part, Moses," Amran said. "When Adam and Eve were apprehended by God, Adam pointed at Eve and said, 'The woman you gave me tempted me with the fruit.' Eve, in turn, pointed to the serpent, 'The serpent deceived me and I ate.'"

Moses laughed, "Yes, in my law studies I have started a court apprenticeship. Right now I'm just observing the cases that come in, and I see many attempts to shift the blame."

"Well," replied Amran, "God would have none of it. He gave them each a punishment. Adam would have to toil by the sweat of his brow, Eve would suffer birth pains, and the snake would crawl in the dust. Actually, God was merciful. Though he had told them they would die if they ate of that tree, he let them live a long life before they died."

Amran continued, "The gravity of what the first pair had done was soon evident when their son, Cain, killed his brother, Abel, in a fit of jealousy."

"Why was Cain jealous?" asked Moses.

His father replied, "Interesting that you should ask that, Moses, because this story also relates to the blood sacrifice. Cain was jealous because God accepted Abel's blood sacrifice but rejected Cain's offering. Abel was a shepherd. He killed one of his flock and brought a blood sacrifice to God. Cain, however, was a farmer and offered produce to God. That wasn't so bad in itself, but God saw that Cain's heart was not right. He had not brought God a blood sacrifice to cover his sin."

Moses thought of the produce offered to Amun. "What makes a blood sacrifice, Father?" he asked.

Amran replied, "The animal must be without blemish. The blood of the animal is sprinkled on the altar, before the burnt offering is presented."

Going back to the story Moses asked, "What happened to Cain?"

Amran said, "Again, God was merciful. Cain was exiled from his family, but he was allowed to live."

"In Egypt, murder is a sin worthy of death," Moses stated. "Perhaps God wanted to give Cain a chance to repent."

"Time to eat," broke in Moses's mother. They talked of other things over the delicious meal his mother had cooked.

Moses asked Amran if they could discuss the afterlife later. "I don't want to tire you, Father."

"Oh, but this gives me new energy, to talk to my son about the stories of God," said Amran, his eyes bright with joy.

"Good," said Moses, "but please have a rest first. It is a holiday for you."

Moses left to give Bekah her exercise. He had her on a leash because he did not know what animals they would encounter. It was in Bekah's blood to give chase.

"We do not need that kind of blood sacrifice, Bekah," he said as he pondered the morning's discussion.

Later, as father and son resumed their discussion, Amran stated, "There is a bit more I want to tell you about the blood sacrifice, Moses."

"All right, father," replied Moses. "I want to hear it all."

"Besides the examples of the first family that I spoke of this morning, there are examples of blood sacrifices offered to Adonai by the patriarchs, Abraham, Isaac, and Jacob. Abraham was even willing to sacrifice his own son, but God provided a ram instead."

"Now, Son," continued Amran, "you wanted to ask about the afterlife. I must tell you we don't know much about that."

"But Father," said Moses, "you do believe in life after death, do you not? The Egyptians make so much of that."

As his father lifted his head, he had a faraway gaze in his eyes. "A long time ago there was a patriarch named Enoch. It was said that he walked with God. Then one day, he was gone, because God took him."

"Do you mean he died?" asked Moses.

"No, all the other accounts of our ancestors end with: 'and then he died.' This one is different."

"Well," said Moses, the student of law, "was there any evidence? Were there any witnesses?"

"Amran looked directly at Moses and said with conviction, "God took him."

"So you believe God took him to Paradise," stated Moses, not willing to pursue his arguments for evidence.

"Yes, and there is something else that causes me to believe there is more that God has yet to reveal to us." Moses leaned forward, intrigued, as his father continued, "It is something God said to the serpent when he was meting out the punishment. God told him that he would put enmity between him and the woman and between his offspring and hers. God said, 'He will crush your head, and you will strike his heel.'"

Moses puzzled over this saying.

His father said, "Many people think God was referring only to the antagonism between people and snakes, but some believe there is a deeper meaning, and so do I."

"What do you think it means, Father?" asked Moses.

"I think God was addressing Satan, because he was the one who inhabited the snake for the purpose of deceiving Adam and Eve. Satan was trying to thwart God's purpose for them, and he will continue to struggle against God. But God said to Satan, 'He (an offspring of the woman) will crush your head.' That signifies Satan's defeat."

"Who would this man be?" asked Moses.

"I don't know," said his father, "some future deliverer who would restore our relationship with God, I think. You see that is what Satan wanted to ruin—our relationship with God."

"But we can still know God, can't we?" asked Moses.

"We can't approach him the way Adam and Eve did before they sinned. He is holy and cannot tolerate sin; therefore we must atone for our sins through the blood sacrifice. It may be that the restoration may occur when we return to the land promised to our fathers. On the other hand, it may not be in this life but in the next."

This was a great mystery, Moses thought. He thanked his father for revealing to him his hope for paradise. He thought about the Egyptian beliefs regarding the afterlife.

"The Egyptians have a justice system in this life that is related to the justice system in the afterlife," said Moses. "There is a growing belief in the cult of Osiris.[28] . "In the Egyptian belief system, Osiris was a son of Amun, god of gods, who was killed by his brother Seth, now equated with evil. Osiris was resurrected and subsequently opens the way to paradise in the afterlife.

"At first it was just for the pharaoh," said Moses, "but the people begged to be included in this resurrection, so the opportunity has been extended to them also.

"This is where the justice system comes in," explained Moses. "The heart is weighed on the scales. If it is light as a feather, Osiris will open the gate, but if it is heavy with sin, that person is devoured by a beast made up of three fierce animals."

Moses kept his explanation simple, not explaining all the other gates that had to be negotiated with the help of the Book of the Dead.

Amran asked Moses, "So then Osiris is supposed to be both judge and savior?"

"In a way," replied Moses. "But there is no blood sacrifice that people are required to make. They must make a confession in the afterlife, but it

---

28 In Egypt *cult* did not designate a false belief, but a belief held by a particular group of people.

is the weighing of the heart that really matters—whether or not the heart is heavy with sin."

"I like that part," said Amran. " Because God sees the heart, I believe. He knew Cain's heart was not right but Abel's heart was right."

Then peering intently at Moses, his father asked, "You don't believe as the Egyptians do, Moses, do you?"

"To be truthful, Father, I don't know what to believe. That is why I am talking with you—to help sort it out. All I know is that when I am at the festival at Thebes, that form of worship doesn't seem right for me. When I am here with the Hebrews, I can worship from my heart."

"That is good," said Amran gently. "Look to Adonai, Moses. He will guide you."

Memphis
1510 BC

Amenhotep I was concerned about his successor, as he had no male heir, and Moses had shown no interest in wearing the double crown of Egypt. His thoughts turned to General Thutmose. He was a good man, loyal, a good leader and, though he was middle-aged, he was still an attractive man. True, he had fathered a child with a harem girl, but a match with Princess Ahmose would firmly establish him in the royal family.

He sought out his sister and found her in the garden, admiring flowers that Meryet had planted.

"Princess," he said, "I've been wanting to talk to you about General Thutmose. What do you think of him?"

Ahmose replied, "I enjoy talking to him. He's your friend so, of course, we are friendly."

"You have been spending a good amount of time together lately. He seems quite taken with you; I've noticed this at our dinners together." He paused, waiting for her reaction to his bold observation.

She replied, "Yes, I've noticed it too, and I have to admit the idea of marriage to him appeals to me." Then she added, "But then there is Moses. Moses is not interested in being Pharaoh; I know that. But I'm concerned about how things may change for him at the palace if I should marry."

Amenhotep replied, "Without a male heir, the situation may change anyway," he said. "Seriously, my sister, will you consider a union with my commander? I can see he is attracted to you, but I wanted to speak with you before I brought the subject up to him."

Before she could reply, he hastened to assure her, "I will talk to Moses. After all, he is a man now, away at school and soon to be away in military training. For the next four years, he won't even be around the palace, so why be worried about changes for him? You've devoted your life to him. It's time you thought of your own life. Maybe it isn't too late to have an heir."

"Would my child be the heir? The general's son, Little Thut is older," she said.

Pharaoh said, "But you are royalty. Your child would come before the general's other son, who has no royal blood. Your child will come first if you have a son."

* * * * *

Moses was home from school after his second year of higher education.

He was called by his uncle and was asked to meet him in the pharaoh's private chambers. As Moses came in, his uncle instructed the guard not to disturb them. Then he led Moses to a small side chamber and motioned to him to have a seat.

Sitting opposite him, Amenhotep said, "It is good to have you home, Moses. Your mother told me you have a letter from the school, a report of your progress there."

"Yes, Uncle," replied Moses, reaching into his robe and pulling out a letter bearing an unbroken seal.

Moses watched anxiously as the pharaoh broke the seal. He wanted to please his uncle. He knew he had worked hard, but he had no idea what his teachers would say about him.

His uncle said, "Moses, before I read this letter I want you to know that I have confidence that you have done well in your studies."

After reading the letter, he broke into a large grin. "Well done, Moses! This letter says you are an excellent student, polite and well-behaved, as well as diligent in your studies. Your teachers say that you have a good grasp of the knowledge areas that were covered this year, and they all give you high ratings. One teacher notes that you were having difficulty expressing yourself, so he encouraged you to read your writings to the group of students. He states that this solution was successful in that the students enjoyed your stories, and you became articulate in public speaking."

Moses was relieved to hear these words of commendation. Pharaoh rose, so Moses immediately did the same.

Patting Moses on his shoulder, Amenhotep said, "I am so proud of you, Son."

Moses was touched that he called him son.

"Now please sit down," his uncle said, "for I have something important to discuss with you. Moses, I have an idea that you do not wish to be Pharaoh, is that correct?"

"Yes, Uncle," answered Moses without hesitation.

"Well, I wanted to be sure about that because I must make another choice then, since I do not have an heir. How well do you know General Thutmose?"

"I know he is a good general," said Moses.

"Yes, I am very pleased with his military service. But as a man, I mean, what do you know of him as a man?"

Moses searched his memory for times when he might have had personal contact with the man. "I remember several times when he was a guest at our table. He seemed pleasant enough, interesting, as I recall. Oh, and he liked Bekah. He joined me in the garden when I was walking there with her. I remember Bekah took to him and that is always a good sign. I think dogs are sensitive to a person's true character."

Amenhotep laughed, "Perhaps I should have consulted Bekah. Moses, you may be wondering why I'm asking you these questions. You see, General Thutmose has been spending more time at the palace these two years while you have been in school. He has not had to be out on campaigns as much, because the frontiers are quiet, for the moment at least. Your mother and the general have taken an interest in each other. In fact, I believe they desire to marry."

Moses was taken aback; he had never thought of his mother getting married. His uncle had always been like a father to him.

"Would he be my father then?" Moses blurted out.

"Actually, he would be your stepfather, but I would still act as your father, just as I always have."

Moses was trying to make sense of it all. He had always had Princess Ahmose to himself. "What does Mother say?"

"First of all, Moses, she's concerned about you—how you would feel about it. But you are already sixteen years old. You will be away at school another year, and then you will be gone for three years of military training. Wouldn't you feel better if she had someone to comfort her in your absence? General Thutmose is middle-aged, but he is still a handsome man. Your mother is beautiful and still able to have a child, though she is thirty-one years of age. Perhaps there is still time for our family to have an heir to the throne of Egypt."

Moses wished that his world weren't changing, but he did not want to be selfish in regard to his mother. During his holiday, he had more time to spend with her and the general. They seemed to respect each other, and he could tell they enjoyed each other's company. He had several more private discussions with his uncle. During one of these, Amenhotep divulged the information that General Thutmose had fathered a child with a harem girl named Mutnofret. This woman would not to be part of the family except to raise the child, little Thutmose, now five years old. The child was not robust. Amenhotep described him as pale and sickly with limited energy.[29] Because Thut stayed close to his mother, Moses would not be seeing much of him.

Moses wished his mother well, but as he left to return to school, he felt the loosening of ties to his Egyptian family and that saddened him.

---

29 According to Egyptologists, he was thought to have had heart problems.

The Delta
1509 BC

It was Moses's last year at the House of Wisdom. In the early harvest season, in the last stretch before graduation, Moses had a short holiday. Before leaving for the palace, he made a brief visit to his Hebrew parents. He had no questions about religion this time. Instead they talked about the changes that were occurring at the palace. "Princess Ahmose has married General Thutmose," said Moses.

"We heard about that," replied his father, who was much more interested in palace affairs now that he was in contact with his son.

"Egyptians don't make much of weddings," explained Moses, "Only coronations, funerals, and religious festivals rate a public celebration. Oh, they will have a party for almost any reason. They love their parties, but I don't like to go to them. Anyway, they told me it was not important for me to attend the simple marriage ceremony of General Thutmose and Princess Ahmose. However, now they want me to come to the palace to see their new baby girl, Hatshepsut."

"Now you will have an Egyptian father," said Amran.

"What!" exclaimed Moses, "Oh, you mean General Thutmose?"

"Yes," replied his father, appearing anxious. "I've heard he is a tough warrior. People say he returned from Nubia with the body of one of the rulers hanging head down from the prow of his bark."

Moses wondered why it was always the most gory story that was spread around; but he supposed that was the purpose—to strike fear in the hearts of Egypt's enemies and enlist the confidence of Egypt's citizens.

He reassured his father, "Pharaoh will be my mentor as he always has. He assured me of that. Pharaoh encouraged this marriage, hoping for an heir to the throne of Egypt as he has no heir himself."

"But the baby is a girl," said Amran.

"Yes, but maybe they will have another child. The general already has a son. Did you know that?"

"No, why don't we ever hear of him."

"He is not of the royal line, and he is sickly I've been told. You will always be my father, but Pharaoh has been good to me."

Amran replied, "But his father gave the order to kill the Hebrew babies!"

Moses responded, "I never knew that other pharaoh, Father; but his son is a good man."

"The wife of Ahmose I is still alive, isn't she?"

"Yes, father, she is the queen mother." Moses thought it best not to say anymore. He couldn't expect his parents to understand how this kind grandmother of his could stand by while her husband slaughtered the Hebrew babies.

Amran, sitting across the table from Moses, reached out to him, and Moses took his hand in both of his.

"Such a terrible day, Moses. It was the worst day of our lives when we had to put you in that little basket on the Nile!"

"But it turned out well, Father. Adonai watched over me, and I was rescued by the princess."

"Yes, Moses, and we are thankful for that. But we were robbed of your growing up years."

"I know, Father, but I am here now, and I've been coming to see you for three years."

Jochebed came over and sat down beside Moses putting her arm around him. "Amran," she said, "don't think about the past. Let us be grateful we have our son back."

"How has it been for the Hebrew workers, Father?" Moses asked, taking the opportunity to change the subject.

"They say that the work is going a little better in the fields and in the quarries. It seems that Pharaoh has issued an order for the taskmasters to let up on the workers. Of course, they still work very hard and there is no choice of work. We must serve where we are needed. However, I do not hear as much complaining as before."

"That is good father," Moses replied, thinking Pharaoh was at least trying to ease the plight of the workers.

His father looked wistful. "Most people seem to have forgotten about the promise of God to go back to Canaan. I think about it though, Moses. We have been here a long, long time."

Memphis
1509 BC

Moses received a warm welcome home from his royal family. He looked in on the new princess as soon as he arrived. Bekah chuffed at his side when he cuddled the pretty infant.

"What's the matter, Bekah? Are you jealous?"

Moses looked at the twinkling eyes of the three-month-old baby. "Hatshepsut," he said, "your name means 'Foremost of the Noble Ladies' I am told, but it is too long. What do you say we call you 'Hat'?"

Baby Hat gurgled back at him.

"I'll take that as a yes. All right then, 'Hat' it is."

* * * * *

General Thutmose had invited Moses on a lion hunt. In Egypt, lion hunting was considered a sport of kings, but it was also necessary to keep down the numbers. Lately, the lions had outstripped their natural food supply and ventured into the cattle breeders' territory. They had become so brazen in picking off straggling members of the herds, that recently a man had been killed while attempting to fend them off.

Nevertheless, Princess Ahmose hated that this "king of beasts" was now considered to be vermin by the herders. She recognized the danger of the hunt and could not breathe easily until Thutmose and Moses returned home safely. Ahmose went out to meet their chariots as they pulled up before the palace gates. When they showed her the lion pelts with their ferocious heads, she winced and turned away. General Thutmose took her arm and drew her to himself. "Don't you like the gifts I brought you?" he teased. "Think what beautiful rugs they will make!"

"Give them to the nobles." she replied. "I prefer turquoise and gold jewelry."

"Oh, but I have something better than that," he said. "We managed, with great difficulty to capture a young male lion, just for you. The cub will make a fine addition to the palace menagerie. He will be your pet, and you may name him and train him too, if you like. Would you like to see him?"

All distaste for the hunt fled from her mind, as she anticipated holding the little animal and making him feel safe.

"Where is he?" she asked eagerly.

Laughing at her abrupt change of mood, Thutmose embraced his wife. He knew her so well.

"So, it's 'welcome home' then," he confirmed.

Later, Moses found Princess Ahmose with the cub.

As she soothed the baby lion, she said, "Moses, I've named him Khufu, after the ancient pharaoh who built the Great Pyramid."

"That's a regal name, Mother," he replied.

"Moses, do you remember the carved lion I gave you when you were a child? You loved that toy, and you were so delighted when you made it roar."

Moses smiled, "I remember, Mother. I wonder what happened to that lion."

"You probably wore the thing out, but that's all right, we have a real lion now!" she said as she cuddled the cub.

Then she looked up and said, "Moses, would you do something for me?"

"Of course, Mother."

"Please go to the kitchen and ask Cook to warm some milk in a bowl. I also need some meat chopped finely in another bowl. This cub looks to be about three months old, so he can eat meat now. Oh, and bring a fine linen cloth. Thank you so much, Moses."

When Moses returned with the items his mother requested, he watched her try to feed Khufu. Princess Ahmose wrapped the linen cloth tightly around her finger and dipped it in the warm milk. Then, she offered the makeshift nipple to the cub, who took it eagerly. Moses laughed to see his mother dip her finger repeatedly in the milk bowl until all the milk was gone. Then she scooped a little meat from the second bowl and let the cub nibble from her fingers.

"Now you have two babies, Khufu and Hat," said Moses.

"Hat?" asked Princess Ahmose.

"I suppose I should have asked you first, but I've shortened Hatshepsut's name to *Hat*," explained Moses.

The princess smiled at him, "Do you like your little sister, Moses?"

"Yes, she's pretty special," he replied.

"Indeed she is," agreed the princess.

The following day, Moses was able to converse privately with his uncle as they walked with Bekah in the garden.

Moses told Pharaoh, "Uncle, I've looked up my Hebrew family. I don't want Princess Ahmose to know, because it may hurt her. She may feel as though she hasn't been enough for me. But I am almost a man now, and she has her own child."

Amenhotep was trying to absorb what Moses was saying. At the same time, he was feeling somewhat hurt himself. Hadn't he given Moses everything, including his own time and love?

"You see," Moses was saying, "I have been studying Egyptian theology, and I wanted to know about the religious beliefs of the Hebrews. So I had a special reason for visiting my family, besides finding out if they were alive and faring well."

Amenhotep managed to get out the words to ask Moses, "And are they doing well?"

"They are not complaining, Uncle, but they work very hard. They wish you well, Pharaoh. They recognize you have been trying to ease their burdens." Then Moses looked at his uncle.

"Uncle Tep, you are the best father to me that anybody could ever hope to have. I told my Hebrew father that you have been very kind to me. I could see the sadness in his eyes for all the years he could not be my father, so I didn't tell him any more about you. I also mentioned that I have a stepfather I barely know."

Pharaoh asked, "But did you enjoy the lion hunt, Moses?"

"Yes, I did, Uncle, but I wish you could have come along. We've had such good times, hunting together."

"I really wanted to go on the lion hunt, but I had such a blinding headache, I thought it not wise to go, with the bright sun and the dust of the desert. Actually, it was good that you had a chance to become acquainted with the general. He has been away on a campaign in Syria. That has been a great help to me, as I have so much to do here, and I don't have the energy I used to have."

"Are you all right, Uncle?" asked Moses, suddenly concerned.

"Oh, I'm fine, except for these headaches I've been getting lately. The doctors don't know what is causing them. I just have to rest more often. When I lie down with a poultice on my head, it helps. The doctors have been treating me with the crushed boughs of the Dgum tree. Don't worry, Moses, I'm learning to slow down."

Then, cheered by Moses's reference to their hunting days, Pharaoh said, "Tell me about your Hebrew family, Moses. Were they surprised to see you?"

"Oh yes, my father Amran embraced me, weeping. I didn't think my mother was going to let me go, she clung so tightly to me. Miriam, my older sister, and Aaron, my brother, were both crying for joy."

Pharaoh was moved. He told Moses that he should take them gifts and say to them that Pharaoh wished them well. Moses was grateful for Pharaoh's response and relieved that he had finally told his uncle about his Hebrew family.

Several days later, Moses was at dinner in the palace. He enjoyed intimate family gatherings. The conversation was always interesting and lively. As he often did, Ineni, the noted architect, had joined the family at the king's table. Ineni asked about the priests of Amun. There was talk in Memphis about how the power of these priests of Thebes was growing.

"Most of that talk is a result of jealousy," said Amenhotep. "The priests of Memphis stir up the people. I will pay those priests a visit. As for the priests of Amun, we need not be concerned about their power. They have a good life, too good to cause any trouble."

Speaking to his general, he said, "Why, the gifts we showered on them from your last campaign alone will keep them happy for a long time to come. Isn't that so, Thutmose?"

"Indeed," replied the general. "Speaking of my last campaign, while I was in Syria, I managed to kill an elephant, and I've brought home the tusks. My lovely wife here suggested that I give them to you Pharaoh," he said.

It was true that when the general had presented the ivory tusks to her, Princess Ahmose had said, "I think you should give them to Pharaoh."

Then she had embraced him with such ardor and relief for his safety that he told her, "My, my, I should hunt elephants more often."

"No, no, I will love you more if you do not," she had exclaimed. It was bad enough that he had to go away to battle so much. She didn't see why he had to go on these dangerous hunting expeditions besides.

Now, at the dinner, course after course had been served, and the servants had temporarily withdrawn. Thutmose leaned forward in the light of the flickering oil lamps and addressed the pharaoh.

"I have an idea for the perfect place to hang those tusks I'm giving you," he told the pharaoh. "I'm suggesting we build a place to stay near Nubia."

The family appeared surprised at this idea, as Nubia was far from Thebes and much farther from Memphis.

Thutmose continued, "Recently I cleared Senusret's canal, near the first cataract. It gets clogged with stones and really needs to be cleared annually. I should be making regular trips to that area to see that our forts are secure. Those Nubians are constantly pushing the boundary."

He went on, "So I was thinking of building a retreat at the second cataract, where I could stay when I'm in the area."

Princess Ahmose asked, "Would it be safe there?"

Her husband replied, "I've repaired the fort that was damaged during the last Nubian siege. That fort is close to the spot I am considering, and the palace itself would be guarded at all times. It may not be an actual palace, just a frontier lodge, but comfortable. What do you think of the idea, Pharaoh?"

"It makes good sense," replied Pharaoh. "Our presence there may serve as a deterrent to the Nubians. I think I know the site you are speaking of, but I would like to see it soon."

"I would like to see it too," said Queen Meryetamun, "It sounds like a beautiful area there above the waterfall."

"You shall go with me," said Pharaoh. "We should go soon," he paused, looking at Thutmose with a twinkle in his eyes, "before my general here tears up the whole place for a construction project."

Thutmose laughed, "Then I take it you approve, Pharaoh?"

"I don't see why not," offered Pharaoh. "Our treasury is full to bursting, even after all the gifts to Amun at Karnak."

"I have a suggestion regarding building materials." said Pharaoh. "We might use limestone, rather than brick—and how about using wood in the construction? I know wood can be expensive, but I think we have the funds to import cedar wood from Byblos. I would like to see the lodge fitting into the natural surroundings. After all, we are not building a monument there. But I am getting ahead of myself. What am I thinking? Too much wine, I suppose. Here sits Ineni, the best architect in all of Egypt, and I'm going on with my petty ideas."

"No, no," protested Ineni. "You have been inspiring me."

Ineni's eyes were bright with the vision of what could be built, but he replied thoughtfully, "What you are speaking of, my Lord, is different from anything I have done. You honor me with your confidence in my skills. I shall do my very best not to disappoint you, Sire."

Pharaoh told Thutmose, "When you and Ineni are working on the plans, I would like to see them too."

Thutmose looked over at Ahmose, "I've heard," he said, "that there is excellent rhinoceros hunting in Nubia." At the sight of his wife's grimace, he was encouraged in his mischief. Perhaps he, too, had imbibed too much wine.

"The rhino hunt is the most dangerous of all hunting," he emphasized. But he realized he had gone too far, as he noticed Princess Ahmose starting to push her chair away from the table.

"No, my dear wife, do not leave us. I promise you, I will not hunt the rhinoceros. But I will take you to Nubia when the retreat is finished. Then when I must be there on business, you may come and visit me. We will have Nubian slaves to serve us there. The decorations will be exotic, with the ivory tusks in a prominent spot surrounded by animal pelts and brightly woven rugs and cushions. Too bad we won't have a rhinoceros head, but, oh well. I can imagine an aviary with tropical birds. And we could keep a couple of monkeys. They are entertaining to watch, and I know how you love animals, dear Ahmose," he said, now trying to make up to her.

"What about Khufu?" she asked him, remembering her cub. "Might we bring him too?"

"We will have an enclosure made for him," Thutmose promised, wondering what he had gotten himself into with his exotic gift. That lion was going to get big, and he would not exactly be portable. Thutmose would have to deal with that when the time came. Right now, he was caught up with the excitement of his new building project.

Not wanting to leave Moses, his new stepson, out of the plans, Thutmose told him, "Moses, you may come to the Nubian retreat also when it is ready. Perhaps you could write your stories and songs there. I must warn you though: it may be a bit noisy with the roar of the cataract, the chirping of birds, and the chattering of monkeys."

He leaned back and laughed, "I can picture it already. Now, let's have some entertainment. I heard you have written a new song, Moses. The musicians and singers have put your words to music. So we shall have a treat now," he announced.

Then Pharaoh clapped for the servants to remove their dishes and for the musicians to be ushered into the central dining salon.

Moses smiled. He felt loved and included in his Egyptian family. It was good to be home. Soon he would be leaving for military training. General Thutmose had already informed him that it would be rough but had added the encouragement, "You have a head start, Moses, you are already an excellent archer."

Moses knew that military training was required for every young Egyptian man. Even the princes were not exempt, including those who chose to be priests. In fact, the war annals of Egypt were full of the brave deeds of the princes. For instance, they were often the first to scale the battlements of the enemy. Moses hoped that he would have that kind of courage when the time came for him to serve.

Moses had just enough time before his classes resumed to make a visit to his Hebrew family, bearing the generous gifts that Pharaoh had sent along in the royal bark. Moses told them that he would make one more visit before graduation, and then he would not see them for a long time, as he had to leave for military training. They understood because his brother Aaron was just completing his own training.

After graduation, Moses fulfilled his promise to the royal family that he would go along with them to the Beautiful Festival at Thebes. The same people would be going this year as before. General Thutmose was off on another war campaign, and little Hatshepsut remained at home with her wet nurse. As Moses watched the proceedings at Karnak, he found that he felt very different from the first time he had observed the Egyptian religious ceremonies. Then he was a bewildered young boy, full of questions and confusion about what it all meant. Now he watched calmly and breathed his own prayers to Adonai. Thanks to the intensive discussions with two people who loved him, his uncle and his father, he was grounded in his faith and open to what Adonai would reveal to him.

On the way home, he and his uncle had their time under the stars. There were no deep discussions on love, sex, and marriage, or even religious beliefs. Instead, there was an easy camaraderie as there would be between intimate friends. They talked and laughed and enjoyed each other's company. Bekah snorted occasionally in her sleep.

"Oh," said Amenhotep, "she's caught another ibex," and Moses laughed.

They finally drifted into slumber themselves, under a canopy of twinkling stars.

Memphis
1505 BC

"Kicheche"

Military training was behind Moses. It had been grueling, especially when the weather was hot. His uncle had been right when he predicted the training would toughen him up. Sometimes he wished it could have toughened him inside.

Moses was going through a rough time emotionally. His dear Grandma "Nefer," Queen Mother Ahmose Nefertari, was dying, and his beloved Uncle Tep was ill. General Thutmose was acting as co-regent to relieve his friend, the pharaoh, of the weight of responsibility for the country.

The one bright spot was little Hat, who was quite a handful but so engaging. Hat was a chubby child with a healthy appetite. She had a round face with dimples at the sides of her pretty mouth. Her most arresting feature was her large round hazel eyes that changed color in different light. Moses's nickname fit her in more ways than one. Because of her fair skin, she needed to wear a hat whenever she was out in the Egyptian sun. Bright ringlets would poke out of her hat and, when she took it off, the red highlights in her auburn hair would gleam like copper in the sunshine. Hat spoke very clearly for a four-year-old, and she was full of questions.

She took to Moses just as Moses had taken to his Uncle Tep. She told Moses, "When I grow up I will wear a crown. I will be pharaoh, and I will marry you, Moses."

Princess Ahmose appreciated Moses's help at this difficult time, so he tried to be patient with Hat's endless questions: "Why is Grandma Nefer sick, Moses? But, why?" "Does Amun want her in Paradise? Will Grandma Nefer walk around in the afterworld? Will she like it there? Better than here?"

"But, why?" she asked, when he tried to give her an answer. "I want her to stay here!" she demanded.

"I know," said Moses as he hugged her. "I do too, Hat."

Moses knew his mother was in deep grief, as Princess Ahmose had always had such a close relationship with her mother. His uncle wasn't well, and it was difficult for him to be losing his mother who was his great supporter. Moses was grieving too. Ahmose Nefertari was the only grandmother he had ever known, and she had been so good to him.

The Queen Mother was a powerful woman. She had protected Moses from the usual palace gossip and intrigue. She would not tolerate any demeaning reference to his different origin. Taunts such as "you are not a real Egyptian" were squelched as soon as they left the lips of the speaker.

"You are the son of the pharaoh's daughter," she would say.

Yet as he grew older, Moses identified less with that title and more with his own people. But he would not say that to Princess Ahmose. She needed him now.

Moses decided he would write a story to amuse Hat and take her mind off all the sad events happening in the palace. He soon found that his little project was helping him too; he wrote "The Little Mongoose," a story about the banded mongoose.

It was early evening when he finished writing, and Moses realized it was past Hat's bedtime. He found her with her nurse and was glad to see she was still awake.

Hat's nurse liked Moses. She said to him, "You would think the child would have worn herself out, running around the palace as she does, but she seems to fight sleep. I think she is upset by all this sadness around her now."

"Well," said Moses, "maybe this will help, and he held up his papyrus. I've written a story for her."

"Good," said the nurse, motioning to a chair by Hat's bed. "Let's hope it settles her down."

"Hello, little one," Moses said.

"Hello, Moses, this is Miu," she said, holding up her new kitten, a fuzzy little tiger-striped, orange ball.

"I have a story for you," Moses said, after dutifully petting her cat.

"What's it about?"

"It's about a little mongoose named Kicheche. Now listen while I tell it to you."

Moses began to read.

The Little Mongoose

Once upon a time, there was a little mongoose by the name of Kicheche. One morning Kicheche came out of his burrow to find his mother fixing their breakfast. She was standing with her back to a big rock. In her front paws, she held a crocodile egg. She scooted the egg between her feet so it would hit the rock behind her. The egg broke.

Suddenly Hat slipped out of bed to demonstrate the scene.

"Like this?" she asked Moses as she mimicked Mother Mongoose.

Moses glanced at her nurse, "Sorry, I don't know if this is going to work," he said.

The nurse tucked Hat back into bed and told her to stay there.

"Like that, Moses?" Hat persisted.

"Yes, just like that," replied Moses as he continued with the story.

Kicheche ran to the egg and sucked at the crack.

'Mmm,' he said as he ate the yolk.

After breakfast, Kicheche looked around for something to do, and he saw a little green frog. The frog hopped this way and that way, so Kicheche hopped this way and that way.

Moses held up his hand as he saw Hat stir under the covers.

"Don't show me, Hat, stay in bed."

Kicheche followed the frog a long way. Finally, the frog stopped and looked sideways at him. He made his neck stick out like a big bubble.

Hat giggled.

Kicheche thought that was funny, but suddenly he looked around. He couldn't see his mother. He did not know where his burrow was. He was lost!

Then Kicheche saw a hippopotamus wallowing in the mud by the Nile.

"Hippo," he asked, "do you know where my burrow is?"

"No," said the hippo, "where did you leave it?"

Hat giggled again. "A burrow is not something to carry around like a toy," she said.

She was so sharp to catch that, Moses thought.

"I didn't misplace it," said Kicheche, "I just can't find it."

"So sad, so sad," said the hippo as he slid into the river.

Kicheche walked on and saw a big crocodile sunning itself by the Nile. He hoped that she didn't know he ate her egg that morning.

"Crocodile," he asked. "Do you know where my burrow is?"

"Can't you see I'm trying to take a nap?" snapped the crocodile.

"But I can't find my burrow," wailed the little mongoose.

"Dig another one," said the crocodile.

"But I want my old one. My mother is there," said Kicheche.

"Too bad, too bad," said the crocodile, and slipped into the river.

Kicheche walked on and saw a flamingo, wading through the reeds by the Nile.

"Flamingo," he asked, "Have you seen my burrow?"

"No," said the flamingo. "Be glad, be glad, Here's your mother!"

Sure enough, Kicheche's mother popped out of the reeds and hugged her little mongoose.

"I've been looking all over for you," she said.

"How did you find me?" asked Kicheche.

"Well," said his mother, "I asked a hippopotamus, 'Do you know where my baby is?' He said, 'No, I don't. So sad, so sad,' and slid into the river. Next I asked the crocodile, being careful not to get too close, 'Do you know where my baby is?' She said, 'No, I don't. Too bad, too bad,' and she slipped into the river."

"Finally, I asked the flamingo, 'Do you know where my baby is?' She said, 'No, I don't, but be glad, be glad; we will find him.' Then she told me to hop on her back, and we flew over the reeds."

"Then I spotted you."

"'There he is, there is my baby!' So she set me down right here."

Then mother mongoose thanked the flamingo for her help, and she took Kicheche home to his own burrow.

"I like that story, Moses," said Hat.

"I'm glad," said Moses. Then he said, "I have a question for you. Which was the real friend in the story? The hippo, who said 'So sad, so sad,' the crocodile who said 'Too bad, too bad,' or the flamingo who said, 'Be glad, be glad, I will help you'?"

"The flamingo," said Hat, triumphantly.

"Tell it to me again, Moses, please, please, she begged.

Moses looked to her nurse, who nodded assent.

"All right, Hat, one more time, just one," he emphasized, knowing how persistent Hat could be.

As Moses repeated the story, he purposely told it in a gentle, singsong voice and was rewarded by Hat's drooping eyes as she went to sleep before he was halfway through the story.

Miu was curled up beside Hat, purring softly. Moses slipped quietly out of her bedchamber after exchanging conspiratorial smiles with her nurse.

* * * * *

Frantic screams were coming from the courtyard. It sounded like Hat.

Moses rushed out and was shocked to see Bekah chasing Miu, with Hat desperately trying to save her pet. Khasha burst onto the scene and helped Moses restrain Bekah.

"I'm so sorry, Moses," the handler blurted. "I was trying to adjust her leash when she dashed away from me. She must have spotted the cat."

Moses held Hat, who was shaking like a leaf.

"Bekah tried to eat Miu," wailed Hat.

"There, there," said Moses, pulling Hat on his lap to comfort her. "It's all right, Miu is safe," he said. "Look, she has scrambled up that tree."

When Moses reached for the cat she hissed and batted his hand with little claws extended. He pulled away just in time.

"Well, I don't blame you, Miu," he said. "You had quite a scare.

"Khasha, take Bekah away and come back with something to protect our hands, will you please? We need to get Miu out of the tree."

Later, he said to Khasha as they were retrieving the kitten, "I am surprised that Bekah had the energy to chase a cat like that. She seems so listless lately."

Khasha replied, "I've noticed it too. I asked Princess Ahmose to look at her. She said that Bekah is just getting old."

Moses was stunned. He hadn't even thought of the possibility of losing Bekah.

Grandma Nefer, Uncle Tep, and now Bekah too?

Memphis
1504 BC

Queen Ahmose Nefertari was buried with great honors and public lamentation. She was considered the great matriarch, the cofounder of the New Kingdom, Divine Wife of Amun. To the family, she was beloved mother and Grandma Nefer. Her son, Pharaoh Amenhotep I, rallied from his own illness and was able to attend the memorial for his mother.

Six months later, Bekah died, and Amenhotep suggested to the grief stricken Moses that the dog be mummified. He said that Bekah could be buried in the tomb that had been prepared by Ineni for himself, the pharaoh.

Moses liked that idea. "You gave Bekah to me, Uncle," he said tearfully. Then he added, "I like to think of the two of you together in the afterlife."

Amenhotep was touched, "You do believe in life after death then, Moses?"

"Yes, I do," he said. "The Hebrews don't have details of it like the Egyptians do, but there is a hope for restoration of the relationship with God that we originally had before sin came into the world." He had told his uncle the Hebrew story of the fall of man, so Amenhotep could understand why the Hebrews believed in the necessity of a blood sacrifice to cover sin.

Despite the signs of Amenhotep's flagging energy after the death of the queen mother, Moses was not prepared for his uncle's decline. He had remained at the palace to comfort his mother and Aunt Meryet, and to spend as much time as he could with his uncle.

Nearly a year after the queen mother's death, Moses went to see Pharaoh in his bed chamber. As Moses approached, his uncle held out his hand.

"My son," he said.

Moses fell upon his bed, weeping and embracing him.

"Moses," Amenhotep said, "I know you have a father. I would like to meet him, but I have waited too long. I am now too weak to make the journey. Do you think he would come to me if—" he paused to catch his breath, "if I sent the royal bark for him?"

"Of course he would," said Moses. "But you must rest now, dear Uncle."

"Go, Moses. Go quickly," said Amenhotep.

Moses did not waste any time fulfilling his uncle's wish. With all haste, he returned with his father. When he had introduced Amran to Pharaoh, he left the room, because his uncle indicated he would like to speak with Amran alone. After a long time, Amran came out to his waiting son.

"He asked me to pray for him and to go home and make a blood sacrifice to cover his sin," said Amran, in amazement.

At this statement, Moses broke down and wept in his father's arms.

And so, Amenhotep died.[30] Yet Uncle Tep's love and encouragement would continue to be an influence in Moses's life.

---

30   In the court annals of ancient Egypt, there is a record of a report of a tomb robbery. When the report was investigated it was found to be exaggerated. The tomb of Amenhotep I was uninjured, but his pyramid was damaged. However, the stele, in front of the pyramid, was intact. On the stele was an engraving of Amenhotep I and Bekah, the greyhound. Today the mummy of Amenhotep I rests in the Cairo Museum in Egypt.

Memphis
1503 BC

Moses saw that Pharaoh Thutmose I was making preparations for another military campaign. He wondered why Pharaoh had not told him to get ready to go along, as Moses had completed his military training three years before. He approached Pharaoh about the matter when he found him at the palace stables checking on the horses.

Thutmose told Moses, "No, I need you here at the palace. Your mother needs you. You may continue the practice of law in the palace court, but it will be comforting to Queen Ahmose to have you nearby."

Moses was still trying to get used to her new title. He was present at the coronation, of course, but it was so close on the heels of his Uncle Tep's death that he just couldn't absorb it all. His mother was now Queen of Egypt! He reminded himself that Thutmose was talking.

"She doesn't need to be worrying about both of us off to battle, even as she is still grieving the deaths of her mother and brother." Then he added, "And it doesn't help that her sister, Meryetamun, is taking it so hard."

Moses could only imagine how it was for his Aunt Meryet, who was so in love with her husband, his uncle. Sometimes he missed him so much himself. But Thutmose I was pharaoh now, so Moses knew he'd better pay attention.

Pharaoh walked over to another horse, and Moses followed. "This one looks good," he said, and turned back to Moses. "Besides, Hatshepsut needs you. Your mother says you are able to calm my little Tadpole." He called her that, affectionately, because she would wiggle off his lap when she was little.

Moses knew the pharaoh loved his little princess, but he was away at war so much she had just gotten used to not depending on him. Moses was glad Thutmose was not jealous of the relationship he had with Hat. Moses was seventeen years her senior and a little young to be a father figure, but he did fill a void in her young life. He could be firm with her and she would respect him, but she could manipulate her mother to get her own way.

Six-year-old Hat was studying with Ineni, his old tutor. The wise old man would sometimes shake his head at her struggle to sit still and pay attention. "Do you see any other child around here?" he would ask her. "You are my only pupil, and I have my eyes on you at all times. Just remember that."

He told Moses that he had decided to give her more frequent breaks, so she would have a chance to release that boundless energy of hers. Thutmose had delegated the supervision of Hat's education to her mother and Moses, instructing them to report any big problem to him. Queen Ahmos and Moses labeled most of the problems little ones, so as not to bother Pharaoh.

He had enough problems with his son, Thutmose II, who was now eleven years old. Pharaoh Thutmose never said anything derogatory about his son, but Moses could tell "Little Thut" was a disappointment to his father. Pharaoh did talk occasionally about his aggravation with Thut's mother, Mut, and how she was managing Thut's treatment.

Although the palace physicians were the best in the land, Mut chose to rely on magic. Pharaoh would utter, "Pooh," in disgust at all the incantations and burning of strange substances over his son. It was true that even in the New Kingdom, some magical practices of the doctors carried over from the Old Kingdom, but most physicians relied more on the natural healing qualities of herbs and plants. In fact, it was necessary for these physicians to have a good knowledge of botany to conduct their practice.

However, that was not Mut's emphasis. She wanted the magic of Isis to heal her son, but so far, Thut had not made a magical recovery. He was still puny and susceptible to every illness that came along. Little Thutmose seemed to have a weak heart, so there was actually a basis for the concern about his health.

Pharaoh Thutmose thought sun, a little exercise, good food, plenty of rest, and treatment by regular physicians was a better health regimen. He was concerned that his son would develop an unnatural dependence on magic as the solution to problems. He realized it hadn't helped the situation that he had taken a new wife and fathered Hatshepsut.

Little Thutmose was all Mut had. When the child was small, Pharaoh didn't mind that Mut clung to the child, but now that the boy was eleven, all this clinging and coddling seemed unhealthy to him. *How could the boy become a man with virility, courage, and moral fiber?* he asked himself. When he tried to explain this to Mut, she responded with such vitriol, that he backed off, fearing to make matters even worse.

How ironic, he thought. *I'm going off to save Egypt, but I can't save my own son.*

Memphis
1501 BC

A family outing was in the works. The Royals were going on a fowling trip to the delta. The party was made up of Pharaoh Thutmose I, Queen Ahmose, Moses, Hatshepsut, and three attendants—plus Pharaoh's charcoal greyhound Pehtes and Miu, now a fully grown cat.

Thutmose II, thirteen years of age, was recuperating from his circumcision. He had developed an infection, which wasn't serious, but he had to rest in bed with a poultice. His father, the pharaoh, was between war campaigns and could not postpone the outing. Actually, no one but the pharaoh minded little Thutmose's absence. They headed for the delta in the royal bark, which was carrying a lightweight, papyrus skiff for use when they reached the marshes.

As they reached the familiar territory of the east delta, Moses thought of his Hebrew family. After his military training, he had been able to make a brief visit to them, but with all the changes at the palace, he had not been back. At least he'd had that time with his father when Amran had come to see his Uncle Tep. He hoped his Hebrew family knew he was needed at the palace. He would visit them soon, he decided. Right now, he was having a rare family time with the new pharaoh, his mother the queen, and the irrepressible Hat. He wanted to "spend the day merrily."

They had transferred to the skiff and were edging quietly through the cattails, bulrushes, and papyrus. It was like moving through a maze. Where the water had receded, there were hiding places and nests of birds in the reeds.

Pharaoh was drawing the throw sticks out of a basket. These were the weapons they would use, slightly curved wooden sticks shaped like boomerangs, with crudely carved serpent heads at one end. He handed several sticks to Moses.

Suddenly, Moses's mother exclaimed, "Oh, look," pointing to a lone duckling in a nest among the reeds. She asked the attendant to stop rowing. Then, reaching down, she scooped up the fuzzy little creature into her hands.

"Now what did you do that for?" asked Pharaoh. "The mother is probably around."

"But you will soon kill the mother," she said. "Besides, the mother duck shouldn't have abandoned her baby. There, there, I won't abandon you," she told the little duckling huddled in her hands.

"Oh, all right," said Pharaoh as he dumped the contents of a small covered basket into a larger container and handed his wife the little basket. "Here, you had better keep that bird out of Miu's reach."

Queen Ahmose smiled gratefully at her husband. As she secured the duckling away in the basket, Hat played happily with her doll, a stuffed linen object with a painted wooden head. Miu was perched on her own elevated platform, safely out of the greyhound's reach.

"I'm hungry," said Moses. "Is it too early to eat?"

An attendant reached in a food hamper and took out a meat-filled bread round, and then poured Moses a mug of beer.

"Mmmm," mumbled Moses, his mouth full of his favorite bread treat from his childhood adventures.

"Well," said Pharaoh, smiling at his contented family, "it looks to me like we are on a baby-duck-gathering picnic. And, here I thought we were going on a fowling trip."

As the boat moved through a patch of reeds, a startled goose rose up on flapping wings. With one deft flick of the throwing stick, Pharaoh brought the bird down.

"Great, Pharaoh," cried Moses as Pehtes splashed into the water to retrieve the bird.

"Now let me try," he said, grabbing a throw stick.

When Moses hurled a stick into the air at more birds winging upward, he lost his balance and plopped on his rear in the boat, much to the family's amusement. Pharaoh was laughing and Moses joined in. Hat could hardly catch her breath she was laughing so hard. Queen Ahmose was pleased that Moses could laugh at himself. Nevertheless she offered him encouragement.

"Come on, Moses, you can do it."

Moses got up and moved over to little Hat. He picked her up and put her in his lap, rocking her back and forth. "I'll shake those giggles out of you," he joked.

"Moses," Pharaoh warned. "Stop, you are rocking the boat."

"Sorry, Pharaoh," Moses replied. Then, to his mother and little sister he said, "I'm getting in all kinds of trouble. I should have stayed home today."

"No, Moses," protested Hat, "I want you here."

"All right then, I'll stay. But you'd better not laugh at me so much, silly girl."

"Am I a silly girl, mother?" she asked.

"Sometimes you are," replied her mother.

When the queen wasn't looking, Hat stuck out her tongue. Moses caught the naughty gesture and shook an admonishing finger at her. He wouldn't tolerate disrespect, not even in fun.

Suddenly, Hat caught sight of her doll, now sprawled on the bottom of the boat. "My baby," she exclaimed.

Moses picked up the toy and handed it to her, whereupon she cradled the doll, murmuring sounds of comfort. Moses watched her, thinking she is a child of many facets, sometimes boyishly climbing trees, at other times as feminine as can be. In her nurturing of the doll, he saw the promise of a good mother.

It was Moses's turn to try again, so he stood up with a warning glance at Hat. She immediately clamped her hand over her mouth, her large twinkling eyes betraying her suppressed laughter.

"Now, Moses," said Pharaoh, "put one leg back like this to steady yourself. That way when you hurl the throw stick, you won't be thrown off balance."

Moses tried and missed the fowl, but he didn't topple over. By the end of their outing, Moses had caught on to the rhythm of the throwing action and his aim had improved. He could claim credit for a few of the birds that lay in the big basket at the front of the boat.

"Cook should be happy with the catch of the day," said Pharaoh.

Moses agreed. He was happy too, looking forward to roast goose. He remembered that was Uncle Tep's favorite meal. He had thought of Bekah when he saw Pehtes spring into action. He missed them both and hoped they were enjoying the afterlife together.

"I'm happy with my little catch of the day too," said his mother as she walked beside him, carrying her little duckling up the gangplank to the royal bark.

Memphis
1500 BC

By nine years of age, Hatshepsut had developed more tolerance for sitting still and paying attention to her tutor. Ineni informed the queen that he thought she was ready for the palace classes. Her mother was pleased to hear that, as she thought it would be good for her daughter to socialize with other children. *She will have to learn to share*, thought Ahmose.

Hatshepsut loved being with the other children. It seemed that she managed to get what she wanted most of the time. It wasn't that she bullied the other children, not at all. It was just that she had such good ideas and such an appealing way of suggesting them that the other children wanted her to be the leader. This acquiescence wasn't just because Hat was the princess. She never used her position in the palace to get what she wanted. She didn't have to. She won the others over by her wit and her charm.

During playtime at school, Hat enjoyed the piggyback ball game in which two girls, riding piggyback on two other girls who were the carriers, would play a game of catch. If a catcher fumbled the ball, she would have to switch place with her carrier. Hat much preferred to be a catcher and was very good at it.

Ineni continued to give Hatshepsut instructions in ethics and religion. Sometimes, after class Hat would question her mother: "Who is Sekmet?"[31] "Who is Heket?"[32] She told her mother she thought the animal gods were fun, but that it was a little silly to worship them.

---

31 Cat goddess
32 Frog god

Queen Ahmose explained, "People don't believe the animal statues are the gods. They believe that a spirit enters them, once they are made. It's like the statue is a house for the spirit."

"Oh," said Hat, thoughtfully. "I don't think Moses believes that. Do you believe that, Mother?"

Ahmose sidestepped her question, not wanting her to be dismissive to the other children who might believe in the animal gods.

She told her daughter, "I believe Amun is enough. And sometimes we say, Amun-Re, but Amun is the god of gods."

"Simple," replied Hat as Ahmose later repeated to Moses.

She thought Moses would appreciate Hat's quick grasp of how her mother had wrapped up the nation's polytheism for her in the deity of Amun.

Moses was amazed, "She said that? Good for her."

His own belief in one God was growing stronger day by day as he followed Amran's encouragement to trust Adonai.

Queen Ahmose discussed their daughter's progress in school with her husband, Pharaoh Thutmose I.

He said, "I'm pleased to hear she is doing well in her classes. I wish I could say the same for my son. I guess I shouldn't be surprised that Thut is behind in his work. He misses so much time when he is ill. Ineni says he doesn't have the interest or motivation. I can't help but wonder if he uses his physical condition as an excuse to shirk his studies."

Ahmose told her husband, "I hate to tell you this, but there is another problem with Thut."

"What is it? I should know if he is causing a problem for you."

"He was taunting Hatshepsut yesterday. I know boys like to tease girls, but he had her in tears, and she doesn't cry easily. Besides, he is fourteen and she is only nine."

"Where was this?"

"Out in the garden."

"What's he doing in this part of the palace? He belongs in the shep."[33]

"I asked him that. He said he has just as much right to be here as Moses does."

"That's ridiculous. Thut is just a kid. Moses is a man of twenty-six."

"I know it doesn't make sense for him to compare himself with Moses. Do you suppose he is jealous of Moses?"

---

33 Quarters for the princes.

Thutmose looked at his wife, puzzled, "I don't know, but I do know that Moses is like my right arm, and he is helpful to you with Hatshepsut, is he not?"

Ahmose said, "I don't know what I would do without him. She is a handful, but Moses has a way with her. He is fiercely protective of her too. But he was out on an errand for you yesterday, and I think Thut took advantage of that opportunity to get Hatshepsut alone."

"I will speak to Thut," his father stated.

"No, wait, please, he will know I told you. As it is, he doesn't like me. Maybe it would help if you spent some time with him."

As her husband left her side, Ahmose thought about Thutmose II. She had purposely left out the worst part of the boy's impudence. When the queen had confronted him, Thut had planted his feet firmly in front of her and gazing at her directly, said, "You are talking to the future pharaoh, the ruler of all the land of Egypt!"

The thought of Thutmose II ruling Egypt made Queen Ahmose shudder. He seemed to have no more strength of character than he had strength of body. No doubt, his mother had ambition for him. Mut had lost status when Thutmose I had married Ahmose. She was certain her husband had not returned to Mut's bed, which must have been hard for Mut. Then the queen's thoughts drifted to her adopted son, Moses. What a fine pharaoh he would make, if only he had the heart for it!

Memphis
1496 BC

Moses had gone on several military campaigns with his stepfather, Thutmose I. The purpose of these raids was to secure protection for Egypt and to open trade routes, especially in the Near East. Thutmose I pushed all the way to the Euphrates with his forces. No Egyptian ruler had ever gone that far. In the South, he pacified Nubia even while extending Egyptian control all the way to the third cataract of the Nile. As he fought alongside him, Moses gained a new respect for the warrior king.

At home, Moses accompanied the pharaoh on several business trips to his building sites. The workers' village at Deir el Medina, which Amenhotep I had envisioned, was now buzzing with activity. Known as the *Place of Truth*, it consisted of seventy mud brick houses on stone foundations, arranged in rows within a high enclosure wall. The houses had four to six rooms each, with a cellar, a terrace, and a kitchen that was open to the sky. The artisans were currently busy decorating the tomb that Ineni had designed for the pharaoh. Thutmose I would be the first pharaoh to be buried in the Valley of the Kings. Directly across the Nile at Karnak, a huge building project was underway. Thutmose I had ordered Ineni to restore and expand the ancient temple there. He was building a huge, colonnaded court behind two towering pylons. Beyond that structure would be his obelisk, Thutmose I told Moses.

In Memphis, Moses was occupied in the palace court. His long absence during military training meant that he had much studying to do in order to brush up on his knowledge of the law. Moses thought the Egyptian system was rather harsh, but he noted that the punishment tended to fit the crime. A life for a life was exacted in the case of murder, whether the victim was a slave or a free person. A hand was chopped off if the defendant was found guilty of forgery. The tongue was cut out for treachery. There were laws dealing with marriage and divorce. A divorced woman was entitled to one third of all the possessions that had been accumulated by the couple during the term of their marriage. *Another reason to be good to your wife*, thought Moses wryly as he remembered his uncle's admonitions.

There were laws of permission as well. The priests were allowed to partake of the foods offered to the gods, and the roast thigh of beef, a favorite cut of meat, was reserved for the high priest. A curious result of the Egyptian belief in the double nature of a person was that the monarch in his capacity as a private individual could contract with himself in his capacity as divine king to purchase a choice portion of offering meat, with the approval of the priests.

The structure of the justice system of the New Kingdom was changed from that of the Middle Kingdom. The New Kingdom had a different constitution and a different appeal system. Although the six houses of justice still existed, the house of justice at Thebes far exceeded the others in importance and stood near the Temple of Amun. It was called the *Excellent Gate, Contented About the Doing of Truth*.[34] Of course, the pharaoh was the final word on justice, unless the matter under investigation was related to persons involved in the royal court. In that event, a special commission was appointed to try the case.

Moses did not aspire to serve on the high court of Egypt. He was occupied with matters of contract law and boundary disputes. Fortunately, the palace court where he worked had a rotating system of service, so he didn't have to be there constantly. In addition, the judges, in deference to his status as a prince of Egypt, allowed him the time he needed away from the law court.

Moses had just returned from a military campaign with his stepfather and was looking forward to several days of rest. The palace was quiet. Most of the family were napping in the shimmering heat of midday, but not Hatshesput. She was intent on finding Moses, who she heard had returned from a campaign to Nubia with her father. She caught up with him in a corridor leading to his private chamber.

"Moses," she said softly as she took his hand, "come with me. I have set up the senet board in the salon. Play a game with me, and tell me about the campaign."

---

34 This was the Supreme Court of ancient Egypt.

Moses would have liked to be alone with his thoughts for a while, but as he looked down at his pretty twelve-year-old sister, he couldn't resist her eager invitation.

Walking with him along the corridor, Hat asked Moses, "And what treasures did you bring back from Nubia?"

"Let me think," Moses replied. "Lots of gold, leopard skins, ebony and ivory furniture, jars of incense, ostrich eggs and feathers, weapons, and—" he paused for effect, "a live young giraffe, for Mother!"

"Oh," exclaimed Hat. "She must be wild with joy."

As they walked into the salon, Hatshepsut called for her handmaiden, who was ever alert for a summons from her mistress. "Please bring us a pitcher of pomegranate water."

Moses noticed she treated her servant kindly, rather than imperiously snapping orders as she could have done. At a small table, a rectangular board had been laid out. Moses and Hat took seats opposite each other. Hat opened the little drawer on the side of the board and withdrew the playing pieces. The board was divided into thirty squares on which were written either challenges or rewards. The object of the game was to negotiate one's way through the afterlife to receive the final reward from the god Osiris. The moves were decided by a toss of knuckle bones.

As Hatshepsut sipped pomegranate water, waiting for Moses's next move, she asked more questions about the campaign.

"We routed the Nubians," Moses said. "They are very accurate with the bow, so we lost some men from their arrows, but we managed to extend our control to the third cataract. That's the farthest ever for Egypt!"

Hatshepsut's eyes widened. "Oh, Moses, I should die if you were killed," she exclaimed.

"But I would be a hero, and you would extol my bravery and bring flowers to my tomb among the princes," he told her, milking the moment of her adoration.

"Moses, you are mocking me now. If I were to die, you probably wouldn't notice I was gone," she said with a tinge of anger.

"Now, Hat," Moses soothed, "don't be angry with me. You aren't going to die in battle. Girls don't fight in the army."

At that remark, Hatshepsut lifted her head and, looking Moses squarely in the eyes, declared, "You will see. Someday I will be pharaoh. Then I will be commander-in-chief of Egypt's army."

Moses smiled, "Oh well, Hat, I hear you. But for now, why don't you be content with winning this game, since you are way ahead of me already?"

Hatshepsut noticed that Moses was wiping beads of perspiration from his brow, so she called for a basin of water and a linen cloth.

"The heat is oppressive today," she acknowledged as she used her bejeweled fan to cool her own face.

As Moses gratefully mopped his face and upper body with the water soaked linen, Hatshepsut noticed his muscular arms and chest. She was surprised by the strange stirring she felt in her own body as she watched. Alarmed, she quickly changed the subject to Thutmose II. If anything could cool her down, thoughts of this puny prince could do it.

"Moses," she asked, "can you imagine Prince Thutmose at the head of an army?"

Moses usually thought carefully before speaking on serious subjects, but he answered with an immediate and decisive, "No."

Hatshepsut continued, "I overheard my parents discussing the prince and his military training. He is the heir to the throne, you know. Anyway, every prince is expected to serve in the army. But I think they are going to make an exception in Thut's case. He wouldn't hold up in physical training."

Moses thought of his own rigorous training and couldn't imagine the prince enduring it, given that he could be wheezing shortly after beginning any game, such as wrestling or batting the balls.

"He will probably be taught military strategy at least," Moses suggested.

"Yes, that is the last part of their conversation I heard—that there would be a modified training of some sort," Hat replied.

"Oh, Moses," she exclaimed, as the game continued, "you are stuck in the "weighing of the heart." It looks like your heart is heavier than the feather of Maat.[35] What have you been up to that you haven't told me about?" she teased.

"Before you rush to judgment," Moses countered, "just wait. Anubis is adjusting the scales. I'll make it. Besides, didn't you hear my negative confession—all the bad things I didn't do? The list was as long as yours. Anyway, I don't believe all that stuff about the afterlife."

"Well, well, that's a lot of words out of your mouth at once, Moses. Of course you don't believe this stuff. That's because you are losing the game."

Moses was amused. She was so quick of mind and could verbally spar with him in such a way that it sharpened his own ability to speak. With others, he often found himself tongue-tied, but he could relax with her.

---

35 The goddess of justice who supervised the scales in the afterlife.

"You haven't made it through all the gates yet," he warned her. "Don't gloat, until you have passed through the many coils of The Serpent Alepo."

Later, as he rested alone in his chamber, Moses thought about the Egyptian system of gods and was grateful that he worshipped the one true God, Adonai. He did believe in the afterlife but not the Egyptian version. His people, the Hebrews, believed that God assured Abraham of an afterlife. Moses thought about this patriarch, who had come to Egypt long ago, during an earlier famine before Joseph's time. Abraham had been at the palace, explaining that Sarah was his wife and Pharaoh couldn't have her.

Amazing, thought Moses. *Of all the women Pharaoh could have had, he wanted Sarah.*

I can have anyone I want too, he thought, *but no one appeals to me. Soon I will be thirty years of age. Perhaps Adonai will provide a wife for me.*

Memphis
1495 BC

"Oh, Moses, you should have been there!" exclaimed Hatshepsut as she recounted the experience of her first big party at the palace the night before.

Moses didn't regret his own absence in the least, but he didn't want to spoil his sister's enthusiasm. It was a beautiful morning in the palace garden. He listened patiently as she described in detail the guests and entertainment.

"I sat with Father and Mother. Of course, their chairs were very elaborate. They were elevated above all the others, who were sitting on cushions around the room. The servants scurried around, placing small tables here and there to hold the wine and food. When the noble women arrived in their finest linen gowns and precious jewels, they were each given a cone. These cones held waxy oils, Moses. The servants put them upside down on the women's heads. Can you guess what happened then, Moses?" Moses didn't have a clue.

"Well, as the evening went on, the room got warmer with all the people in it; the wax melted and ran down over the ladies' wigs and robes. The fragrance was sublime." Hat closed her eyes and sniffed as though she could still smell the aroma.

"And the food," Hatshepsut went on. "Such a variety of delicious, small dishes you never tasted in your life, Moses. Then came the main course. The roasts of beef and fowl were paraded through the room. After that the servants carved the meat and served it with more side dishes." She rubbed her tummy. "I don't think I can eat for a week," she said.

Moses doubted that, as Hat had a hearty appetite. The feast did sound good to him; he realized he was getting hungry just hearing about it. When Moses started to rise, Hat stopped him.

"Wait, Moses, please; I have more to tell you. This part is funny. There was a lot of drinking of wine and beer. One noble woman threw up her dinner before a servant could get to her with a basin."

Well, that spoils my appetite, thought Moses.

Hatshepsut was going on about the dancers. "You should have seen the harem women, with their long hair swinging as they moved their lithe bodies in the dance. I tell you the truth: they wore nothing but a thong and jewelry. Some of them had a band around their waist with strings of beads hanging down. You could see everything when the beads swayed apart. Prince Thutmose couldn't take his eyes off them—but more about him later. The music was wonderful."

"The women were really accomplished singers, and the way they played the harp was absolutely divine. When the girls danced to the beat of the timbrels, it made you want to dance with them. Our guests seemed to enjoy it too, as some were swaying and clapping to the rhythm."

Moses tried to picture what he imagined to be a rather hectic scene. Hatshepsut brought him back to the present with another exclamation.

"The acrobats, Moses, you must see the acrobats sometime. They can bend their bodies in ways I never thought possible. If I tried some of their moves, I think my back would snap in two."

Suddenly Hatshepsut's face clouded like a shadow had passed over the sun.

"There is something I need to tell you about Prince Thut, Moses," she said ominously. "I think he wants me—no, I don't just imagine that—I know it. How can I describe the look he gave me at the party?" she said. "It was between a leer and a sneer, as if he desired me and would get exactly what he wanted!"

"Oh, Moses, when he looked at me like that, I felt as if scarabs were crawling all over me. No, it was even worse than that, because the scarab beetle means 'good luck,' and I do not feel that it is good luck that he desires me."

"Listen to me, Hat," Moses told her, firmly taking her shoulders in his two strong hands. "Do not let your young life be troubled by the face of the prince. You had a good time last night. You described the party so well that someday when I think of it I will believe I was there."

Hat smiled at that idea.

"Good, my sunny Hat is back. Hold on to the good memories, Hat. Always think about what is good and lovely."

As he left the princess, Moses hoped he had convinced her not to worry. He hadn't entirely convinced himself, however.

Surely, he told himself, our parents would not consider a union between their darling daughter and that odious son of Mut, even if he was the son of the pharaoh too.

* * * * *

Six months later, Moses was chasing Hat around the courtyard. She had snatched his sandals, and he wanted them back. Both were laughing at Hat's impudence. She would do anything to get his attention. Very agile, she easily weaved and dodged around pots of palms, fig trees, and sculpture. Finally, he caught her, and they sank breathless onto a stone bench. Hat took Moses's shoulders and turned him gently to look in his eyes.

She appealed to him, "Moses, the time is getting short. Soon I will have my fourteenth birthday, and I will be marrying age then." She paused as tears welled in her eyes. "I know you don't want to see me unhappy. You do love me, don't you?"

"Yes, Hat, you know I love you, but not in the way you mean. You are my sister."

"Well, there you go. My grandmother was a full sister to my grandfather. Mother says they were very happy together. Pharaoh Amenhotep and Queen Meryetamun were brother and sister. You told me yourself, they only had eyes for each other. Besides the god Osiris married his sister, Isis."

Moses looked at her. "Hat, you honor Amun, the king of gods. Why then do you bring up other gods as examples?"

She knew Moses was still hoping she would honor the invisible God that he worshiped. She was onto his strategy. If he could convince her to worship one God, and forget the others it would be a step in the "right direction." As much as she wanted him, she couldn't resist the opening he had given her to win their argument.

"You are right," she said. "I used the wrong example. I should have used Amun and Amunet, who were twins and mates at the time of creation."

Moses shook his head. She was impossible! The playful mood had passed, and Moses rose from the bench.

"I should go now."

Hatshepsut realized she had gone too far. "Please, Moses, don't be angry with me. Can't you see I'm frightened?"

Was she really scared, Moses wondered, or was this one of her clever manipulations? He knew her mind was quick and more flexible than the feet of the dancers at the parties he was loath to attend.

"I'm not angry, Hat," he responded. "I'm just weary of your arguments about why I should marry you. You will be all right. Your mother loves you. She will not expect you to marry someone you hate."

Memphis
1494 BC

Queen Ahmose, at the urging of Moses, met with Ineni concerning the working conditions at the quarries and building sites.

Moses had also requested that Pharaoh Thutmose I provide a doctor for the workers at each site, just as physicians accompanied the military expeditions. On the battlefield, most warriors were killed outright. However, when there was a smaller wound, such as a gash, the doctor would cleanse the wound, stitch it up, and apply a poultice of dates and honey. If the injury was caused by a fall from a chariot, the doctor would look for certain signs that would indicate whether the man was untreatable. In that case, it was said that the injury came from outside, meaning that it was the breath of God and he would die.

Sometime after these interventions with the queen and pharaoh, Moses visited his Hebrew family. He asked his father about the workers and was relieved to learn that conditions had improved.

* * * * *

Moses was enjoying the cool, afternoon breeze in the courtyard when Hatshepsut joined him. She was followed by an attendant, carrying an ivory-inlaid, ebony tray. When the attendant set the tray down on a small alabaster-topped table, Hat whisked off the linen cloth that covered it.

"Surprise!" she exclaimed.

On the tray were small rounds of bread made from finely ground grain, toasted in a clay oven. They were topped with goat cheese and pieces of plump figs, drizzled with honey. The tray also held a dish of salted almonds and a mug of Quede beer. Moses bit into a toast round and savored the contrast of flavors, the tang of the cheese, and the sweetness of the figs and honey.

"Mmm, this is good," he said.

"I made this with my very own hands," Hat told him. "Now see what a good wife I would make? I'm grown up, Moses. Haven't you noticed?" she said, coyly looking at him under her long eyelashes. She stood before him; smoothing her hands over her budding breasts, clearly visible through her fine linen gown.

"Stop it!" Moses exclaimed, suddenly angry. Hat jumped back, startled at his tone.

"I'm sorry, little one," he said, relenting, "but you must never do that to a man, not even to me. You could get yourself in trouble!"

Her large green eyes filled with tears. "It's just that I love you, Moses," she said.

Memphis
1493 BC

The following spring, just before inundation time, Moses found Hatshepsut sobbing in the palace courtyard. He sat down on the bench they had shared since she was a tiny child. Moses was moved by her obvious anguish. He slipped an arm around her, but she pulled away and faced him angrily.

Through her tears, she demanded, "How could you let this happen, Moses? You said it wouldn't happen!"

Moses, with a growing sense of dread, asked his little sister, "What, Hat, what are you talking about?"

"I am to marry—" she couldn't say his name. Her voice broke into a wail.

"Not Prince Thutmose?" Moses asked in disbelief. But even as a new wave of grief overwhelmed his sister, Moses knew it was true.

"It can't be!" he exclaimed. "I'm going to talk to Mother."

In large strides, he stomped through the palace, servants staring after him.

Because Moses was normally so calm, they wondered what had gotten into him. What they didn't realize was how fiercely protective he could be.

Reaching the queen's chambers, he told the guard that he wished to speak to his mother. Moses struggled to calm himself as he waited for his mother's appearance. He knew he needed to address her with the dignity accorded a queen. He had to wait for some time. She must have been resting, he thought. Finally she came toward him, and when she saw his face set in such hard lines, she beckoned him to her chamber, leading him to a small side room.

When they were seated, Queen Ahmose said, "What is it, my son?"

Moses took a deep breath and said, "My Mother, great Queen of Egypt, I have always valued your kind spirit and your compassion, which were extended to me when I was a helpless babe set adrift on the Nile. All these years I have experienced your loving care. I have seen your concern and tenderness for animals. Even Khufu, now a great lion, follows you around like a puppy. But now, my heart is breaking for my beloved sister, your precious daughter. Is it true that you have granted permission for Prince Thutmose to marry Hatshepsut?"

"Moses," replied the Queen, in a soft voice, "I see your sorrow and, believe me, I am filled with grief for my daughter. You need to understand, Moses, that when you are the ruler of a country, you have to sacrifice your own wishes for the good of that nation, for the 'higher good,' if you will."

She waited until Moses looked up at her again. He could see the genuine pain in her eyes.

The Queen continued, "I'll be honest with you, Moses. The Prince is not strong enough in body or spirit to lead Egypt effectively, but Hatshesput *is* able. By this union, we can have hope that Egypt will survive the loss of Pharaoh, 'the General.' He is not well, and he must see that his successor is in place before he travels the afterlife."

Moses pleaded, "But, Mother, is there not another way? Why must the prince be the ruler?"

"Because the people expect it," stated Ahmose. "Prince Thutmose is the rightful heir. They would not likely accept a female pharaoh."

Moses, grasping at straws, reminded her that Egypt had been ruled by female sovereigns in the past; he had learned about them in his study of Egyptian history.

"That is true, Moses, you have learned well. However, in most instances the ruler was a co-regent or briefly filled the gap as sole ruler until a male pharaoh was available."

One last time, Moses tried to argue for a different solution. He pointed out, "The general was not of royal blood, and he became pharaoh. Why can't another person of military honor or one of the nobles be chosen for Hatshepsut? Someone she could at least respect."

"Like yourself, Moses?" Queen Ahmose asked gently.

Moses just stared at her. How could she possibly ask him that now? He thought surely he had made it plain how he felt about being pharaoh.

"Never mind, Moses. I know very well that you do not want to be pharaoh, but can you see how that brings us to this impasse? You are the elder son. I adopted you and gave you everything you needed to be pharaoh, but I respected your wish not to be considered for that position. Your uncle, Pharaoh Amenhotep, was the best father he could be to you, and when he had no heir, it was his heart's desire for you to succeed him on the throne. But you did not want that. He chose General Thutmose, because your uncle had no heir, but Thutmose did have an heir. As much as you and I would rather not face that fact, it is true."

"Now I ask you to respect the decision that has been made. You need to think beyond the present. If Prince Thutmose would choose another to be his consort, the royal line that has come down from my beloved father, the Great Ahmose, the founder of the New Kingdom, would be broken. This marriage keeps the line going through Hatshepsut. All she has to do is produce an heir. She does not have to love Thutmose or even like him. From what I hear, he has already set up a section of the harem as his own, and he spends more and more time there. Now I ask you, Moses, do we need another harem-spawned heir like Prince Thutmose?"

His mother leaned forward. "We need Hatshepsut's cooperation now. I was going to talk to you, Moses, but after the trying morning we had with her, I was exhausted."

Immediately Moses felt contrite as he saw his mother's hands tremble. "I'm sorry to have disturbed you, Mother," he said.

"No, it is good that we had this time to talk," she said. Then she reached out and took Moses hands in her own. "My dear," she said, "I need your help now with Hatshepsut. It's best that you leave her alone for a few days to thrash out her feelings of outrage. She is a strong, young woman and will come to see the logic of my decision in due course if we give her time. She wants to be pharaoh. I believe Prince Thutmose may not be long for this world, given his maladies. I know that it sounds harsh, but I can't help but hope that Hatshepsut will not have to put up with him for long. She is young; she will be sixteen when they marry. If she lives above reproach as queen-consort, the people will respect her. She will have the right to take anyone she chooses as pharaoh. Maybe by that time you will reconsider that position yourself. You know she loves you."

Moses felt dizzy. This was too much! He had been pulled from outrage to logic to a future scenario that was incomprehensible to him—and all in the space of an hour! He was confused. Why did they want him to be pharaoh? Is that what God wanted for him? Wouldn't God put that desire in his heart if he wanted that for Moses? As he took leave of his mother, he wondered, was this the way that his people, the Hebrews, would be delivered from oppression, by his having Pharaonic power? His passion for their freedom had been growing. Maybe somehow he was the key. His head spun, and he braced himself at the door.

Queen Ahmose, watching him, called, "Moses, are you all right?"

He knew what would help clear his head—to be out on the Nile in the fresh breeze. "Mother," he said, "I need to get away for a while. May I have your permission to take the royal bark out on the Nile?"

"That is an excellent idea, Moses. Take provisions for several days. Don't worry about Hatshepsut. I will tell her that we talked."

Moses ran to his chambers to pack a few things. He could not wait to get out of this palace of woe.

Memphis
1492 BC

The palace was in mourning for Pharaoh Thutmose I, who had passed away peacefully in his sleep. For a man of war, it was a quiet ending. The elaborate funeral procession had been long and tedious for Hatshepsut, especially as she observed the grief of her mother.

She really did love him, Hat thought as together they stood in the Valley of the Kings where her father's tomb was the first to be cut into the cliffs.

Hatshepsut's own grief for her father was overshadowed by the dread of her upcoming marriage to Thutmose II. She had resigned herself to her fate, determined to rule Egypt as co-regent the best she could. She would need all the cleverness she could muster to let her new husband think he was totally in charge, while she somehow pulled the strings behind the scenes. She would also have to get that nasty business of producing an heir out of the way as soon as possible.

As she left the tomb, Hatshepsut saw Moses coming up the incline toward their mother. He nodded to Hatshepsut and took his mother's arm, opposite Hat.

Queen Ahmose leaned gratefully on her adopted son's arm as she carefully picked her way over the rough surface to the awaiting royal litter. She beckoned to her old nurse and indicated that she wanted the nurse to ride with her and Hatshepsut. Queen Ahmose could do what she wanted now, even ignoring a little protocol. Soon she would be Queen Mother, usually a very powerful position, but Ahmose was not the mother of the pharaoh. Her power would lie mainly in the influence she had with Hatshepsut who would soon be Queen.

As confidante and advisor to the queen, Ahmose would play a vital role, but she would not be as publicly prominent as her predecessors, the Great Ahotep and the Divine Ahmose Nefertari. Seated between her daughter and nurse, Ahmose squeezed her daughter's hand, a signal to be strong. As the litter was lifted onto the shoulders of Nubian slaves and the curtains were closed, Queen Ahmose buried her head in the bosom of her beloved nurse and sobbed like a child.

The marriage of Hatshepsut and Thutmose II was a simple affair, but the coronation that took place after the General's death was an extravagant time of opulent ceremony and feasting. Pharaoh Thutmose II basked in the celebrants' praise and adoration.

If only they knew him as I do, thought Queen Hatshepsut, sitting beside her husband with a smile plastered on her face.

He knew she didn't love him, but that knowledge did not deter him in the least. In fact, it seemed to excite him as he took her again and again and then threw her aside as a conquering soldier might rape a captive woman of the enemy. She tried not to make an enemy of him. Lately, Hatshepsut had taken to pretending she wanted him just to protect herself from his rough treatment. If only she could get pregnant! Now that he had ravaged her, he would soon tire of her if she produced an heir.

Ten months later little Princess Neferure was born. "Beauty Is Here" was the meaning of her name and it fit. She was a beautiful, healthy baby, and Queen Hatshepsut was delighted with her, but Pharaoh Thutmose II was obviously not interested in the tiny new princess. He didn't bother to hide his disappointment that she was not the male heir he wanted.

Memphis
1491 BC

In the early months of the royal marriage, Moses chose to be away from the palace as much as possible.

There was plenty of work for him in the courts. The judges always welcomed him, as he reduced their load of cases, willingly hearing and deciding the most mundane affairs, such as charges of boundary moving. The chief judges recognized his thorough knowledge of Egyptian laws and codes, and they gradually trusted him with more serious cases because of his wise decisions. Wearing the golden feather of the goddess Maat, the bringer of truth, harmony, and justice, around their necks on a chain, the chief judges discussed how strange it was that Moses didn't seem interested in the position of chief judge or even governor. As a prince of Egypt, he had that right, and he certainly had the ability.

"Such a humble man," they marveled.

Moses had his own reasons for not accepting a judgeship. He wanted to have time to visit his own people, the Hebrews. He had been able to attend the wedding of his brother Aaron to a Hebrew woman, Elishaba. Unlike the Egyptians, the Hebrews made a great event of weddings. The celebration went on for days. Although Moses had avoided Egyptian parties since boyhood, he found himself enjoying these festivities. The only problem was that now his mother was looking at him expectantly.

"Moses," she asked, "when are you going to get married? Will you marry a Hebrew girl like your brother has?"

"Mother," Moses replied, "I have plenty of time. I haven't seen anybody I want, anyway."

Jochebed replied, "I hope you don't marry an Egyptian girl, Moses."

Moses thought she was getting a little too personal, so he put up an argument.

"Joseph married an Egyptian girl, Mother. Asenath was the daughter of an Egyptian priest of On."

"Well that was different," she replied. "There weren't any other Hebrews around then. His family was still in Canaan."

"But the marriage seems to have turned out well. They had two sons, who were blessed by Jacob, even having their own tribes."

Jochebed changed the subject, passing him some date cakes, "Here, Moses, have some of these."

Moses thought, *Sure, that will work—just stuff up my mouth with food.* But he said no more about marriage, and the matter was dropped.

Back at the palace, Hatshepsut confided in Moses. "It's a good thing my father secured the country as well as he did," she said. "Thutmose II does nothing but boast about being on military campaigns with his father. Do you remember the campaigns you were on with the General?"

"Of course I do," replied Moses. "I served as a royal charioteer in the squadron of the pharaoh."

"Well, I remember you telling me about those campaigns. Thutmose II tells the same stories, except that in place of your name, he puts in his own as though he had helped fight those battles."

Moses frowned, "Hat," he said gently, still addressing her by the familiar term she loved, "he must have wanted to go, but he wasn't strong enough."

"He wasn't brave enough either, Moses. You are too kind. Everybody knows he didn't go on those campaigns, but they say nothing and neither do I. Why anger him? He is pharaoh. But I hate to see history distorted like that."

"Be patient, dear sister. I have a feeling that you will make history yourself, and it will be good, because you genuinely care about the common people. Even now, you have managed to help so many of them. I have heard the stories of your generosity as I have been out in the world."

Perking up, Hatshepsut replied, "Really, Moses, are the people saying good things about me?"

Having encouraged Hat, Moses went to look in on Neferure, who was with her wet nurse.

"What a perfect little angel," he exclaimed as he took the three-month-old infant in his arms. In her twinkling eyes, he could see the baby Hatshepsut and was reminded of his determination to protect little Hat. Now he felt a sadness for her unhappy marriage and a frustration that he was helpless to protect the adult she had become.

Memphis
1490 BC

There was a breath of fresh air in the palace with the arrival of Senmut, former priest of Amun, now vizier to Pharaoh and chief architect for Hatshepsut's Memorial Temple at Deir el Bahri.

Moses liked the man. For one thing, he provided a buffer between Hatshepsut and Pharaoh. Senmut listened to her, but Thutmose II did not. In his insecurity, the pharaoh was threatened by the queen. He tended to present obstacles to any of her ideas or plans, but she could work through Senmut to accomplish her most important goals.

Moses also appreciated Senmut's personal qualities. He connected with the architect's intellect, creativity, and spiritual sensitivity. Of all the Egyptians Moses knew, he felt he could be a friend with this man. However, Moses was guarded because of Pharaoh. Senmut was Pharaoh's vizier first. As Senmut and Hatshepsut became close friends, Moses could sense a shift in power.

Though Senmut and Hatshepsut were clever, Pharaoh could somehow sense power slipping away from him. From time to time, he would go into a tirade about something unimportant just to assert his own authority.

Often now, Moses would notice Senmut and Hatshepsut standing close to each other, their heads bent over a large papyrus plan for her mortuary temple. Moses had been enlisted to help with the project. Senmut pointed out that it was customary for a man who has served in the the royal chariot force,[36] to serve in stone transport or as an engineer in times of peace. Therefore, Moses had received a leave of absence from the courts and had

---

36   tent-htor (horse estate)

taken on the task of helping Senmut in the selection and transport of the stones for the Memorial Temple.

One day, as they were traveling together, Moses asked Senmut, "Why are the Egyptians so focused on the dead and the afterlife. Take the Saga of Sinuhe, for example. He wanted to return to Egypt for what he considered a proper ushering into the afterlife, though it meant leaving his loved ones behind in his last days."

"From the earliest times, it has been so in Egypt. Just look at the pyramid tombs. Hatshepsut will have a Memorial Temple suited for her greatness. To avoid tomb robbers, she will be buried over three hundred feet below the earth in a rock tomb."

Moses didn't care where he was buried. He only hoped that Adonai would welcome him home to Paradise.

As if reading his thoughts, Senmut asked, "Do you believe in God, Moses?"

"Yes, I believe in the one true God, Adonai."

"Oh, that's the God of the Habiru people. I forgot you came from those people. Do you ever question your belief in Adonai?"

"Not really," replied Moses. "What I question is, what purpose God has for me to fulfill in my life."

"I've heard you are an excellent judge, and you certainly are a help to me on this building project. Your oversight has provided us with the finest blocks for Hatshepsut's Temple."

"Yes, I'm doing this for her, but it pains me to see the Hebrews suffer. It seems to be worse under the new pharaoh. He has abolished the commission that was established in the last reign to see to their needs and complaints."

"I'm sorry to hear that," said Senmut, wondering if there was anything he could do. Pharaoh had acted independently to show his power, Senmut realized. It was just like him to pick on the most oppressed people.

Memphis
1489 BC

Moses knew he had to do something. He had chosen this time to appeal to Pharaoh on behalf of the workers. He had heard that Pharaoh was in a good mood, as he looked forward to the New Year's festival and all the gifts he would receive.

Still, Pharaoh kept him waiting three days for an audience with him.

When he was finally ushered into the ruler's presence, Moses made the laudatory address that was expected. Moses, who was good at poetry, had written and memorized the song of praise with which he addressed Pharaoh. This creative work seemed to surprise and delight the monarch.

Once Thutmose II was placated, Moses presented his case for the oppressed Hebrews. He spoke calmly and logically, including comments of hope for the gracious mercy of Pharaoh.

Thutmose II heard Moses out, though the drumming of Pharaoh's fingers on the arms of his throne warned Moses to cut short the plea for his people. Pharaoh rose on his dais and waved his arms in dismissal as he let out a torrent of invectives against the "vermin parasites" who didn't deserve his consideration.

"How dare you bring up this matter to me?" he roared at Moses. "You are no better than them. Now get out of my throne room!"

Moses backed out of the room, still observing protocol, but his heart was sinking for the future of his people.

Memphis
1487 BC

The temple building was going well, and Queen Hatshepsut seemed happy with the project.

Princess Neferure, who was now five years old, was a continual delight to her mother. However, her father, Pharaoh Thutmose II, spent very little time with his daughter or even his wife. Lately, he seemed to have energy only for his harem. Hatshepsut was relieved. She hoped he had given up trying to produce a male heir with her. He hardly ever called for her, and when he did, he only wanted her to hold him. Like a child in the night, he was given to terrors. Hatshepsut wasn't surprised that he was frightened of death, since he still suffered from frequent illness. She thought that he wasn't helped by all the incantations of the magicians. His superstitions seemed to prey on his mind. In every dark corner there was a spirit waiting to devour him.

Moses was very busy these days but he managed to find time for Princess Neferure. He thought she took after his mother, Queen Ahmose. She was so feminine and sweet natured. The fact that she had a lisp endeared her to Moses, who remembered his own struggle to express himself clearly.

One afternoon, he found her in the garden with her nurse keeping an eye on her. The pretty little girl was bent over her needlework. It was a simple pattern, and her nurse was helping her with it. Moses quietly watched the child, dark hair falling over her shoulders and delicate fingers working the needle in and out of the fabric.

"What are you making?" he asked.

Looking up, she smiled and said, "Thomething for you Motheth."

"Really? That's so nice of you to think of me, Neferure."

They spent some time together, and then Moses left to visit his mother.

Queen Ahmose had not been herself lately. Her husband's death and her daughter's miserable marriage had taken their toll on her mental health. Moreover, she didn't feel she was needed anymore. Her daughter turned to Senmut for advice and encouragement. Queen Ahmose could understand that, but she just hoped Hatshepsut didn't hold any hard feelings against her for her part in the marriage decision. She asked Moses about that when the attendant ushered him into her chamber sitting area.

"No, Mother," said Moses. "I don't believe Hatsheput harbors any ill feelings toward you. She doesn't talk to me that much either, not like she used to. She's focusing on that temple of hers."

"Mother," he asked, "do you find any comfort in praying to God?"

She just looked at Moses as though she was searching for something. He took her hands in his.

"Mother," he said gently, "just say to him quietly, 'I love you, God, my true and only living God.' Don't pray to any other gods, Mother, please."

She smiled at him. "Do you remember, Moses, how I tried to get you to say 'Amun' when you were little, and you always said, 'Adon'?"

"Yes, Mother, I love you so much. You have been a good mother to me. You always wanted the best for me." Then he told her, "You look tired. Rest now, and I will come back to see you later."

Queen Ahmose looked intently at Moses and asked him, "Why did you call me 'Mother'?"

"What do you mean?" said Moses, wondering if she had heard that he had been in contact with his Hebrew family. What she said next made him wish that was all that it was.

"Who are you?" she asked, looking clearly disturbed. "How did you get in here?"

Moses called for her nurse. He was shaken as he left her bedchamber. He didn't say anything to Hat, but he was worried that his mother's mind was slipping.

Memphis
1486 BC

With loving attention from Hatshepsut and Moses, their mother had "come back" to them, and they were able to have some good times with her. However, within a year she slipped away in death. It was especially difficult to say good-bye to this sweet presence in their life. Neferure was heartbroken as she was close to her "Grandma Ahmoth."

Senmut was now at the palace constantly, because he had taken on the additional task of tutoring the princess. One day, after Neferure had finished her instructions, Moses found her in the courtyard playing with Keke, her pet monkey. The little animal, with its black face ringed by a fringe of white hair, gave Moses a grimace that made him laugh. Keke was busy peeling an onion. Neferure popped up from her bench to greet Moses.

"Would you like thome figth, Motheth? Keke will get them for uth."

"All right," said Moses as he watched the monkey scramble up the fig tree to gather the plump fruit from the top branches.

"Here, Keke, drop them in here," she told the monkey as she held up her basket. After dropping the figs, Keke flew from the tree onto Moses's shoulders and wrapped his arms around Moses's neck. Neferure and Moses were laughing at the monkey's antics when Pharaoh came into the courtyard. Instantly, Neferure froze and appeared anxious. She was afraid of him, Moses realized.

"Go to your nurse," Thutmose snapped at the child, and she fled. Keke screeched and scrambled up the fig tree.

"Don't you have anything better to do than waste your time with a useless child?" he demanded of Moses.

"Your Honor," Moses began, but he was interrupted by Pharaoh.

"Go haul some stones, since you love those quarries so much; or is it the people in them that you love?" he said, hatefully.

As Moses slipped out of the palace, he thought about Pharaoh's attitude toward Neferure. He was either disgusted that she wasn't the royal male heir he'd hoped for, or he was jealous of Moses's relationship with her. Either way, Pharaoh's mood didn't bode well for Moses. His remark about the quarries and the workers Moses took as a warning. He had no doubt that this pharaoh would like to get rid of him, especially since Queen Mother Ahmose was no longer around to protect him.

Six months later, it was springtime, which was harvest time in Egypt. Moses had been careful to stay out of Pharaoh's way since the episode in the palace courtyard. He felt his nerves wearing thin. Thutmose II had everyone on edge. Moses felt like he was walking along the rim of a cliff, ready to plunge over at any time.

As Moses entered the quarry worksite, he saw something that made his blood boil. An Egyptian overseer had taken up his whip and was brutally beating a Hebrew worker. Moses looked this way and that, and seeing no one in the immediate vicinity, picked up a rock and hurled it at the Egyptian, killing him instantly. Quickly Moses buried the man in a pile of sand and left the quarry.

What have I done? he asked himself as he drove his chariot back to the palace. *I've got to get hold of myself.*

Moses didn't want to be around the family, so he found a little boat near the palace and went out on the Nile.

The next morning, having calmed himself with the sail and a good rest, he returned to the quarry. After working a little while, he walked around to see if there was any talk about the man he had killed. He heard nothing and breathed a little easier. Then he saw two Hebrews quarreling, so he tried to intervene.

"Who made you the judge over us?" asked one of the men indignantly.

"Are you going to kill us like you killed the Egyptian?"

A stab of fear struck Moses. *Oh, no! Word is out of what I've done.*

He raced back to the palace. Hatshepsut met him at the gate.

"Moses," she said, "Pharaoh seeks to kill you."

As she handed him a knapsack of provisions, she said, "Hurry, you must go now. May God protect you, dear brother."

Moses ran for several hours to get away from the vicinity of the palace. Then he hid in some bushes. In his knapsack, he found a change of clothes. He thought, *I must shed my royal clothes and put these on instead.*

Worried that they might use dogs to track him down, he wadded up his prince's garments, weighted them down with a stone, and threw them in the Nile after dark. Then he made his way under cover of darkness toward the eastern frontier of Egypt.

When Moses finally reached the fort there several days later, it was light. As he crouched in the bushes, waiting for night, he thought of Sinuhe. Just as he did, Moses was fleeing from Pharaoh.

I wonder if I will be living with the Bedouins? he asked himself as darkness fell, and he headed for the desert.

Thebes
1483 BC

After the Beautiful Festival, Hatshepsut and Senmut remained in Thebes to watch the progress on her mortuary temple. The masons were working on the second-level courtyard, which would have two large pools of water. ·Senmut wanted to check on the dimensions of the pools. He also planned to visit the southern quarries. As Grand Vizier of Egypt, he had other business at Thebes, the southern capital. He also had a personal matter in mind.

Because the queen planned to stay several months into the planting season, she had brought Neferure and her nurse along with her. The child was nine years old now and still asking when Moses was coming back. Hatshepsut decided a change of scene would do her good, and Senmut could continue tutoring her.

One afternoon, Senmut invited Hatshepsut to visit the temple. They were standing on the second level as the golden sun slipped behind the cliffs above them and shadows crept over the valley. Senmut had asked the guards to set up torches in the courtyard. For security, the guards were posted on the lower level by the entrance ramp. The temple laborers had gone home to the workers village. The torches were lit. Senmut took Hatshepsut in his arms. "I've wanted you for so long," he said as he pulled her close and kissed her passionately.

"Senmut," she said, when she could catch her breath. "Look at the shadows. It will soon be dark. Shouldn't we be getting back to the palace?"

Senmut called for the guards. She watched in amazement as they set up a tent with cushions and a hamper of food and wine.

"My dear lady," he said as he gallantly motioned to a cushion. "No need to worry, we are spending the night."

They enjoyed a glass of wine. Then he set aside her empty goblet and gently lowered her to the cushions. Leaning on one arm, he slowly undressed the beautiful young woman. Breathing in the scent of myrrh rising from her warm skin, Senmut quoted an old Egyptian love poem:

"If I embrace her and
her arms are open
I am like a man in the
land of perfumes
If I kiss her and
her lips are open
I am drunk
even without wine" [37]

Lying on the cushions under the stars, Hatshepsut melted in Senmut's arms. His lovemaking started, tender and sensitive. She felt her whole body tremble as she responded to his caresses. Soon she was matching him in hunger and passion.

Later, as Senmut lay sleeping, she thought of the romantic dreams she had as a young girl and how she was inspired by the love poetry of Egyptian literature, as well as the stories of her mother about the romances in her family. All those fanciful dreams had been wiped from her mind by her marriage to Thutmose II when she was only sixteen. He had been harsh and forceful, treating her like a possession that was created only for his pleasure. He seemed to enjoy humiliating her, subduing her. His cruel treatment had effectively closed her spirit until Senmut came along.

Hatshepsut had not known love could be like this. She had felt so lonely before, not being able to confide in anyone, not even her mother or Moses. It would have hurt her mother, and Moses would have fought Thutmose, forgetting the danger to his own life in protecting her. But now at last, she had her love. Senmut was so powerful in Egypt that he could have had any woman he wanted, but he had chosen her. She didn't realize how gorgeous she was at twenty-four.

Senmut stirred, and reached for her. The lovers moved toward each other as though it was their natural state to be in union. They fit together;

---

37 *Ancient Egypt, Discovering its Splendors*, 107.

they belonged together. At that moment, a wild animal cried out in the night for its mate.

Hatshepsut laughed as Senmut said with a low growl, "Come here, my little panther. Where have you been?"

"Looking for you, my love," she replied with a little snarl.

Moments later, it was Hatshepsut's cries that rang in the night as her lover brought her to heights of ecstasy.

When the limestone cliffs above them caught the first rays of the morning sun, Senmut and Hatshepsut took off in the royal chariot for the palace across the Nile to the east.

In the months following their tryst at the temple, Hatshepsut was feverish with desire for her lover. She couldn't get enough of him. Senmut would slip away to her private chambers and within moments they would be wrapped in each other's arms.

After they returned to Memphis, Hatshepsut took her nurse, a trusted guard, and a handmaiden into her confidence. These servants guarded her secret, so pleased were they to see their queen glowing with happiness. She had always been so good to them, and they couldn't help but be aware of the misery she had endured from the pharaoh.

Hatshepsut and Senmut were not concerned about Thutmose approaching the queen's bedchamber. He was always weary in the evenings and retired early to his own chambers.

Pharaoh took his own pleasure in the afternoons in his harem. He was so in need of adulation that he believed the flowery praises of the young women there. It was his fantasy that they vied for a turn to enjoy sex with him. One time he had mistaken a spat to be over him, and he had cajoled, "Come, come, girls. Don't fight over me. There is enough of me to go around." The maidens had barely been able to suppress their laughter.

After that incident, they devised a game of mock quarrels, which they would stage for him from time to time to his great delight. During these fights, the girls would express a desire to enjoy this or that part of him, which they would extol in great detail. This verbal foreplay seemed to excite him more than their actual physical ministrations. If they waited too long between the mock fights, he would pout and complain that they didn't love him anymore, because they weren't fighting over him. So they would resume their little game to mollify their child, the pharaoh.

One day, six months later, Isis called the women of the harem to gather around her; she had an announcement to make. She was pregnant with

Pharaoh's child. If it was a male child, he would be heir to the throne of Egypt, because the great royal wife, Queen Hatshepsut, had not produced a male heir.

Isis was one of the most beautiful and intelligent women of the harem, and she was clearly enjoying her new status.

"There will be no more mock fights," she said as those were demeaning to Pharaoh, who was now the father of the child she was carrying. There would be a new system of rewards for the best dancing, singing, and playing of musical instruments for the palace entertainment and for state dinners. Isis, herself, would be the one to decide who would be involved in the "private entertaining" of visiting dignitaries.

Memphis
1482 BC

During the late months of her pregnancy and at other times when she was indisposed, Isis would assign or call a woman or several women from the harem to pleasure the pharaoh in his private chambers. Thutmose II treated Isis with special attention throughout her pregnancy, spending time talking with her, playing senet, rubbing precious oils on her body, and even kissing the growing bulge. Isis hoped she would have a boy, thinking that the pharaoh's attention and special favors would continue if she did produce a male heir.

When the baby came, he was a healthy boy, and Pharaoh promptly named him Thutmose III. He called for a celebration throughout the land. Even Queen Hatshepsut was delighted. Thutmose II had his male heir. Now maybe he would be kinder to Neferure.

When Thutmose III was three months old, Pharaoh called Isis to come to his private chambers with the baby. She noted as she approached his suite of rooms that there were two guards. Usually one guard was sufficient. As Isis entered, she bowed low to Pharaoh, addressing him with the expected praise, "O. Divine Lord, to whom we owe our very existence." Even as these words came from her lips, she thought it an odd contrast to her experience of him cavorting in the buff with the naked women of the harem, including herself.

Finally, he stood before her. "Give me the baby," he ordered. Proudly she laid the infant in his arms. Then he looked at her.

"As a common harem girl, you are not worthy to raise this child. From this day forward, you will have no contact with him. You will remain in the harem for my pleasure, and you will come to my chambers whenever I call you. The great Royal Wife, Queen Hatshepsut, Royal Consort of Amun, will raise this child to be a proper pharaoh. He will be her son. He will be to you, your future pharaoh."

"Guards!" he called as Isis screamed and fell to her knees, clutching at the hem of his robe and pleading for her baby.

As the guards took her away, she begged them to kill her.

"Stop," ordered Pharaoh to the guards. Isis turned hopefully toward Pharaoh.

He told her, "I can have another child by another harem girl if I choose. If you want this child to live to be pharaoh, you will pull yourself together. I will expect you back here in my bedchamber this very day, willing and eager to delight me after my midday meal."

Memphis
1482 BC

Hatshepsut heard, via palace gossip, how Isis had been treated.

That poor girl, thought Hatshepsut.

She knew that the harem was kept under guard, so she couldn't go to see Isis, but she found a way for her trusted handmaiden to get messages through to Isis about how the baby was doing. She had found a good wet nurse for the child.

Neferure was delighted with her baby brother. Keke, the monkey, displayed some jealousy, so Hatshepsut warned her to keep the monkey away from little Thutmose III.

The baby was good for Neferure, who was still hoping for Moses's return. Senmut had worked with her on her lisp, and she would say, "Mother, won't Moses be proud of me? How well I can talk now? He will be proud of me when he comes home."

How sad, thought her mother. *She never asks for her father.*

Hatshepsut had been concerned that the pharaoh would be frequenting her quarters now that she had the baby there, but he wasn't feeling well and was having breathing difficulties at times. Thutmose also was suffering from a skin disease that left scabrous tissue and scarring on his face. When he was feeling better, he would call for Isis and spend the afternoon in bed with her. The word around the palace was that this desperate young woman was bending to Pharaoh's every demand, no matter how outrageous, in the belief that she was protecting the life of her baby.

While Pharaoh ignored his little son, Senmut was tender with baby Thutmose and attentive to Neferure. As her private tutor, he appreciated Neferure's good mind, but it was the little princess's sweet personality and sensitive spirit that had captured his heart. Moreover, Senmut was deeply in love with Hatshepsut. Never had he known anyone like her. Their lovemaking continued unabated. Her spunk sparked a fire in him. Her wit and sense of humor constantly amused him. What he didn't realize was that *he* had awakened these qualities that had been dormant in her for some time.

Senmut enjoyed watching people who were meeting Hatshepsut for the first time. They literally stopped in their tracks. Those large eyes, with flecks of green and gold, sparkled like jewels in her gently rounded face. When she smiled with those perfect lips, dimples formed at their sides.

He loved the simple, fine linen gowns she wore, the clingy material showing off her curves and her small waist, which he loved to embrace, pulling her body tightly to his. The tanned, bare arms encircled with golden bracelets, belonged around his neck, and her warm, shapely legs were at home wrapped around his body. He did not mind others admiring Hatshepsut, because he knew she was totally his, body and soul. He loved taking off her jewelry, the elaborate collar, her crown, and all the rest. She took off her braided wig only for him. When she shook free her auburn ringlets, he felt kissed by the sun. Her people wrote of her, "She is beautiful to behold." But only he beheld her full natural beauty.

The Desert
1486 BC

Moses wanted to get as far away from Egypt as he could. He avoided the Egyptian outposts, traveling south along the Red Sea in the Sinai Peninsula.

He was grateful for the goatskins of water Hatshepsut had given him. She must have known he would head for the desert. Unlike Sinuhe, he was not tempted by the water of the Bitter Lakes, for he rationed his water until he could refill his skins at the Oasis of Elim. He was grateful his escape was taking place in the spring. The desert could be unforgiving in the summer. He avoided the copper mines at Dophkah. They would be in full swing at this time of year and would have many Egyptians working there. Moses didn't know how far the news of the slain Egyptian overseer would have traveled by now, but he wasn't taking any chances.

He continued his lonely journey, traveling north along the eastern arm of the Red Sea, the Gulf of Aqaba. Walking by day now and resting at night, he encountered the occasional flock of goats. He thought again of Sinuhe. This was Bedouin territory, he realized. Would he stay with the Bedouins like Sinuhe did?

I will need a place to live, he thought. *It will be a long time before I can return to Egypt.*

Moses went around the tip of the Gulf of Aqaba at Ezion Geber. He was now in the heart of Midianite territory, which flanked the Gulf on both sides and stretched from Western Asia to South Central Arabia. As he turned south again on the eastern side of the Gulf, he started to breathe more easily. He felt safe here, far from the pharaoh who wanted to kill him.

On this day he had been walking since early morning. Now it was midafternoon. His food rations were gone, and his water supply was dwindling. Then, in the distance, he saw a flock of goats beside a well. As he drew nearer, he could see a group of women drawing water from the well. They were pouring it into troughs for their animals. Suddenly, shepherds came and drove the women away, taking the water for themselves. Ever the protector, Moses ran to the rescue. Swinging his walking stick in wide arcs, he drove the men off. Then he motioned to the women that they could return to the well, and he helped them water their flocks.

When the seven daughters of Ruel[38] returned home early, their father asked them, "Why are you home so early?"

They explained how Moses had helped them.

"Well," he asked his daughters, "where is he? Did you leave him there? Why didn't you bring him back here for something to eat? Go and invite him to dinner."

Hospitality was of primary importance in those parts. Besides, Moses had done a special favor for the daughters of the family.

Ruel, or Jethro[39] his address as a priest of Midian, welcomed Moses into his home and invited him to stay.

So it was that Moses found a home with the Bedouins, just like Sinuhe. Moses felt comfortable with the Midianites, who were descendants of Abraham by Keturah, whom Abraham married after Sarah died. Their son, Midian, was the forefather of Moses's new hosts. The people worshiped Adonai but were also influenced by the religious beliefs of surrounding tribes. Their territory was generally dry and desolate, so the people had to wander some distance to provide water for their flocks. Many also worked as coppersmiths, fashioning tools and other utensils from the copper that was mined in the Sinai. They would trade the articles they made with the caravans that came through that area in exchange for certain items they could use. The people lived in goats-hair tents, which were as colorfully decorated as the Egyptian camping tent that Moses had shared with his Uncle Tep on their antelope hunt.

Moses's new home was certainly a stark contrast from the palace in Egypt, but he was safe and he was comfortable. For that, he was grateful to Adonai. Moses enjoyed the camaraderie of the nightly campfires, when family and friends would gather round to sing and tell stories.

---

38 Meaning a friend of God.
39 His Excellency.

Soon after Moses arrived, he began to notice one of Jethro's daughters, Zipporah. What first got his attention was her hearty laughter whenever she was with her sisters. It reminded him of Hatshepsut, although Zipporah's appearance was not like Hat's. Zipporah was taller and more full-figured. Her long, dark, wavy hair fell forward from under her head covering when she bent over the cooking pot. She had warm brown eyes and full lips. He had kissed those lips once, when they had left the family campsite to sit apart and talk. He had not gone any further with her than that kiss out of respect for her and for Jethro, who had been so kind to him. He did wonder, though, what it would be like to have her in his bed, holding those curves in his arms.

Jethro gladly gave his daughter, Zipporah, to Moses in marriage. The wedding was celebrated in the family and community with days of joyful singing, dancing, and feasting. His new bride surpassed all of Moses's ideas of what she would be like in bed.

She was worth waiting for, decided Moses as he lay spent beside her. *I found the right one, Uncle Tep!*

Memphis
1480 BC–1479 BC

Queen Hatshepsut was numb with grief. Her precious daughter, Neferure, had passed into the afterlife. The eleven-year-old princess had come down with a fever and died within two days.

In her anguish, her mother had cried out to the loved ones who were no longer available to her.

"Mother, I wish you were here. Oh, Moses, where are you when I need you so? Why haven't you come back? Where is your God, Adonai, now? Where is my god, Amun, now? Am I being punished for loving Senmut? Which god is punishing me?"

Senmut tried to comfort her, even while his own heart was breaking for his beloved little student.

Little Thutmose III was only two and half years old, but he knew his 'Nefer' was gone. "Where is Nefer?" he kept asking.

Even Keke wasn't swinging from branches now. The little monkey just sat around looking forlorn.

Thutmose II couldn't face Neferure's death. Even though he was never close to his daughter, he was prostrate and couldn't get up to attend her funeral ceremony. Before she died, he had been troubled by nightmares and feared his own death. Now his nightmares were more frequent. Hatshepsut thought that his superstitions were getting the best of him.

Those incantations the magicians chant over him are only making matters worse, she thought.

Once when Thutmose III was sick in bed, she had observed his doctors as they medicated him. As they were preparing the medicine, they chanted:

*"That Isis might make free,
that Isis might make Horus free
from all evil that Seth has done
to him when he slew
Horus' father Osiris."*[40]

Then, as he took the medicine, they chanted to give the remedy more power:

*"Come remedy, come drive
the disease from my heart
Make me strong in magic power
with the remedy."*[41]

Finally, the doctors chanted:

*"Oh, Isis, great enchantress
free me, release me from
all evil red things, from
the fever of the God and the
fever of the Goddess, from death,
and death from pain, and
the pain which comes over me,
as thou hast freed, as thou
has released thy son Horus
whilst I enter into the fire, and go forth from the water."*[42]

Less than a year after Neferure's death, Thutmoser II died at the age of thirty-four.

Senmut, as Grand Vizier, made all the arrangements. Thutmose II had stipulated, before his final illness, that he wanted both the amulet of Isis, the goddess of protection, and the Ded amulet placed on his mummified body. The Ded amulet was a small pillar, topped by discs, which symbolized the sacred backbone of Osiris. It was believed that the Ded amulet would indicate that this man belonged to Osiris, so that when

---

40   Erman, *Life in Ancient Egypt,* 356; Eb., 1, 12 ff.
41   Erman, 356; Eb., 2, I ff.
42   Erman, *The Great Dynasty Papyrum,* edited by Ebers 356

Osiris recognized it, he would open the gate. Thutmose II wanted to make sure he wasn't thrown to the monster instead.

Hatshepsut managed to get through the funeral. Only once did Thutmose III ask, "Where is Father?"

She had simply said, "He is gone far away to the afterlife, my dear boy."

He replied, "Oh." And that was that.

They were now co-regents, the tiny child and Queen Hatshepsut. She would focus on raising Thutmose III to be a mighty pharaoh.

The Desert
1479 BC

Moses was settled in with the Midianites. They treated him as one of their own, and in a way he was, through his marriage to Zipporah.

Life around the campfire was jovial. Some of the songs they sang now were those written by Moses. The people shared amusing stories and tales of adventure. The latter were often told by Hobab, Zipporah's younger brother, who liked to explore the areas beyond the borders of their tribe. Moses liked him and often chose to tend the flocks with him.

Moses had listened to the Midianite stories before he started to tell his own. They often clamored for more stories from him. They wanted to hear all about life in Egypt, especially life in the palace. Moses told them about his Uncle Tep, Bekah, and Hatshepsut, as well as about his Hebrew family. He noticed that they weren't as interested in "those relations" of his, as much as in the Egyptians, possibly because the Hebrews were more like themselves, except that they lived in mud-brick houses and were forced to work for the Egyptians. The stories of the palace and hunting with Uncle Tep were much more exotic.

Scratching out a living in the desert was not easy, but it was a slower-paced life than Moses was accustomed to. There were occasional skirmishes with neighboring tribes, but mostly they had a peaceful coexistence with other desert peoples. There was not much in the way of spoils to tempt others to attack—no gold, no horses or chariots, and no costly incense.

Most of their jewelry and colorful clothes were made by the tribespeople themselves, of materials available to anyone who lived in the desert. Wells were their main treasure, and they had to be guarded. Moses took his turn at that task.

He ate well. There was always the delicious flatbread he enjoyed so much, and there was goat meat and goat milk. Occasionally, during the migratory season, there were quail that flew over the Gulf of Aquabah. Fish, fresh from the gulf or dried, was a staple. They ate fresh vegetables from the little garden patches by the base camps, which they irrigated with well water carried painstakingly in buckets. Moses continued to enjoy dates, figs, olives, and honey. The food was plain, but tasty, and eaten by using one's fingers. Moses liked eating his evening meal from a bowl while sitting by the fire. He could always look forward to the night in his tent with Zipporah.

She conceived and bore Moses their first son. Moses named him Gershom,[43] for he said "I am an alien in a strange land."

His wife was puzzled. "Don't you feel at home here, Moses?" she asked.

Moses replied, "You and your family, and everybody else, have done everything to make me feel welcome here, and I appreciate that."

He paused, and then said, "I don't know why, but I just think maybe this isn't the end of my journey. But I don't know what is," he said. "Maybe it is Canaan, the land that was promised to my father."

Zipporah just shook her head, "I don't know about you Moses. I don't know what more you could want," she said, as she looked lovingly at their baby son.

Moses smiled, "You are right, Zipporah. Adonai has blessed us. When the baby is circumcised, we will have a family celebration."

---

43   Literally, *alien there* in Hebrew.

Thebes
1474 BC

Hatshepsut's mortuary temple was almost completed. It had taken fifteen years. Her affair with Senmut had lasted a decade, and she still loved him with every fiber of her being. She hadn't made him pharaoh, for that was a position reserved for her nephew and stepson, Thutmose III.

In the meantime, Senmut was working behind the scenes to establish Hatshepsut's own ascendance to the throne. She was now Queen and co-regent with the eight-year-old boy, but she would soon be pharaoh, ruler of the Two Lands of Egypt, the upper and lower. She would have at least a decade and maybe more, she thought, before the boy would be ready to rule by himself.

Senmut had invited Hatshepsut to the mortuary temple at Deir el Bahri to repeat the experience of their tryst there—a sort of private anniversary celebration. He also wanted to show her the mural the artisans were currently working on. The first part of the relief, depicting her childhood, was finished now.

He pointed out the relief panels of her conception. The great god, Amun, disguised as Thutmose I, was shown appearing before Hatshepsut's mother. The inscription explained that "Amun took the form of the noble King Thutmose and found the Queen sleeping in her room. When the pleasant odors that proceeded from him announced his presence, she awoke; he gave her his heart and showed himself in his godlike splendor. When he approached the Queen, she wept for joy at his strength and beauty, and he gave her his love."

Hatshepsut studied the relief. Both figures were nude, except that the queen was wearing her uraeus[44] crown. The scene was explicit, clearly portraying the sexual union between Amun and Queen Ahmose.[45]

Senmut explained, "This is to show your divine origin."

"Let's move on," he said, pointing to the next scene.

Hatshepsut's father, Thutmose I, was instructing Khnum, the creator-god, who fashioned mankind of clay on his potter's wheel: "Go to fashion her better than all the gods. Shape for me this, my daughter, whom I have begotten."

Khnum replied: "Her form shall be more exalted than the gods, in her dignity as King."[46]

Senmut explained: "This is Khnum, forming your *Ka*, your soul or double. See that little nude figure on his potter's wheel?"

"But it's a boy," she said.

"Yes, that's the whole idea of this mural. It shows your divine origin and your male Ka. Both give you credibility to rule as pharaoh. That is what you want the mural to depict, isn't it?"

"Yes," Hatshepsut replied, smiling at her lover. "Maybe I should wear the false beard and the male kilt also."

Senmut laughed at the idea of this feminine woman, still beautiful at thirty-four, wearing a false beard. Then he scooped her up in his arms, carried her out to the cushions in the courtyard, and asked, "What do you say we make love, before you put on that beard?"

---

44 The cobra that projected from the crown of the pharaoh and was often worn with the blue and gold striped headcloth, the *nemes*.
45 This relief can be seen at Deir el Bahri.
46 Chip Brown, *National Geographic*, April 2009, 102.

Thebes
1473 BC

The coronation of Pharaoh Hatshepsut was magnificent, beyond anything that had taken place before in Egypt. Hatshepsut was radiant as she waved to the crowd from her splendid sedan chair, which was supported by two carved lions in full stride. The procession went on as far as the eye could see. The Grand Vizier, Senmut, carrying incense, led the priests. Following Hatshepsut's raised carrier were the nobles, courtiers, and royals. Then came the musicians and row after row of soldiers, marching in their finest regalia.

The official party was followed by the people, who also lined the way, throwing flowers before the royal procession that was making its way to the temple of Amun. Everyone waited outside the temple while Hatshepsut descended from her carrier and entered the temple to present her offerings and beseech Amun's blessings on her reign.

When Hatshepsut emerged from the temple, she took her place on a throne in front of the sanctuary in full view of all her people. The throne was placed atop a raised platform, shaded by a beautiful multicolored canopy. On the two front corners of the structure stood tall staves, holding flags bearing the royal insignia. Attendants stood on both sides of the throne, waving long plumed fans. Hatshepsut looked down the broad walkway, lined with people all the way to the small sanctuary of Min at the other end. It was a lovely day, a propitious sign from Amun, she thought.

As Hatshepsut waited for the Min ceremony to begin, she spotted nine-year-old Thutmose III running around, darting here and there in the crowd.

That boy has such boundless energy, she thought, *and on top of that he is excited about this event, his first big public festivity.*

Oh my, she realized, *there is nothing I can do now to settle him down.* When she saw that Senmut had collared him, she breathed a sigh of relief. What would she do without his help?

Senmut was the only "father" the boy knew, since his own father had died when he was only three years old. Senmut had been his tutor for the early part of his education. Now Thutmose was in palace classes, but he still received religious instruction from the Grand Vizier, a former priest. Both he and Hatshepsut had emphasized the worship of Amun as god of gods, the other gods being only manifestations of Amun. The boy was as quick of mind as he was of body. Thank god for Senmut's help, especially today.

Hatshepsut thought of Moses. He had predicted this day. She wished he were here to see her crowned. When Thutmose III was younger, she had told him adventure stories of the Egyptians. He loved the stories she told about her brother. However, she had given Moses a fictitious name to protect his identity. She did tell the lad that her brother had killed an Egyptian who was cruel to slaves, and that he had to escape from Egypt to save his life.

"Maybe he will come back like Sinuhe did," said the boy, who had already heard from her a simplified version of that classic Egyptian tale.

"I hope he does." Hatshepsut said. "What he did was wrong. You must never take matters of justice into your own hands." Then she added, "But he is a good man and a good friend despite what he did."

Hatshepsut was drawn back to the present when she saw that the ceremonial procession of Min, started from the other end of the walkway, was moving slowly toward her. Twenty priests bore the covered stand that held the upright image of Min, the god of fertility, wrapped tightly as a mummy. His face and long beard were black like the fertile soil of the Nile. Hatshepsut glanced back at Senmut and Thutmose III, noting that Senmut had lifted the boy onto his shoulders to have a better view.

"Look, look," said the boy, laughing and pointing to a unique feature of the god Min, his erect penis protruding from his mummy wrapped body.

Senmut reached up and grabbed the boy's finger. "No, Thutmose, we don't point, and we don't laugh at the god."

"But, Teacher," he said, "don't you think it's funny how Min can do that, under all those tight mummy wraps?"

Senmut couldn't help but smile. He had never thought of that. He remembered how he had taught the boy the facts of life, including how to treat a woman. Senmut thought Thutmose was fortunate, in a way, not to have known his father, who couldn't have been a good influence on him. For Hatshepsut's sake, he had done everything he could to help the boy develop a good moral character. Actually, it was not difficult to love him. First of all, he was the image of Hatshepsut, whom Senmut adored. It was amazing how much the boy looked like her, seeing that they only shared one ancestor, Thutmose I, the "General." Hatshepsut's father was the grandfather of Thutmose III. The boy could have been Hatshepsut's son with his handsome fine featured face.[47]

Now Senmut told him, "Look, my son, see that white bull? Isn't he grand?"

Hatshepsut also saw the white bull, sacred to the gods. He was still some distance away, walking between the image of Min and the priests. They were reciting from the papyrus the blessing of the God Re, the sun manifestation of Amun.

Suddenly the procession stopped, and the crowd hushed. The priests of Amun stopped before the royal platform, carrying the Pschent, representing the lands of Upper and Lower Egypt.

The Red Crown, throne-shaped and fronted by a cobra head, represented Lower Egypt and held the white, cone-shaped crown of Upper Egypt. They solemnly placed the double crown of Egypt on Hatshepsut's head. Then, as the musicians began to play, the people cheered and a priest let fly four geese to carry the news to the four quarters of heaven that Hatshepsut, protected by Horus, son of Isis and Osiris, had received the white and the red crown of Egypt.

After the monarch had been proclaimed pharaoh, she offered her royal sacrifice in the presence of the statues of her ancestors, which were borne by priests behind the image of Amun. A priest presented her with the golden sickle with which she cut a sheaf of corn. She strewed it before the white bull, which had been prodded forward before her throne. This symbolized the offering of the first fruits of her reign.

Next, she offered incense before the statue of Min, which the priests brought forward as the bull was led away. Her offering to Min would ensure a good flood and healthy crops for Egypt.

---

47 The resemblance between Hatshepsut and Thutmose III has been noted by Egyptologists when comparing their statues.

Finally, the pharaoh received the congratulations of her court. Much later, after the feasting and dancing, Hatshepsut lay in Senmut's arms, and they discussed the events of the day.

She laughed when he told her the comments of Thutmose III. "He really is my son, you know. He is like my own son."

"Yes, I know," he murmured, placing a gentle finger on her lips. Then he lovingly kissed the new pharaoh of Egypt.

The Desert
1472 BC

Moses was having a rough time in the desert. Zipporah was not herself after the birth of their second child. Moses named the boy, Eliezer, meaning "God is my helper," for he said, "My father's God was my helper. He saved me from the sword of Pharaoh."

Everyone noticed the change in Zipporah. She had wanted the second child. They had waited a long time for him. Gershom was ten years old already. However, now that he was born, she was not rejoicing with Moses. Much of the time, she just sat with her head down. She wasn't well, and though she had always had a hearty appetite, now she just picked at her food.

Zipporah had no appetite for sex either, even six months after the baby's birth. Moses could wait, but he was worried about his wife. She nursed little Eliezer, but afterward she would hand the infant to Moses or one of her sisters. She had loved holding Gershom, Moses remembered.

What could be wrong? he wondered.

"Adonai, you are my helper. That's why I named my son as I did. Please help me now. Help Zipporah to be herself again."

Finally, Jethro told Moses, "Get away with Hobab for a while. The well water is getting low in this area, so take the flocks to the other side of the Gulf."

Moses hated to leave Zippora, but Jethro said, "The situation is getting you down, Moses. You need a rest from it. Go now, we will take care of Zipporah and the children."

Memphis
1472 BC

Within a year of Hatshepsut's coronation, she lost her friend and lover. They were walking in the palace garden, when suddenly Senmut clutched his chest and crumpled to his knees. Frantically, she called for help as she held him in her arms. But it was too late. He was gone, even more suddenly than her daughter, to the life beyond the setting sun.

Hatshepsut was grateful that the priests made most of the arrangements. Senmut was one of their own, as chief priest.

This time, it was Hatshepsut who lay prostrate in her bed. She told her beloved nurse that she didn't want to live anymore. Her nurse held and soothed her. Then she said, "Would Amun be pleased with this?" indicating her rumpled bed, the refuge she had sought in her overwhelming grief.

"My precious child, you are dead while you yet live."

"But I feel dead inside," she moaned.

"Little Thutmose has been asking for you," the nurse informed her.

"Thutmose!" said Hatshepsut, startled from the stupor of her private grief. "He has lost his teacher, his father. I forgot about him," she said incredulously.

Suddenly concerned for her stepson, she asked, "Where is he?"

Her nurse replied, "He is with his own nurse, but she is having a difficult time with him. He is as inconsolable as you."

"Oh" said Hatshepsut, "I must go to him."

Her nurse called for attendants to fetch warm water for a shower, and then she began to lay out her clothes.

Hatshepsut found Thutmose III with his nurse. As he raised his tear-stained face to her, Hatshepsut held out her arms to him.

He came running to her crying, "Mother, I thought you'd never come!"

She took him on her lap and rocked him as she soothed, "It's all right. I'm here now. I'll always be here right beside you. My precious son, I will never leave you."

As soon as her son was settled in his bed, Hatshepsut took a small papyrus, and on it, she wrote the poem that Senmut had recited to her on that first night together at her mortuary temple. The following morning she called for a carriage and went to the embalmer, where he was working over Senmut. She asked the man, who was wearing an Anubis mask, to leave her alone with Senmut's body, just for a few moments. His body had been dried in natron and was in the process of being wrapped with strips of linen. Hatshepsut wrapped her arms around him. Tearfully, she took the poem papyrus, scented with myrrh, and tucked the tiny roll in Senmut's wrappings.

"Good-bye, my love," she whispered. Brushing away her tears, she motioned to the embalmer to proceed, and she left to spend the day with her son.

Senmut was buried in a tomb with a splendid ceiling. Major constellations were depicted as mythological figures. The display revealed the extensive knowledge of the sky and the movements of the stars and planets. Under this magnificent canopy, the great supporter of Hatshepsut was laid to rest. He had completed his work on earth: He had finished his greatest architectural achievement, Hatshepsut's mortuary temple. He had established her as pharaoh in her own right, and he had groomed her successor, Thutmose III, for the first ten years of his life.

Hatshepsut would take over now.

Senmut had been the love of Hatshepsut's life. She would not have another.

The Desert
1470 BC

Moses was relieved that Zipporah had recovered from her listlessness. She was eating and sleeping as well as before Eliezer's birth. She was energetic now and welcomed Moses's loving embraces again. However, she was also more critical of him. Though he tried to meet her demands for more help with the children, it seemed that he could never do anything right.

Zipporah could out-argue Moses, even with his logical mind. She was vocally quick and articulate. Although in the House of Wisdom, Moses had proven his ability to express his thoughts, he was no match for his wife. When he could not keep up with her, he kept quiet. Gradually he regressed and began to lose confidence when he was around her. Then she complained that he never talked to her.

Moses remembered his Uncle Tep's words about how to treat a wife and he got tears in his eyes. He missed him, although he realized God had provided a wise, new advisor in his father-in-law, Jethro. When he was alone with Jethro, he would relax and gradually be able to freely discuss a range of topics. But, of course, he couldn't tell Jethro about his difficulties with Zipporah. After all, she was his daughter. Moses realized, wisely, that doing so would put Jethro in the middle, a difficult place to be.

Jethro would ask Moses, "How is it going with Zipporah? She is a good woman, is she not?"

"Yes, Father," he would always say. "She is a good woman."

And she was, thought Moses. She was a passionate woman. He had to admit that she had never short-changed him in bed. The full curves he had admired when he first met her were as attractive to him as ever, and she satisfied him in that way.

It was just that, she was a "take charge" kind of woman, and though she certainly managed the home and the children well, she tried to manage him too. To be honest, thought Moses, sometimes it was just easier to let her.

Then he remembered his Uncle Tep's advice: "Be kind and loving to your wife. Do not let your wife take charge of you, or she will not respect you."

Well, thought Moses wryly, his uncle didn't know Zipporah. He supposed Uncle Tep was right though. It seemed that the result of Moses taking the easy route with Zipporah was that she had lost respect for him. He didn't know how to turn it around, but he could try to be more loving and helpful and could also pray about it. That was always Jethro's answer, "Let us pray about it."

He had enjoyed many good talks with this priest of Midian about the nature of God. Sometimes they disagreed about some aspect of God, and Jethro would say amiably, "All right, Moses. Don't try to convince me. You worship your God, and I'll worship my God."

Living in the desert and on the grassy slopes of the vast wilderness areas was to be confronted with one's own insignificance. It drew one to want to magnify God and to realize one's own dependence on him. Moses would need help from God to discern when and how to answer Zipporah and when to remain silent. Then he remembered a wise saying he had learned in Egypt:

"Before all things, guard thy speech
for man's ruin lies in his tongue.
Man's body is a storehouse,
full of all manner of answers.
Choose, therefore, the right one and speak well,
and let the wrong answer
remain imprisoned in thy body."[48]

For now, Moses would pray about his relationship with Zipporah. He would try harder to be a good husband. The most difficult part would be to make an effort to stand up to her anger. For that, he would especially need God's help.

Sometimes he would get away for a while. He enjoyed tending the flocks with Zipporah's younger brother, Hobab. When he would come back, after several nights away from his wife, she seemed to appreciate him more. He decided that he should probably do that more often. A little absence could relieve the tension between them. Moses expected the tension would increase if he stood up to her more often, so he would need those times of peace under the stars.

---

48 New Empire Instruction, Erman, Ancient Egypt.165.

Memphis
1470 BC

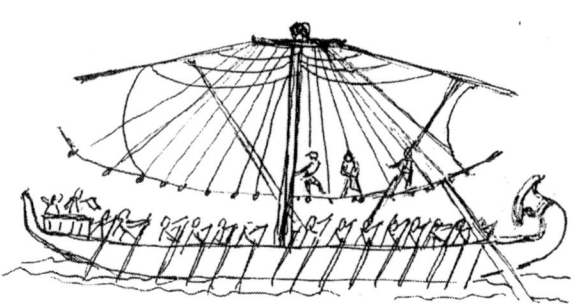

It was several years after Senmut's death, and Hatshepsut missed him every day. She wished he were here to take part in her new venture.

For three hundred years there had been no trade with the incense lands to the south at the farthest reaches of the Red Sea. She intended to open up trade with the mysterious land of Punt. Egyptians viewed this land as mythological—God's Land. But Hatshepsut believed it was a real place, and she planned to send a trade expedition there.

She stated, "Amun of Thebes, the Lord of gods suggested this thought to me, because he held this ruler so dear."[49]

In preparation, Hatshepsut had ordered cedar wood imported from Byblos. The fine, straight-grained wood, from the forests of Lebanon, was an excellent material for use in building ships. Five ships, each measuring about sixty-five feet in length, were now ready for the voyage. Their gigantic sails, when unfurled, stood out like great wings from the sides of each ship.

Pharaoh Hatshepsut and twelve-year-old Thutmose III, her co-regent, stood together at the port of departure on the Red Sea. They had come to see their ships off on this historic expedition, which would be the highlight of Hatshepsut's reign. As they watched, the ships were laden with goods to exchange for the treasures of Punt. Large jars, holding provisions for the journey, were being toted up the gangplank of each ship. Hatshepsut was sending a contingent of armed soldiers along, because they were not sure what kind of reception they would receive in Punt. The soldiers boarded the ships, most of them stationed in the lead ship.

Finally, prayers for fair winds and calm seas were lifted to the skies, and the monarchs bade the captains and their crews, "Farewell, safe journey."

---

49   Erman, *Life in Ancient Egypt*, 511.

Thebes
1470 BC

"Mother, when are the ships coming back?" asked Thutmose III one afternoon in Thebes.

"I'm sorry, Son, but it's been centuries since anyone has been to Punt, so we don't know how long such a journey takes," replied Hatshepsut.

"Didn't anyone record the early journeys?" he asked, accustomed to the diligence of the scribes.

"If they did, the records were destroyed in the time of the Hyksos."

"What if they got shipwrecked?" he replied, referring to the current expedition.

"Let's not imagine such a tragic event. Anyway, we sent five ships. If they were caught in a storm, surely some of the ships would make it back."

"What if they were all murdered by the people of Punt?" persisted Thutmose, lost in his catastrophic scenarios.

Hatshepsut responded, "I don't think the people of Punt are a warring nation, but we sent soldiers along in case the expedition encountered any opposition. Let's get our minds off the ships for a while. I'll play you a game of senet."

Every day, Pharaoh Hatshepsut prayed to Amun that he would bring the ships back safely. Thutmose III was learning to depend on Amun too, for he was Hatshepsut's pharaoh-in-training, besides being her nephew and stepson. He watched and emulated everything she did.

They were still waiting in Thebes when the expedition arrived. Over sea and over land, through the streets of Thebes to the palace came the procession from the ship. With joy and exultation, Hatshepsut, Thutmose

III, and the people of Thebes, as well as many from Memphis, welcomed the adventurers home.

It was a triumphal pageant, as the exotic cargo was paraded through the streets. Some of the people of Punt had returned with the expedition. The festive procession also included baboons, monkeys, greyhounds, a leopard, panther skins, sweet scented woods, white gold, electrum,[50] ebony, ivory, heaps of incense, ointment, and the myrrh resins, which were used by the Egyptians in their cosmetics and for their religious ceremonies.

Most amazing, were the thirty-one live myrrh trees. Besides all of this magnificent array, there were "two live panthers, which were to follow her Majesty," a personal gift to Pharaoh Hatshepsut.

"You may have one of the panthers," she said to her stepson, as he oohed and aahed over the astonishing gifts.

The palace scribes were busy recording all the items. It was written that "no one has ever seen the like since the world was created."[51]

Hatshepsut wanted a full report of the expedition. She asked, "What were the people like? Describe their appearance, their homes, and villages. Tell me about their plants and animals."

They replied, "We were met by the King and Queen of Punt, who indicated that they came in peace to greet us. The queen was riding on a donkey, because she was so fat she could not walk. The people wore their hair plaited in a long tail, which hung down in the back. The men wore pointed beards. Everybody was dressed in a simple shirt. Their conical houses were made of reeds and were elevated on poles, so that a ladder was needed to enter the door. Donkeys and short-horned cows milled around the village. The land was lush with tropical plants and palms. There were terraces of myrrh trees."

"How did the trading go?" Hatshepsut asked.

"For one thing, it was mostly done in silence," explained the ship captains, "for we could not speak or understand each other's language. We put up tables on the beach and laid out our wares, such as beads, small statues, copper, turquoise and gold jewelry, and weapons. When everybody was satisfied with the trading, we ushered their king and queen and the elders into a tent, where we had prepared a feast of the specialties of Egypt for them."

---

50   A natural amalgam of silver and gold
51   Erman, 514.

"Good," exclaimed Hatshepsut. "Very well done. You are my heroes, and you shall be rewarded. Now let the festivities begin!"[52]

Hatshepsut's limbs were "fragrant as the dew of the gods with ointment and myrrh."[53] She shared the treasures with Amun by planting many of the myrrh trees in the temple garden. Hatshepsut thanked the god for a successful mission .

She said, "I have made a Punt in his garden, just as he commanded me."[54] In this way, Hatshepsut demonstrated to Thutmose III that the first fruits and spoils of every expedition, whether of war or trade, were to be given to Amun. The rest of the myrrh trees, she planted in the lovely, first-level gardens at her mortuary temple.

Though Hatshepsut accomplished much in her reign, the expedition to Punt stood out in the imagination of her people. Ineni, the famous court official who had served and outlived three pharaohs, used nautical terms when he wrote of Hatshepsut, his former pupil.

"Egypt was made to labor with bowed head to her, the excellent seed of the god—bow rope of the South, stern rope of the Northland is she, the mistress of command, whose plans are excellent."[55]

---

52 On the walls of her Memorial Temple, on the second level, there are detailed paintings that commemorate the expedition to Punt, including the parade of exotic cargo, and the king and corpulent queen with her donkey. The poor woman probably suffered from a disease that is still prevalent among African women, a disease that causes gross swelling in various parts of the body.
53 *Ancient Egypt, Discovering its Splendors*, 223.
54 *Ancient Egypt*, 223.
55 *Ancient Egypt, Dicovering Its Splendors*, 223.

Memphis
1467 BC

After the successful expedition to Punt, Hatshepsut spent as much time with Thutmose III as she could. Whenever he wasn't in classes, she had him accompany her on her rounds of duties as pharaoh. She realized that in less than two years, he would be gone to the House of Wisdom in On. The three years of higher education would be followed by three years of military training. Then, if she felt he was ready, she would make him an officer in her army and he could gain military experience by going on campaigns for her.

In the meantime, there was so much for him to learn. Actually, she was just giving him an introduction to life as a pharaoh. Her plan was that when he was older, in his early twenties, between military campaigns she would give him more in-depth instructions in the various aspects of the pharaoh's responsibilities. There were domestic, as well as foreign areas of concern. In Egypt, Thutmose III would need to be acquainted with the court system. He was already planning to study law at the House of Wisdom, at Hatshepsut's urging.

Now she was planning a tour of the kingdom and wanted Thutmose to go along.

"You summoned, Mother?" asked Thutmose as he stood before Hatshepsut. He was wearing only a kilt and sandals, having come directly from a wrestling match with friends.

Hatshepsut looked at her stepson with his bronzed, muscular chest, glistening with perspiration, and she couldn't help contrasting him with his pale, sickly father, long deceased.

"Yes, I called you," Hatshepsut told Thutmose. "I need you to get ready, as we are leaving on a long trip tomorrow."

"But, Mother, I have plans," he stated.

Hatshepsut was used to Thutmose III making his own plans. She knew that once he made up his mind, he did not like to be deterred from his course.

"Thutmose," she said, "this trip is important. Soon you will be going away to school. I want to make use of this time to give you an overview of the kingdom and your duties as future pharaoh."

"But why do I have to go with you, Mother? Can't you just tell me?"

"Thutmose, I know you are a good listener. Yes, I could tell you, but it would not be as comprehensive. I want you to experience the various aspects of the kingdom first hand. Besides, it is important for you to be seen by the people, so they can be assured of their future pharaoh. Of course, you already are pharaoh, in a way, as my co-regent. All the more reason why you should be at my side on this tour."

"What about next week? Could we leave then instead?" asked Thutmose, now trying to negotiate with his mother.

"Thutmose, do you realize the extent of the preparation I've had to make to get time away in my busy schedule?" said Hatshepsut, annoyed by his persistence. Then she softened as she noted his expression of disappointment.

"Look, Thutmose, I realize you are reluctant to leave your friends for so long, so I have planned a special treat for you if you give me your full cooperation during this trip."

"What kind of treat?" he asked, intrigued.

"A chariot race," declared Hatshepsut.

"A chariot race!" exclaimed Thutmose. He heard that they had chariot races in other countries, but he had never seen one.

"Yes," said Hatshepsut. "Normally, we use our horses and chariots only for serious purposes, like defending the country, not for entertainment. But I have made an exception. I have arranged for a one-time event—a chariot race just for you and your friends. Now, what do you say? Do I have your cooperation?"

"You do!" said Thutmose, now grinning from ear to ear. He could hardly wait to tell his friends.

* * * * *

Pharaoh Hatshepsut's entourage, including her co-regent, departed in the royal bark the following day. Fortunately, the sites Hatshepsut wanted to show Thutmose were situated along Egypt's major highway, the Nile.

As future pharaoh, Thutmose would need to be apprised of the ongoing needs of the common people, the *rekyt* as Hatshepsut called them, for they were as numerous as the delta marsh birds, the lapwings or *rekyt*. Agriculture, which included the canals and general irrigation systems, concerned these people who provided food for all of Egypt. In times of good floods, the granaries would need to be stocked to supply food in times of poor floods. The 20 percent tax for Pharaoh must be collected. Any attempts by tax collectors to skim off the top of these revenues must be prevented. The transportation system was important too.

"That canal that Senusret built for boats to circumvent the rapids at the first cataract of the Nile is always getting clogged up, so be sure to keep it clear," Hatshepsut told Thutmose III. She also informed him that she had reinstated the workers labor commission, which tended to the needs of the workers, especially in the limestone, granite and alabaster quarries and the copper, turquoise, gold, and galena mines. Thutmose gave Hatshepsut his full attention as she explained about the workers, but as they moved from site to site, he wondered what his friends were doing. Then he would distract himself with thoughts of the chariot race to come.

"Brickyards are included," Hatshepsut was saying. "Many of the Hebrews work at brick making. We don't need an uprising from any workers," she added. "The best way to prevent that is to treat them well. After all, we treat our horses well, feeding them, seeing to their health needs, and not running them into the ground. Why should we not treat our slaves well also? They are our possessions too, and besides that, they are human beings, whom Amun has formed. I believe he will withhold his blessings and protection from us if we mistreat them," she warned.

As Hatshepsut and Thutmose stood in the Valley of the Kings, she emphasized maintaining good security in important places. "The tombs of our ancestors must be guarded against robbery," she told him. "It is important to pay the artisans in the workers' village in a timely manner for their work, so as to prevent the temptation to rob the tombs."

At Karnak, Thutmose's interest was aroused as he reviewed the building projects in progress. "When I am pharaoh," he said, "I will erect a magnificent building here, and I will have my own obelisk too."

"Thutmose," said Hatshepsut, "I know it is more enjoyable to build new buildings, than to repair the old, but we must maintain our existing structures. I have started a project to repair the public buildings, monuments, and temples. Look, already your grandfather's hypostyle hall is in need of repair."

Then she thought of another concern that might escape his attention if he were involved in more exciting projects. "Another thing," she said, "Make sure there are enough scribes being trained, as we need them in all areas of our life so as to keep good records."

"Now, Thutmose," said Hatshepsut, "I know you have received excellent instructions from the priests on the religious duties of the pharaoh at the ceremonies and festivals. The priests officiate at over sixty each year, and you won't need to be present at all of them, of course. However, I do want to encourage you to bring your daily offerings and prayers to Amun in the palace chapel. As pharaoh of Egypt you will need his divine help and blessings."

On the way home to Memphis, Hatshepsut discussed foreign affairs. She cautioned Thutmose III to carefully review the trade contracts and peace treaties with foreign nations. She stressed the importance of monitoring the tribute countries on a regular basis.

"They will need your visits to remind them of whom they serve," she said. Hatshepsut barely touched on military concerns, because he would receive detailed instructions in his military training. She simply mentioned the contrast between the two theaters of war, Asia and Nubia.

"Remember the rich resources of gold in Nubia," she said. "Maintain a viceroy there, and be sure you have good Nubian representation in the royal court. The tribal rulers there are prone to rebellion," she continued. "As for the Asians, they are too far away to keep them completely subjugated, especially if they combine forces against us. Therefore, we have various policies for maintaining those nations in a tributary allegiance to us. We train their future rulers as princes in the palace school and sometimes accept their princesses in marriage. From time to time, however, war is necessary to maintain our own security."

Thutmose thought how exciting it would be to drive his chariot into battle in those exotic places. Then he thought of the chariot race he would soon enjoy, and he wished he could will the bark to sail faster.

Ineni was right when he noted that Hatshepsut made excellent plans. Moreover, she followed her plans to successful completion. Her successor was well-prepared for the position of pharaoh.[56] During her protégé's

---

56   Thutmose III is considered by present-day historians, to be one of the great Pharaohs of Egypt. He has been admired for his excellent administration of the nation, as well as for his military genius.

years at the House of Wisdom and in military training, Hatshepsut built new structures, besides repairing the old. She began to erect a beautiful sanctuary at Karnak called the Red Chapel, named for the color of the quartzite stone used in construction. She also started work on an obelisk to commemorate her accomplishments.[57] On various structures at Karnak, and elsewhere, her stepson, Thutmose III, was depicted also as pharaoh, standing by her side, or receiving honors from the gods, particularly Amun. Hatshepsut, herself, was often depicted as a male king, wearing the nemes crown with full ureaus, the *shendyt* kilt, and the false beard.

Occasionally the "she-king" actually appeared in public thus arrayed, in order to reassert her authority to rule. When she did don the false beard, she remembered Senmut's remarks to her and his laughter.

Now she could almost hear him say, "My love, why would you cover that pretty chin?"

---

57 Hatshepsut's obelisk still stands at Karnak.

The Desert
1465 BC

Moses was in the desert, tending the family flocks with Hobab. They were far from base camp and had been out about a week. As they sat by the campfire one night, Hobab was telling Moses about some interesting places he had explored.

"One such area is about halfway between the Red Sea's the Gulf of Aqaba and the Dead Sea," he said.

He described a narrow canyon of light red rock that opens up after about an hour's walk.

"If you look closely at the two sides of the canyon in the narrow part, it looks like they could be fit together, because the patterns in the two sides match.[58]

"Do you know what I mean, Moses?" Hobab asked.

"You mean they might have been one rock that split?" asked Moses.

"Exactly. The main thing to remember," he warned, "is that you don't want to be in that narrow canyon during the rainy season when it can flood. The walls are so sheer and steep, that there would be no place to escape."

"How far is that from here?" Moses asked.

"About a week of walking; we are on the edge of the Edomite country, but they don't usually bother a single traveler or two, unless they decide that they are spies and then—" he paused, ominously.

"Stop right there," interrupted Moses, "None of your horror stories just before bed!"

---

[58] Siq of Petra

After his brother-in-law was asleep, Moses lay quietly, looking at the stars. He had offered to take the first watch and keep the fires going. The flock was huddled in a protective bundle of wool and hair, with the dogs spaced at intervals, their ears alert for any sound of a wild animal. When Hobab was telling about the area around the narrow canyon, Moses realized that would be close to Canaan, the land of promise. His father, Amran, had talked about the promise given to Abraham by God. It was at the same time Abraham was promised a son at the age of ninety-nine.

God also told Abraham that his descendants would go down into Egypt, where they would remain for about four hundred years. Eventually they would become slaves[59] but God would punish the nation that mistreated them, and the oppressed people would be brought out to the land of Canaan. By Moses's calculations, when he was at the House of Wisdom, it should be getting close to four hundred years. He hoped he didn't miss the big event while he was living with the Midianites.

The next morning, Moses asked Hobab if it was possible to see Canaan from the area he talked about.

"Here's what you do," explained Hobab. "When you get through the narrow red canyon I was telling you about, you turn toward your left hand and go straight until you see white cliffs. Not far from there, about a three-hour walk, is a mountain, which is easy to climb. From the top of the mountain, you can see the land all around in every direction. To the northwest, you can see the southern edge of Canaan. A little further west from the mountain, there are great springs and a wide grazing area. There were nomadic settlements along the way when I came through that area, so I was able to buy provisions to supplement my own."

Hobab was getting enthusiastic now, as he could see Moses's growing interest in such an adventure.

So he continued, "I think we should take the basic foods and, of course, water. We can take our bows and hunt for small game. Surely our family could watch the flocks while we are gone."

Moses asked how long he thought the trip would take.

"Probably about a month," he replied. "We would want to rest a few days on the other side of the rock canyon before turning back. It just depends on the weather. If we should run into a *Khamsin* in the desert, we would have to stop."

Moses knew about the *Khamsin*, those biting cold winds that could come down suddenly from the mountains. When they hit the hot desert

---

59   After Joseph's time

air, a whirling, blinding blast of sand would result. It would become so dark that you could not see your way even a few steps ahead.

Moses knew he would not really get to see Canaan, but just to be that close would be amazing. Zipporah would probably not like him going away that long. They were getting along better these days, but she always had so much for him to do. He thought about the trip and felt he was due for a little adventure. He would get everything caught up. If Jethro approved of Hobab and Moses going on the trip, he would go.

Memphis
1461–1459 BC

Hatshepsut saw that Thutmose III was ready to go on military campaigns after his training. His excellent performance in battle prompted her to make him her general. She thought of her father, Thutmose I, the original Pharaoh General.

"Your grandfather would have been so proud of you," she said.

After the third campaign of Thutmose III, Hatshepsut told him, "You have proved to me that you can lead an army. Now you must prove that you can produce an heir. It is time for you to consider taking a wife, Thutmose."

"Mother, I am so fully occupied with all the responsibilities you've placed on me. How am I to find a wife too? I don't want just anyone. She would have to be lovely to look at as well as wonderful to be with."

"Fine, my son. Then I shall take on the responsibility of finding you a suitable wife, with your approval, of course."

"Yes, Mother, go to it. Let us see who you come up with," said Thutmose, laughing now.

The Desert
1460 BC

For five years, the adventure that Moses and Hobab had talked about was put off. There was always something that stood in the way of their month-long getaway—something to be done first or a wedding, or birth or skirmish at a well or a burial that could not be missed. Finally, they were on their way.

As they crossed the red sands of Wadi Rum, marveling at the majestic jebels[60] rising against the blue sky, Moses felt every weight drop from his shoulders.

"Thank you, Adonai, for this precious gift, this respite from the daily toils and cares of my life."

As much as Moses enjoyed the venture with Hobab, the highlight of this trip was the contact that was made with a passing caravan, which provided him with news from Egypt.

"What do you know of Egypt?" Moses asked. "Who is pharaoh now?"

Moses could understand most of what the traveler was saying, and Hobab filled in the rest.

"A lady pharaoh rules, now," replied the caravan leader.

"Oh, it has to be Hatshepsut!" Moses exclaimed. "She made it—she did it!" He clapped Hobab on the shoulder.

"Is her name Hatshepsut?" he asked the leader.

"That sounds right. I just remember it started with 'Hat," he said.

"Hat," Moses repeated. "My little sister, Hat, is the mighty Pharoah of Egypt!"

---

60   Stone crags.

"She's mighty, for sure," remarked the leader. "We hear that she has a general as her strong right arm. They call him pharaoh too," he said, now curious as to what Moses's reaction would be.

"A general pharaoh?" puzzled Moses. "That couldn't be Thutmose II. Could it be that she had a son after I left?"

Calculating the time lapse, Moses said, "It could be. He would be in his early twenties by now."

"Do you remember his name?" he asked the caravan leader.

"No, they just call him *the general*. I don't even know if he is a general, but they say he wins every battle he fights and he leads the army, so that's what they call him."

Moses gave the man a gold coin for sharing information, and the caravan went on its way. He was thoughtful now. What did this news mean for him? Could he go back?

"Huh?" Moses asked. Hobab was asking him a question.

"Would you want to leave us now?" he asked. "To go back to Egypt, I mean?"

"I don't know, Hobab. That's what I'm wondering about. I'd like to see the pharaoh. You see I was raised with her."

"Is she the same 'Hat' of your stories?"

"She's the one," said Moses. "But what I'm trying to figure out, is the identity of the pharaoh general whom the caravan leader was talking about. He would have to be the son of Thutmose II, the man who wanted to kill me. There is enough of a chance that he told his son about me—"

"To make it unsafe for you return to Egypt?" Hobab said, finishing Moses's sentence.

"Yes," answered Moses.

"Good," replied Hobab. "Well, I mean, I don't want you to go back, but I suppose you would like to see your family."

"Yes," said Moses. "I would at least like to make a visit." Then he added sadly, "But that's not going to happen."

Hobab left Moses alone with his thoughts. Moses thought about his Hebrew family. *I'll probably never see them again.* His heart was heavy, so he prayed for his family. Then he prayed for his little sister, now the mighty pharaoh. How he wished he could see her and congratulate her.

"See," he would say, "I told you that you would be pharaoh someday."

Now that day had come and he couldn't even see it. He had done it to himself, thinking he could save the Hebrews with his own strength.

Actually, he didn't remember even thinking. He had just acted out of anger. How foolish! He could see that now—one man against Egypt? No one but God could save the Hebrews. God had promised to deliver them, and Moses wondered how he would do that.

Thebes
1459 BC

Hatshepsut had searched far and wide for a suitable mate for Thutmose III. One day, as she was getting ready to meet another young woman who was to be presented to her at the palace, she looked at herself in the mirror.

"I'm getting old," she said to her faithful nurse, who murmured assurances.

"No," said Hatshepsut, in honest self-assessment, "I'm old and I'm fat."

She put her hands on her thickened waist. "I used to have such a tiny waist," she said, wistfully. Then she shook off her reminiscence, with a laugh. "It must be all these little sylph-like beauties I'm looking at. Oh well, at least I'm not as fat as the queen of Punt," she said. With that remark, she and her nurse had a good laugh.

Hatshepsut took her seat on the throne, and the latest applicant for the position of Great Royal Wife was ushered in.

"Meryetre Hatshepsut, Your Majesty," announced the Royal guard.

Pharaoh took one glance at the gorgeous maiden standing before her and was certain she was beholding the most beautiful woman in all of Egypt. Her petite frame featured a tiny waist, full breasts, and hips that Hatshepsut guessed were just wide enough to give birth to a healthy child. Meryetre had dark, flowing hair that reached halfway down her back and long dark eyelashes that fringed her almond-shaped eyes, which were the color of amethyst. Her facial features were fine and perfectly formed, including her full rosy lips.

Oh my, thought Hatshepsut, *she is like an exquisite doll and just the right size for my handsome son.* Thutmose III was slightly over five feet tall. Hatshepsut noted that when the girl smiled, she revealed even, pearly white teeth.

Dear me, thought Hatshepsut, *I feel like I'm judging a horse!*

Even so, she had been drawn to Meryetre, and she didn't think it was only the name. Her parents, who were a nobleman and his lady, had named their daughter Meryetre Hatshepsut after two royal women they had admired: Hatshepsut's Aunt Meryet and Pharaoh Hatshepsut herself.

Queen Meryet's full name, Meryetamun, contained the name of the god Amun, whereas Meryetre's name ended with the name of the sun aspect of Amun, the god Re. The latter name seemed to fit the girl, Hatshepsut thought. She seemed to have a cheerful, sunny attitude. Hatshepsut already liked her easy, warm laugh. She talked with the girl briefly and then thanked her for coming.

In order to get to know her better, Hatshepsut arranged to see Meryetre at her home with her parents, who were awestruck to have the great Pharaoh Hatshepsut as their guest. The evening went well, and Hatshepsut was pleased with the girl's good breeding and the respect she showed her parents.

Soon after the home visit, Hatshepsut gave a dinner party at the palace at Thebes for all the nobles and their ladies, as well as their adult children. Of course, Meryetre attended with her parents. It was a lively party, with music and dancing for entertainment. Hatshepsut noticed that Meryetre appeared to be elegant, yet friendly and warm as she mingled with the other guests. She was showing an interest in them and drawing them out. The others seemed to enjoy her amusing comments, which were never at the expense of anyone else.

Thutmose was excited about Meryetre, and after all the guests had left the palace, he wanted to discuss her with Hatshepsut. He had observed many good things about the girl, as well as her beauty, of course.

Finally he said, as he took yet another sip of wine, "Well done, Mother, you have found the right girl for me."

"Hold on, Thutmose, Meryetre is not like that wine you are enjoying, which you know you want more of after a taste."

"But, Mother," he said, "I am a man who knows what he wants. It doesn't take me that long to make a decision."

"Well, it should when it comes to a life partner. Remember, she would be the Great Royal Wife, the Queen of Egypt."

"But I already know I want her, Mother. Why are you being difficult about this?" he asked, puzzled. After all, Meryetre had been his mother's choice, and he reminded her of that.

She replied, "That's just it, Thutmose, your wife must be your choice, too."

Then she looked at him hesitantly and said, "I haven't said much about the marriage of your father and me. You see, we were forced to marry, and our marriage was not a happy one, although I tried to be a good wife to him. In his final illness, it was me he wanted, because he knew I would be kind to him. So you see, I didn't have a choice, but you do. You must be sure Meryetre is the right one for you."

"All right, Mother. What do you want me to do? What will convince you that I am making my own choice?"

Hatshepsut replied, "Spend the next month talking with her. Walk with her in the palace gardens. Take the royal bark out on the Nile for the day, now and then. Take her to see my mortuary temple across the Nile. Walk among the myrrh trees in the gardens. Sit on the edge of the pools on the second level and dip your legs in the cool water. Take a basket of food and wine along."

"Mother, that is quite a plan for lovers. One would almost think you had enjoyed such pleasures yourself," he teased.

Hatshepsut smiled and told him, "It is late, time for sleep. We will make arrangements tomorrow."

THEBES
1459 BC

After a month of courtship, Thutmose wanted more than ever to marry Meryetre Hatshepsut. Before their wedding day, Hatshepsut took him aside for a private talk.

"Thutmose," she said, "I know you are a passionate man. As you know, many kings and nobles keep a harem. Both your father and your grandfather did so. I have learned that Meryetre's father also has a harem. Yet people say that he and her mother are happy together, and they appear to love each other, at least at the times I've been able to observe them."

"What are you getting at, Mother," Thutmose asked her, impatient to complete his own preparations for the wedding.

She continued, "I am thinking that Meryetre may expect that you will keep a harem too. That is your choice, Thutmose. I want you to know that. You may also be given royal women from foreign lands to seal good relations with those countries. Their rulers will expect you to take their daughters as wives. However, they must only be side-wives to you. Meryetre must always come first in the kingdom, in the palace, and in your bed. You must see to her desires and needs first. You are a man of boundless energy. I would be surprised if one woman could satisfy you. Just remember my words. Do not neglect your Great Royal Wife. Be patient, and she will present you with an heir."

"Is that all, Mother?" asked Thutmose. "I don't want to be disrespectful, but I really have a lot to do."

As he was leaving the chamber, he looked back at her, and said, "Thank you, Mother. I do appreciate your advice, but all I want is Meryetre."

Hatshepsut smiled. She knew her stepson better than he knew himself.

THEBES
1458 BC

Shortly after the royal wedding, Thutmose left his new bride to go on another war campaign, his seventh so far. He came home to find his stepmother very ill. Hatshepsut was suffering with an infection, resulting from an abscessed tooth. She had always loved the Egyptian bread, sweetened with dates and honey, but all the years of crunching on fine grains of sand embedded in the bread had gradually worn down the enamel on her teeth, leaving them open to decay and infection. Hatshepsut's resistance to this latest assault on her body was low, because of several chronic diseases she had.[61] The doctors had done everything they could. She knew she was dying, so she summoned her stepson and his wife to her bedside.

"I'm about to travel to the afterlife," she told them. Looking at Thutmose, she said, sadly, "I don't know why Amun is taking me now. I haven't finished the sanctuary of the Red Chapel at Karnak."

"Mother," he assured her, "you have made excellent plans. I will follow them and complete the chapel for you."

"Thank you, Son," she said weakly.

Then she turned to Meryetre. "I've prayed to Amun, that he will bless you. I know you will have a son, but I will not see him. You have been a good wife to my son as I knew you would be."

Meryetre was now sobbing.

Hatshepsut turned to Thutmose, "My son, you will be such a good ruler. Remember, when you have your heir, prepare him well, as I have tried to prepare you."

---

61 Egyptologists suspect diabetes and bone cancer based on the CT scans taken of her mummy.

Thutmose tried to speak, but he choked up and could not continue. Instead, he squeezed her hand and, bending down, kissed her gently on her forehead.

"Good-bye, Mother," he managed to whisper.

"Amun?" murmured Hatshepsut. Then as her eyes widened, she breathed, "Adonai."

Hatshepsut was only fifty years old when she died, but when she lived, she was larger than life. She accomplished what no other woman had done before her: she ruled the most powerful, advanced civilization in the world, successfully, for twenty years. Hatshepsut had cared about her people, and they had responded to her with their allegiance. Her monuments held many inscriptions in which she referred to the rekhyt or common people. She spoke of *my rekhyt* and asked for approval of the rekhyt.

She also cared about how people would view her in future generations. On her obelisk, at Karnak, was the touching inscription: "Now my heart turns this way and that as I think about what people will say—those who see my monuments in years to come and who shall speak of what I have done."[62]

---

62 *National Geographic*, April 2009, 96.

THEBES
1458 BC

The coronation of Pharaoh Thutmose III, took place about six months after Hatshepsut's death. The affair was as lavish as Hatshepsut's coronation had been. However, the Ceremony of Min, associated with the coronation, was celebrated with a different emphasis by Thutmose III.

As in Hatshepsut's Ceremony of Min, the god of fertility was recognized as important in an agricultural country, but Thutmose emphasized that the mummy god with the erect penis also symbolized sexual potency. He had a stele made, depicting himself standing before the god, whose sexual member reached across to the pharaoh like a phallic handshake.

He also had a goblet engraved with the Min figure.[63] It seemed that Thutmose III, who valued these symbols of virility, was greatly hoping for an heir. However, his own part in producing that heir had to be postponed, because the situation in Asia was heating up, and Pharaoh Thutmose had to ride swiftly to battle in his war chariot.

---

63   Both the stele and the goblet are in existence today.

Megiddo
1457 BC

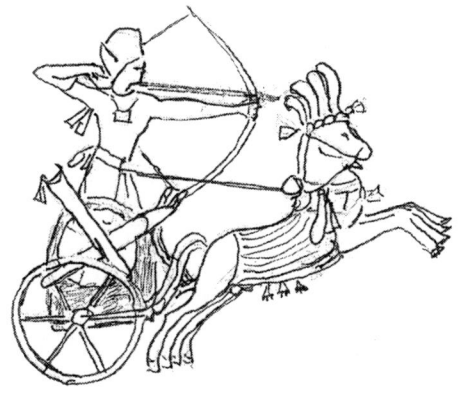

Within months after Thutmose III acceded to the throne at the age of twenty-four, the army of Egypt marched into Asia with the pharaoh at the head. Palestine and Syria consisted of a loosely held group of city states that had been subjugated by Thutmose I. Now these city states, at the instigation of the King of Kadesh, had formed a coalition to revolt against the domination of Egypt. They had gathered their armies at Megiddo, a city elevated above the plain of Esdraelon.[64] Megiddo commanded the pass through the Carmel ridge on the main road to the upper Euphrates.

Though his officers urged a less dangerous route, Thutmose, in his gilded chariot, bravely charged through the narrow pass. Not anticipating such a daring move, the enemy had not posted a single guard on the pass. Thutmose led his army through, emerging in open territory in the plain below the city. The Egyptians overwhelmed the enemy, who fled to the city, abandoning their horses so that they could scramble up the walls. That was a boon to the Egyptians, and they took the horses and chariots for themselves. Thutmose laid siege to the city for seven long months, finally taking the city and more loot. A battle scribe recorded the spoil: 340 prisoners, 2041 mares, 191 foals, 6 stallions, 924 chariots, 200 suits of armor, 502 bows, 7 tent poles wrought with silver, about 24,000 head of cattle and other livestock, plus over 100,000 bushels of grain, standing ready for harvest in the fields.[65]

Hard on the heels of Megiddo, Thutmose III marched his army into southern Lebanon, taking more cities and building a fort before returning

---

64 The biblical Armageddon.
65 *Ancient Egypt, Discovering its Splendor*, 224

to Thebes. The Lebanon expedition added 175 days to the lengthy campaign.

After the battle, while his lovely wife and his captured harem beauties awaited his attention, Thutmose gave his first adoration to Amun. Records and pictures on temple walls at Karnak attested to his copious gifts and his outpouring of gratitude to his god for helping him triumph over Egypt's enemies.

After his devotion at the temple, Thutmose called his nobles and courtiers together for a dinner to celebrate the victories. The oil lamps were lit. Dish after dish of Egyptian specialties were served to the guests. The talk became louder and more effusive as the wine flowed. Everyone wanted to hear about the campaign. With great charisma, Thutmose told highlights of the battle, often laced with amusing incidents, such as the clutching of the clothes of the escaping enemy as comrades pulled them up the battlements. Meryetre listened along with the rest, but she was also searching for a clue. Would he be coming to her bed tonight, or would he want to sample the prize of his spoils, those three Syrian maidens he had captured? Then she saw it—their signal. Her husband had picked up his special goblet and was fingering its bowl. Yes! He was smiling at her, as he rubbed the part of the engraving that signaled he wanted her. She would be the one to welcome him home.

Thebes
1457–1455 BC

After having quashed the revolt so soundly, Thutmose III was able to focus on affairs at home for two years. However, he did make an appearance in Syria and Palestine every year, at the end of the rainy season there. The reputation Pharaoh had made at Megiddo spared him any aggressive action during this time. He spent more time with Meryetre, and she became pregnant with their first child, which they hoped would be the son that Hatshepsut had predicted.

Thutmose fulfilled his promise to her to finish building the Red Chapel at Karnak, just as she had completed her father's unfinished construction projects. He also reformed the government by appointing two viziers, one for Memphis and one for Thebes, whereas there had been only one. Memphis and Thebes were over three hundred miles apart. It made sense to have a top official in each place. Moreover, Thutmose anticipated his future absences for war campaigns and wanted to be sure that government affairs were administered well at home.

In the second year after his return, a healthy son was born to Thutmose III and Meryetre Hatshepsut with great joy and celebration. Thutmose decided to name his son *Ahmose II* after the founder of the New Kingdom and the Eighteenth Dynasty of Egypt. Thutmose thought would go down the line, naming his second son, *Amenhotep II*, and his third son, should he have one, *Thutmose IV*. Shortly after the birth of his son, Pharaoh Thutmose was off to war again.

Memphis
1455–1447 BC

Year after year, for nine years, Thutmose III conducted war campaigns, most of them in Asia. He moved his family to his Memphis palace, to be nearer the Asian theater of war. He assured Meryetre that she could make trips to Thebes, where her family lived, whenever she wished, as long as she was in Memphis to welcome him home from battle. He would send messengers ahead to announce his return home. His wife was happy to oblige her husband whom she adored.

Thutmose III liked to enjoy his harem after his campaigns, especially when he had added several beauties to his collection. When the women were prepared by fragrant oil massages, so that their pores exuded the scent of myrrh or lotus blossoms, and they had been bedecked in their finest robes and jewelry, they were brought for inspection to the harem matron. Finally, they were ready to be presented to the pharaoh for his pleasure.

He didn't always keep the women for himself. Occasionally he would make a special gift of one of them to a deserving noble or officer of his army. Often the happy recipient would tell him later, "That girl you gave me—whoa! What a frisky filly she is!" Pharaoh would smile and wonder fleetingly if he should have kept her for himself. But he would reassure himself with thoughts of Meryetre. *No one could be as frisky as she is*, thought Thutmose.

The Great Royal Wife was aware of her husband's sexual appetite and was not troubled, because he had heeded the advice of Hatshepsut. Whenever he came home from an expedition, he would make love to his Queen exclusively for many days. He brought her exquisite gifts and treated her as though she was the best jewel in his crown, his own special love. And she was; Thutmose believed that to be true and held Meryetre in his mind and heart.

Thutmose loved to talk with Meryetre, because she always listened with sincere interest to everything he told her about his exploits just as Hatshepsut did when she was alive. His mother had always wanted a full report of his campaigns, with all the nuances included. Now, he would tell Queen Meryetre both the exciting and the mundane details; she wanted to be able to picture his life when he was away from her, she said. He would discuss political issues with her also. She helped him weigh his options when he needed to make a decision, and she helped him slow his racing thoughts so he could think more clearly.

There was one subject that Thutmose wisely never talked about to Meryetre. That was, the topic of his sexual exploits at home or away. Before her marriage, Meryetre's mother had told her, "The pharaoh is a virile man with strong passions. Undoubtedly, he will have a harem. You must never give the slightest indication that you object to his harem visits, and you should never question him about it. Remember, there will be only one Great Royal Wife, and that will be you!"

Therefore, this Great Royal Wife viewed that part of her husband's life to be as natural as his need for food. He was always eager to be in her arms, and that was all that mattered to her. Thutmose could sense when Meryetre was ready for a rest, and then he would go to enjoy the women of his harem. Besides the sex, he enjoyed their singing and playing of the harp and flute. The music and the fragrant oil massages they gave relaxed him when he found it difficult to unwind.

During the nine years of regular campaigns, there were two incidents from different battles that provided entertainment as Thutmose III recounted them to guests in his home. The first event involved the King of Kadesh, a persistent enemy of Egypt. The king, having noted that the Egyptian chariots were drawn by stallions, released a mare in their midst to cause a disruption in their ranks and upset the impending battle charge. The brave officer, Amunemheb, rising to the challenge, pursued the mare, slashing her with his sword. After the battle, he presented the mare's tail to Pharaoh.

When the laughter at the dinner table died down, the company clamored for the Gold of Valor to be awarded to Amunemheb for his quick and courageous action.

"Indeed," replied Thutmose, "I am at this time trying to decide the form of the award. The Gold of Valor was not merely a gold medal, but an expensive and elaborate piece of jewelry, such as only a king would wear or present to a worthy subject.

Thutmose told his distinguished guests, "I need your help, as the artisans have fashioned several equally magnificent pieces. I'm sure your advice would help me make the best decision."

The second incident was a ruse perpetuated on the enemy by the Egyptians. In order to capture the city of Joppa in Palestine, General Thutiy faked a surrender. Thutiy hid two hundred soldiers in the panniers used to carry heavy burdens on the backs of donkeys. Then, purporting to share booty with the city, the Egyptians entered the city gates. At a strategic moment, the soldiers burst from their hiding places and took over the city. This story was one that Thutmose III told with animation to his son, now eight years old, to the boy's great delight.

Thutmose remembered Hatshepsut's words, "Prepare him well to be pharaoh."

The Desert
1447 BC

Moses was tending the family flocks on the far side of the desert in the Sinai region, and he came to the mountain of God. There he saw a bush that was burning but was not consumed.

He thought to himself, *I will go over and see this strange sight—why the bush does not burn up.*

"Moses, Moses," came a voice from within the bush. Moses stopped in his tracks. Up until this time, Moses had prayed to Adonai, but now he was actually hearing the voice of Adonai. Moses was awestruck.

Trembling, he answered, "Here I am."

"Do not come any closer," said the voice. "Take off your sandals, for the place where you are standing is holy ground."

Then Moses heard a voice say, "I am the God of your father, the God of Abraham, the God of Isaac, and the God of Jacob."

At this, Moses hid his face, because he was afraid.

The Lord said, "I have indeed seen the misery of my people in Egypt. I have heard them crying out because of their slave drivers, and I am concerned about their suffering. So I have come down to rescue them from the hand of the Egyptians and to bring them up out of that land into a good and spacious land, into a land flowing with milk and honey. So now, go. I am sending you to Pharaoh to bring my people, the Israelites, out of Egypt."[66]

Moses asked God, "Who am I, that I should go to Pharaoh and bring the Israelites out of Egypt?"

---

66 Exodus 3:7–10.

God told Moses that he would be with him, and he would give Moses a sign that he had sent him. He told him that when he had brought the people out of Egypt, he would worship God on this mountain. Moses asked God what he should tell his people when they asked what God's name is.

God told him, "I Am Who I Am."

He told Moses, "Say that *I Am* sent you. Tell them the Lord [67], the God of your fathers, the God of Abraham, the God of Isaac, and the God of Jacob has sent me to you."

Then God told Moses to assemble the elders of Israel and tell them God has seen their misery and sent Moses to bring them up out of Egypt into the Promised Land. God said that the elders would listen to him, and they were to go to the king of Egypt and ask him to let them go for three days into the desert to sacrifice to their God.

He told Moses that the king would refuse, but that God would perform wonders so that the king would let the Israelites go.

Moses asked God, "What if they don't believe me?"

Then God gave Moses two signs to give them so they would believe. One sign was to throw his staff down and it would become a snake. The other was to put his hand in his robe, and when he took it out, it would be leprous. God would restore both his staff and his hand. God demonstrated the signs to Moses in the desert.

Then he told Moses, "If they don't believe the first two signs, give them a third. Take some water from the Nile and pour it on the dry ground. The water will become blood."

Moses pleaded, "Oh, Lord, I have never been eloquent. I am slow of speech and tongue."

The Lord said to him, "Who made your mouth, is it not I? Now go, I will help you speak and will teach you what to say."

But Moses said, "Oh, Lord, please send someone else to do it."

The Lord was angry at Moses's resistance. He said, "What about your brother, Aaron? I know he can speak well. He is already on his way to meet you, and his heart will be glad when he sees you. You shall speak to him, and he will speak for you. I will teach both of you what to say and do."

Moses was excited as he returned to Jethro. Aaron was coming! He hadn't seen Aaron in forty years.

Moses asked Jethro, "Let me go back to my own people in Egypt to see if any of them are still alive."

---

67 Adonai

Jethro said, "Go, and I wish you well."

God spoke to Moses in Midian and told him not to be afraid to return to Egypt, for the men who wanted to kill him, Pharaoh Thutmose II and his guards, were dead.

Moses packed up his wife, Zipporah, and his sons, Gershom and Eliezer, and put them on donkeys. Then he took the staff of God in his hand and set out for Egypt.

When they had gone a day's journey, they stopped at a lodging place. As they were still in Midian territory, a comfortable tent was made available to them. However, Moses was in trouble with God, because he had neglected a very important responsibility—to see that his second son was circumcised. This ritual signified that a male belonged to God and was usually carried out when the child was eight days old.

However, when Eliezer was born, Moses was so worried about Zipporah's state of mind that he hadn't circumcised his son. Later, Zipporah had reminded him several times, but Moses had resisted her because that was when they weren't getting along. Then Eliezer was grown, and Moses dreaded to do the procedure. But in putting off this important requirement of God, Moses was in disobedience, and God was angry with him. Zipporah was angry too.

"I told you to do it, but no, you didn't listen to me," she shouted at Moses, waking up both of their sons.

"What's wrong?" they asked.

Zipporah snatched a flint knife and a small copper pan from their sack of belongings.

"Hold his arms," she ordered Gershom.

Before Eliezer knew what was happening, she stripped off his loincloth, shoved the pan between his legs to catch the blood, and cut off his foreskin. Then she threw it at Moses feet.

"There it's done!" she exclaimed. "Surely, you are a bloody husband to me!"

Moses realized that Eliezer would be sore for several days, certainly too sore to walk, or ride a donkey. They would be safe here with their people. He arranged for an escort to accompany his family back to their home with Jethro so Moses could travel on and meet Aaron. He promised his family that he would come back this way for them when the Israelites left Egypt.

Moses realized his failure. Though he knew how it happened that he had neglected his duty to God and to his son, he knew there was really no excuse for it. He asked God to forgive him and make him worthy of the task ahead.

When Moses spotted Aaron walking beside his donkey, he ran to meet him. Aaron embraced Moses and kissed him. They met at the mountain of God. Moses told Aaron everything that the Lord had told him to say and about all the miraculous signs he had commanded him to perform.

As they traveled together toward Egypt, Moses asked about his parents. He was sad to hear that his mother had died.

"She was 110," Aaron said, "and she was still hoping to see you again." He added quickly as he saw Moses' tears, "She said to tell you, she would see you in paradise."

"She believed in the afterlife then?" asked Moses.

"Oh, yes," said Aaron. "More so as she got older."

Moses was almost afraid to ask about Amran. "And Father?" he asked.

"Father is going strong at 116," replied his brother. Then he laughed, thinking of his father. You should see him with Phinehas, his great grandson. He loves to play with him. Miriam worries about Father, but I tell her that Father enjoys his great-grandson, and it keeps him young to be around Phinehas.

"My oldest sons have no boys, so Phinehas, Eleazar's son, is Father's first great-grandson. I think Eleazar was born after you left Egypt, Moses. He married an Egyptian girl. Mother wasn't too happy about that, but it turned out she was Mother's favorite. Now tell me about your family."

Moses told his brother about Zipporah and his own sons. They laughed about the similarity of their son's names, Eleazar and Eliezer.

"It's difficult to believe it's been forty years," said Aaron. "But you are coming back to us at last, Moses. Father is full of joy that you are coming."

Moses was thoughtful. He supposed not everyone would be happy to see him back. He wondered what kind of reception he would get from Pharaoh.

Asia-Memphis
c 1447 BC

"I set the war cry of your Majesty throughout the Nine Bows."[68]

The words of Amun proclaimed Egypt's dominion over its known world—the Nine Bows—and hailed the conqueror, Thutmose III. He had led his army to challenge the powerful king of the Mitanni, who inhabited the area between the upper reaches of the Euphrates and the Tigris rivers. It was along these riverbanks that the Mitanni elite group, the Marya[69], loved to race their horses.[70]

The Mitanni were influenced by cultures farther east, such as India. They intoned magic incantations from the Rigveda in front of images of Mithras, the victorious goddess of light over darkness. They also worshiped at shrines to Ninurta, the war goddess. Egypt had shared common boundaries with the Mitanni since Thutmose I had pushed to the Euphrates on his war campaigns. The two powers were continually conducting raids on each other. Now, Thutmose III was riding to battle in an attempt to defeat the Mitanni.

Thutmose provided his army with boats to the coast of Lebanon. From there they continued overland. The most amazing part of the plan was that they hoisted the boats onto oxen-driven wagons, and dragged them all the way to the Euphrates in order to ferry the army across the river. What a sight that must have been—the plodding oxen towing the land-borne fleet,

---

68 The nine enemies of ancient Egypt.
69 Young warriors.
70 Hundreds of clay tablets have been found on equestrian matters—a veritable library of information on breeding, care and grooming, breaking of horses and racing, as well as regulations for operating horse stables.

followed by horses and chariots, marching soldiers with bows and spears, and a donkey train bearing provisions bringing up the rear.

Thutmose III triumphed over the Mitanni, who were willing to negotiate a peace settlement because the powerful Hittites were threatening them from the West. Thutmose accepted a sumptuous gift from the ruler—two beautiful daughters of the king of Mitanni. Then he erected a stele there to commemorate his victory. Before returning home with the Mitanni princesses, he allowed himself a respite: an elephant hunt in the nearby marshes. Amemenheb, trusted officer of Thutmose, was with him and wrote in his diary, "The Lord of the Two Lands hunted 120 elephants for their tusks."

Upon return from his campaign to Syria, Thutmose presented the first fruits of his victory to Amun as Hatshepsut had taught him to do. An inscription at Karnak recorded the gifts that Pharaoh gave to Amun: fields and gardens, exclusive plots of land overgrown with "sweet trees" or orchards, cattle, quantities of gold and silver, and lapis lazuli. In addition, Asiatic prisoners, at least 878 men and women, were to fill the granaries of the god, and spin and weave and till the ground. Finally, Thutmose III settled upon three of the conquered towns that had to pay tribute to the god. He also established additional sacrifices for the festival days.

At home in Memphis, a victory celebration was planned. It would include a large parade to honor the great warrior hero. On the eve of the public festivities, the pharaoh was enjoying an intimate dinner with Meryetre, his favorite nobles and their ladies, General Amemenheb, and the Vizier of Memphis.

Meryetre looked ravishing in the special gift Thutmose had brought her from Asia. Cascades of golden rosettes formed a stunning headdress that she wore over her long black hair. This gift, made of gold and precious stones, sparkled in the flickering lamp light.[71]

Pharaoh stood to make an announcement. "My Queen, my friends," he said, "for the first time ever, in Egypt, I am introducing chicken to the dinner table."

Then, as he clapped his hands, the servants came from both sides, bearing platters heaped with chicken, which had been cut in pieces and simmered in the most delectable spices until tender. The guests savored the tasty dish, and they cleaned the last bit of meat from the bones.

Thutmose pointed to the empty platters. "I think you like my treat just a bit."

---

71 Meryetre's magnificent headpiece was discovered in pieces by tomb robbers at Qurna in 1916. When reassembled for museum display, it weighed four and a half pounds.

The guests nodded their heads vigorously as they dipped their hands in the finger bowls.

As dessert and more wine were served, Thutmose began to tell his guests about the elephant hunt.

"Now, I don't know if you are aware of this," he said. "When an elephant roars he is warning you to back off, but when he charges, he does not give a warning first."

"So, here I am in the thick of the hunt," he continued, "and I have no idea this huge bull elephant is bearing down on me from behind. I was headed for the afterlife—no doubt about it. Then who should come to my rescue? My faithful General Amemenheb here," and Thutmose gestured toward him. "He came racing from the side and lopped off the elephant's trunk, even while the beast was attacking me. He saved my life! I would not be here to tell this tale, but for the bravery of my trusted friend, Amemenheb!"

All the guests rose to their feet with the king and queen and chanted, "Amemenheb! Amemenheb! Hail to Amemenheb!"

The pharaoh motioned everyone to sit down and again clapped his hands. Attendants entered the dining room with an inlaid jewelry chest.

Thutmose said, "I wanted you to have a close up view of the Gold of Valor piece, which I shall officially award to Amemenheb tomorrow in a special ceremony as part of the festivities. While I was honoring Amun in Thebes, my artisans were working day and night to complete the piece, and here it is."

With a flourish, Thutmose III motioned to the attendants to carry the splendid piece around the room for all the guests to see.

"Now, one more surprise before I call for the musicians and acrobats. I am formulating plans for a special expedition—to hunt the fierce rhinoceros in the upper regions of the Nile in Nubia. Who would like to go with me?"

As the room buzzed with animated talk of the anticipated hunt, Thutmose looked at his wife. The thought of her husband, battling such fierce horned beasts did not worry her in the least. To the contrary, it excited her. Thutmose could see the sparks in her eyes and the flush on her cheeks. Ah, he would have a wild time tonight with Meryetre. The Mitanni princesses would have to wait.

* * * * *

The following night, when the public festivities were over, Thutmose walked in the palace garden, unwinding after the long day of fanfare.

Who else has accomplished the great things I have done? he thought. *My grandfather, Thutmose I, went to the Euphrates, but I have gone beyond the Euphrates. He extended Egypt's southern boundary to the third cataract, but I have stretched it to the fourth cataract. I have a wife to match my passion, and the most beautiful women in the world to entertain me. My buildings are of the finest design and there will be more to come. My army is a mighty force, and I am the commander in chief. My heir will follow in my footsteps. Ahmose II will be even greater than Ahmose I. I am the most powerful man in the world. I am the mighty pharaoh, Lord of the Two Lands—King of the Nine Bows!*

If there were an Egyptian equivalent for the proverb "Pride goeth before a fall," Thutmose III was not aware of it, but he was about to experience it firsthand.

The Delta
1447 BC

Amran was overjoyed to see his son Moses. Moses embraced and kissed his father.

"Adonai has been gracious to me, Father, that I may see your face again," he said.

The family group around the dinner table represented four generations, as joining Amran, Moses, Aaron, and Miriam were Eleazar, his wife, and their son, Phinehas. Moses was reminded of former times around the same rough-hewn table when as a youth, a mere schoolboy, he talked of the ways of Adonai with his father. Only Jochebed was missing, but Moses could feel her presence even as Miriam bustled about serving hearty food, which they enjoyed after their long journey and spare rations.

That night, after visiting with his family, Moses went to bed early, but he tossed and turned.

What if Thutmose III realizes I'm the man who killed the Egyptian overseer? he thought. *Maybe I should change my name.*

Moses prayed, "Adonai, please banish from my mind that horrible scene with Pharaoh Thutmose II, when I pleaded for my people, to no avail, and please keep Aaron and me safe when we confront Thutmose III."

Then he remembered God's words to him, "Do not be afraid. I will be with you," and Moses drifted off to sleep.

In the morning, Amran said to Moses, "Let's go to the elders without delay, so that we may then go to Pharaoh as soon as possible."

Moses agreed, but told Aaron, "You do the talking, my brother. They know you and will be more likely to believe you."

So Moses and Aaron gathered all the elders of the Israelites together, and Aaron told them everything the Lord had said to Moses. They also performed the signs before the people and they believed Aaron and Moses. The elders were touched to hear that God had seen their misery and that he was concerned about them. They were filled with gratitude and bowed down and worshiped.

Memphis
1447 BC

At long last, after over four hundred years of oppression in Egypt, it was confrontation time.

Moses and Aaron had to wait a few days for an audience with Pharaoh Thutmose III.

When they appeared before the king, they said, "This is what the Lord, the God of Israel, says: 'Let my people go, so that they may hold a festival to me in the desert.'"

Pharaoh said, "Who is the Lord, that I should obey him and let Israel go? I do not know the Lord and I will not let Israel go."[72]

Moses and Aaron replied, "The God of the Hebrews has met with us. Now let us take a three-day journey into the desert to offer sacrifices to the Lord, our God, or he may strike us with plagues or with the sword."

This was a veiled threat of what was in store for Egypt if Pharaoh did not grant their request. Instead of granting permission, however, Pharaoh refused to let the people go.

"Moses and Aaron," he demanded, "why are you taking the people away from their labor? Get back to work!" Then he added, "Look, the people of the land are numerous, and you are stopping them from working!"

As soon as Moses and Aaron left, Pharaoh gave the order to the slave masters: "You are no longer to provide straw for the people to make bricks. Let them get their own straw, but do not reduce the quota of bricks they are expected to produce each day. They are lazy; that is why they say, 'Let us go and make a sacrifice to our God.' Make the work harder for them, so they won't pay attention to these lies."

---

[72] Exodus 5:2.

Later the Hebrew foremen, appointed by Pharaoh's slave masters, were beaten for not meeting the quota, so they brought their complaint to Pharaoh.

"We cannot do this," they told him. "It is not our fault, but the fault of your own people for not supplying us with straw!"

Pharaoh said, "Lazy! That's what you are, lazy! Now get to work! You will not be given straw, but you must still produce the same number of bricks as before."

Forgetting Hatshepsut's warning to treat the workers well lest Amun withhold his blessings, Thutmose III was following the ways of his father in piling an extra burden onto the backs of the Hebrews. Now the foremen knew they were in trouble. They had been given an impossible task. As they left Pharaoh, they came upon Moses and Aaron, who had been waiting for them.

The foreman said, "May the Lord look upon you and judge you, for you have made us a stench to Pharaoh and his officials. You have handed them a sword to kill us."

The mission was not going well at all. Moses was burdened with the people's plight, so he went to the Lord in prayer. "Oh, Lord, why have you brought trouble upon your people? Is this why you sent me? Ever since I went to Pharaoh to speak for you, he has brought trouble on this people, and you have not rescued your people at all."

The Lord answered Moses, "Now you will see what I will do to Pharaoh. Because of my mighty hand, he will let my people go. I appeared to Abraham, to Isaac, and to Jacob, but by my name *Lord*,[73] I did not make myself known to them."

Then God told Moses that he had heard the people groaning, and he was going to fulfill his promise to their fathers to give the people the land of Canaan. God told Moses what to say to the Israelites, who were struggling under an even heavier burden.

"Tell them that I will bring them out, and I will be their God and they will be my people. I will free them from slavery, and I will redeem them with mighty acts of judgment. Then they will know that I am the Lord who brought them out from under the yoke of the Egyptians. I am the Lord."

Moses reported this to the Israelites, but they would not listen because of their discouragement and cruel bondage.

---

73   The name *Lord* refers to the redemptive aspect of God, which would be experienced by the Israelites when they were delivered from Egypt. They would come to know God in a special way.

God told Moses, "Go and tell Pharaoh, king of Egypt, to let the Israelites go out of his country."

Moses replied, "If the Israelites will not listen to me, why would Pharaoh listen to me, since I speak with faltering lips?"

The Lord told Moses, "See, I have made you like God to Pharaoh, and your brother Aaron is your prophet. You are to say everything I tell you. When Pharaoh's heart is hardened, I will stretch out my mighty arm and multiply my miraculous wonders in Egypt. Pharaoh will resist you, but I will bring my people out."

And so the two elderly men[74] again went before the powerful Pharaoh Thutmose III, who at thirty-six was in the prime of life. No wonder the king questioned the authority of these men. He demanded they show him a sign.

Aaron threw down his staff and it became a snake. Pharaoh summoned his wise men and sorcerers, who were able to duplicate the miracle. However, when their staves became snakes, Moses's snake swallowed up their snakes. Yet Pharaoh's heart became hard, and he would not listen.

That night, when Thutmose talked with Meryetre about Moses and Aaron, she said, "Oh, why do you let those *sandramblers*[75] bother you? Here you are, the mighty pharaoh. It's only been a few weeks since your victory celebration, and you saw how the people admire you. Don't pay any attention to those troublemakers. Come now, let me take your mind off that nonsense."

As Thutmose took her in his arms, Meryetre smiled. He still had not been to visit his new side-wives!

The next morning, Pharaoh emerged from the palace with his officials to go down to the Nile to bathe. There, on the river bank, he found Moses and Aaron waiting for him.

What is that pesky pair doing here? he thought. *I haven't granted them an audience today.*

Moses said to Pharaoh, "The Lord, the God of the Hebrews, has sent me to say to you, 'Let my people go so that they may worship me in the desert.' But until now, you have not listened. Therefore, the Lord says, 'By this, you will know that I am the Lord.'"

Then Moses told Aaron to stretch his staff over the Nile, and it turned to blood. Some said the reddish brown color was from the sediment that washed down from the Ethiopian highlands at flood time. Others insisted

---

74 Moses was eighty and Aaron was eighty-three.
75 A perjorative term referring to nomads.

it was actual blood. One thing was certain, the waters became unfit to drink. Pharaoh did not get his bath that day as the water in every wooden bucket and every stone jar had turned to blood too. Every canal, stream, and pond was blood red.[76] The fish died, and the water stank. God had rendered judgment on the life-sustaining river Nile and its god, Hapi.

But Pharaoh would not listen. He turned from Moses and Aaron and went into his palace with his sorcerers, who had been able to produce bloody water also. That was not a difficult feat, as all the water was already tainted. The Egyptians desperately dug trenches alongside the Nile in order to get water that had been filtered through the sand layers along the bank. They were thus able to survive the first plague.

Seven days later, Moses and Aaron again approached Pharaoh and gave him the words of God, with a warning of another plague to come if he did not let the people go.

Aaron again stretched his staff over the waters of Egypt. The Nile teemed with frogs, which came up out of the river and went into the palace, into the pharaoh's bedchamber, and onto his bed. Then the frogs went into the houses of the officials and the people. Frogs were everywhere—in the kitchens, in the ovens, and in the kneading troughs. The magicians claimed they produced some of the frogs. The people didn't want to kill the frogs, because the little creature was believed to be the representation of the god Heket, who was credited with helping Egyptian women in childbirth.

Pharaoh summoned Moses and Aaron and said, "Pray to the Lord to take the frogs away from me and my people, and I will let your people go so they may offer sacrifice to the Lord."

Moses replied, "I leave to you the honor of setting the time for us to pray for the Lord to rid you of the frogs, except for those that remain in the Nile."

"Tomorrow," said Pharaoh.

The next day, Moses and Aaron prayed, and the frogs died. Dead frogs were stacked in heaps all over Egypt, and the land reeked with them. Still, as soon as the frogs were dead, Pharaoh broke his promise to let the people go.

As a result of the pharaoh's refusal, God sent a plague of gnats. When Aaron struck the ground with his staff, the dust became a swarm of gnats that spread across the land, coming upon men and animals alike.

The magicians said to Pharaoh, "This is the finger of God."

---

76 Ironically, Egyptians believed that the Nile was the bloodstream of Osiris.

But still the pharaoh would not heed the word of the Lord.

The fourth judgment God sent to plague Egypt was flies. During the end of flood season, flies were a common problem in Egypt. However, this plague was so severe that the people ran out of their usual remedy for fly stings—the fat of the woodpecker. Another more expensive remedy for both gnats and flies was called "the Phoenician remedy," as it was imported from Byblos. It is no wonder that flies proliferated with the mawkish water of standing ponds and all the dead frogs! The magicians were not able to produce either gnats or flies. With the fourth plague, God made a distinction between the Egyptians and the Israelites. There would be no flies in Goshen where most of the Hebrews lived. Pharaoh was told this, when Moses and Aaron warned him before the plague.

Thutmose summoned them, as people cried out for relief from the flies.

Pharaoh said, "Go, and sacrifice to your God, but do it here in Egypt."

Moses said, "That would not be right. The sacrifices we offer the Lord would be detestable to the Egyptians. We may incur their wrath. No, we must make a three-day journey into the desert to make our sacrifices."

Pharaoh replied, "I will let you go into the desert then, but you must not go far. Now pray for me."

Moses promised to pray and ask for relief from the flies, and he added, "Only be sure that Pharaoh does not act deceitfully again by not letting the people go."

The flies left; not a fly remained after Moses prayed. But this time also, Pharaoh hardened his heart.

The Lord sent Moses to Pharaoh again and told him to warn the King that if he did not let the people go, if he continued to hold back, the Lord would send a terrible plague upon all the livestock of the Egyptians. Moses gave Pharaoh the warning, along with the distinction between animals of Egypt and those of Israel. No animals belonging to the Israelites would die.

"Tomorrow," warned Moses, "the Lord will do this in the land."

The next day the Lord caused a deadly disease to fall upon all the animals of Egypt.[77] It wasn't just that the Egyptians lost their livestock. It was also a judgment on all the animal gods in polytheistic Egypt.[78]

---

77 The animals had been out in the fields after the receding of the flood waters and probably were infected by anthrax bacteria carried by the flies of the fourth plague.
78 Apis, the bull god, was so revered in Memphis that a sacred bull was kept within the temple and when it died, it was given an elaborate burial at Saqquara, near Memphis. Hathor, the cow goddess, was considered to be the protector and nurturer of life.

Pharaoh investigated the area of Goshen and found, just as Moses had predicted, that not one animal of the Israelites had died. Yet Pharaoh's heart was unyielding.

Next, the Lord instructed Moses and Aaron to take handfuls of soot from a furnace and have Moses toss the soot up in the air in the presence of the pharaoh. The soot would become fine dust over the land to bring festering boils to men and animals.

When Moses did that before Pharaoh, the magicians, who were still impotently standing by, immediately broke out with such painful, festering boils[79] that they collapsed. The sores were black burning abscesses that developed into pustules, causing great suffering for the afflicted. Pharaoh's heart remained hardened.

---

79   Probably a type of skin anthrax

Memphis
1446 BC

The Lord told Moses, "Get up early in the morning, and meet Pharaoh at the water. Confront him there, and let him know that if he does not let my people go, I will unleash on Egypt the worst hailstorm that has ever occurred in the history of the country. Tell him that I am ready to send the full force of my plagues against him and his officials and his people, so they may know that there is *no one* like me in all the earth."

This was a direct contradiction to Pharaoh's self-aggrandizement.

God told Moses to say, "By now I could have stretched out my hand and struck you and your people with a plague that would have wiped you off the face of the earth. But I have raised you up for this very purpose, that I might show you my power and that my name might be proclaimed in all the earth."[80]

The Lord said that if Pharaoh does not listen, then he should give an order to the people to bring their livestock and everything in the fields to a place of shelter, because the hail will kill all that is left out in the field, both men and animals.

The officials of Pharaoh who believed the word of the Lord, hurried to bring their slaves and their livestock inside. But those who ignored the word of the Lord, regretted it later.

Moses stretched out his staff to the sky. Lightning flashed to the ground and thunder pealed. Hail rained down as the lightning flashed back and forth. The hail struck the men and animals. It beat down everything growing and stripped every tree. The only place it did not hail was the land of Goshen. The Israelites were safe.

---

80   Exodus 9:15, 16.

Pharaoh summoned Moses and Aaron and said, "This time I have sinned. The Lord is in the right, and I and my people are in the wrong. Pray to the Lord, because we have had enough thunder and hail."

The storm was especially frightening to the Egyptians, including the pharaoh, because hailstorms were extremely rare in Egypt. The storm was a judgment on the sky gods, particularly the weather god of the Hyksos, Baal, who was the Egyptian Seth. The flax and barley were destroyed by the hail, as the barley had headed and the flax was in bloom, however, the wheat and the spelt would ripen later. Moses told Pharaoh he would lift his hands to the sky and pray to the Lord and the hail would stop, "So that Pharaoh and his officials may know that the earth is the Lord's."

Then Moses added, "But I know that you and your officials do not fear God."

Moses was right.

As soon as the hail stopped, Pharaoh changed his mind.

The eighth plague was to be a terrifying invasion of locusts that would devour all that was left of the fields after the hail.

The pharaoh had been duly warned and given a day to think about it, but the Lord told Moses that Pharaoh would not listen, because this time, after all his refusals, God had hardened his heart. The Lord said that his purpose was to perform more miraculous signs in Egypt, so that his people would tell their children and grandchildren how God had delivered them and they would know he was the Lord.

Moses and Aaron went to Pharaoh and said to him, "This is what the Lord says, 'How long will you refuse to humble yourself before me? Let my people go, so that they may worship me. If you refuse to let them go, I will bring locusts into your country tomorrow.'"

Then Moses turned and left Pharaoh.[81]

Pharaoh's officials said to him, "How long will this man be a snare to us? Just let the people go, so they can worship their God. Do you not yet realize that Egypt is ruined?"

That evening, Thutmose was troubled.

"What is it?" asked Meryetre.

"All my officials think I should give in to the Hebrew demands and let them go into the desert to worship their God."

"Well, do you want to let them go?" she asked.

Thutmose replied, "No, I don't. There is so much building to be done. All those slaves I brought back from Asia need housing. In three months,

---

81 Exodus 11:4–7.

I'll be going back there to check on the countries and collect tribute, so I wanted these projects completed."

"These officials of yours," said Meryetre, "aren't they just advisors?"

"Yes," said Thutmose.

"You are pharaoh; you make the final decision, don't you? Then do what *you* think best," urged Meryetre.

In the morning, Pharaoh ordered his officials to bring Moses and Aaron back to see him.

He told them, "Go, worship the Lord, but just who will be going?"

Moses replied, "We will go with our families and our livestock to celebrate a festival to the Lord."

Then Pharaoh said, "The Lord, be with you. But you will take only the men. If you take along your women and children, you clearly are bent on evil."

Then Thutmose III ordered Moses and Aaron to be ushered out.

Moses stretched out his staff, and the Lord brought an east wind that blew all day and all night. By morning, the wind had brought the locusts. The ground was black with them. They devoured all that was left from the hail—every green plant. The locusts filled the houses, something that had never been seen in the time of their fathers or forefathers.

Where was Min, the god of fertility? Where was Nepri, the goddess of grain? Locusts were a frequent calamity in mid-east countries, but this plague was far more severe than any before.

Pharaoh quickly summoned Moses and Aaron and said, "I have sinned against the Lord, your God, and against you. Now forgive my sin once more, and pray to the Lord to take this deadly plague away."

Moses prayed, and the Lord changed the wind to a strong west wind that carried the locusts into the Red Sea. Not one was left. But Pharaoh refused to let the people go.

Moses then was told by God to stretch his hand to the sky to bring darkness over Egypt, a blackness so thick it could be felt. Darkness was a harbinger of death to the Egyptians; it was connected to the afterlife. People got out their wedjet eye amulets to guide them, but it didn't help. This darkness was an insult to Re, the sun aspect of Amun, and to Pharaoh, the incarnation of the sun god. People were accustomed to the Khamsin, the sand-filled wind that blew off the desert and turned day into night, but this darkness was worse. It could be *felt,* and it lasted for three days. Yet the Israelites had light in their places.

Then Pharaoh summoned Moses and said, "Go, worship the Lord. Even your women and children may go with you, but leave your flocks and herds behind."

Moses replied, "You must allow us to have sacrifices and burnt offerings. We must take all our animals with us into the desert, because, until we get there, we will not know what we need for the offerings."

God hardened Pharaoh's heart and he said, "Get out of my sight! Make sure you do not appear before me again for, if you do, you will die."

"Just as you say," said Moses. "I will never appear before you again."

Then Moses told Pharaoh, "This is what the Lord says, 'About midnight I will go throughout Egypt. Every firstborn son in Egypt will die, from the firstborn son of the pharaoh who sits on the throne, to the firstborn son of the slave girl who is at her hand mill. There will be loud wailing throughout Egypt, worse than has ever been or will ever be again. But among the Israelites, not a dog will bark at any man or animal."[82]

Moses, now hot with anger, told Pharaoh, "All these officials of yours will bow down before me saying, 'Go, you and all that are with you.' After that I will leave." Then Moses left Pharaoh.

Moses and Aaron instructed the people of Israel to slaughter a lamb without blemish. They were to take some of the blood and smear it on the sides and tops of the doorframes of the houses where they ate the roasted lamb. They told the community of Israel that they should eat the lamb while they were standing with their cloaks tucked into their belts and their sandals on their feet. Each one was also to have his staff in hand. This was to demonstrate the haste with which they were to leave Egypt.

Pharaoh had until midnight to issue a stay of execution, as it were, but he did not budge.

Finally, the finger of death moved across the land, taking every firstborn, from Pharaoh's palace to the humblest hut.

The Lord had told Pharaoh, "You have oppressed my firstborn, Israel, now I will take your firstborn."

The shivering dread that many years before had come over the Great Queen Ahmose Nefertari, had now come to pass. Then, it was the Hebrew families crying out in anguish for their dead children. Now, it was the Egyptians' cry that was heard throughout the land.

---

82 Exodus 11:4–7.

The Israelites were spared now by the sign of the blood on their doorways.[83]

In the early morning, Pharaoh Thutmose III and his Great Royal Wife were awakened by the cries of their son's nurse, "I can't wake him. I can't wake him!" she shouted. Thutmose and Meryetre rushed to Ahmose, and found him, their precious nine-year-old son, unresponsive in his bed. The heir to the throne of Egypt was dead. As word of all the deaths came streaming into the palace, Pharaoh summoned Moses and Aaron.

He told them, "Go, worship the Lord as you have requested. Take your herds and flocks too." Then he added, "And also, bless me."

---

83 Throughout the ages, Hebrews would keep the Passover to remember how the Angel of Death passed over their houses that were marked by the blood of the lamb. Christians would take the same event as a sign of salvation, pointing to the ultimate blood sacrifice of Christ, the Lamb of God.

The Red Sea
1446 BC

The children of Israel marched out of Egypt en masse, in full view of the Egyptians who were burying their dead. They did not go empty-handed, for Moses and Aaron had told them ahead of time to ask their Egyptian neighbors for gold, silver, and clothes to take with them. So the Israelites were somewhat compensated for all the lost wages of so many years, as the Egyptians heaped on them great quantities of treasure.

By now, the Egyptian people and Pharaoh's officials had great regard for Moses. He had the power to do great miracles with the help of his God.

After 430 years, the Hebrews were finally leaving Egypt.[84] The first stop for this huge company was Succoth, in southeastern Goshen. There they paused to bake cakes from the dough of unleavened bread, which they had hurriedly wrapped in their clothing as they left their homes.

When Pharaoh Thutmose was told that the people had fled, he and his officials looked at each other and said, "What have we done? Most of the labor force and our trained military reserve have left us. We have lost their services!"

Pharaoh called for his chariot. Then he called together his army, including six hundred of his best chariots driven by an elite division of officers and the other chariots of Egypt with officers over them.

Thutmose III was used to getting his way. Now he thought, *I've been pressured and I've been duped. Those Hebrews aren't coming back. They are*

---

84 Just how many there were has been a point of debate. The NIV, a scholarly version of the Scriptures, states that there were 600,000 men on foot. When you add the women, children, and elderly people, as well as the "many other" people who went up with them, a conservative estimate would be two million people along with large flocks, herds, and many donkeys.

trying to escape, but I will get them back. When I do, they will have so much work they won't have time to plan anything like this again.

The Egyptians—all of Pharaoh's horses and chariots, horsemen, and troops pursued the Israelites and overtook them as they camped by the sea.

When the Israelites looked up and saw the Egyptians approaching, they cried to Moses saying, "Was it because there were no graves in Egypt? Is that why you brought us out here in the desert to die? What have you done to us? Didn't we say to you in Egypt, 'Leave us alone; let us serve the Egyptians?' It would have been better for us to serve the Egyptians than to die in the desert!"

Moses was getting an early taste of what it would be like to lead these people, who were so quick to blame him when faced with an obstacle. Moses, however, remained calm.

He told them, "Do not be afraid. Stand firm, and you will see the deliverance the Lord will bring you today. The Egyptians you see today, you will never see again. The Lord will fight for you. You need only to be still."[85]

The Lord told Moses to raise his staff over the sea to divide the water so that the Israelites could go through the sea on dry ground. The cloud that had been leading them, moved between them and the Egyptians.

When the Egyptian officers attempted to pursue the Israelites by entering the cloud, they could not see anything. They told Pharaoh, "If we try to fight in these conditions, we could wind up killing each other."

Pharaoh replied, "Wait it out. The cloud will lift and we will continue our pursuit. Remember Megiddo? We waited seven months in that siege, and at the end of it, we took the city. This is easy compared to that battle. Sit tight. We will prevail."

All that day and all night the Israelites marched through the sea to the other shore, for God had sent a great wind to divide the waters for them.

As the last of the Israelites were climbing up the bank of the opposite side, the cloud lifted, and the Egyptians plunged into the sea bed in pursuit of their escaping servants.

For once, Thutmose III did not lead his army as he usually did. This was such an easy task—there was no need to provide an example of bravery by taking the forward position. Thutmose waited on the near bank, expecting to enjoy the spectacle of the Israelite round-up. He would wait to give Moses and Aaron the special greeting he had in mind: *Thought you*

---

85 Exodus 14:13, 14.

fooled me? You underestimated the pharaoh. This should teach you never to do that again!

The Lord waited until all of Pharaoh's army was in the path between the walls of water, and then the army began to have trouble with their chariot wheels.

"My wheels are coming off!" yelled one officer.

"Mine too," shouted another. And so it went down the line.

"The God of the Israelites is fighting for them. Let's turn around," they shouted over the whinnying horses.

But it was too late. The walls of water were collapsing over them. What the shocked pharaoh saw was a brief, tumultuous bobbing of the horses, chariots, and men; and then they all sank to the bottom of the sea, and a deadly quiet settled over the scene.

Pharaoh Thutmose was shaken to his core. His eyes were riveted on the sea, which had just swallowed the best of his army. He turned to his driver and swore him to silence on threat of death to him and his family. Above all, the news of this humiliating defeat must not reach the ears of the nations he had recently conquered. They were sworn to pay tribute to Egypt. If they knew of his weakened position, all his campaigns could come to naught. No, they must not learn of this. Then it hit him like a biting wind, sucking the breath from him—his son was dead! His precious son, in whom he had invested the hope for Egypt's future.

"Stop the chariot," he ordered the driver, who had turned back toward Egypt.

"Wait here," he said as he descended to the desert floor. To one side rose a rock outcropping covered with thorn bushes. He headed for this screen. Then, shielded from the driver's view, Pharaoh Thutmose III sank to the earth and let the wave of grief wash over him unabated.

"My son, my son!" he wailed in anguish.

All those archery lessons, all those plans for the future, swept away in a moment like the sand beneath his knees. How could he have forgotten his son? Anger at the escape of the Hebrews and the rush of excitement in pursuing them, followed by the shock of seeing his army submerged in the sea, had left no room for thoughts of his son until now.

"The young prince is gone. How can it be? I will never embrace him again," mourned the pharaoh.

Finally, when his emotions were spent, his thoughts began to clear.

"I must get home to Meryetre," he realized. "There is so much to do. We must prepare the burial for Ahmose II. Then I must focus on a new successor."

Thutmose stood and brushed the sand from his clothes.

I must build a new army. That could take years, he thought as he returned to the chariot.

The pharaoh mounted his chariot, gave the driver the "Speed up" order, and raced back to his mourning wife and country.

The Desert
1446 BC

On the opposite bank of the Red Sea, there was a much different scene. A mood of celebration reigned, as Moses and the Israelites sang this song to the Lord:

> "I will sing to the Lord,
> for he is highly exalted.
> The horse and its rider
> he has hurled into the sea.
> The Lord is my strength and my song,
> he has become my salvation.
> He is my God, and I will praise him,
> My father is God and I will exalt him.
> The Lord is a warrior;
> the Lord is his name.
> Pharaoh's chariots and his army
> he has hurled into the sea.
> The best of Pharaoh's officers
> are drowned in the Red Sea.
> The deep waters have covered them;
> They sank to the depths like a stone.
> Your right hand, O Lord,
> was majestic in power,
> Your right hand, O Lord,
> shattered the enemy.
> In the greatness of your majesty

you threw down those who opposed you.
You unleashed your burning anger; it consumed them like stubble.
By the blast of your nostrils
the waters piled up.
The surging waters stood firm like a wall;
the deep waters congealed in the heart of the sea.
The enemy boasted,
I will pursue, I will overtake them.
But you blew with your breath, and the sea covered them.
They sank like lead
in the mighty waters.
Who among the gods is like you,
O Lord? Who is like you
Majestic in holiness,
awesome in glory,
working wonders?
You stretched out your right hand
and the earth swallowed them.
In your unfailing love you will lead
the people you have redeemed.
In your strength you will guide them
to your holy dwelling.
You will bring them in and plant them
on the mountain of your inheritance—
the place, O Lord, your hands
established.
The Lord will reign forever and ever."[86]

Then, Moses's sister, Miriam, the prophetess, took a tambourine in her hand, and all the women followed her with tambourines and dancing. Miriam sang to them the song of Moses.

After the people had celebrated and rested awhile, Moses led them from the Red Sea into the desert of Shur. For three days, they traveled without finding water. They complained to Moses, "What are we to drink?"

Moses knew they were still a day's journey from the Oasis of Elim, and it was obvious the people wouldn't be able to make it there without water. Now they were crying out beside a sulfurous waterhole.

---

86 Exodus 15:1–18.

Moses's heart sank, as he looked over a seemingly endless throng of thirsty people. He prayed to the Lord for help, and God sweetened the water so that the people and their animals could drink it. Moses named the place Marah, meaning *bitter*. It was here that God promised good health to the Israelites.

He said, "If you listen carefully to my voice and do as I say, then I will spare you the diseases that befell the Egyptians; for I am the Lord who heals you."[87]

Within a day, the company of Israelites came to Elim, a fine oasis with seventy shady palm trees and plenty of water from twelve wells. That night, as the starry sky stretched like a twinkling canopy over the earth, Moses lay with his head resting on his arms and gazed at the heavens. The stars seemed so close. He thought of God's promise to Abraham—that his seed would be as the stars of the heavens and as the sands of the earth. Moses had seen the vast, golden sands of the Sahara and the stretches of brick-red sands in northeastern Midian. God was keeping his promise. The children of Israel had certainly increased; Their numbers had doubled nearly every generation of their stay in Egypt. No wonder the Egyptians had been threatened. The sheer number of people with all their needs was overwhelming to Moses.

"Adonai, my only God, these are your children. Help me to be faithful and trust you each step of the way," he prayed.

After Elim, began the Wilderness of Sin, on the shore of the Red Sea. The Israelites had come no great distance, but they were not used to privation after what was, despite its rigors, a well-fed, well-ordered existence in Egypt. The whole community grumbled against Moses and Aaron.

They complained, "If only we had died by the Lord's hand in Egypt! There we sat around pots of meat and ate all we wanted, but you have brought us out in the desert to starve us all to death!"

Then the Lord promised Moses to provide food, so Moses and Aaron reassured the people, "In the evening, you will know that it was the Lord who brought you out of Egypt, and in the morning, you will see the glory of the Lord, because he has heard you grumbling against him."

Then Moses added, "Who are we, that you should grumble against us? You are not grumbling against us, but against the Lord. At twilight, you will eat meat, and in the morning, you will be filled with bread. God said, 'Then you will know that I am the Lord.'"

---

[87] In Hebrew, *Jehovah Ropheka*.

Just as the Lord had promised, at twilight quail came up and covered the camp. It was spring in the Sinai, the time of the great bird migration. From Africa, which became extremely hot in the summer, the birds migrated along two routes. The eastern route lay directly across the Israelites' campsite. Quail and other birds had flown across the Red Sea, where, exhausted by their long flight, they alighted on the flat shores to gather fresh strength for the flight over the mountains to the Mediterranean.[88] In the evening, the Israelites enjoyed roasted quail around their campsites. In the morning, they came out of their tents to find the bushes covered like frost with a white substance.

"What is it?" they asked each other.[89]

Moses explained, "It is bread from heaven, which you are to gather early each morning, an omer[90] for each person, which is enough for the day. On Friday, you are to gather enough for two days, so that you may rest on the Sabbath."[91] The manna, a white, round, flaky substance, looked like coriander seeds and tasted like honey that had set and crystallized. It could be crushed to make bread cakes, or it could be roasted or boiled.[92]

The next stop was Dophkah. The Israelites had traveled inland from the Red Sea and were now moving slowly along the old road that the labor gangs had traveled to the copper and turquoise mines in the area. The Egyptians had employed Canaanites to work the mines, which were closed from time to time.[93]

---

88 The Bedouins today still catch the exhausted quail by hand.
89 *Manu* is Hebrew for "What is it?"
90 About two quarts.
91 This was an early application of the principle, which would later be given in the Ten Commandments, to keep the Sabbath Day holy.
92 Some scholars have surmised that the manna of the Israelites was a natural secretion of the tamarisk bush, which occurs when it is pierced by a small, hard-shelled insect, Najococci. This substance, which is sweet to the taste, is sold by Bedouins today as "mannite." However, as a main ration supplemented only occasionally by birds, game, or fish, it is doubtful that mannite would have contained sufficient nutrients to sustain the people for forty years in the wilderness.
93 In modern times, inscriptions were found here that were not cuneiform or hieroglyphics, but a different linear system of writing. In 1948, a team of archaeologists from the University of Los Angeles found the key that made it possible to make a literal translation of the characters on the Sinai tablets. Without a doubt, the inscriptions had their origin about 1500 BC and are written in a Canaanite dialect. They were determined to be the first step of a Phoenician form of writing, which is the ancestor of our own alphabet. These intriguing inscriptions could have been made by the mine workers, or possibly written by the people who camped there in 1446 BC on their way to Mount Sinai. It is interesting that the first time the word *write* was used in the Old Testament is at the next camp, Rephidim.

Walking along the plateau above the Red Sea, the only things that broke the bright yellow flatness of the sand were camel-thorns and sparse brushwood. But looking up, an amazing scene appeared; the Israelites got their first glimpse of Mount Sinai.

The mountain range rose up from the earth in a rainbow of hues. It was as if all the colors of an artist's palette had been brushed onto this serrated cathedral of stone.

From place to place, the Israelites traveled as the Lord commanded them.

On the way to Rephidim, there was no water. The people quarreled with Moses, demanding water.

Moses cried out to God, "What am I to do with these people? They are almost ready to stone me!"

Moses was instructed to take some elders and go ahead of the people. There, he obeyed God's command to strike the rock with his staff, and water gushed forth. Moses gave the place two names: *Massah,* which meant testing, and *Meribah,* which meant rebellion.

The children of Israel pitched camp at Rephidim, a main oasis in this Sinai area. Shortly after arriving, they were attacked by Amalekites,[94] who may have been trying to protect the water supply they used. They began the attack by picking off stragglers on the edge of the group. Hostilities could not be avoided, so Moses appointed Joshua to be his general and prepared for battle.[95] Moses stood on a hill above the battlefield and held up his staff. As long as he did so, the Israelites prevailed. When his arms grew tired, Aaron and Hur each held up an arm and found a rock for Moses to sit on. Bitter fighting continued all day, until sunset, when Joshua won a decisive victory for Israel.

The Lord told Moses, "Write this on a scroll as a memorial to put in a book," so Moses wrote about the battle with the Amalekites. Then he built an altar and called it *Jehovah Nisi,* the Lord is my banner.

The next day, Moses received a welcome surprise. As they had begun their journey south from the Red Sea, Moses had sent a message to Jethro, his father-in-law, that they were on their way to Mount Sinai. Now his father-in-law arrived with Moses's family: Zipporah and their sons, Gershom and Eliezer. Moses went out to meet Jethro and bowed down and kissed him. He embraced his wife and sons with joy.

---

94 The Amalekites were descended from Amalek, a grandson of Esau, Jacob's twin brother.

95 Joshua became Moses' close assistant and eventually his successor.

Later, in the tent, he told Jethro about everything the Lord had done to Pharaoh and the Egyptians for Israel's sake and about all the hardships along the way. He told Jethro how the Lord had saved them in every difficulty. Jethro was delighted to hear about all the good things the Lord had done.

He said, "Praise be to the Lord. Now I know that the Lord is greater than all other gods, for he did this to Pharaoh and the Egyptians, because they had treated Israel arrogantly."

Then Jethro brought a burnt offering and other sacrifices to God, and Aaron came with all the elders of Israel to eat bread with Jethro and Moses in the presence of God.

The next morning, Moses took his seat to serve as judge for the people who stood around him from morning to evening.

When Jethro saw this, he asked Moses, "What are you doing? Why do you sit alone as judge?"

Moses explained, "Because the people come to me to seek God's will. Whenever they have a dispute, it is brought to me, and I decide between the parties, and inform them of God's laws."

Jethro told him, "Moses, what you are doing is not good. You, and the people who come to you, will only wear yourselves out. The work is too heavy for you. You cannot handle it alone."

Then Jethro suggested a plan whereby Moses would select capable men from the camp and set them over divisions of thousands, hundreds, fifties, and tens. The people could bring their disputes to these judges first, so that they would handle the simpler cases. If they encountered a difficult case, that could be brought to Moses to decide.

Jethro said, "May God be with you, and if he so commands, this plan would make your load lighter because those others would share it. That way, you will be able to stand the strain, and all these people will go home satisfied."

Moses recognized the wisdom of Jethro's advice, so he did all that his father-in-law said. Then he sent Jethro on his way back to his own country.

SINAI
1446 BC

Exactly three months after leaving Egypt, the Israelites came to Sinai. They camped there in the desert in front of the mountain. Moses remembered God's assurance to him almost a year before: "As a sign that I have sent you to Egypt, you will come back here and worship on this mountain."

Moses started up the mountain, and God called to him. He told Moses to say to the people, "You, yourselves, have seen what I did to Egypt, and how I carried you on eagles' wings and brought you to myself."

God was using an endearing illustration of nature. A mother eagle nudges her baby from the nest. Then as the eaglet plunges, the mother swoops under the little bird and catches it on her wings, then carries the eaglet back to the nest. She repeats this "training" until her baby learns to fly. How apt this illustration actually was for God's children in the desert, would be borne out by their series of plunges into disobedience and danger when they would need to be rescued by God. They had started out as a loosely joined community and would need to be trained and forged into a nation.

God renewed his covenant that he had given earlier at Marah: "If you obey me and keep my covenant, then out of all nations, you will be my treasured possession. Though the whole earth is mine, I will make you a holy nation."

Moses was sent back to speak to the elders. They promised to do everything the Lord said.

When Moses relayed their response to God, he told Moses that he would speak to him in a dense cloud so that the people could hear and would put their trust in Moses as their leader. Following God's instruction, Moses told the people to prepare themselves to approach God. They were to be ceremonially clean, which meant several days of cleansing themselves, washing their clothes, and abstaining from sexual relations. Under no circumstances were they to go near the mountain, until they heard the long blast of the ram's horn.

On the morning of the third day, there was a thick cloud over the mountain. Thunder and lightning came from the summit along with a very loud trumpet blast. Everyone in the camp trembled. Moses led the people to meet with God at the foot of the mountain. The Lord descended on Mount Sinai in a spectacular display of fire and smoke. The whole mountain trembled violently, and the trumpet blast grew louder. When the people saw the thunder and lightning, they were afraid and backed up some distance from the mountain.

They told Moses, "Don't let God speak to us or we will die. Let him speak to you instead, and then you can tell us what he said."

Moses spoke to them gently, "Do not be afraid. God has come to test you so you will have reverence for him that will keep you from sinning."

Then, as God had promised, he spoke to Moses out of the dense cloud in a loud voice so that the people could hear. He called Moses to the top of the mountain. After his climb, Moses was rewarded with an amazing experience.

Growing up in Egypt, Moses had been interested in law and the ways of Adonai, the one true God. Now he was about to receive the greatest code of law on earth directly from the hand of the living God.

Moses stood transfixed as he watched the finger of God inscribing in stone the following words:

I am the Lord your God who
brought you out of Egypt,
out of the land of slavery.
You shall have no other gods before me.
You shall not make for yourself
an idol in the form of anything in
heaven above or on the earth beneath or in the waters below.
You shall not bow down to them
or worship them; for I., the Lord
your God, am a jealous God,
punishing the children for the
sin of the fathers to the third
and fourth generation, of those
who hate me, but showing love to

a thousand generations of those
who love me and keep my
Commandments.
You shall not misuse the name of
the Lord your God, for the Lord
will not hold anyone guiltless
who misuses his name.
Remember the Sabbath day by keeping
it holy. Six days you shall labor
and do all your work, but the
seventh day is a Sabbath to the Lord your God. On it you shall not
do any work, neither you, nor your son
or daughter, nor your manservant
or maid servant, nor your animals,
nor the alien within your gates.
For in six days the Lord made the
heavens and the earth, the sea, and
all that is in them, but he rested on
the seventh day. Therefore, the Lord,
blessed the Sabbath day and made it holy.
Honor your father and your mother so that
you may live long in the land the Lord, your God is giving you.
You shall not murder.
You shall not commit adultery.
You shall not steal.
You shall not give false testimony
against your neighbor.
You shall not covet your neighbor's
house. You shall not covet your
neighbor's wife, or his manservant
or maid servant, his ox or donkey,
or anything that belongs to your
neighbor.[96]

God gave Moses three types of laws, (1) the moral law or the Ten Commandments, (2) the civil law, and (3) the ceremonial law, which included instructions for worship, priests' duties, sacrifices and offerings, and special feast days.

---

96   Exodus 20:117 NIV.

The civil law was similar to federal law for a nation. As Israel would be a theocracy, this law, too, came from God. Civil law covered such subjects as Hebrew servants and slaves[97], personal injury, protection of property, social responsibility, justice and mercy[98], and Sabbath laws.

For the ceremonial law to take effect, the Israelites needed a place where the priests could bring offerings. The most important object in that place would be the Ark of the Covenant. Before giving instructions for the building of the ark, God renewed his covenant with Israel. Because a covenant is between two parties, God sent Moses back to the camp to obtain the renewal of the Israelites' part of the covenant. Moses told the people all that God had said.

They responded with one voice, "Everything the Lord has said we will do."

Moses wrote everything down. Early the next morning he rose and built an altar at the foot of the mountain. He also built twelve pillars of stone representing the twelve tribes of Israel. He offered a blood sacrifice on the altar and read from the Book of the Covenant in the presence of the people of Israel.

Again they responded, "We will do everything the Lord has said; we will obey."

Then Moses took Aaron, Aaron's two oldest sons, the seventy elders, and his assistant, Joshua, part way up the mountain. There God gave them a vision of himself seated on his throne, with his feet resting on a pavement of sapphire. They ate and drank in celebration of the renewed covenant.

Moses told the group, "I will leave you now to go up again to God. While I am gone the people can bring their disputes to Aaron and Hur to be heard."

Then he took Joshua up farther with him and waited six days for God to call him. On the seventh day, the Lord called to Moses from within the cloud, and Moses entered into the presence of God. From the desert floor, what the people saw as they looked upward was the glory of the Lord like a consuming fire on top of the mountain. The fiery mountaintop could be seen for miles by other people and tribes as well.

"Look, look," they exclaimed. "That is where the people are, who came out of Egypt!"

Moses was safe with God, but the people of Israel did not know that. They watched the mountain, anxiously awaiting his return. They would wait a long time—forty days and nights.

---

97 They were to be set free after seven years.
98 Do good to those who abuse you; do not oppress an alien.

Meanwhile, on the mountaintop, God was instructing Moses how to build the Ark of the Covenant. He was to build a chest of acacia wood forty-five inches long, a little over half as wide and deep. It was to be overlaid with gold, with golden rings at its feet to hold gold-covered wooden poles for carrying. The lid was to be made of pure gold and hold two hammered gold cherubim, one at each end. The angels were to be made one with the cover and their wings were to be spread upward and over the cover, toward the center, where the presence of God would rest. The ark was to hold three objects: the stone tablets containing the Ten Commandments symbolizing God's justice, the sealed jar of manna symbolizing God's caring love and provision, and eventually, Aaron's staff, which God would cause to turn into a budding, blossoming almond branch to prove that Aaron was his choice as high priest. The latter symbolized the mediation between man and God.

God further instructed Moses on the building of the tabernacle. It was to be forty-five feet by fifteen feet and fifteen feet high. Its walls would be made of acacia wood poles and crossbars, covered with gold and set in gold-covered silver bases. Between these poles would be hung curtains of finely woven linen in scarlet, purple, and blue, skillfully embroidered with cherubim. The curtains would hang by loops and would be pinned together at the sides by gold clasps to make a unit. To form a roof, three coverings were to be made for the tabernacle: one of goatskins, dyed red and supple, like Moroccan leather, one of goat hair, similar to the goat hair tents of the people, and one of sea-cow,[99] that would be waterproof.

The furnishings of the tabernacle were to be as exquisite as the surround. There would be two parts: the Holy Place and the Holy of Holies, which would contain the ark. The two sections were to be separated by a curtain similar to that of the walls.[100] In the Holy Place, on the north wall, was to stand the golden table, holding the bread of the presence.[101] Opposite the table was to be the pure gold lampstand, its seven arms formed like branches, buds, and blossoms.[102] The priests were to keep the lights of the candelabra burning throughout the night.

The atmosphere in the tabernacle would be pleasant because of the sweet aroma wafting from the golden altar of incense standing before the curtain of the Holy of Holies. God stipulated that the incense and the

---

99 A type of seal that was native to the Red Sea.
100 This curtain was a forerunner of the curtain in the temple, which would be rent from top to bottom at the time of Christ's crucifixion, symbolizing for Christians the access to the presence of God made possible by Christ's ultimate blood sacrifice.
101 Christ was later to announce, 'I am the Bread of Life.' John 6:35, 48.
102 Jesus would say, "I am the Light of the World." John 8:12.

anointing oil used by the priests were to be the work of perfumers.[103] Very expensive substances were to be used in the recipes God gave—such as resin of myrrh, frankincense, cinnamon, and the extract from the root of a flower that grew in Syria and Persia. The recipes were to be sacred and not used by anyone else

Then God gave Moses instructions for the courtyard in which the tabernacle would stand toward the back. This open courtyard was to measure 150 feet by 75 feet and was to have the same type of construction as the tabernacle, with wood poles and curtains between. The wooden posts were to have silver bands and hooks and bronze bases. The altar for the burnt offering, toward the entrance, was to be bronze and all the utensils would be bronze.

A large, bronze basin for the ceremonial cleansing of the priests would stand between the altar and the tabernacle.

At this point, God interrupted his instructions for the tabernacle.

---

103 It may be that some of the Egyptians that came with the Israelites when they left Egypt were skilled in the art of making perfume, or some Israelites may have been trained in this important Egyptian skill.

SINAI
1446 BC

God told Moses, "Go down, because your people, whom you brought out of Egypt have become corrupt."

He said, "Go down to them, for they have been quick to turn away from what I commanded them and have made themselves an idol cast in the shape of a calf. They bowed down to it and sacrificed to it, and have said, 'These are your gods, O Israel, who brought you out of Egypt.'"

Then God said, "Now leave me alone with my anger, so that I may destroy this stiff-necked people. Then I will make you into a great nation."

What is the Lord saying? thought Moses. *He wants to wipe out these people and start over with me? I would be the new Abraham? That's not what I want. What about the people?*

Moses pleaded with God for the Hebrew people, "O, Lord, why should your anger burn against your people whom you brought out of Egypt with your mighty power?"

Though Moses interceded with God, he did not want to identify with the rebellious people of Israel.

God has just told Moses: "*Your* people, whom *you* brought out of Egypt," and Moses said to God: "*Your* people, that *you* brought out of Egypt."

Moses tried to persuade God with two reasonable arguments, "What would the Egyptians say? Think of the havoc you have wreaked on them so they would let your people go. They will say that it was your intent to get them out in the wilderness to kill them all. Moreover, there is your promise, your covenant with your servants, Abraham, Isaac, and Israel, to whom you swore by your own self. Remember you promised them to be their inheritance forever."

God relented and did not bring upon the people the disaster he had threatened. Moses turned and went down the mountain with the two stone tablets of the Ten Commandments, inscribed on both sides. Joshua was waiting where Moses had left him, part way down the mountain. As they descended together, Joshua heard noises coming from the camp.

He said to Moses, "There is the sound of battle in the camp."

But Moses replied, "It is not the sound of victory. It is not the sound of defeat. It is the sound of singing that I hear."

Even though Moses had been alerted by God as to what the people had done, his anger burned when he saw them dancing around the calf. He threw the stone tablets he was carrying and smashed them against the rocks at the foot of the mountain.

The next thing Moses smashed was the golden calf. In righteous fury, he crushed the idol to fine dust, threw it in the stream, and made the people drink it.

Then he asked Aaron, "How could you allow this?"

There were echoes of Eden in Aaron's answer as he first blamed the people, and then indirectly pointed to Moses for staying away so long with God.

"Do not be angry, my Lord," he answered Moses. "You know how prone to evil these people are. They said, 'We don't know what has happened to that fellow, Moses, so make us gods who will go before us,'" Aaron explained.

"So I told them to give me their jewelry, and I threw it in the fire and out came a calf. I saw that they were worshiping the calf, so I called for a festival to the Lord the next day. We presented burnt offerings to God, but then they just went back to indulge in this revelry."

Moses saw that the people were running wild. Aaron had let them get completely out of control, so Moses stood at the entrance of the camp and called for those who were for the Lord to come to him. The Levites rallied to him. Then Moses called for the execution of those who had led the rebellion. Three thousand people died that day.

Moses was troubled that night. How could he possibly help these people who had sinned so grievously against the Lord? By morning, he knew what he must do.

Moses gathered the people and said to them, "You have committed a grave sin, but now I will go to the Lord. Perhaps I can make atonement for you."

Moses went back up the mountain to the Lord. He said, "Oh, what a great sin these people have committed, but I plead with you, forgive their sin, but if not, then blot me out of your book." Moses's voice broke, for what he was proposing was the ultimate sacrifice—to forfeit his own soul, The Lord would not accept Moses's sacrifice no matter how sublime. Only a sinless person could be such a Messiah.

So God told him, "You are to lead my people. I will punish with a plague those who took part in the rebellion. Now take the people from this place and go to Canaan. I will send an angel to lead you, but I will not go with you, lest I destroy the people in my anger."

Moses went down to the camp and told the people God's words. God would not go with this stiff-necked people, lest his anger burn against them and he destroy them on the way. He had promised to send an angel to lead them the rest of the way to Canaan. The people mourned and stripped off their ornaments at the foot of the mountain. Moses went to pray at the Tent of Meeting, which he had put up outside the camp as a place to meet with God.

When the people saw Moses go out to the Tent of Meeting, they would stand at the entrance of their tents. When Moses went inside, the pillar of cloud would come down and stay at the entrance while Moses spoke with God.

The people would then worship at their own tents. The Lord spoke to Moses as one would speak to a friend. Then Moses would return to the camp, but his young aide, Joshua, would remain in the Tent of Meeting.

Now Moses prayed to the Lord in the Tent of Meeting. "O Lord, you have been telling me to lead the people, but I don't want to take a step ahead unless you go with us."

Then Moses made three requests of God. First, he prayed, "I want to get to know you better. If you are pleased with me, teach me your ways."

Secondly, he reminded God that the nation of Israel was God's people. He prayed, "If your presence does not go with us, do not send us up from here. How will anyone know you are pleased with me and with your people if you don't go with us? What will distinguish us from any other people if your presence is not with us?"

Finally, Moses asked God, "Show me your glory."

The Lord responded, "I will do as you have asked, because I am pleased with you and I know you by name."

As for Moses's third request, God promised to pass in front of Moses with all his goodness and to proclaim his name in Moses's presence. "But," he said, "you may not see my face, for no one may see my face and live."

God told Moses that on the mountain there was a place where he could put Moses in a cleft of the rock and cover Moses's face with his hand as he passed by, then remove his hand so Moses could see his back.

Sinai
1446 BC

The Lord told Moses to chisel out two new stone tablets and take them back up the mountain the next day. No one was to come with him. Even the flocks and herds were to stay off the mountain.

God said, "Be ready in the morning, and then meet me at the top of Mount Sinai."[104] Moses was to start out early, and the Scriptures say he carried two stone tablets in his hands.[105]

When Moses reached the mountaintop, the Lord came down to the mountain in a cloud. He passed in front of Moses as he said he would do and proclaimed, "The Lord, the Lord, the compassionate and gracious God, slow to anger, abounding in love and faithfulness, maintaining love to thousands, and forgiving wickedness, rebellion, and sin."[106]

God finished his instructions to Moses regarding the ceremonial law by describing the vestments and duties of the priests, the offerings they would present to the Lord, and the annual festivals that they would lead the people in celebrating. God wanted his people to be joyful in contrast to the unbridled, drunken orgy that they had just exhibited around the golden calf.[107]

---

104 Mount Sinai is 7500 feet in elevation. This would seem to be a miracle in itself: for an eighty-one-year-old man to carry two stone tablets unassisted to the top of Mount Sinai. Today, people can ascend by donkey trail, but they must travel most of the night to arrive by morning.
105 Exodus 34:4.
106 Exodus 34:6, 7a.
107 The people's revelry harked back to the Egyptian worship of Apis, the bull, and particularly the worship of Hathor, the cow goddess. In addition to succoring the pharaohs, Hathor was the goddess of the parties, flowing with alcohol. According to Egyptian mythology, Hathor at one time thirsted for blood. To deceive her, the Egyptians had poured brown beer into the Nile, making it appear to be blood. She drank so much of it, she became drunk, and she happily abandoned her thirst for vengeance.

As God described the ceremonial dress that the high priest would wear, Moses imagined Aaron, his brother, arrayed in such splendor, more beautiful than anything the Egyptian priests ever wore. He would be dressed in a tunic of linen, woven so finely that the cloth would be indistinguishable from silk.[108] The sash of blue, purple, and scarlet linen, would be the work of an embroiderer. The vest, or ephod, of the same embroidered colors, with hammered, fine gold strips woven in, would hang from his shoulders. Two onyx stones, set in gold filigree and engraved with the names of the twelve tribes, would be on the shoulder pieces, signifying that the responsibility for the spiritual welfare of the people of Israel would rest on his shoulders.

Over the ephod an embroidered, multicolored pouch or breast piece, was attached to the ephod by fine ropes of braided gold, strung through golden rings, and fastened to the shoulders. On the front of the breast piece were attached four rows of three stones—ruby, topaz, and beryl; turquoise, sapphire, and emerald; jacinth, agate, and amethyst; chrysolite, onyx, and jasper. The twelve stones were set in gold filigree and each was engraved with a name of one of the twelve tribes. In this way, the priest wore the stones over his heart to show his love for the people he represented to God.

Over the tunic, the priest was to wear a long robe, open at the front. To the hem of the robe were sewn pomegranates of blue, purple, and scarlet yarn, with gold bells between, so that the balls of yarn and the bells alternated around the hem. There was a purpose for the bells, besides beauty. Once a year, the high priest would enter the Holy of Holies to bring the sin offering for himself and the people. He was to sprinkle some of the blood of the sacrifice on the lid of the Ark of the Covenant on the *Mercy seat* or place of reconciliation. Thus, symbolically, the blood would cover the law tablets held within the ark. The laws that the people had broken that year would be forgiven because of this atonement. If for some reason this priestly duty was carried out insincerely or incorrectly, and the high priest was struck dead, the other priests would know, because they would not hear the ringing of the little bells. In such a case, they could slide a crook under the curtain and pull out his body, as they were forbidden to enter the Holy of Holies.

The final part of the priest's vestment was the headpiece. This was to be a white turban with a pure gold head plate engraved with the words, *Holy to the Lord*, attached to the turban with a cord. Above the head plate,

---

108 Such garments were found by archaeologists in Egyptian royal tombs.

a diadem would be set over the turban. Aaron's sons would wear only the tunic, sash, and headband as well as simpler linen robes. The priests were not to drink alcohol before or during their ministering, and they were to perform only authorized procedures.

They were to officiate at five types of offerings. The first three were for the community: a burnt offering for sin, by a blood sacrifice in which the entire animal was burned on the altar; a grain offering, which consisted of finely ground grain mixed with oil and salt, presented as a thanksgiving gift to God; and a fellowship offering or peace offering, whereby confession of sin was made over the head of an animal.[109] The other two offerings were made for individuals. A sin offering was made for those who sinned against another unintentionally, and a guilt offering was made for someone offering restitution for harm done to another person or their property.

God told Moses, this is how Aaron is to bless the people:
"The Lord bless you
and keep you.
The Lord make his face
to shine upon you
and be gracious to you
The Lord turn his face
toward you
and give you peace." Numbers 6: 24–26

---

[109] Blood was sprinkled on the altar, but only the fat and kidneys were burned so the rest of the animal could be eaten by the people in fellowship.

Sinai
1445 BC

God instructed Moses to observe and celebrate three annual festivals. The first was the Passover, which was a remembrance of how Israel was delivered from bondage in Egypt and from the Angel of Death. The second festival was the Feast of Weeks, when the first of the grain harvest was brought in. The third was the Feast of Ingathering for the products of the orchards and vines, and was also called the Feast of Tabernacles and commemorated the Israelites' sojourn in the wilderness when they camped in temporary shelters.[110]

In addition, there was the Day of Atonement, which was a day of soul-searching, confession, and fasting rather than feasting. A goat was slaughtered for a blood sacrifice. Then another goat was taken, the sins of the people symbolically placed on its head, and it was released into the wilderness.[111] Every fiftieth year was the Year of Jubilee.[112] This came after seven sets of seven years or forty-nine years. Then the land was to be returned to its original family owners.[113]

When God had finished all his instructions to Moses and he had written again on the stone tablets, he handed them to Moses and told him to return to the people and start building the tabernacle. Moses's face glowed with such radiance when he descended the mountain that the

---

110 The feast was called Tabernacles because of the booths made of branches and palm leaves that the people lived in for four weeks during the festival.
111 A *scapegoat* for "escape."
112 Today this is observed by Jewish people as Yom Kippur.
113 There came to be, over time, an emphasis on returning people to the land, rather than returning land to the people. The words on the American Liberty Bell in Philadelphia echo the words from the Year of Jubilee: *"Proclaim liberty throughout the land and to all the inhabitants thereof."*

people could not bear to look at him, so he covered his face with a veil until the glow had faded.

Moses called for the people to contribute the materials needed to construct the tabernacle with all its furnishings as God had instructed. God filled Bezalel and Ohaliab with his spirit and gave them special gifts, skills, ability, and knowledge to master all kinds of arts and crafts that God's design required. They taught and supervised others whom God also blessed with special gifts. The people gladly gave up all the treasures they had, much of which the Egyptians had heaped upon them at the time of the Exodus.

In six months, all the parts of the tabernacle, courtyard, and furnishings were completed. The entire structure was portable and designed to be assembled and taken down quickly. Moses saw to the setting up. When it was completely assembled with everything in place, including the oil and incense and the contents of the Ark of the Covenant, God descended in the Shekinah cloud and filled the entire tabernacle.

However, a black cloud had descended on Moses and his family. Zipporah had died. She had been a good mother. Moses, watching his weeping sons, knew they would miss her as much as he would. Yet he could not cry. He felt numb and empty.

"Adonai," Moses prayed, "please help me get through this. I'm so weary."

After the official mourning period had passed, Moses spoke to the people of Israel. He praised God for his provision. He blessed the people for their obedience in building the beautiful tabernacle. When they left Egypt, they had only the stories of the patriarchs and a promise of deliverance. Now they had their deliverance, a complete system of law, a place of worship, and a priesthood with ceremonies and festivals.

Best of all, they had a renewed relationship with God, the God of love and mercy, who had graciously consented to guide them all the way to the Promised Land.

Memphis
1444 BC

Egypt was obsessive about keeping records. The scribes recorded everything in great detail, but throughout the country there was not a hint of what had happened at the Red Sea. Pharaoh's driver had kept the secret of the humiliating defeat. Thutmose III had conducted at least seventeen campaigns in nineteen years. Every year, like clockwork, his chariots would appear in Asia or Nubia. Then suddenly, all war activity stopped abruptly without any decisive battle.[114] He did have soldiers at the frontier outposts and a small contingent at Thebes that he hadn't wanted to wait for in his haste to overtake the Hebrews. But the best of his army, soldiers, horses, and chariots lay at the bottom of the Red Sea.

In two years, he had made a start of building up his army, and when he made his annual visits to Asia, it was horses and chariots that he demanded as tribute, because he needed to have a show of force for the security of Egypt.

However, he had lost his taste for battle. The defeat ushered in twenty years of peace. He and Meryetre clung together in their grief. The death of a son can drive people apart, but that didn't happen in the royal couple's case.

Only one year later, another son was born to them.

As Thutmose III had previously determined, he named the infant after the second pharaoh of the Eighteenth Dynasty, Amenhotep I, Moses's Uncle Tep. Amenhotep II was a healthy boy, and Queen Meryetre was fiercely protective of him, as though she could somehow prevent this boy from also being snatched by death. The child's wet nurse, Amenemopet,

---

114 Egyptologists puzzle over this sudden cessation of warfare.

lived at the palace with her own son, Kenamun. It was reassuring to have someone to keep an eye on Amenhotep at all times. Amenemopet, his nurse, became as one of the family.[115]

Thutmose III was not quite the same as he had been before the loss of his first son and his army. Less arrogant, more settled, the man was probably a better parent to Amenhotep II than he had been to Ahmose II. He was certainly around him more. No six-month absences for campaigns any longer. That is a long time in the life of a child.

Thutmose III was also able to focus on other affairs at home with greater diligence. It had previously taken a great deal of energy to balance both the war campaigns and the administration of the country. One of his current efforts was to keep open the canal that Senusret III had built at the first cataract of the Nile. Hatshepsut had reminded him of the need to clear the waterway of debris regularly. He was reminded again when he made a trip to Nubia and couldn't get through.

He had the canal cleared and named it, *"Opening of This Way in the Beauty of Thutmose III,"* demonstrating a lingering tendency to pat himself on the back. The pharaoh left orders with the fishermen at Elephantine to clear the channel annually. Other more ambitious projects were in the design stage at this time. With the loss of such a large service sector of the population, the Hebrews, the building projects would take longer to complete. However, the first signs of recovery were now evident in Egypt.

---

115 A colorful mural, discovered in Egypt, depicts the young, future pharaoh on the lap of his wet nurse. Kenamun was described as Amenhotep's foster brother. The boys were brought up together, and when Amenhotep II later became Pharaoh, he named Kenamun, his chief steward and vizier.

Sinai
1444 BC

Moses's old buddy and brother-in-law, Hobab, had come for Zipporah's burial. Now he was preparing to leave, but Moses told him, "We are setting out for Canaan, the land God promised us. Come with us and we will treat you well."

Hobab replied, "No, I will not go. I'm going back to my own people."

But Moses said, "Please do not leave. You can be our eyes in the desert, because you know where all the good campsites are. If you come with us, we will share what the Lord gives us."

Hobab agreed to go along, and Moses was comforted in his grief for his wife, Zipporah[116]

The tribes of Israel had been organized to march in a set formation, with the Ark of the Covenant in the forefront, carried by the Levites. Following the ark were the disassembled parts of the tabernacle and behind that, the furnishings.

Silver trumpets were made to announce the march. Before leaving Sinai, the Israelites celebrated Passover at twilight on the fourteenth day of the first month. On the twentieth day of the second month of the second year, the cloud lifted from above the tabernacle.

Whenever the ark set out, Moses said:
"Rise up, O Lord!
May your enemies be scattered,
May your foes flee before you."

---

116 There is a record in Judges 1:16, of the Kenites or metal workers, who were the descendants of Moses's brother-in-law, having a part in the inheritance of Israel and settling in Judah.

Whenever the ark came to rest, Moses said:
"Return O. Lord,
to the countless thousands of
Israel."[117]

Now the cloud had lifted. Spirits were light. It was spring again, and they were on their way to Canaan. The Israelites headed northeast, about thirty miles inland, along the eastern arm of the Red Sea.

The high spirits did not last long, for at the very next camp the people complained bitterly. They had been roused by certain "rabble" elements who were not Israelites and only came along on this journey to escape their own miserable existence in Egypt. Now, however, all they could remember of Egypt was the good food, free fish, cucumbers, melons, leeks, onions, and garlic.

"We have lost our appetite," they complained. "We never see anything but this manna."

Moses heard all the families wailing at the doors of their tents and went to God in despair, "Why have you brought this trouble on your servant? What have I done to displease you that you put the burdens of all these people on me? Did I conceive all these people? Did I give them birth? Why do you tell me to carry them in my arms as a nurse carries an infant to the land you promised on oath to their forefathers? Where can I get meat for all these people? They keep wailing to me, 'Give us meat to eat!' I cannot carry all these people by myself. The burden is too heavy for me. If this is how you are going to treat me, put me to death right now if I have found favor in your eyes—and do not let me face my own ruin."

The Lord did not become angry with Moses for pouring out his heart in honest despair and anger. God was angry at the people too. Besides, he knew what Moses had been through in the past two years: first, confronting Pharaoh for six months or so, then the difficult journey to Sinai, followed by going up and down the mountain, mediating between the people and God, and finally, the death of his wife. Moses was exhausted physically and emotionally, so the Lord told him he would put the same Spirit on seventy elders as he had given to Moses.

"These leaders will help you so you won't have to carry the burden alone," he said.

Although Moses thought it would be impossible to feed meat to so many people, God said, "Is my arm too short?"

---

117 Numbers 10:35, 36.

Again it was migration time. A wind went out from the Lord, and drove the quail in from the sea, so that they landed and piled up, three feet deep, for the distance of a day's walk in every direction from the camp. There was meat to eat for a month. However, God punished the people with the plague for complaining, because by now they should have known better. Many died, so Moses named the place *Kibroth Hattaavah,* meaning graves of craving, for the people who were buried there.

The next camp was Hazeroth, and it was here that God gave a special gift to Moses to comfort him. Moses looked upon the people. Now that his wife was gone, it seemed as though everyone was in couples. He hadn't noticed that before, but now his eyes were drawn, however unwillingly, to the clasped hands of husband and wife and to the affectionate embraces around the campfires. There was something else he was noticing now, a Cushite woman. It dawned on Moses that he was lonely. Had she looked up at him under those thick lashes and held his gaze a little longer than usual when she brought him his food? No, what would a young woman like that want with an eighty-one-year-old man?

True, he didn't look his age or feel his years. God had been good to him, giving him strong bones and muscles, agility, and the energy he needed to lead the people. He looked at his arms, noting that his flesh was tanned and firm. His senses were working also. He could still enjoy the cool evenings when the people would sing and dance around the campfires. Moses began to single out the Cushite, appreciating the way her lovely, lithe body swayed to the rhythms of the tambourines and the haunting sound of the flutes.

Increasingly, as she served him his meals, he would catch the subtle aroma of her perfume rising from her ebony skin, warmed by the sun. One day, to his utter amazement, she knelt by him and took his hand.

"You are lonely, dear Prophet?" she voiced, in a rich mellow tone.

Tears welled in his eyes. She leaned forward and embraced him as he wept. Finally, she withdrew and gently wiped his face with the soft linen towel she carried with her water bowl.

"There is no need, Moses, for you to be lonely," she addressed him, now more intimately.

"Do you mean," Moses murmured, "you would be willing to be my wife?"

"If that is your wish, I would be so honored," she replied firmly.

So they married, and the Israelites rejoiced with them. Moses had thought his days of sensual delight were behind him. This was not the case, he realized, as his beautiful bride caressed him and brought him to heights of pleasure and then sweet release.

As she lay sleeping beside him, he prayed, thanking God for this gift, adding, "Please do not let me adore her so much that I lose sight of you, my Lord."

Not everyone was happy for Moses and his new wife.

"Moses has disgraced us," complained Miriam to Aaron.

"How do you mean?" asked her brother.

"Marrying that Cushite woman!" she said in disgust. "She's not our kind, with that black skin and Nubian background. Why did he have to remarry anyway? It should be enough that God speaks through him. Even that isn't so special anymore, now that God has put his Spirit on seventy elders."

Aaron was thoughtful. Miriam was usually right. Moses did not consult with them as much anymore, now that he had all that help. He spent time with his new wife too. Aaron's own wife, Elishaba, had not been herself since the death of their two oldest sons at Sinai—a punishment for irreverence and disobedience in their ministry as priests.

Aaron looked at Miriam, who had always focused on the work of the Lord and seemed satisfied with her role as a prophetess.

"Miriam, it *is* still special that God speaks to us," Aaron encouraged her.

"Then let's tell Moses that," she insisted.

"Has the Lord spoken only through Moses? Hasn't he also spoken through us?" So she stirred up Aaron against Moses.

Moses was shocked that his sister and brother were challenging his leadership. But what had he done that they should oppose him? Moses was more humble than any man on the face of the earth. He did not defend himself, but God did. Immediately, God called Moses, Aaron, and Miriam to the Tent of Meeting.

"All three of you," he said. Then he came down in a pillar of cloud and stood at the entrance. He summoned Aaron and Miriam to step forward. Then God told them to listen to his words:

"When a prophet of the Lord is among you,
I reveal myself to him in visions.
I speak to him in dreams,
but this is not true of my servant, Moses;
he is faithful in all my house.
With him I speak face-to-face,

clearly and not in riddles; he sees the form of the Lord,
Why then were you not afraid
to speak against my servant, Moses ?"[118]

The Lord was angry! When the cloud lifted, there stood Miriam, leprous, her skin as white as snow. Aaron pleaded with Moses to help her, "Please do not hold against us, the sin we have so foolishly committed!"

Moses cried out to the Lord to heal her. She was told to stay outside the camp for seven days. After that time, Miriam was completely healed and the Israelites could move on.

---

118 Numbers 12:6–8.

KADESH-BARNEA
1444 BC

Normally, the distance between Mt. Sinai and Kadesh Barnea could be walked in less than two weeks, but the people of Israel found the trek very difficult.[119]

Kadesh-Barnea was about halfway between the northern tip of the Gulf of Aquaba and the southern point of the Dead Sea. The weather was now getting warm. The cloud of the Lord spread out over the travelers to provide cover from the beating sun. Still, the going was rough as they picked their way over rocky terrain and loose scree. Finally, they reached Kadesh-Barnea, not far from Canaan.

Moses told the Israelites, "See, you have reached the hill country of the Amorites. Go up and take possession of the land of Canaan. Do not be afraid and do not be discouraged. The Lord is with you."

But the people suggested that men be sent ahead to spy out the land. God instructed Moses to pick a leader from each tribe, twelve in all including Joshua, his aide, and Caleb, a man who was not Israelite by birth, but was very loyal to the nation. Moses told them to go up from the Negev into the hill country to see what the land of Canaan was like. Were the towns walled or not? Were the people strong or weak? What about the soil, the crops? Was the land beautiful?

It was the time of the first grapes. "Try to bring back the best fruit," Moses called to them as they left, eager to be on their way.

---

119 Deuteronomy 1:19 records that they traveled "through all that vast and dreadful desert." The book of Numbers states that Moses was asked by God to record all their camps. It lists nineteen camps from Hazeroth to Kadesh Barnea, which would be their base camp. This was the grassy place with the springs that Hobab had described to Moses, as they tended flocks in Midian.

The spies were gone for forty days. When they came back, they gave a mixed report. Ten of them said the city walls were high and strong and the people were huge. Caleb gave an impassioned speech, declaring that the cities could be taken, because God would give them victory. Joshua supported this claim. Everyone agreed that the land was beautiful and bountiful. They brought back a vine so loaded with grapes that it took two men to carry the pole holding the fruit. This was indeed tempting to the desert-weary people.

The ten dissenters spoke up again, exaggerating their original claims—the walls weren't just high, they were impenetrable. The people weren't just big, they were giants! At this, the people cried out with fear. When Joshua and Caleb tried to speak, the people threatened to kill them. Suddenly, in their midst, there appeared the glory of the Lord at the Tent of Meeting.

A voice boomed, and the Lord spoke to Moses:
"How long will these people
treat me with contempt?
How long will they refuse
to believe in me, in spite of
all the miraculous signs
I have performed among them?
I will strike them down with
a plague and destroy them,
but I will make you into a
nation, greater and stronger than they."[120]

Again, Moses pleaded with God for Israel, using the same arguments: God's reputation among the nations, especially Egypt, and God's character: his being slow to anger, abounding in love, and forgiving sin and rebellion, as well as being faithful in keeping his promise to bring the people into the land.

God said, "I have forgiven them as you asked. Nevertheless, as surely as I live and as surely as my glory fills the earth, not one of the people who saw my glory and the miraculous signs I performed in Egypt and in the desert, but who disobeyed me and tested me again and again—not one of them will ever see the land I promised to their forefathers. These people have treated me with contempt and they will not see the land. Only Caleb and Joshua will go in. Your children will go in and enjoy the land you have rejected. For forty years, one year for every day that you explored Canaan,

---

120 Numbers 14:11, 12.

you will wander in the desert until this sinful generation has passed away. Then I will bring your children into the land."

The spies who brought the bad report were struck with a plague.

The people's response was to go into the land that they had rejected and try to take it anyway, but Moses warned them, "Don't do it. The Lord is not with you."

In their presumption, they went in to attack the inhabitants and were beaten back.

Kadesh-Barnea
1440 BC

One day, as Moses communed with God in the early desert morning, he recalled his education in Egypt and recalled how he had excelled in the House of Wisdom. He remembered reading stories that he had written and remembered how others had responded.

"Why, Lord, am I thinking about this now?" he asked God. "Is there something you want me to do?"

A strong conviction came over him. *I must write about the great deliverance of God for future generations. We are living an important story!*

True, he had kept records of the many laws given to him by God, as well as the instructions for making the tabernacle and its furnishings. God had told him to write about the battle with the Amalekites and the covenant. He had also told Moses to record all the stages of their journey, and he had done that, naming all the campsites. But he had not filled in all the human elements that would reveal God's mercy and loving provision for his people.

He had to write the story of how the Israelites came to be in Egypt in the first place. That was his favorite—the story of Joseph. But what about God's promise to Abraham, concerning the deliverance of his people from Egypt? For that matter, how about Abraham's response to God's call to come out from Ur to a land, "which I shall give you." *That relates to us too,* he thought.

Once Moses had papyrus, a reed pen, and ink in hand, he wrote, to his surprise: "In the beginning, God created the heavens and the earth."

Well, how about that? God knew all along where Moses should start the story. He would look to God for inspiration. He would interview the people to hear all the stories that had been handed down over the generations by oral tradition, but God would reveal to him what to include.

Yes, his story would be God-breathed. Moses was fully occupied throughout the thirty-four-years that were left before they could enter the Promised Land.[121] He enjoyed his activities of ministering to the people as teacher and judge. But most of all, he enjoyed communing with God and writing the story of God and his relationship with his people.

---

121 God had given them credit for the two years of their journey from Egypt to Kadesh-Barnea.

Kadesh-Barnea
1437 BC

Moses sat on a flat rock of an outcropping at Kadesh Barnea. He looked over the sea of people. More than half of them would die in the desert because of their disobedience. It was important that they be honest with their children and teach this new generation wisely, so that they would be faithful to God. Thirty-one more years to go!

Much had been accomplished thus far. The people had the law to tell them how to live. The Ark of the Covenant went before them as they moved from camp to camp seeking out water holes and pastures. They had the tabernacle as a place of worship. These people knew how to live in the desert now.

Moses counted his own blessings. God had prepared him for life in the desert by the forty years spent in Midian. The Lord had blessed him with a loving wife who was a comfort to him after Zipporah's death. Aaron and Miriam were respectful and helpful after their brief rebellion. He was grateful for time with his father, Amran, still going strong at 125 years of age. Most of all, Moses treasured his time with his heavenly Father. Remembering his petition to get to know God better, he realized that the Lord was granting that request day by day as Moses communed with him in his writing.

He thought of Egypt. Moses had no desire to go back there, for the people he loved were gone. He thought of Thutmose III and had no bitter feelings. The judgment on him had been swift and deadly. Moses knew how difficult it was for Aaron to have lost two sons, even though Aaron bore their death with resignation and patience. He wondered how Thutmose was bearing up in the loss of his son. Did he have another son to succeed him on the throne? That was so important to the Egyptians. After his son's death, Thutmose had asked Moses to bless him, so Moses prayed for him now. He wondered if Thutmose did have a son, would he tell him about his defeat at the Red Sea or would he only boast of his military victories?

Thebes
1437 BC

Thutmose III was enjoying a time of peace throughout his land. However, he wanted to prepare his son to lead a strong nation. To accomplish that, there must be military might. His army was rebuilt after the fiasco at the Red Sea, and he had employed the best archery instructor in the land to teach his son the important military skills with the bow. From the pillared gallery of his palace, Pharaoh observed this training take place in the courtyard.

"Span your bow to your ears," the instructor was saying.

When Amenhotep II was good enough with the bow, he would take him lion hunting. He knew Meryetre would not want the boy to go, but it was time for the prince to participate in "manly" activities. What better way to grow up than facing a fierce lion in the wilderness? But he would wait a few more years.

After the archery lesson, Thutmose retreated to the privacy of his chambers. He gave the order to his guard that he was not to be disturbed. Something was troubling him, and he needed to think it through. He had figured out that the Moses of the plagues was the same Moses Hatshepsut had told him about—the one who grew up in the palace with her as her brother.

But there was something else that he couldn't put his finger on. The problem he pondered had to do with Hatshepsut. On the one hand, she had been good to him in many ways, especially in his training to be pharaoh. The harem girl who had given him birth meant nothing to him. Since infancy, Hatshepsut had been the only mother he had known. But to see her dressed as a male pharaoh on temple walls, in statuary and on obelisks was too much. Amenhotep was already asking who that was. Thutmose did not want to leave that kind of legacy to his son.

Something else was eating at him. The stories about Moses, that he had loved hearing from his stepmother when he was a boy and always clamored for more, now left him cold. He knew his own father was a weak man, just from palace gossip. He supposed his stepmother wanted him to have someone strong as an example, even though as a child he had never laid eyes on Moses. Now, as he thought about Moses and the damage he had done to him personally and to all of Egypt, he wished that he had *never* laid eyes on him. What was it that was nibbling at his memory—just at the edge of it? Aha, it was the question of Moses's escape. He had fled from Egypt after he killed the Egyptian. Thutmose knew that his father had wanted to kill Moses—and rightly so. Hatshepsut had told him that. What else had she told him?

His tension was building and blocking his memory. Thutmose breathed deeply and calmed himself. Then it came. Hatshepsut had warned Moses. That was it! It hadn't seemed important when she had said it. Moses was gone—in the desert somewhere, no threat to Thutmose, but Moses had come back, hadn't he? Suddenly it was clear to him, the import of that warning given so long ago. Without Hatshepsut's interference, Moses would have been killed. She saved him! Even though Thutmose knew that Hatshepsut would not have knowingly caused her stepson any harm, he was furious that her action, her cursed interference, had cost him his son, Ahmose. Why hadn't he thought of this before? he asked himself, but he knew the answer.

It had taken all his energy to grieve his son, rebuild his army, and prepare a new successor. The memory he had just retrieved had been buried, waiting for the time he should act on it, and now he would do just that.

Hatshepsut had erected an impressive obelisk in Karnak. Thutmose was in the process of building a magnificent, hypostyle hall there, and he was designing his own obelisk. Thutmose would give the order to have her structure covered in stone. No one would ever see all those inscriptions and reliefs of her exploits. He thought of her mortuary temple in Deir el Bahri, He would leave that. He was building his own mortuary temple beside hers. Thutmose decided to leave the wall paintings in her temple, because he, himself, was depicted in many of them, but he would smash her statues. He got some satisfaction just thinking about that. He would watch those proud figures topple to the ground!

Now that his anger was slightly abated, Thutmose thought of Hatshepsut's place as consort of his father, Thutmose II. He would honor his father as commanded in the Code of Egypt, he thought self-righteously. He would leave the images of Hatshepsut as his father's queen. All the other images he would order to be scratched out with precision by his workmen. He would change the labels of other images, attributing the deeds to his grandfather, his father, or himself. He smiled as he thought, she has made it easy for me—in many of the images she is already in male dress!

Having reached a decision, Thutmose III strode proudly out of his chamber and promptly ordered the guard to summon his vizier. He did not want to waste any time getting rid of Hatshepsut's images of power. He couldn't order the execution of Moses, who was out of his reach and probably dead by now anyway, but he could wipe out Hatshepsut's portrayal of herself as a male pharaoh. He could also omit her name from the official list of Egypt's kings. He would leave his own well-earned legacy for his son, Amenhotep II.

Kadesh-Barnea
1425 BC

In Kadesh Barnea, the people were mourning with Moses, Miriam, and Aaron, for their father had passed away at the age of 137 years. He had far exceeded what Egyptians considered the ideal lifespan, one hundred ten years.

The burial was simple. Aaron, as high priest, officiated, aided by his younger sons, Eleazar and Ithamar. Moses wrote a song, which Miriam sang.

Then Moses addressed the people: "We gather today to honor Amran, to mourn his death, and to celebrate his life. This man of God worked hard in his life, but he considered that his greatest task was to teach his children the ways of God. With my mother, he taught my brother Aaron, now your high priest, and my sister Miriam, your prophetess, and also myself, your prophet. You have heard the story of how I was rescued from the Nile by Princess Ahmose. My parents were allowed to keep me only three years before I was brought to the palace to live with the Egyptians.

"In that short time, my parents instilled in me the concept of one God whose name is Adonai. At three years of age, I could not say the Lord's full name, so I said, *Adon*. My Egyptian family would try to get me to say, *Amun*, but I would insist God's name was *Adon*."

A murmur of amusement and appreciation rippled through the crowd as they pictured the little boy, Moses, standing up to the regal Egyptians.

Moses continued, "When I was sent to study at the House of Wisdom, I found my Hebrew family. My father and I had long talks about God. Adonai inspired my father as he prayed for wisdom to answer my questions. As a youth, I was truly impressed with the love and faith I saw in my father's life. Now you have an opportunity to teach your children about God's wonderful works for his people. We are now about halfway through our desert wanderings. Your children are the ones who will face the giants and the fortresses of Canaan that intimidated you. Teach them that God is our fortress and no one is more powerful than he.

"If anything should have convinced you of God's superior power, it was the plagues. When the Nile was turned to blood, where was Hapi, the river god? Where was Heket, the frog god, when the frogs got out of control? Hathor is widely admired as a nurturing goddess of Egypt, but where was this cow goddess? And where was Apis, the bull god, when the cattle were stricken with a deadly disease? Where was Isis, when the people contracted the disease? Could this healer goddess help? And where was Min, the god of agriculture, so celebrated at every coronation? Couldn't he rescue the fields when the locusts were stripping them bare? Was the weather god, Baal, asleep during the hailstorm that pounded down the rest of the crops? Where was Horus, the great warrior god, protector of the pharaohs? Could his wedjet eye guide the people when the thick darkness fell upon them?

"Finally, when the finger of death struck every Egyptian household, where was Osiris, the Egyptian savior god? Most of all, where was Amun and his potter god, Khnum? Could they restore the Ka of the eldest son? But what about you? You were saved by the blood on the doorway, the Passover blood.

"The Egyptian gods are worthless and so are the gods of the nations surrounding you, yet, you are tempted by these other gods. Don't you think I was tempted in Egypt? The pharaoh and the princess loved me. I'm sure they would have been pleased if I had worshipped their gods, but I could not be unfaithful to Adonai. They wanted me to be pharaoh, but God had other plans for me.

"You have about twenty-five years left before we enter Canaan. Make good use of the time, I beseech you. Teach this new generation from infancy to adulthood. Teach them that the Lord God is one God. Instruct them in the ways of God that they may live to please him. Comfort them as you reassure them of Adonai's unfailing love. I am so grateful to my father and mother for their faithfulness. Their faith that God had a special purpose for me prompted them to put me in that basket on the Nile, and God did the rest. May you have such faith for your children."

Then the people sang, Aaron led prayers to God, and Amran was laid to rest.

Thebes
1425 BC

In Egypt, Thutmose III was dead at the age of fifty-seven. His was an elaborate funeral. On the Nile a great procession of barks traveled across the river from Thebes to the Valley of the Kings, where the mortuary temple of Thutmose III awaited beside, and a little above, Hatshepsut's famous temple.

The bark immediately following Pharaoh's bark held women on the deck. They lamented and called out to the helmsman: "Steer to the west, to the land of the justified. In peace, in peace, to the west, thou praised one, come in peace. When time has become eternity, then shall we see you again, for behold, thou goest away to that country in which we are all equal."[122]

From the river, the whole procession transferred to land for the journey to the tomb, the elaborate bier traveling ahead. Everything the pharaoh could possibly use in the afterlife, including food, furniture, chests of clothes and jewelry, writing materials, and weapons were carried along to the tomb.

A great outpouring of grief echoed against the steep canyon walls as the people exclaimed, "How can our great leader be no more? He was strong, he laughed at the years. How can it be that the one who was always arrayed in the finest robes must now be wrapped as a mummy?"

Meryetre threw herself on the mummy of her husband and cried:
"I am thy wife, Meryetre.
Thou great one, forsake me not,
Thou art so beautiful.

---

[122] Erman, *Ancient Egypt*, 321, 322.

What does it mean that I am
now far from thee? Now
I go alone…Thou, who didst
love to talk with me --thou
art now silent and dost not speak."[123]

Thutmose died before he could erect his obelisk, which was designed to be 105 feet tall, five feet higher than Hatshepsut's obelisk. In his lifetime, he could not experience even this small triumph over his stepmother. His obelisk lay in a workroom in Karnak for many decades.[124]

The great Thutmose III was succeeded by his twenty-year-old son, Amenhotep II. Thutmose III had given excellent supervision for the training of this young prince, who showed great skills in handling boats and chariots.

He was a warrior like his father had been in his youth, and he was a great archer.

It was said of Anmenhotep II, "No one could draw his bow!"

---

123 From an ancient papyrus, Erman, *Ancient Egypt*, 321.
124 Thutmose IV, the grandson of Thutmose III, added his own cartouche to the obelisk of his grandfather and erected it east of the temple in Karnak. Later, it was moved and can now be seen in Rome.

The Wilderness
1406 BC

The children of Israel were gathered at Kadesh Barnea, where they mourned the death of Miriam, their prophetess. Except for her brief rebellion, Miriam had been a constant support for Moses. Now the people were so close to entering Canaan. Sometime this year their long sojourn in the wilderness would be over. Moses remembered how Miriam had spoken in glowing terms of the Promised Land. How sad that she would not get to see it, he thought.

However, Moses could not linger with his thoughts of Miriam. The people were grumbling again, and he had to see to their needs.

Why did they have to be so demanding? Moses wondered. The springs had dried up, and the thirsty people confronted Moses and Aaron:

"If only we had died before this. Why did you bring the Lord's community into this desert? Why did you bring us out of Egypt to this terrible place? There is no grain or figs or pomegranates or grapevines, and there is no water to drink!"

Had they not learned anything in all their years of wandering? This was a new generation, a generation that would be taking possession of Canaan. All but a few of the previous generation had died.

Moses and Aaron prayed to the Lord. He told them to gather the people together in front of a rock that he would show them. Then Moses and Aaron were to speak to the rock, and water would gush forth.[125]

Moses said to the people angrily, "Listen, you rebels, must we bring you water out of this rock?" Then Moses raised his staff and struck the rock twice.

---

125 There are two springs in the general area of Kadesh-Barnea that today are called "Aina Musa." One of them is at the entrance to Petra. We do not know the exact location of Moses's spring, but we are told that Moses and Aaron dishonored God there.

The Lord said to Moses and Aaron, "Because you did not trust in me, enough to honor me as holy, in the sight of the Israelites, you will not bring this community into the land I give them."[126]

Moses and Aaron were stunned. They asked each other, "Did God really say we are not to enter Canaan?" They began to realize the consequences of disobeying God by striking the rock instead of speaking to it. Still, they held out hope that God would relent.

It was time to move on. With their thirst slaked, the Israelites were now ready to approach Canaan for the second time. Moses sent messages from Kadesh to the King of Edom asking for safe passage. He addressed him as "brother," because the Edomites were descended from Esau, the twin brother of Jacob. Moses asked if the Israelites might pass along the King's Highway.[127] He promised they would not enter a field or vineyard, nor would they drink from their wells. However, the King's response was to send his army to block the way. The Israelites would have to go around. God would not allow them to attack Edom because of the ancient family relationship.

While they were still at Kadesh-Barnea, God told Moses and Aaron that it was time for Aaron to be gathered to his people. God told Moses to accompany Aaron and the eldest of Aaron's surviving sons, Eleazar, to the top of Mount Hor, the easy-to-climb mountain near Petra that Hobab had described to Moses. When the three men reached the top, Moses did as God instructed and removed the garments of Aaron, putting them on Eleazar who would be the new high priest. Then Aaron died.[128]

Moses and Eleazar went down the mountain and told the people that Aaron had died. The whole community mourned for thirty days. Moses wrote the following Psalm, which is apt because it speaks of the eternal grandeur of God, the frailty of man, and the need for God's grace:

Lord you have been our dwelling place
throughout all generations.
Before the mountains were born
or you brought forth the earth and the world,
from everlasting to everlasting, you are God.
You turn men back to dust saying, "Return to dust, O sons of men."
For a thousand years in your sight

---

126 Numbers 20:12.
127 Still in existence today.
128 Today, on *Jebel Haroun* (Muslim for Aaron), there is a small, white shrine over what is thought to be Aaron's grave, located about a three-hour walk from Petra's canyon.

*are like a day that has just gone by,
or like a watch in the night.
You sweep men away in the sleep of death.
they are like the new grass of the morning --
though in the morning it springs up new,
by evening it is dry and withered.
We are consumed by your anger
and terrified by your indignation.
You have set our iniquities before you,
our secret sins in the light of your presence.
All our days pass away under your wrath;
we finish our years with a moan.
The length of our days is seventy years—
or eighty, if we have the strength;
yet their span is but trouble, and sorrow,
for they quickly pass, and we fly away.
Teach us to number our days aright,
that we may gain a heart of wisdom.
Relent, O Lord! How long will it be?
Have compassion on your servants.
Satisfy us in the morning with your
unfailing love,
that we may sing for joy and be glad
all our days.
Make us glad for as many days as
you have afflicted us,
for as many years as we have seen
trouble.
May your days be shown to your servants,
your splendor to their children.
May the favor of the Lord our God
rest upon us;
establish the work of our hands for us -
Yes, establish the work of our hands.*[129]

Aaron, the high priest, brother of Moses, was 123 years of age when he was gathered to his people.

---

129 Psalm 90:1–10, 12–17.

Border of Canaan
1406 BC

Mt. Nebo

The decision was made for Israel to enter Canaan from the east, above the Dead Sea across the Jordan River. Five nations blocked the way.

An early skirmish with King Arad of the Canaanites ended in a victory for Israel. When Moses's request to the King of Edom for safe passage was rejected, the Israelites were required to backtrack to the Red Sea, swing eastward, then north around Edom. Three nations were protected by God because of his promises to the patriarchs: Edom, children of Esau (Jacob's brother); Ammon, children of Lot (Abraham's nephew); and Moab, also children of Lot. The children of Israel were allowed to defeat the Amorites, about whom God said that their iniquity was full, meaning they were due for judgment because of their evil practices.

Next, the Israelites faced the giants that had terrified the ten spies on their first attempt to enter Canaan. King Og of Bashan was one of a remnant of very tall people, the Rephaites, and David later faced such a giant.[130]

With God's help, Israel easily defeated these Amorite people. The people of Israel moved onto the plains of Moab. Balak, the King of Moab, was in a panic. He had heard of his defeated neighbors and knew he couldn't match the military strength of the Israelites. Moreover, he didn't know about God's protection of Moab as a nation. In his desperation, he resorted to magic as a way to defeat the Israelites. The most famous magician, or diviner, of this time was Balaam who lived near the Euphrates. The king of Moab sent his swiftest chariot to bring him back, promising a hefty fee for his services.

---

[130] The iron bed of King Og was described as measuring six feet by thirteen feet.

Unfortunately for the King, however, the curses that Balaam prepared for Israel turned into blessings as they came out of his mouth. Balak was furious, so Balaam, not wanting to lose his fee, suggested another ploy.

"Let your wives, daughters, and sweethearts seduce the young men of Israel into worshipping Baal with them. That will weaken Israel," he said to the king.

"Excellent idea, why didn't I think of that?" he said as he saw Balaam's hand stretched out for payment.

It was an effective but deadly snare for Israel that Balak and Balaam set in motion. Some of Israel's young men succumbed to the temptation and took part in the orgies that ensued. Israel struck back, swift and hard, and God sent a plague to kill the offenders. One brash, young Israelite had dared to bring a Moabite woman to Israel's camp. They were locked in a sexual embrace in front of the Tent of Meeting. Phinehas, grandnephew of Moses, in his zeal for the Lord, ran them through together with one thrust of his spear. Then the plague stopped. Phinehas, the hero who "cleansed the camp" of corruption that day, would later succeed his father Eleazar as high priest.

The children of Israel were about to enter Canaan. Moses pleaded with God to let him go in with them. He prayed, "O Sovereign Lord, you have shown me your greatness. There is no one in heaven or earth who can do the mighty works you do. Now, please let me go over and see the good land beyond the Jordan."

Finally, God said, "Enough!"

Then he told Moses that he would not let him enter Canaan, but he would let him view the Promised Land from the top of Mount Nebo.

Moses accepted God's offer gratefully. For five weeks at the end of the year, Moses taught the people. He reviewed their history, describing the burden he had carried in governing so many people and the frustration he felt at their unbelief when they had first reached the borders of Canaan. Moses told of the prolonged weariness of the desert wanderings. He reminded them that God had protected them and fed them the entire forty years. God had prevented their clothes from wearing out and their feet from swelling. Then came the happy defeat of the Amorite kings, Sihon and Og. Moses told them how he had begged God to let him go in with them to Canaan, and how God had said he would let him see the land from the mountain. He assured them that Joshua would lead them into the Promised Land.

The Prophet Moses exhorted them to obey God's law, "Be careful not to forget the covenant of the Lord, your God that he made with you."[131]

---

[131] Deuteronomy 4:23.

Moses spoke to them about the law, starting with the Ten Commandments. Then he summed up the commandments in these words:

"Love the Lord your God
with all your heart and
with all your soul
and with all your strength"[132]

Almost fifteen hundred years later, Israel's leaders would test Jesus with a question, which is the greatest commandment of all? He would answer by quoting Moses's words "Love your neighbor as yourself,"[133] thereby summing up one's duty to God and to one's fellow man.

Moses enjoined the people to keep the commandments upon their hearts. "Impress them on your children," he said.

"Talk about them when
you sit at home, when you walk along the road,
when you lie down and
when you get up."[134]

The Israelites took Moses's words literally when he said to bind the commandments on their hands and foreheads. They put Bible verses in little boxes[135] and fastened them to their wrists and foreheads.

Repeatedly, Moses said in his farewell speech, "Hear, O Israel, the Lord our God, the Lord is one."[136]

This eloquent, farewell speech demonstrated that Moses had mastered his speech problem.[137] After reviewing the history and the laws of Israel with the people, Moses gave this warning to them:

"See, I have set before you today life and good, death and evil."[138]

"Therefore choose life, that both you and your descendants may live; that you may love the Lord your God, that you may obey his voice and that you may cling to him; for he is your life and the length of your days;

---

132 Deuteronomy 6:5.
133 from Deuteronomy and from Leviticus 19:18.
134 Deuteronomy 6:6–9.
135 Phylacteries.
136 This was a clear statement of monotheism, one of the earliest in the history of mankind. Moses had clearly rejected the polytheism of his life in Egypt.
137 The New Testament martyr, Stephen, in reciting Israel's history, said that Moses was powerful in speech and action.
138 Deuteronomy 30:15.

and that you may dwell in the land which the Lord swore to your fathers, to Abraham, Isaac, and Jacob, to give them."[139]

Moses then raised his voice in praise. He had started the long desert sojourn with a song at the Red Sea and now he ended it with a song on the shores of Jordan:

"Listen, O heavens and I will speak;
hear, O earth, the words of my mouth.
Let my teaching fall like rain
and my words descend like dew,
like showers on new grass,
like abundant rain on tender plants.
I will proclaim the name of the Lord.
Oh, praise the greatness of our God!
He is the rock, his words are perfect,
and all his ways are just.
A faithful God who does no wrong,
upright and just is he."[140]

"For the Lord's portion is his people,
Jacob his allotted inheritance.
In a desert land he found him,
in a barren and howling waste.
He shielded him and cared for him;
He guarded him as the apple of his eye,
like an eagle that stirs up its nest
and hovers over its young,
that spreads its wings to catch them
and carries them on its pinions.
The Lord alone led him;
No foreign god was with him."[141]

Finally Moses blessed the tribes of Israel:
"The eternal God is your refuge,
and underneath are the everlasting arms.
He will drive out your enemy before you --
so Israel will live in safety alone.

---

139 Deuteronomy 30:19, 20.
140 Deuteronomy 32:1–4.
141 Deuteronomy 32:9–12.

Jacob's spring is secure
in a land of grain and new wine,
where the heavens drop dew.
Blessed are you, Oh, Israel!
Who is like you
a people saved by the Lord?"[142]

Moses bade the people farewell and retired to his tent. He knew that in the morning, the people would be preparing to enter Canaan, and he would not be with them.

If only I had not struck that rock in anger, he thought, as he lay down on his bed. Waiting for sleep to come, Moses thought of his Uncle Tep and the story of Sinuhe.

"Everyone wants to go home, Moses," he remembered his uncle saying. For over forty years, Moses had looked to Canaan, the home of his ancestors, as his own home. He fell asleep and dreamed of the land of milk and honey.

In his dream, God spoke to Moses, "I am taking you home, Moses. *I am your home.* Tomorrow you will be home with me."

Early the next morning, Moses awakened, refreshed. After breakfast and prayer, he set out for Mount Nebo as God had instructed him to do. On the lower slopes of the mountain, pomegranate trees grew, their limbs heavy with the deep red fruit. As he walked through the orchard, Moses considered his life.

He looked to the heavens, "O Lord, my two greatest desires were to know you and to fulfill your purpose for my life." Moses was comforted to know that those desires had come to fruition in his lifetime.

Farther up the mountain, Moses stopped to rest and to survey the camp below. He was confident that the people were in good hands. Joshua was a strong leader, and God's presence would go with them.

Though Moses was 120 years old, his strength was not gone and his eyes were not weak. At the top of Mount Nebo, he stood looking out over the panorama below. Down to his left, he could see the Great Salt Sea. Beyond the Jordan stretched the fertile fields of Canaan. To the north, Moses could make out a series of mountain peaks rising above the plains. He could see clearly, yet he was surprised to find that there was no tug at his heart. The intense desire to enter Canaan was gone. In its place was a stirring excitement to be with God.

---

142 Deuteronomy 33:27–29.

I'm not a son of Egypt, he thought. *I'm not a son of Israel either.*

"Adonai, I'm *your* son," he said.

Then Moses lifted his arms to the heavens, "I'm ready, Father, take me Home."

Legacies

Legacy of Thutmose III

What of Thutmose III, who had been concerned about the legacy he would leave for his son? What was his legacy? He overcame Egypt's enemies and brought twenty years of peace to the nation. His brilliant military strategies, especially at Megiddo, are studied to this day in military academies. He has been called the "Napoleon of Egypt." Since he measured slightly over five feet tall, he fits that title in more ways than one. James Henry Breasted of the University of Chicago called him the "first world hero."[143]

At Karnak, Thutmose III built the magnificent Jubilee Hall, which is the earliest known building created in the basilica style. He rebuilt the hypostyle hall, which his grandfather, Thutmose I, had erected in the main sanctuary of the Temple, and he constructed the seventh pylon. His obelisk now resides in Rome, where it is known as the Lateran Obelisk.

The refined features of Thutmose III are apparent in a finely carved statue, which can be seen in the Luxor Museum. His features resemble Hatshepsut's so much that one could imagine him to be her biological son. Did he order the statue to resemble her face as his ideal image? Or- did he really look like that?

The mummy of Thutmose III was found by a goatherd in 1881, among others hidden from tomb robbers in a cache near Hatshepsut's Memorial Temple.

He was later given a second funeral procession on the Nile as his body was brought to Cairo where it rests in the Egyptian Museum. Recent DNA tests of his mummy indicate that Thutmose III was not the biological son of Thutmose II. However, there is always the question of accuracy when testing a body that is 3500 years old. On the other hand, one might wonder, did Isis have a liaison with one of the harem guards and try to palm off her offspring as the son of the pharaoh?

What is so fascinating about ancient Egypt, is that for every question answered, there are many more questions raised.

---

143 *Ancient Egypt, Discovering its Splendor,* National Geographic Society, April 2009, 226.

Legacy of Hatshepsut

Hatshepsut remains an intriguing figure. Her stepson, in sheathing her obelisk with masonry, inadvertently preserved it for generations to come. Hatshepsut's magnificent obelisk, sculpted from a single block of granite, soars one hundred feet above the ruins of Karnak. Defying the attempt to erase her name from history, it stands as the tallest structure of its kind in Egypt. As they were in Hatshepsut's time, artisans are busy at work in her temple. Presently, they are restoring the stunning images that depict her life from conception to her adult exploits, including a marvelous depiction of her trade expedition to the mysterious Punt, and the treasures gleaned from that exotic land. The temple, itself, is an architectural masterpiece, a labor of love designed by her adoring architect.

Today, at Karnak, tourists admire the Red Chapel, the beautiful rose quartzite sanctuary, which she added to the temple complex. Hatshepsut favored the worship of one god, the God of gods, as did Moses. However, she called him Amun. Did Moses influence her? What effect did this strong-willed sibling have on Moses? For Egypt, Hatshepsut bridged the gap between Thutmose I and Thutmose III, and she raised and trained her successor to provide strong leadership for Egypt.

The search for this Queen's mummy has gone on for many years. It appears to have been hidden by Egyptian priests around 1000 BC in the tomb with her wet nurse. Howard Carter first observed this tomb, labeled KV60, in the Valley of the Kings in 1903. He noted that there were two mummies there, one in a coffin and the other on the floor. Over the years, Egyptologists lost track of the entrance to KV60. Then in 1989, Donald Ryan, an Egyptologist from Tacoma, Washington, went exploring in the Valley of Kings and rediscovered KV60.

He was amazed to see a well-preserved female mummy lying in a heap of rags on the floor of the tomb. Her left arm was crooked on her chest in a royal pose. She could be a queen, Ryan thought. Was it Hatshepsut? He thought the indignity of her situation should be remedied, so he did what he could by obtaining a simple wooden coffin for her. He and a colleague gently settled her into the coffin and closed the lid. Then they left the tomb.

For almost two more decades, the mummy waited. Then Zahi Hawass, head of the Egyptian Mummy Project and Secretary-General of the Supreme Council of Antiquities, asked the curators of the Egyptian Museum to round up all the unidentified female mummies from the Eighteenth Dynasty. In late 2006 and early 2007, the mummies were passed through a CT scanner, so archaeologists could gauge their age and cause of death. During this process, the CT scan revealed a tooth in a corner of a canopic box containing the liver of Hatshepsut and labeled with her cartouche.

The team dentist identified the tooth as a secondary molar with part of its root missing. In an examination of the CT scan of the mummy from KV 60, the Egyptologists discovered a root with no tooth. Measurement of the root in the mummy and the tooth revealed that they matched. This finding is a good indication that Hatshepsut's mummy has at last been identified. She now rests under a protective glass case in one of the two royal mummy rooms in the Egyptian Museum of Cairo. The label on the display reads:

"Hatshepsut-the King, Herself."

In Egyptian literature there is a poem dedicated to Hatshepsut:
"God has created her
in order to exalt his splendor.
She whose diadems
shine like those of
the God of the horizon."[144]

---

144 Erman, *Life in Ancient Egypt,* 396.

Legacy of Moses

And what of Moses's legacy? He is honored as one of the greatest prophets who ever lived by three of the world's religions: the Jewish, Christian, and Muslim faiths. Pointing to one God, Adonai, the Invisible One, he provides an early example of monotheism. Although a few cultures in ancient times had attempted an amalgam of gods, these efforts often deteriorated into a panoply of grotesque imagery. Such was the tendency of the people Moses led. The persistent penchant for idols had to be checked constantly.

Moses led a "stiff-necked," disorganized lot of people for forty years through the wilderness to become a nation. He was God's instrument to give us the Ten Commandments, the clear moral mandate, which undergirds the system of law and justice for Western civilization.

Moses's leadership of the people out of Egypt and through the Red Sea to the Promised Land symbolizes for Christians the delivery from the bondage of sin, through salvation by God's grace and Christ's blood, to inherit eternal life. How did Moses accomplish what he did? His secret for success was the abiding of his soul in God. Though he was an imperfect human being, he trusted his Lord, and God used him mightily to fulfill his divine plan. Moses became the emancipator of his people, a great prophet, and an inspired law-giver.

What was God's own evaluation of Moses's life? We read in Deuteronomy 34:10–12, the words penned by Moses's successor, Joshua, God's assessment of his Prophet, Moses:

Since then no prophet has risen
in Israel like Moses, whom
the Lord knew face to face,
who did all those miraculous
signs and wonders the Lord
sent him to do in Egypt—
to Pharaoh and to all his officials
and to his whole land.

For, no one has ever shown the
mighty power or performed the
deeds that Moses did
in the sight of all Israel."

Most importantly, Moses left a record of God's unfailing love. He wrote the first five books of the Bible, the best-selling book of all time.

Acknowledgments

My gratitude goes to Shirley Huston, literary agent and friend, for her encouragement and her faithful work in typing the many revisions of the manuscript.

Heartfelt thanks to my husband, Pete, my sister, Nancy Corwin, and my friend, Sharon Miles, for their patient attention and insightful feedback as I read aloud from my book-in-progress.

Many thanks to my lovely daughter, Cheri Dixon, her husband, Dean, and my long-time friend, Cathy Garcia, for their reading and helpful suggestions.

A special thank you to my grandson/fellow author, Peter Bekendam, for his loving support and technical help in this project.

Thanks go to Travis Dixon, graphic artist extraordinaire, for his striking cover design. Thanks also to Echo Fluharty, coordinator, and the editorial staff at Westbow Press for helping me to launch my first novel.

Finally, I am indebted to all my family and friends for their love and prayers without which I could not have completed this project.

Sources

Bangs, Richard and Pasquale Scaturro. *Mystery of the Nile.* New York: New American Library, 2006.

Brown, Chip. "The King Herself." *National Geographic*, April 2009.

Butzer, Karl. "The People of the River." *In Ancient Egypt, Discovering its Splendors.* Wash. D.C.: The National Geographic Society, 1978.

Davis, Virginia Lee. "Pathways to the Gods." *In Ancient Egypt Discovering Its Splendors.* Wash. D.C.: The National Geographic Society, 1978.

Erman, Adolf. *Life In Ancient Egypt.* New York: Dover Publications Inc., 1971.

Grosvenor, Gilbert M., ed. *Ancient Egypt, Discovering Its Splendors.* Wash. D.C.: The National Geographic Society, 1978.

Keller, Werner. *The Bible As History.* New York: William Morrow and Co., 1956.

Lawrence, T. E. *Seven Pillars of Wisdom.* New York: Double Day and Co., 1935.

Magi, Giovanni. *Valley of the Kings, Valley of the Queens.* Firenze, Italia: Casa Editrice Bonechi, 2009.

Mayhew, Bradley. *Jordan.* Oakland, Ca.: Lonely Planet Publications, Pty Ltd., 2006.

Mertz, Barbara. "The Pleasures of Life." *In Ancient Egypt Discovering Its Splendors.* Wash. D.C.: The National Geographic Society, 1978.

Scott, Jonathan. *Safari Guide to East African Animals.* Nairobi, Kenya: Kensta, 2006

Silverman, David P., ed. *Ancient Egypt.* New York: Oxford University Press, 1997.

Simpson, William Kelly. "The Gift of Writing." *In Ancient Egypt, Discovering its Splendors,* Wash. D.C.: The National Geographic Society, 1978.

Spalinger, Anthony J. " The Crest of Empire." *In Ancient Egypt Discovering its Splendors*. Wash. D.C.: The National Geographic Society, 1978.

Strudwick, Helen. ed.. *The Encyclopedia of Ancient Egypt*. London: Amber Books, Ltd., 2006.

The Holy Bible. New International Version. Grand Rapids, Mich.: Zondervan, 1985.

Von Geldermalsen, Marguerite. *Married to a Bedouin*, Great Britain: Virago Press, 2006.

Illustration Credits

The book jacket, map and geneology were designed by Travis Dixon, graphic artist.

All chapter illustrations are the work of the author.

CPSIA information can be obtained at www.ICGtesting.com
259890BV00002B/2/P